crushing it

A ROAD TRIP ROMANCE

EMERALD BAY
BOOK 2

THEA LAWRENCE

EDITED BY
BEN BROWNING

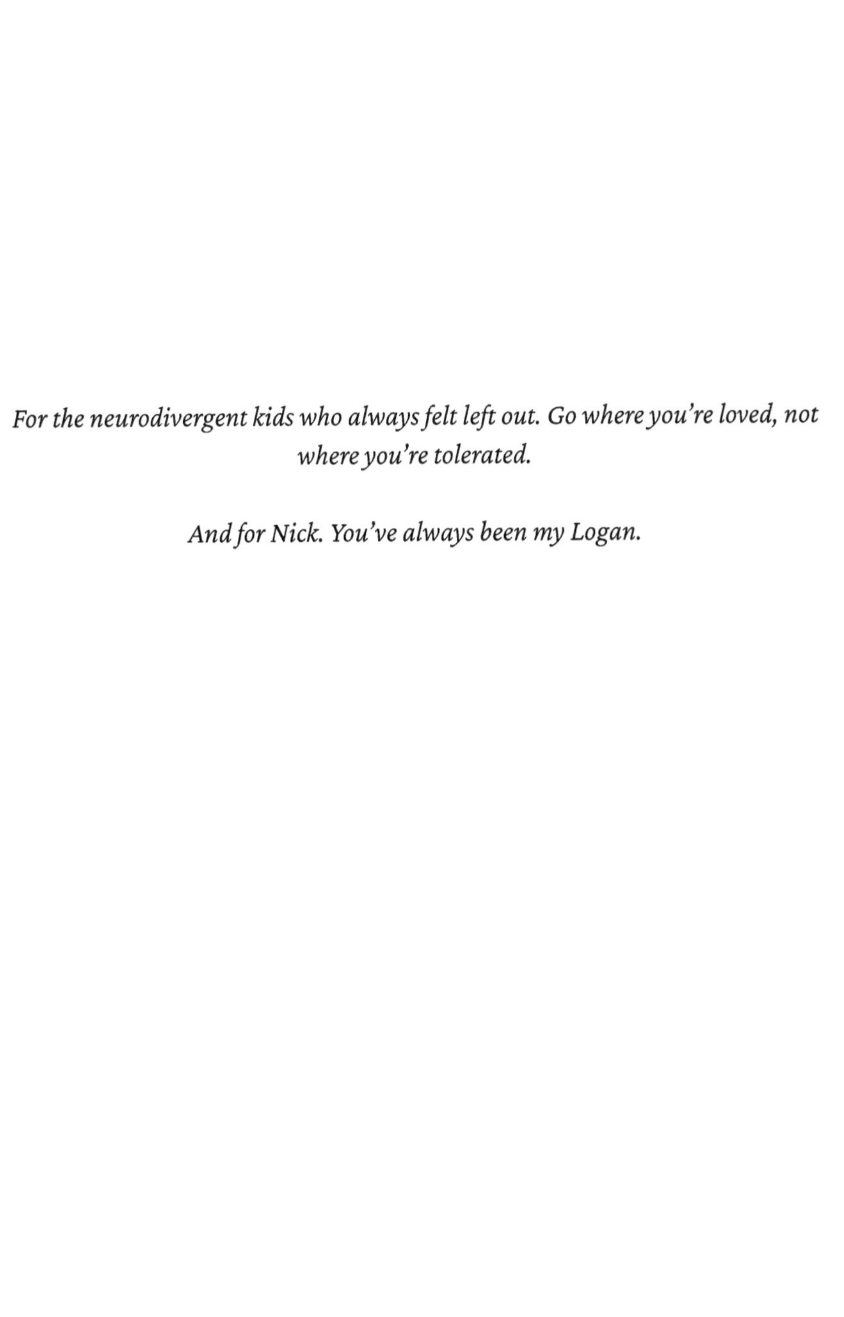

For the neurodivergent kids who always felt left out. Go where you're loved, not where you're tolerated.

And for Nick. You've always been my Logan.

Crushing It is the **second book** in the Emerald Bay series. While reading Swipe Right is recommended, it's not necessary as this is a standalone book. I've included a character catch up section titled *Who's Who in Emerald Bay*, that outlines the characters who appear in this book. There is also an academic glossary at the back of this book for readers curious about some of the academic jargon and concepts that are brought up in the text.

Logan's ADHD is undiagnosed and comes out in his actions: his impulsivity, his temper, his quirks, and his racing thoughts. This is all based on my own experiences living with undiagnosed ADHD for 30+ years. Your experiences may differ from mine.

Trigger warnings include: the death of a parent, brain cancer, discussions of medically assisted death, paternal abandonment, spiders, discussions of drug overdoses/being the child of a parent in active addiction, anxiety, abandonment issues, grief, discussions of bullying, harassment, violence, blood/wounds, open door sex scenes, rimming, anal sex, butt plugs, spitting, hand necklaces, degradation kink, oral sex, and exhibitionism.

If you or someone you know is experiencing addiction issues, and need help, please go to https://www.smartrecoveryinternational.org/ to find resources for your country.

who's who in emerald bay

Dr. Roman Burke was a professor of Sociology at Emerald Bay University. He is a widower and a former cowboy who grew up in Montana. After accidentally meeting and falling for his best friend's sister on KinkFinder, a local hookup app, Roman left his job as a tenured professor to attend culinary school. He now lives with his girlfriend, Imogen, in Emerald Bay, Washington.

Imogen Flynn is a former Emerald Bay PhD student who got into a secret relationship with her brother's best friend, Dr. Roman Burke. Since their relationship has gone public, she's transferred to the University of Washington where she continues to do her research on kink and stigma. Imogen is Logan's sister.

Dr. Frankie Hughes is the head of the Sociology Department at Emerald Bay University. He's also Logan and Abi's boss. His story will be in book 3.

Piper Morgan is Imogen's best friend and a friend of Abi's. She moved from New York to Emerald Bay with Imogen in book one to pursue her PhD in Psychology. Her boyfriend is Jason "Jay" Mills, who is featured in book one. **Please note that Jay does not appear in this book.**

dicktionary

A handy dandy (pun intended) guide to all of the spicy chapters in this book.

book playlist

The Goo Goo Dolls - Slide
The Strokes - Is This It?
Sabrina Carpenter - Sharpest Tool
Taylor Swift - The Prophecy
Chappell Roan - Casual
Alanis Morissette - Head Over Feet
Taylor Swift - The Archer
The Tragically Hip - Courage (For Hugh MacLennan)
Joni Mitchell - A Case of You
Taylor Swift - The New Romantics
Shania Twain - No One Needs to Know
Nitty Gritty Dirt Band - Fishin' in the Dark
Neil Young - Harvest Moon
Taylor Swift - Paper Rings
Sparks - Coldplay
Taylor Swift - Guilty As Sin?
Mitski - My Love Mine All Mine

The Neighbourhood - Pretty Boy
Hozier - Do I Wanna Know?
Otis Redding - Try a Little Tenderness
The Strokes - Trying Your Luck
The Barenaked Ladies - Call and Answer
The Tragically Hip - Ahead By a Century
Queen & David Bowie - Under Pressure
The Tragically Hip - Bobcaygeon

character playlists

ABIGAIL KING

LOGAN FLYNN

If you're reading this on your phone/tablet, the images are linked to the playlists.
Happy reading!

CHAPTER ONE

is this it?

LOGAN

EMERALD BAY, WASHINGTON
PRESENT DAY

I think I've been stood up.

No, I *know* I've been stood up, but saying *I think* makes me feel a little better. It gives me a dash of hope, you know? Hope that maybe I haven't wasted an entire night buying flowers, ordering champagne, and lying to the server that my date is just 'stuck in traffic.'

But it's been 45 minutes and there's no sign of Theresa.

I tried calling and texting, but she hasn't responded. She's a lawyer, so maybe she's busy? But we confirmed everything this evening.

Should I text her again?

No, that seems desperate.

It was pouring rain when Theresa and I met on campus. She was having trouble with her umbrella, I helped her fix it, and before I knew it she'd given me her number. We've been texting all week so I thought we hit it off. She's even been laughing at my shitty jokes.

Okay, so maybe she just responded with some laughing emojis, but that's still something, right?

I take another look around, hoping to see her walk through the door but only finding my server shooting furtive glances over at the table, her eyes bouncing between me and a new couple at the front of the restaurant.

This place is packed, and I managed to snag a spot at the last second, but only under the explicit condition that we'd be out in an hour.

I guess my time is almost up.

"Fuck it."

ME

Hey! Are you on your way?

I hope I don't sound too clingy.

Just as I hit send, I feel someone looming over me and glance up to see an apologetic look on my server's face.

"Hi," she says softly. "I'm really sorry, but the people at the front have this table booked for 9:00pm."

My stomach sinks.

"Sure, I'll just pay for my stuff."

I move to grab my wallet. I've been humiliated enough for one night.

"Oh, no. It's– it's fine. It's on the house."

Great. She feels sorry for me. That's fucking *awesome*.

"That's... kind of you. Thanks."

"No problem." She tucks a strand of blonde hair behind her ear. "I've been there before. It sucks. I'm really sorry."

Oh god, the shame spiral is starting, I need to leave immediately. I pick up the flowers, thank her again, and scurry out of the restaurant as quickly as I can with my metaphorical tail between my legs. Of course the moment I step outside the sky opens up, drenching me within seconds.

It's about a 15 minute walk back to my place and I left my AirPods at home, primarily because I thought I'd be going on a date with a hot lawyer.

I didn't even bring a jacket.

"Gotta love the PNW," I grumble.

I've been on a lot of first dates in the last three years, never making it past a few weeks before things fall apart. One of us always loses interest, or we realize we're both forcing a connection that wasn't really there to begin with; I'm 36 and I've never once been in a serious relationship.

I've either been too focused on my career or my family, and bounced around from partner to partner, always looking for that *thing*. That spark. That hook that tells me 'this is the person I want to spend the rest of my life with.'

Frankie says I should just enjoy the ride, but that guy is going to be a bachelor until he's 85. He had one big heartbreak and never looked at love the same way again.

I don't want to be like that. I still believe in people, and I still believe in love even after getting let down so many times. I want someone to wake up next to, someone I can brush my teeth with in the morning, someone who sees the ugliest parts of me and loves them anyway. So I guess it's back to the dating apps to try again. Statistically, I'm bound to meet *someone*.

That's math, and you can't argue with math.

Growing up, it was clear my parents were head over heels for each other. Every morning, my dad would leave mom a little note at the bottom of the stairs with his agenda for the day, all the way down to what time he'd be home, and when he might call to check in. My sister and I sat on the floor after he passed, going through his things, and reading all those little notes:

Picking up your dry cleaning on the way home from work.

How do you feel about tacos tonight?

We bawled our fucking eyes out.

They were the smallest fragments of love but my mom held on to all of them.

Rain pours down my face as I find myself glancing down the street toward Abi's apartment. There's a light on in her unit, which hopefully means she's home, and I can't think of anything more pathetic than sitting in my living room alone waiting for a text from Theresa. I need the distraction.

Normally I'd ask before showing up at someone's door on a random Thursday, but Abi and I have the kind of friendship where this is par for the course. I know the second I buzz her apartment, she'll greet me with open arms because she's always had my back, and I've always had hers.

It'll be nice to be able to vent a little, after all I can tell Abi anything—

Correction.

I can tell Abi *almost* anything.

Nobody will ever hold a candle to her, but dating just wasn't in the cards for us, and I have... thoughts about that.

Still, we're co-workers. We're friends.

That ship has sailed.

I find myself at her doorstep, my finger hovering over the buzzer as I stare at the little faded bat sticker next to it. It makes me smile like it always does, but just as I move to buzz her apartment, the front door swings wide open.

"Oh my gosh, Logan, you're soaked to the bone!"

Mrs. Russell, Abi's building manager. I'm pretty sure she thinks I'm Abi's boyfriend, even though we've told her a thousand times that we're just friends. She's in a rain jacket, with a chihuahua barely the size of a football tucked underneath her arm.

And he's... *also* wearing a raincoat.

"Forgot my umbrella, and I figured I could borrow one from Abi!" I laugh. "Are you taking Todd for a walk?"

I move my hand to pet the dog, as slowly as I can, trying my absolute best to not terrify the most neurotic creature I've ever met.

"Oh, yes. He loves the rain, don't you, Toddie?" She ushers me inside as the little beast trembles like a leaf, every single sight and sound adding to his mounting anxiety. "Come in, come in!"

I slip inside, trying to shake off some of the water before realizing how futile it is. My clothes cling to my skin, raindrops splattering against the floor. I have to resist the urge to gag as I suddenly become aware of the water sloshing around in my socks. I can't stand wet socks. It's in the top five on my list of worst sensations.

"For Abi?" Mrs. Russell asks.

I look down at the flowers still clutched in my hand. They're pink and white lilies. I thought they were pretty, sitting all by themselves outside the flower shop this afternoon.

"I guess— yeah. Yeah, they are."

Mrs. Russell winks at me.

"You're a good man, Logan."

"Thanks, Mrs. Russell. Have a nice walk, and try to stay dry!"

CHAPTER TWO

slide

ABI

EMERALD BAY, WASHINGTON
PRESENT DAY

When I first moved to the Pacific Northwest, everyone told me it was beautiful, but with some of the dreariest weather you'd ever seen. Luckily I've always loved the soothing sound of the rain.

I'm hunched over, as usual, my laptop resting on a couch cushion while the wind howls just outside my window. Whenever I work, it's total chaos. Coffee and wine-stained papers are scattered all over the table beside me. The burrito bowl I made for dinner sits mostly uneaten in my lap.

"Wednesday, Lydia! No!"

I snap my fingers and my two pet rats stare up at me, frozen mid-movement but practically begging me for a bite.

I'm allergic to cats despite growing up with them, and no matter how much I love having them around, I can't go through 24/7 congestion again. For dogs it's even simpler: the idea of keeping one in my tiny apartment just felt cruel.

Rats were a good compromise. There are so many misconceptions about them, and people really underestimate their intelligence.

Just before Wednesday can make the leap straight into my burrito bowl and start chowing down, I scoop the two up and plop them back in their cage.

"I know you were both counting on getting some of that chicken," I murmur, locking everything up tight. "But mama's gotta work on her journal article. That way she can become a big, fancy academic and buy you more treats."

Last week I got the email no postdoc wants to get, but always knows is coming. Frankie let me know that my contract is up at the end of December, that my fate now lies in the hands of the budget committee. Universities only have so much money to go around, and everyone has to tighten their belts... All while the President makes a hefty salary and approves tuition hikes.

Did that sound bitter?

I'm stuck halfway through the scholarship application that could save my job here in Emerald Bay, so you'll forgive me if I'm a little stressed. If I can get the funding, the school doesn't have to spend as much money to keep me on; they get to cheap-out on paying their staff, and I get to keep working.

Win win.

Besides, it's worth $175,000, and that comes with some serious bragging rights for me as an academic. More importantly though, it means that I could get my dream project off the ground.

I've been collecting data for a pilot project that will provide a safe place for people to use drugs, including clean needles and testing kits, with the main goal being the reduction of overdose-deaths in the area. While Emerald Bay is quaint and picturesque, there's a much darker underbelly to it that people don't really like to talk about.

Just as I'm about to take the second big bite of my late dinner, a rap at the door nearly makes me knock everything over. I look at the clock, 9:00pm on a Thursday?

I didn't order more food, and I'm pretty sure I'm up to date paying my rent, so it can't be my landlord. Mom's all the way back in Ontario, and unless something absolutely insane's happened, there's no way she'd be on my doorstep unannounced.

I stand and tuck my hair behind one ear, suddenly hit with a brief moment of shock when I realize it's a lot shorter than I'm used to. I got it cut this morning, but time just seems to blur together when you're on a deadline.

There's that knock again, rattling me even more.

But then I hear the voice.

"Shortcake? Are you home?"

"Logan?"

Shortcake's a nickname he's had for me since I started at EBU. I'm 5'10", but compared to his 6'4", I guess I am a little short.

I crack the door open, greeted with the sight of his sandy, usually shaggy hair sticking to his head. He's in a purple dress shirt that's drenched and clinging to his chest, water dripping from his black skeleton tie.

"What happened? Where's Theresa?"

His big hazel eyes don't have their usual sparkle, and all of a sudden I know exactly what he's going to say.

"She stood me up." He thrusts a dripping bouquet of pink and white lilies out at me. "So, I suppose now these are for you."

Even soaked in rainwater, they still have a lovely smell.

"Get in here. We'll get you warmed up."

I walk him in, heading toward the kitchen as Logan takes off his shoes and sets them down by the radiator.

"Did she even text you?" I ask, grabbing a vase and filling it up with water.

"Nope," he sighs, heading straight into my bathroom before emerging with a towel to dry his hair. "I tried to make the best of it and ordered some appetizers, but I felt like everyone could tell, you know? When the server said it was all on the house, I knew I had to get out of there— oh, shit."

He glances at the giant pile of books and papers I've left on the coffee table. My apartment's pretty open concept, so unfortunately I can't escape the mess I've made no matter where I go.

"I'm sorry. I should have called," he sighs.

"It's *fine*. Besides, I've been working through most of the night. I probably need a break."

I move to the fridge, grabbing a bottle of chardonnay and pouring us two massive glasses before heading back into the living room. Logan takes his, slumping against the sofa and staring into his wine.

"I'm sorry. You seemed to really like her."

Over the years, I've seen him get ready for more than a few first dates. I've helped him fix his perpetually crooked ties and watched as he tried in vain to smooth down his unruly curls. He tries so hard, and he really puts himself out there.

It takes courage to do that.

"Yeah, I thought we were cool." He shrugs. "She left me on read, too."

"What?! What a bitch," I snort as I take a sip of my drink.

"Abi!"

"Hey, it's straight up rude to stand someone up and then not even apologize. So, Theresa can fuck right off."

Logan's been one of my closest friends since I got here three years ago. Even though we got off to a bit of an awkward start, I think things have really blossomed between us. He's one of the first people I come to when I have news— good *or* bad. We text all day, we love the same movies, the same music...

"I really thought this one was going to work out," he mumbles.

Logan is more optimistic when it comes to love, willing to try over and over again, whereas I'm much more cynical. The collapse of my previous relationship really did a number on me, and in a lot of ways, it's been hard to find myself again. He once told me that healing is like a cat: it shows up whenever it wants, but you have to be patient with it.

"I mean, there are plenty of fish—"

"It's more like a pond, Abi," Logan chuckles sadly to himself. "The smallest pond imaginable."

"Okay, sure, we don't have the biggest dating pool. But there are good people out there who won't ditch you. You know there are. Sometimes it just takes a while to find your person."

This town has a fairly transient population of university students who ebb in during the fall and rush back out once summer hits, but obviously they're off-limits. When it comes to the locals, it's slim pickings. Unless you want to date a professor, but a lot of them live in Seattle or even further into Washington.

"Yeah, maybe you're right," he sighs.

"So? You gonna soldier on and try again?"

Logan shakes his head.

"I'm gonna delete the dating apps. All of them. Maybe this is the universe's sign to get me to stop trying so hard."

"You? Giving up on love?" I ask, pressing a hand to my chest. "I'll alert the press."

He rolls his eyes, giving me a gentle shove with his shoulder.

Logan's been in exactly one meaningful relationship since I've known him. Her name was Jennifer. She worked at Black Dog Video, the only rental store in town until it closed late last year. Whenever we'd go in there to rent a movie, the two of them would *always* flirt, so I made him get her number.

They lasted about three weeks before she moved back to her parent's house in California. It took him a while to get his spark back. But I was here with booze, and as many horror movies as it took to get him through it.

"More wine!" he shouts, downing his drink before getting to his feet dramatically. "God, I should have taken that champagne from the restaurant."

He doesn't make it more than 3 steps toward the kitchen before he stops, a disgruntled groan following the disgusting sound of his wet socks sloshing and slapping against the floor. It's hard not to laugh, and even harder not to gag.

"Let me get you some fresh clothes."

I head for the bedroom, rummaging around in my drawers until I find his big Snoopy Christmas sweater and a pair of obnoxiously bright short shorts that he wore to the gym one time. Maybe twice.

"Damn, I left clothes here?"

I look up, finding him standing in the doorway, dripping water into his wine glass.

"You leave something here every time you're over. Get out of those and I'll get them cleaned up."

"You don't—"

I put my hands on my hips and give him a faux scowl.

"Don't argue with me, Logan Michael Flynn."

"Oof. Middle-named," he sighs. "I am definitely in trouble."

I slip past him, patting him on the shoulder as I go.

"I'll pick a movie for us to watch and get out some blankets and pillows. You can stay over tonight, and before you say anything: It's *not* pity, I want to do this."

He grins, the first real smile I think I've seen all night.

"Thanks, Shortcake."

I nod, heading back into the living room while Logan shuts the bedroom door, grabbing some bedding from the closet and setting it aside for later. I toss his clothes into the wash and grab some snacks. Popcorn, chocolate, and sour keys. All his favorites.

Logan emerges from the bedroom, all smiles as he sticks out his arms and does a little spin.

"You think I could teach in this?"

"Absolutely. How could anyone possibly have a problem with that?"

"Right? I think my sweet thighs would actually be a benefit to pedagogy." He leans over, slapping them with a big, goofy grin.

There's that sparkle I missed.

He settles down next to me and I load up The Thing on Netflix. It's one of his favorites, and I can see it catch his attention immediately. This has always been one of my favorite things to do with him. We trade horror movie trivia, talk about what makes a movie work, and dissect every other shot. He knows so much about the genre from his dad's work, it's like getting a PhD all over again.

"Did you know that the sound effects on the autopsy scene of the face splitting Thing were done by soaking paper towel in egg yolk?"

I've heard this one, but I pretend I haven't.

"That's so cool!"

He's about to turn back to the screen before doing a double-take, reaching out and plucking something from my hair.

"You party hard, Dr. King."

He's holding a piece of popcorn, playfully examining it like it's evidence of some crime.

"What can I say? I know how to have a good time. Pajamas, popcorn, and the single glass of wine that'll put me to sleep..."

Logan snickers, leaning up against me. I can be a lot to deal with. Obsessive about my work, introverted, and more than a little awkward at times. I mask a lot of my neuroses when I'm around other people, but I feel so at home when I'm with him. It's that kind of feeling where you can just be yourself.

People have always drifted past me in life, and I've rarely felt like I belonged anywhere. Trying to make genuine connections feels like standing in a crowded room trapped in a glass box. People can press their hands up to it, walk past it, even talk to me through it, but nobody gets in.

Because I don't know how to let them.

We watch the rest of the movie, gentle conversation floating between us, until at one point I grab my phone off the charger.

"See? The tentacles in the dog cage *are* whips!" I flash him the IMDB page. "You owe me five bucks."

"How about a coffee and a croissant on Monday?"

"Ooh, the cheese ones?" I ask, batting my eyelashes at him.

Logan smirks, munching on another piece of popcorn.

"Anything for you."

sharpest tool

ABI

TORONTO, CANADA
MAY 2021

Holy shit it's loud in here. Maybe I made a mistake agreeing to this.

That, or I haven't had enough to drink yet.

But I have to admit, Kat was right. This feels a lot better than locking myself in the hotel room and watching romcoms. I feel free, and I'm actually *smiling*. And what's even better? The music is so loud that I couldn't think about Brendan if I tried.

It's 80s night, and a lot of people are dressed on-theme, the dance floor smelling like sweat and cheap perfume as Revolver pounds through the speakers. This was my mom's favorite band when she was a kid. She used to play their records all the time, in the house, on road trips, you name it.

The song reaches its peak, and just as I'm losing myself in the crescendoing rhythm, someone crashes into me. My drink tumbles from my hand and spills all down the front of my dress, soaking me completely.

"What the fuck?!"

Dammit, I've even got ice in my bra.

"Oh my God, I'm so sorry!"

I can feel my temper rising, but funnily enough I can't stay mad when I get a good look at him, his soft hazel eyes slightly obscured by unruly dark blond hair, and a clearly apologetic smile on his face. He's dressed in black, everything except for his tie, which I'm almost certain is a pattern of the cover of Mary Shelley's Frankenstein.

The man holds out both hands, his thick brows knit together as he starts to stammer.

"I'm— I— I'm so, so sorry! I was looking for my friend, and…"

I'd definitely put him over six feet, despite the fact that he's hunched over, looking like he wants to run far away from me but just a bit too intrigued to do it.

"It's okay," I laugh, as what's left of my anger slips away. "It's just a dress, right?"

With everything that's happened lately, I've been trying to be someone who looks on the bright side of things. Sure, my $13 cocktail just got spilled down my tits, and I'll smell like Smirnoff for the rest of the night, but at least the guy who did it's really hot.

"Can I at least buy you another one?" He asks sheepishly.

Even in the dim light I can see the red in his cheeks. He looks so frazzled that I'm starting to feel sorry for him.

"You can watch the bartender make it and everything, I promise! I just… I feel awful. That's a really nice dress and I totally ruined it."

Anything can be dry-cleaned, but I kind of want to keep talking to him; he gives me butterflies. I glance over at my friend Kat who's noticed something's up. She raises a brow alongside a little smirk, and I can tell exactly what she's thinking:

Go get him.

And I know I shouldn't. I should be focusing on me, not some random guy, and work on my own recovery before getting back on that horse. Then again, how does that old saying go?

The best way to get over someone is to get under someone else.

"That sounds great."

He claps his hands together, flashing me a charmingly confident smile, and I notice he's suddenly standing up much straighter.

"Perfect! I'll ask the bartender for some paper towels, too." He guides me toward the bar, and I watch him bob his head along to the music. "Gosh, I can't tell you how sorry I am!"

"It's really okay," I chuckle. "It's a black dress, so it's not like it's totally ruined."

It's a little quieter away from the dancefloor, and we manage to wedge ourselves in between a small crowd of people.

"Can I get an *extra* dry martini, and—" He turns to me with a prince charming grin that makes my knees a little weak. "For you?"

"Vodka diet coke."

"A vodka diet coke, for the mysterious woman in black!"

The bartender starts making our drinks, flashing the two of us a bemused look while my new friend takes the opportunity to offer me a handshake, along with his hopeful expression. I'm a little surprised by how much he's got going on just with his hands, catching sight of a gold pinky ring, black nail polish, and A, D, and I tattooed on his knuckles.

"I'm Logan."

"Abi," I laugh, gently taking his hand with a brief shake. "Cool nail polish! And I love your tattoos!"

"Oh, thanks!" He chirps. "They're for my family."

He gives me a little awkward smile before pointing directly at my face.

"I like your lipstick! Is that a weird thing to say?"

"No," I giggle. "I mean, it wasn't cheap, so thank you."

"How much?"

"About $65."

He whistles, shaking his head as he begins to worry at his lip with his teeth.

"Well, it looks great!" He pauses for a moment, starting to seem a little unsure of himself all over again. "So, are you, uh… are you from here?"

"I'm actually from Blackburn Falls."

"Oh, cool!" He nods sagely. "I have no idea where that is!"

I let out a laugh, much louder than I intended. Normally I'd feel humiliated, but somehow I don't care.

"It's about two hours from here."

"That's awesome! I'm from Washington— well, originally New York and I moved—" He stops himself, shaking his head. "Sorry, you probably just want the drink without my autobiography."

"I don't mind, it's always nice to meet new people." I'm starting to wish we were someplace quieter, maybe a little more private. "Are you liking Toronto?"

"Yeah, it's great! From what I've been able to see of it, at least. I'm here for a work thing. This is actually the first time I've gotten out in a couple of days."

The bartender slides my new vodka diet coke across the countertop, and a martini for Logan. We clink glasses, each of us taking a quick initial sip before his face twists up in disgust.

"Oh Jesus, that's awful!" He coughs into his elbow. "I thought I was gonna look so cool sipping this."

He shakes his head and sets it down on the counter, struggling not to gag.

"I'm guessing you don't like martinis?"

Even under the dim lights it's clear that he's blushing.

"Apparently not," he laughs. "I'll choke it down, though."

"But... why did you order it?"

He shrugs, sucking in a deep breath.

"I wanted to look suave, debonair, you know? Sure, I could get whiskey, but I'm just not a whiskey girl."

I don't know what it is, but everything about this guy puts me at ease.

"Me neither," I laugh, gently resting my hand on his forearm. "I think you're at least a little suave, by the way. Not quite sold on the debonair part yet."

I sip my drink as an awkward silence nestles between us, and suddenly I feel myself wanting to sink back into the crowd. Was telling him he's cool too forward? Before now I'd been with one guy since I was 17 so it's hard for me to gauge this whole flirting thing.

"Would you want to dance?" Logan asks, his eyes quickly flooding with worry. "Or am I reading our whole serendipitous meeting wrong?"

"Ooh, good word! Invented by Horace Walpole who wrote—"

"Castle of Otranto!" He finishes, practically bouncing on the balls of his feet. "I love that book."

"Me too!"

There's a bit more awkward silence as we grin like idiots, but he breaks it up by motioning toward the dance floor with a goofy little wiggle of his shoulders.

"So, um… is that a yes?"

I look around at all the bodies writhing beneath the flashing lights, covered in glitter and sweat. After what Brendan did to me, I think I deserve a little bit of freedom. After all, tonight was supposed to be a celebration.

I drain my drink, setting it down on the counter.

"I'd love to."

"Cool." He dips his head so that his lips just barely brush against my ear. "You're really beautiful, by the way."

Logan leads me to the dance floor, Revolver still pouring out of the speakers, and the two of us bounce along with the beat, laughing and trying to mimic each other's dorky dance moves. Flailing arms, the chicken dance, the twist, we do it all while struggling not to double over with laughter. Every time I look at him, I'm hit with a kind of buzz the booze can't provide, like when you first step out into the sunshine on a beautiful summer day.

As the song slows down, I wind my arms around his neck.

His hands hover over my waist, slightly unsure.

"You can touch me," I breathe.

He grabs me by the waist, the look in his eyes shifting from warmth to desire. My heart pounds and I lick my lips. He mirrors me, his eyes fixed on my mouth as we begin to sway to the next song. I never do stuff like this— obviously. I'm not the kind of girl a guy picks out of a crowd.

"My fiancé just dumped me!"

Logan stares at me in shock.

Oh god, why the fuck did I say that?

It feels like all of the air just got sucked out of my lungs.

I wish I could snatch the words up and shove them back into my mouth.

But it's only a moment before his smile returns.

"Well, then he's an idiot." His eyes darken. "I really want to kiss you right now."

Relief fills me up, and I try to regain my composure as quickly as I can.

"You're a little shameless."

Logan dips his head, one of his hands sliding around my body to rest on my lower back. His mouth hovers over mine and I can feel my heart thumping violently, threatening to run out of control.

"Is that going to be a deal breaker for you?"

I give in, those big doe eyes nearly bringing me to my knees.

"Not at all. I think shame's overrated these days."

a case of you

LOGAN

EMERALD BAY UNIVERSITY
PRESENT DAY

Some people race cars for an adrenaline rush, some people sky dive...

Me? I've been teaching for a long time, but I still get a thrill just before I start a lecture; standing up at the front of a room full of students gets me that same hit.

"Okay, so, when we examine the idea of research historically, we're looking at a very *smash and grab* kind of situation." I pull up a slide, taking an instinctual look at my notes even though I've got most of it memorized. "Researchers often come into communities, remove specific pieces of knowledge out of context, and write about these things as though they invented them. Now, what can we do to combat that?"

I glance around the room, watching my four PhD students scroll through their laptops as they search for an answer.

"Exercising critical reflexivity?"

Audrey. I learned her name before everyone else's because she emailed me directly to be her supervisor.

"Okay." I nod. "Now what does that look like to you?"

Methodology courses are my favorite, and today we're doing a unit on the deconstruction of research, something that always gets at least a couple students buzzing.

"Well, for example, I'm writing an entire chapter about my background and all of the biases I can think of. I'm also going to go into the fact that this entire thesis is just my interpretation of all my interviews and my readings."

"That's great! Exactly! Knowledge isn't held by one person, it's a community effort, and it takes all of us. When I first started doing research on medically-assisted death, I walked into the field totally ignorant outside of my experience. What I've learned is each person is an expert in their own lives—"

I glance down as my phone buzzes on the table next to me, the name on the screen making my stomach drop to my feet.

THERESA

Hey, Logan! Just touching base about the other night. Things were chaotic at work and by the time I'd looked at my phone, it was so late I figured you'd gone home already. But I'd love to reschedule if you're free.

Is she serious? She ghosts me, deletes her profile on the app, and now she just crawls out of the woodwork like it's a missed doctor's appointment?

"Dr. Flynn?"

I'm yanked out of this waking nightmare, looking up to see my students still hanging on to the sentence I left half finished. It's about 10 minutes until the official end of class, but clearly, I've already checked out.

"I think we'll leave it there for today. Really excellent work, everyone. Let's pick this up again next week, and remember your final papers are due on the last day of class. If you need anything or want me to look over your outlines, shoot me an email. I'd be happy to chat."

Everyone starts packing up as I grab my phone, staring at the text message, my stomach tightening with each passing second.

I'd love to reschedule if you're free.

What's to say she won't ghost me again?

I slump back in my chair as the last student makes their way out the door, my phone still clutched in my fist. Should I give Theresa the benefit of the doubt? Maybe she really *was* just busy. She's a lawyer. It makes sense that her life is kind of chaotic.

But then again, so is mine, and I still manage to show up to shit on time.

Okay, maybe ten minutes late, but at least I *tell people.*

And why, pray tell, didn't she reply to the text I sent her the next day?

I really like Theresa. We bonded over a mutual love of theory and comic books, but she's also *cool.* She dresses like an eccentric high school art teacher: boldly colored earrings matched with chunky necklaces, and a collection of eyeglasses that she wears depending on her mood.

She's so much like Abi, it—

My stomach sinks and I squeeze my eyes shut.

Three years of trying to get over Abi and I pick someone who's just like her.

Okay, no. Not right now. Focus, Flynn.

A half-assed apology a week later isn't going to cut it, but I don't want to be rude or push her away, because what if I'm pushing away a real chance at love?

My mom's always said I give people the benefit of the doubt too often. I wish I was more like my sister in that respect. You push Imogen Flynn to her breaking point and she's got no problem cutting you out of her life. Meanwhile, I hold on to threads of past relationships with a desperate hope that someday, they can be repaired.

I don't even think my standards are crazy or anything. I want someone who shares at least a couple interests, someone who can introduce me to new experiences, and who makes my heart race when they walk into a room.

Like Abi did.

Last week, after that date, she made me feel so much better. Arriving at her apartment was purely instinctual; it seems like my heart always knows where to go when I need comfort.

But Abi and I work together, and besides, she's not interested in a relationship, she's interested in her career. It's never going to happen for us, and I've accepted that.

A sharp knock drags me back into the moment, where I find Roman standing lazily in the doorway. His eyes glimmer with mischief as he flashes me a cocky smile.

"Hey, I'm looking for this guy Logan," he drawls. "Big nerd, glasses, talks *way* too much... You know him?"

This is the most relaxed I've seen him, wearing his standard black t-shirt and blue jeans, his cowboy hat tipped back on his head. I grin, pretending to scratch my eye with my middle finger. It's crazy the difference a few months makes.

"I think he's waiting at the corner of *go fuck yourself avenue* and *get bent street*, but who knows."

Roman chuckles, opening the door a little wider as he leans in to make sure no one else is around.

"Ready for lunch? I'm buyin'."

I glance down at the text that's still open on my phone, my stomach flipping as I consider what I should do. Ghost her back? No, that's rude. I don't want to take the low road. Relationships are so fucking complicated sometimes.

"Hey, Big Bird?" Roman cuts in. "You okay?"

"What?" I slide my phone into my pocket. "Oh, yeah. Busy day is all."

He narrows his eyes, tipping his head to the side as I shove everything into my messenger bag and haul it over my shoulder.

"Bullshit."

"I'm good!" I exclaim, my voice cracking a little as I involuntarily rise in pitch. "Let's just go, okay? I'm starving."

Roman raises a brow, scratching his salt and pepper beard.

"You're not good. Your voice did that weird thing it does when you lie, like you're going through puberty again. That, and you were staring a *little* too hard at your phone."

I let out a deep sigh, stuffing my hands into my pockets and glance down at my mismatched converse— one green, one pink.

"I got stood up last week."

Consistent inconsistency.

"Ah," Roman murmurs. "And I take it you're still not over it?"

"No— I mean, yeah— I mean..." I take a breath. "I just got this really lame-ass excuse and— God, this feels so..."

I laugh, shaking my head.

"Stupid."

"It's not stupid," Roman replies. "Come on. Lunch special is vegan sloppy joes on a kaiser roll with caesar salad. Made it all myself."

"So, what should I say?" I ask, taking a napkin and wiping some of the sloppy joe juice off my chin.

We're in *Simmer Down*, the quirky little diner Roman works at as a prep cook on the weekends when he's not in culinary school. It's a decently popular lunch spot on the edge of town, but last month a video of him went kind of viral. He wasn't even doing anything, just standing talking to a server but I guess if you caption a video with *Chef DILF*, it tends to catch on. The comments were insane, but it's gotten the restaurant a hell of a lot more business.

My sister thinks it's hysterical.

"You said you called her? Texted her?"

"Yeah, and no response until today."

"Doesn't take much to just text someone back... trust me, I'm the expert on fucking *that* up. If it were me, I don't know if I'd want to reschedule."

"And you apologized too," I reply, pointing at my phone. "There's no apology here."

Roman and Imogen had a bit of a rocky start to their relationship, what with it being secret and all. She was his teaching assistant and they met on a dating app, neither of them having a clue who the other person was. Once their jobs and livelihoods were threatened by the university, Roman retreated and didn't text her for weeks.

I was afraid it would be the end for them.

"Maybe she's saving it for in-person," he mutters halfheartedly, picking at his food for a moment or two before looking me right in the eye. "Okay, look, do you like her?"

I sit with the question, bouncing it around in my head the way my dad used to throw his tennis ball at a little spot on his office wall. He said it helped him think. Mom said it made her want to smack him. Either way, I always knew dad was working when I heard that *thud, thud, thud* from downstairs.

"I... think I do."

Roman sips his beer, smearing the sweat gathering on his glass with a thumb.

"And I think you're a bullshitter, Flynn. I think you want everyone to like you so when there's conflict, you can fawn and tell people it's okay. You never stick up for yourself—"

"Hey, I yelled at the two of you when I found out about Iggy."

"That's not sticking up for yourself," he chuckles. "That's being taken by surprise."

I slump back down in my chair, suddenly deflated.

"You really think I don't stick up for myself?"

"I think you're afraid of what's going to happen if you do." Roman leans forward, lowering his voice like he's about to reveal a terrible secret. "You're afraid you're going to push people away, that you'll lose a connection, but the fact of the matter is this woman stood you up. Are you willing to forgive someone who doesn't even care enough to apologize?"

If there's one thing Roman's gotten really good at since he's started dating my sister, it's speaking his mind.

"We haven't even been talking that long. I mean, what's there to forgive?"

Roman stares at me, giving that *don't bullshit me* look he's so damn good at.

"Leaving you alone at a restaurant, all dressed up with a big bouquet of flowers? Call me crazy, but it seems a little thoughtless regardless of the excuse, especially one she came up with a week later."

I stare at him, suddenly grinning from ear to ear.

"Hot damn, partner, when did you become a therapist?"

"Since I started going to therapy," he chuckles. "Seriously, though. You want people in your life who make you a priority; who love you and respect you enough to be up front. And maybe she'll end up apologizing in person, but I think she may have already shown you who she is."

I stare at the phone sitting next to my plate and take another deep breath.

"Yeah, to tell you the truth, I always have more fun watching horror movies than I do going on any of these first dates. I'm sick of them."

Roman gets a twinkle in his eye. He'll never say it, but I know he and Imogen think there's something going on with Abi and I. Nobody really knows what happened between us, and that's the way it's gotta stay.

"First dates aren't all bad. You just have to find the right person."

"That's easy for you to say, dude. You and Iggy were made for each other."

"Good point, just start taking every girl you meet out to play mini golf."

I snort.

"Hey, change of topic: how are the two of you doing?"

I ask every time we talk like this, figure I'm just doing my brotherly duty.

"We're great." Roman beams, glancing around the restaurant before pulling out a small box from his bag and sliding it across the table. "I got her something. Wanted to, uh…"

I swallow the little burst of jealousy at the back of my throat. Sure, Roman and Imogen's relationship was paved with secrets and catastrophe, but it all ended so perfectly. I don't think it's selfish of me to want something like that.

"If you say you want my blessing, I'm gonna beat you with a Judith Butler book," I laugh.

"No, no, I just want your opinion on it."

I pop the box open, and my jaw practically hits my plate. Sitting inside is a big pink diamond with some smaller ones clustered around it, all resting on a rose gold band. I don't know much about jewelry, but I do know he paid a shitload of money for it.

"Dude… When did you… when are…?"

"I'm biding my time," Roman says with a curt nod. "She's going to be *All But Dissertation* in a year and a half. I've been saving up, and I'm gonna take her to Italy for a few months so she can decompress, write a little, and then I'll pop the question."

"This is beautiful, dude," I manage to choke out before sliding the box back. "I'm really happy for you. For both of you."

Roman flashes me another softer smile as he tucks the ring back into his bag.

"It'll happen for you too. I have faith."

"Glad someone does." I raise my beer, matching his grin. "To becoming brothers."

Roman clinks his glass against mine.

"Finally."

oh, pretty woman

LOGAN

TORONTO, CANADA
SUMMER 2021

I'm in love—

Alright, no. No, I'm not.

I can practically hear my sister screeching, *Red flag, red flag!*

But whenever I look at Abi, when her whole face lights up and she draws me toward her like a magnet, I feel like the air has been sucked right out of my lungs.

"Oh my God, it's so much nicer out here!" She giggles, fanning herself as the rush of cool air hits us. "I'm so sweaty!"

The alleyway is empty, and all I can hear is the music back inside the club. It smells like stale cigarettes, spilled beer, and the faintest hint of what I am *pretty* sure is urine. I try to push that last part out of my head.

I don't want to think about urine at a time like this.

I've only known her for about half an hour, but she's the hot goth girl of my dreams. I wouldn't say it out loud, but I'm actually kind of glad I spilled that drink on her.

"Are you okay?"

She's trembling and I brush a strand of hair away from her face.

"I've never made out with someone in an alley before."

"Never?!"

Abi beams, relaxing a little.

"I take it you have?"

"Oh, all the time! I'm the King of Makeout Alley."

She laughs.

"Is that what they call you?"

I love her laugh, this little witch cackle that's making me blush.

"No," I confess. "Actually, I'm a huge dork. I spend my time watching horror movies and reading textbooks."

"Oh, me too! Do you have a favorite movie?"

No fucking way.

"The Thing."

"A classic!" Her eyes glitter with excitement. "Wait, original or—"

"Original," I scoff. The two beers I had before that martini are starting to catch up to me. "John Carpenter just does it better."

"I have to agree on that."

No. Fucking. Way.

I reach over and cup her cheek, feeling her skin warm against my touch. She gives me a little quizzical look, her dark brows furrowing until a little crease forms between them.

"Do I have something on my face?"

It's adorable the way she scrunches her nose up when she smiles.

"No!" I squeak, my voice breaking just enough to make me even more nervous. "I— I just can't stop thinking about kissing you again."

Abi grabs my tie and pulls me toward her until our bodies are pressed right up against each other.

"Well then, it would be wrong not to use this dark creepy alleyway for its true purpose."

This is the most impulsive thing I've done in a while. A long while. Most of the time, when I meet someone new, I feel like the nerdiest person in the room, but somehow I charmed the shit out of her.

"That's true, it really does have the perfect atmosphere." I breathe deeply as my lips hover over hers. "We could fit a lot of making out in this bad boy."

"Yeah?" Her voice has a playful and teasing edge to it. "And is that something you'd like?"

"If you'd let me."

She licks her lips, her grip on my tie refusing to loosen. My heart starts to thump chaotically against my ribcage as I watch bright pink burn into her cheeks.

"I'd let you do a lot more than that."

I sink into the kiss, pressing my body against hers as we devour each other. The combination of her perfume and the alcohol on her tongue causes something in me to snap. A growl rumbles in my throat and I start to grind against her thigh. She giggles, wrapping one leg around my waist as we deepen the kiss. I can still hear the pumping bass inside shaking the building like a beating heart, but I keep my focus on Abi.

And to think I almost didn't come out tonight.

No, I think I'll just stay home and work on this paper.

That Logan's an idiot. I'm so glad I didn't listen to him.

I slide my hands down her body, squeezing her ass. A sinful little moan spills from her lips as I tear my mouth away to suck on her neck. I hit a little spot underneath her ear that makes her gasp, and feel my cock start to strain.

Abi claws at my arms and down my back, gasping for breath as I find the slit in the side of her dress. I play with the fabric, teasing her until she grasps my wrist. We're practically dry humping like a couple of teenagers on prom night.

"Keep touching me." She guides my hand between her thighs. "Here."

"Are you sure?"

Abi grins, and desire sinks its teeth into the back of my neck.

"Logan, I'm a big girl. I know what I want."

"Yes, ma'am."

I've never had something like this happen before. Making out with random girls in alleys isn't really my thing. A bucket list item? Absolutely. But it wasn't something I ever thought would really happen to me… until now.

I tease her through her lace panties as my free hand glides up to her breast, tugging on a perky nipple before moving on. She shivers and I kiss her again, making gentle circles around her clit while I pull down one of the straps on her dress. She's getting wetter by the second and I need *more*.

"Good?"

The answer comes in the form of a hungry kiss, and I slide a finger inside of her. She's tight, quivering gently as soft shuddering breaths slip from her throat.

"Curl your fingers and press— fuck yes, just like that!"

I hear a *thunk* as her head smacks against the wall. Shit. I just wanted to have a good time, not give her a concussion.

"You okay?" I ask, pulling away a little to make sure she's not seriously hurt.

"Got a little too excited."

Abi blushes furiously, but continues rocking her hips with a grin, putting my mind at ease as I follow suit, and press soft kisses up and down her neck.

"Careful, beautiful. I can't have you hurting yourself."

"I'm fine," she breathes, digging her nails into my back. "Worry about yourself."

This is way beyond my own personal definition of making out, but I'm not about to stop now. I slide a second finger in and she melts at my touch. Who am I to deny a woman in need?

"Someone could walk out here any minute," I murmur. "And you look so fucking pretty I don't know if I could stop."

"I wouldn't want you to."

"Yeah?" I'm getting harder by the goddamn second. "You'd let them watch?"

The way she looks at me sets my skin ablaze. I want her to rip this stupid shirt right off me. I wouldn't even care if she popped the buttons. What are the odds I'd meet a gorgeous woman with an exhibitionist streak?

"Dirty girl," I purr, pistoning my fingers until she starts to tremble.

Abi hooks one leg around me, her back arched and her tits thrust into my face. She's practically begging to come, and I hope to god I get to spend the rest of the night watching her fall to pieces.

"Logan," she gasps. "Logan, I'm coming!"

"Eyes on me," I murmur.

Sweat on her brow, flushed cheeks, bitten red lips, and the light from the street makes her olive eyes pop. She shivers, clawing at me as her eyelids flutter.

"Good girl." I kiss her, slowing the speed of my thrusts. "Good fucking girl."

She whimpers as we break apart and I slowly slide my fingers out of her pussy, staring straight at her as I lick them clean. I want more. So much more. All I can think about is pinning her to a mattress and devouring her until we get a fucking noise complaint.

"I have a hotel room. Do you want to..." Abi winces, like she doesn't know what she's about to say until the last word comes falling out of her mouth. "Fuck?"

I let out the dorkiest chuckle I've ever heard as I finish cleaning my fingers. Abi blushes, flashing me a bashful smile as she tucks a strand of hair behind her ear.

"Sorry, I didn't mean to laugh at you," I murmur, wiping my hand on my pants. "I just didn't expect you to read my mind."

She gnaws on her lip, her big doe eyes sparkling.

"It's been a really long time since I've been kissed or touched like this, and—" She grimaces. "God, I'm so bad at this."

"I think you're doing great," I whisper.

And then we just stand there, staring at each other while my mind goes a thousand miles a minute. Should I do this? Will she regret it in the morning? I'm almost certain I won't.

She pulls her dress back down, wobbling a little on her heels.

"Hey so, I don't want to be rude but uh... How drunk are you? I don't want to take advantage or anything."

Abi grins, closing her eyes and stretching out both arms, touching her nose as she walks a perfectly straight line.

"How'd I do?"

"Tens across the board."

And then a gut-wrenching realization washes over me; I can feel myself go pale in an instant.

Shit.

"I don't have a condom."

"Oh..."

I can feel her disappointment as if it were my own...

And then I remember Frankie.

"Listen, my friend's just inside—"

God bless that fucking horndog. He's always got a shitload of them.

"I was going to say, there's a Circle K down the street. We could go there."

I clap my hands together.

"Okay, here's the plan: I'll go talk to my friend. If he doesn't have one, I'll meet you out front and we'll go on a little adventure."

"Like The Fellowship of the Ring, but hornier!"

Fuck, she's funny.

"I'll text my friends, and order us a car," she says softly.

"Do you wanna go half, or—"

"Depends on the sex," she giggles.

I'm a fucking mess right now, and I'm about to have my first one night stand.

Is it weird to be this excited about it?

"Okay. I'll be right back. Promise."

I rip the door to the club open, practically tripping over my feet as I sprint toward the dance floor.

"Alright, curly blond hair and..."

I turn the corner to see an ocean of white dudes, flailing around the dance floor in tank tops.

"Curse you, 80s night," I mutter, shoving my way through the mass of rhythmically deficient bodies until I finally spot him.

It looks like he's making out with someone, but without my glasses, it's a little tough to see the details.

"Frankie!" I cry out. "I need you!"

People turn and glance over their shoulders, shooting me weird looks, but I pay them no mind. This is a fucking emergency. *Literally*. A *fucking* emergency.

Normally I'd never intrude, but tonight I have no qualms about striding forward, grabbing him by the shoulder, and tearing the two of them apart.

"What the hell, dude?!"

Frankie stumbles, giving me a shove back.

"I need a condom!" I bellow.

He blinks, wasted as hell. There's beer spilled on his shirt and he's got bright pink lipstick smeared all over his mouth. The brunette behind him is giving me the death glare, and I flash her what I hope is an apologetic smile.

"Frankie, please, I—"

He grins, raising a hand and reaching into his jeans pocket and handing me an entire row of condoms.

"You just have these on you?"

"Hey, I was a boy scout," he replies with a smirk. "Have fun— and remember, we catch that flight back to Seattle tomorrow at 1:00."

I reach out to ruffle his sweat-logged hair, grinning like an idiot.

"O Captain, My Captain!"

Frankie snorts, giving me another quick shove.

"Get the fuck outta here, and be safe!"

"I will! I deeply appreciate your friendship!"

"That's a weird thing to yell, man!"

But I have no time to quip back, I'm already shoving my way through the crowd, trying to make my way to the door. By the time I get outside I'm breathless, but there she is, waiting by a small white car with a little smile on her face.

She looks almost relieved that I showed up, like she was half expecting me not to walk back out that door, staring into my eyes like I'm the best thing she's seen all year.

And then the driver honks his horn.

"I'm gonna start charging—"

"Yeah, yeah!" Abi groans, rolling her eyes and climbing inside.

We buckle our seatbelts as the driver takes off, whizzing past people and parked cars in equal measure. Our conversation is... well, chaotic, in between the makeout session. She points out some of her favorite coffee shops and restaurants while I spend most of the conversation just staring at her. Eventually Abi's hand finds my thigh, and she gives it a gentle squeeze, lighting up all my senses just as her purse starts to buzz. I try to ignore it as long as I can, but it seems to get louder with each passing second.

"Do you need to get that?"

"What?"

"Your purse is vibrating."

"Oh!" Her cheeks turn bright pink. "I didn't even notice."

She rummages around in her bag for a moment before retrieving her phone, and it's only a couple seconds before her expression shifts.

"Everything okay?" I ask.

I watch her jaw tick, and she turns to me with an exasperated smile.

"Yeah. It's just been a weird day. My fiancé kinda dumped me tonight. Did I already say that?"

"You did." I chuckle. "Don't worry, I'm cool with being a rebound."

Ever wish you could hop just a few seconds back in time and punch yourself in the face for being a braindead idiot? Because once they invent time travel, kicking my own ass is going to be at the top of my list.

Actually, maybe it'll be second, right after winning the 7th grade spelling bee instead of Jason Sanderson.

That Scholastic Book Fair gift certificate was supposed to be *mine*.

"We don't have to do this," she says softly. "I can have the driver—"

I reach out and grasp her face, pressing a sweet little kiss to her lips.

"Sometimes, my mouth opens and words come out before my brain can stop them. I'm sorry. That wasn't cool."

She's blushing again.

I stroke her cheek, getting totally lost in... well, everything about her. Tears glimmer like little diamonds in her eyes, but she doesn't let a single one fall.

"Let me help you forget, okay? I'll buy you waffles in the morning. You like waffles, right? Everyone likes waffles."

"I do," she chuckles. "Thank you, Logan."

We stop outside of a swanky looking hotel, the two of us each thanking the driver as we tumble out of the car. All it took was a single glance from this woman and I'm considering telling Frankie that I want to spend another week here, but...

Goddammit, that Flynn intensity is kicking in again.

I cannot freak this woman out.

The elevator ride is agonizing, and it's difficult to keep my hands off her as people keep getting on and off at every floor. It takes an eternity to get upstairs, but when we finally make it into her room, her mouth is on mine again.

We're tearing at each other's clothing and stumbling toward the bed. Her fingers fumble with the knot on my tie and I hear a frustrated snarl as she breaks the kiss.

"How tight did you tie this?!"

Her angry little pout just makes me want her even more.

"It's a Trinity knot." My voice is a little sheepish. "I was afraid it would come undone."

"More like an impossible knot," she grumbles.

"I'll be sure to alert the knot police."

Abi snickers, the two of us working together to loosen it before she moves on and unbuttons my shirt, slipping it off my shoulders. My muscles tense in anxious anticipation. I've always been a little ashamed that I'm on the scrawnier side, but she just smiles, biting her lip as she drinks me in.

"Damn."

The way her eyes dance around my naked torso gives me the kind of confidence that makes me want to take the lead.

"Look who's talking." I nip at her bottom lip just to listen to her moan again. "Let's get you out of this dress."

Whoever dumped this woman must be the stupidest man alive.

CHAPTER SIX

under pressure

ABI

EMERALD BAY, WASHINGTON
PRESENT DAY

"Anomie is a kind of vanishing of morals and values that were previously common in society. Durkheim posits that it occurs during massive upheavals— so, we're talking things like social structures, economic collapses, and big shifts in political ideology."

"Like the recession?"

"Precisely!" I nod. "So, when you guys go to write your papers, one of the things that might help is focusing on a particular time period and analyzing how parts of society shifted or broke down. Remember, anomie isn't necessarily a bad thing. We need things to break down in order to make room for change, right?"

I look around at a sea of slightly confused faces. I get it. These are dense topics to teach and to learn, but so far, everyone's doing really well.

I think I'd be a shitty professor if they weren't. I always hated the ones in school who would announce things like *'nobody in my class gets an A.'* Learning should be challenging, yes, but students shouldn't have to sacrifice their sleep or their sanity to get a good grade.

I check the clock. We've only got about five minutes left and I've got to submit my scholarship application tonight, which means that I'm going to need all the caffeine I can get. My plan was to head over to Déjà Brew to do some last minute revisions and enjoy a little oat milk latte while I work.

Roman gave me his old Keurig machine, but I ran out of pods for it, only to find out the horrifying truth of how expensive they are, so the coffee shop has been my new sanctuary lately.

"Good work today, everyone! We'll dive deeper into Durkheim next week. Go and be free!"

As my students make their way out and I scoop up the last of my things, I notice an obnoxious buzz from my phone, and pluck it out of my bag.

KAT

Did you get the invite?

I frown.

ME

What invite?

KAT

Check Facebook. I can't believe this shit.

At first I think she's talking about her husband Marcus, but if they were fighting, it wouldn't be on Facebook. That and she would have sent me the evidence to analyze: screenshots, memes, voice memos, you name it.

Kat and Marcus hooked up the same night Logan and I did, but it turned out a lot better for them. They work as realtors in Blackburn Falls and have a little boy named Dylan who's just turned two. Kat got the life that I wanted— deep down, at least. Yes, I want a career in research and teaching. Yes, I want to write articles and change the game, but I also want a family.

All of these things feel so far out of reach right now.

I don't even know if I'm going to stay in Emerald Bay.

I haul my bag over my shoulder and head out of the classroom, starting my little Facebook investigation as I walk.

I haven't logged on in about half a year, so I have to sort through a bunch of notifications before I find the one that stops me in my tracks.

EVENT: Blackburn High 10 Year Reunion
WHEN: June 20, 2024
WHERE: Reynold's Vineyard
HOST: Carly Howard

It takes me a moment to even recognize her. Her hair is lighter, her face looking so different than it did in high school, but it's her last name that catches me off guard. Howard. As in Brendan Howard. As in Brendan and Carly got married. *Just* married, by the looks of it.

There are dozens of wedding pictures, all from about three months ago. I keep swiping, madly flipping through photo after photo as a thick knot of jealousy begins to grow in my gut. I nearly drop my phone when I see a picture of Carly holding a baby.

Connor Burlington Howard, born February 14, 2021. Our Valentine.

I think I'm going to be sick.

He's three. Brendan left me three years ago. That means...

I feel myself start to spiral, furiously swiping and swiping as it all sinks in. I sift through three years of pictures. A trip to Italy, to France, and their honeymoon in Australia.

> KAT
>
> Did you see?

Shit, I got so caught up in all of this, I forgot I was texting her.

> ME
>
> Yeah. I saw.

> KAT
>
> You have to go.

My eyes are blurry with tears. I'd have respected him more if he told me he was fucking my high school bully behind my back.

ME

Why the fuck did they invite me?

KAT

Probably to show off the fact that Carly's really good at spending her parent's money.

I can't help but let out a little snort of laughter, even as the tears run down my cheeks.

KAT

Fuck that bitch, but FUCK HIM especially. Not in the sexy way. Like with a giant lego dildo covered in hot sauce.

If there's one thing Kat's incredible at, it's making me laugh at my lowest moments. Since I moved away from our hometown, our relationship has turned into almost daily text messages, video calls, and the traditional swapping of memes. It's hard being so far away from her, but whenever we talk, it's like no time has passed.

ME

Why would I want to see either of them?

Carly tortured me in high school— all because she couldn't have Brendan. He asked me to the school dance instead of her. After that, she made my life a living hell until graduation. Years of torment.

Turns out all she had to do was be patient, and count on the fact that Brendan Howard always takes the easy way out.

KAT

Come on! Reunions are all about reconnecting with people and showing them up after high school! You've got a big fancy professor job and a boyfriend. Show up at Reynolds Vineyard and shove that shit in their faces!

Shit. I forgot that I *sort of*... well, lied. It was after I got the news about my contract being up. Kat was asking me how life was going and I didn't want it to be a pity-party, so I came up with the best possible version of things I could think of. Pretty sure I even said I was making like 80 grand a year, which is pretty depressing when you consider that was my highest hopes.

I should never text someone after I smoke a joint.

ME

I don't know.

KAT

Come on! We haven't seen you in so long, and
Dylan misses his Auntie A. You've got to have
PTO or something, right?

I groan as the elevator doors open to the ground floor and I head toward Déjà Brew, following the path through beautiful towering cedar trees. I'm alternating between trying not to trip on fallen branches, and texting madly.

ME

You can't use your child as a bargaining chip.

KAT

I can do whatever I want! See?

She proceeds to send me six pictures of Dylan and I at the park last summer, wearing matching sunglasses and eating ice cream. He's so fucking cute, with his chubby little cheeks and his curly dark hair. He looks so much like his mom.

ME

This is manipulative.

KAT

But is it working? Look at how much that baby
loves you!

I sigh.

ME

I'll think about it, okay?

KAT

Okay! Just let me know! I'm sure your mom would love to see you, too! We could celebrate your big promotion!

I slide my phone into my pocket as I approach the coffee shop. I can't think about that fucking reunion anymore, I have to get this scholarship submitted and save my job.

I get up to the counter and order an extra hot vanilla oat milk latte with a sprinkle of cinnamon and nutmeg on top. It's the closest I can get to fall right now, so I'll take it. I manage to find a quiet seat near the back of the café and pull out my laptop, but I only make it 5 minutes before I find myself on Facebook again.

I scan the invite, looking for clues that couldn't possibly be there. *Why* did she invite me? Was it a sense of obligation? The chance to show off the fact that she got what she always wanted? No explanation is going to be good enough, not after what the two of them did, but a part of me still wants to hear it directly from the horse's mouth.

I start clicking through all of the people who said they'd attend the reunion. They're lawyers, entrepreneurs, teachers... most of them have really beautiful families.

I know it's social media and I'm comparing my own current mess of a life to everyone's highlight reels, but I can't help but feel like I'm falling behind. I live in a shitty one bedroom apartment with two pet rats; I'm probably going to lose the best job I've ever had and have to move back to Blackburn Falls with my tail between my legs.

My stomach twists, the cursor hovering over the giant blue **ATTEND** button.

"Abi, you look like you're going to throw up."

A familiar voice comes crashing down, nearly making me jump as I find Piper Morgan standing over me. She's sipping an iced latte, dressed in a pale purple tank top and a pair of jeans. Her dark hair is pulled back into a big messy bun, with a few stray pieces framing an audacious pair of heart-shaped sunglasses.

When Piper and Imogen arrived at EBU, the three of us just clicked. We have drinks together, go on shopping trips, and complain about anything and everything related to academia.

"I'm okay."

How long has she been standing there?

"You sure?" She asks. "I've been watching you for a couple minutes and it looks like you've gone through all five stages of grief in rapid succession."

"You've been watching me?"

"Well, I was worried," Piper replies, gesturing to the empty chair in front of her. "I assume I can sit down?"

"Fill your boots."

"That's a weird expression," she chuckles.

"Yeah, it's something my mom used to say. I guess it sorta stuck."

She pauses for a moment, her eyes newly-fixed on my laptop.

"So what's going on? Are you fighting on the internet again, some dude bothering you or something?"

I rub my face and let out a groan.

"If only my day were that good. I got invited to my ten-year reunion."

"Aren't you like 26?"

"I graduated early."

"Ah," Piper replies. "I guess you and Logan have another thing in common."

I flash her what I hope is a confident smile, but she only tilts her head, looking more worried than before.

"So, what's wrong with the high school reunion?"

"Well, for one, I got bullied, like… the *entire* time. I was a huge loser who spent more time in the library playing Dungeons and Dragons than trying to be cool. Anyway, a couple months ago I *sort of* told my friend Kat that I have a boyfriend, and tenure… and that I make 80 grand a year."

Even saying the last part makes me wince.

"You Romy and Michele'd yourself."

"What?"

"You never saw that movie?" She laughs.

"No, I did, but—"

"They said they invented Post-Its."

"Okay, right but," I wave my hands in front of my face. "This isn't quite like that. I mean it's…"

Piper snorts.

"Pretty similar, actually?"

I shrug, sighting deeply.

"The real problem is that it's being hosted by my ex's new wife."

Piper gasps.

"The dickhead who dumped you after the two of you got engaged?"

I nod, taking a big sip of coffee. I've told Piper and Imogen this story before, over too many glasses of shitty sangria at The Hi-Dive. It's nice to have someone to confide in other than Logan. I love the guy, but he can *barely* keep a secret.

"Assclown!" Piper hisses. "And he seriously got married?"

"Yeah. Has a kid too." I pull up Carly's profile and show her the picture. "The baby's about three."

Piper's jaw practically hits the table, and she yanks the laptop toward her, scrutinizing every single detail. I watch her eyes bounce around as she clicks away; I almost tell her not to type anything, but she's on her best behavior, keeping her finger on the track pad the entire time, her eyes still wide in shock.

After about a minute, she slides it back over to me.

"Well, you have to go."

I raise a brow, staring at her in total disbelief.

"What?"

"You have to go!" Piper laughs. "Show them both up. Lean into the lie."

"I think you're supposed to be talking me out of this," I grumble.

"No, think about it!" Piper leans forward, her eyes gleaming with excitement. "Who's going to know you're lying?"

"The faculty section on the EBU website is a pretty good clue," I groan.

It's got our dorkiest pictures, our most recent publications, and the department we teach in along with our positions. It's a dead giveaway I'm not a real professor if someone googles me.

Piper rolls her eyes.

"You're gonna let that stop you? The EBU website looks like it was designed by a blind chimp who just learned how to use clip art, okay? It's terrible."

"Okay, but my LinkedIn says—"

"Fuck your LinkedIn! Just *lie!*" I can see the gears spinning in her head as she sips her coffee. "Look, a sane person would tell you not to go, but a woman bent on vengeance would tell you to Romy-and-Michele that shit! Just, you know... be more careful about it. Don't say you invented something that's easily Googleable."

She pauses.

"Is that a word?"

"These days? Probably," I sigh, staring at her with disbelief. "You really think I should do this?"

"What better way to get closure than to bring a hot guy to your reunion, and rub it in your ex's face!"

"Hot guy?" I laugh. "Don't know any."

Piper's eyes narrow, and before she even utters another word, I know exactly what's going to come out of her mouth.

"No." I shake my head. "Absolutely not."

"Oh, come on! It's all fake, and you two are super close! It would be easy to fool anyone— and besides, he's totally into you."

I roll my eyes. It's been a running joke amongst our group of friends. Except for Frankie. After what happened with Roman and Imogen, we've been very careful not to make those kinds of comments around him. I don't need him getting an embolism.

"I'm not asking Logan to be my fake boyfriend just to get back at my ex."

"Why not?" She shrugs. "You're too nice, Abi, you gotta stick it to that dickhead, make him realize how much he fucked up! Logan's cute, he's charming, he's pretty famous in academic circles, and... Oh, doesn't he do magic tricks?"

"You sound like you want to date him," I laugh.

"Nah, he's cute, but he's not my type." She grins. "But he's yours... and I see the way you look at each otherrrrr!"

There's only so many times I can object before I have to accept that it's futile.

"Look, I know there's lots of rules and stuff so you guys can't date, but you can *fake date* for one night, can't you?"

My eyes flick back down to my laptop. The idea is tempting, and she's right... Who would find out? Logan and I post pictures of each other all the time on Instagram. We're always together, and it's not that big of a leap given how we started.

The problem isn't that I think he'd say no.

The problem is I know he'd agree.

And that's the part that makes me nervous.

CHAPTER SEVEN

the meeting

ABI

EMERALD BAY UNIVERSITY
PRESENT DAY

"Did Frankie say what he wanted to talk to us about?"

"No," Logan replies, cleaning his glasses on his rumpled shirt. "Nothing."

We were planning to go to the Hi-Dive after work with a bunch of people from the sociology department. It's our way of celebrating the end of the spring semester, but Frankie sent out a message at the 11th hour asking the staff to come in for a 'mandatory department meeting'.

I got the email when I was sitting with Piper at Déjà Brew and my first thought was that it was about the budget cuts, that we were getting called in so I could be let go in front of all of my friends and colleagues. I bumped into Logan in front of the elevator on the way up, and when I told him, he said I was being paranoid. Maybe I am, but he's not the one whose future is at the mercy of the fucking budget committee.

As we reach the seminar room, the door swings open and we're greeted with a big Frankie smile. There's a slightly manic energy to him, which somehow makes me a little less nervous, but a lot more curious about what the hell's going on.

45

"Hey, stragglers! Come on in. We're just about to start. There's coffee and donuts if you want them."

"Chocolate sprinkles?" Logan asks, his voice hopeful.

"You think I'd forget your favorite?" Frankie chuckles as we slip inside.

"You actually forgot it on September 25, 2022," Logan reminds him. "It was 4:18PM and the pain was—"

"Okay, that's enough," he snaps back as he does one last scan of the hallway before shutting the door. "I should be asking *you* for donuts, Flynn. As a pain in the ass fee."

"I don't have donuts, but you're welcome to some of this cake," Logan replies, popping out a hip and giving his ass an exaggerated smack.

Frankie frowns, the whole room completely silent, and then I see the words scrawled on the board:

WORKPLACE HARASSMENT & RELATIONSHIP POLICIES

Oh, god.

Logan instantly turns red and nods at Frankie.

"Right. Of course. I was just demonstrating what *not* to do."

"I think Dr. Flynn might have given us an excellent segue into a particularly difficult topic. Have a seat, guys."

I don't think I've seen a department meeting this packed. Even the adjuncts who barely teach part time are here. Logan's not paying any attention to them though, his lips practically disappearing in a frown as we settle into our seats. He reaches for a big chocolate donut, taking an aggressive bite out of it and chewing violently as his face glows even pinker.

Logan always eats when he's nervous. I remember one time we were at a conference and he spotted one of his academic heroes across the room. Before he built up the courage to talk to the guy, he managed to devour half the plate of coconut shrimp, even though he said he didn't even *like* coconut shrimp that much. He made himself so sick he could barely go to any panels the next day.

"So, due to an incident earlier last year involving a department member and a Teaching Assistant, the Dean wants me to conduct a quarterly review of the workplace harassment and relationship policies…"

Frankie gestures to the board behind him. "Now, keep in mind, the department sprung this on me about an hour ago, so there may be some technical issues."

Logan grabs another donut as Frankie clears his throat, and boots up his powerpoint presentation.

"We're going to start with the first question: What is workplace harassment?"

He clicks the remote before launching into the different definitions.

I can tell he got this presentation directly from admin. It's so packaged and… dated.

Out of the corner of my eye, I catch Dr. Barnes checking his watch, an extensively irritated look on his face.

"If anyone should be listening to this, it's Dicky over there," Logan grumbles in my ear. "Creepazoid."

Dr. Barnes is somewhat infamous for the kind of behavior Frankie's currently going over. There was even a rumor going around campus that he's got a whole secret family his wife doesn't know about, and may have even started relationships with students. I don't know how much truth there is to that, but the guy *is* a legit creep. I've caught him checking me out a few times when he thought I wasn't looking.

If anything, we should be talking about *that* kind of stuff, instead of this toothless corporate bullshit. Besides, most harassment at work is *far* more insidious than what's in this training package.

"Logan," Frankie interrupts. "Can you give us some examples of workplace harassment?"

Logan's eyebrows fly up his forehead and he sets his newly acquired *third* donut down onto the table.

"Um… Creepy unwanted hugs? Massages?"

Frankie nods, moving to the white board to write them down.

"Good, good. I also would have accepted smacking your ass in front of your boss and telling him he's welcome to 'some of this cake.'"

Logan puts his head in his hands and the room is quiet as Frankie clicks to the next slide that says **INAPPROPRIATE NICKNAMES**.

"We have to be careful about the nicknames that we use in the workplace, because some of them could cross boundaries."

A brief flash of panic rockets through me. Logan and I aren't inappropriate with our nicknames, but sometimes he calls me 'Shortcake' in front of the other professors. It's not a big deal, and most people don't bat an eyelash. It's just how we've always been.

Okay, sometimes we answer our office phones with shit like *'Hey Hot Stuff'* or *'Talk to me, Big Daddy'*. But those are jokes! They're consensual, they're just between us, and no one's getting hurt.

Oh my god is the university spying on us?

If it was his call, Frankie would be having an open and compassionate discussion about any concerns we may have. But after what happened with Roman and Imogen, it seems like all the administration is worried about is covering their own asses rather than actually looking out for their staff and students.

"So, what are some examples of nicknames that could be considered inappropriate? Things like..."

The words flash on the screen as he moves to the next slide.

"Dr. Sexy. Okay, *wow*."

He advances the slide forward in a vain hope that the next one will be better.

"Or... Sugar Boobs— for real?" He sighs. "Who the hell wrote this?"

Laughter begins to fill the room and Frankie's face twists up in a scowl.

"Guys, this is serious! You're all adults, we have to be able to have adult conversations."

Even Janine Rogers is chuckling, and she's the most staunch feminist I've ever met.

"Frankie, no offense to the department's stellar and *very* up to date examples... but we should be talking about some real issues we face in the workplace." She subtly tilts her head toward Dr. Barnes who is now scrolling through his phone. "These bloated corporate slideshows are just the university ticking off boxes and saying they trained us. And besides, there are better ways to do this than with a half-assed PowerPoint that was created in 2007."

She's right. I'm pretty sure I saw this *exact* slideshow when I went to U of T about ten years ago. Talk about administration being behind the times.

"Actually, I think it was 2005," Frankie says with a grimace. "I don't think it's been updated either."

Janine shakes her head.

"This has to be some kind of end of the semester prank. Which one of you made this?"

Logan puts up his hands, shaking his head in denial.

"You'll never pin this on me! Never!"

"Okay, you know what? I can think of some more nicknames that department members *have* exchanged over the past year."

Frankie's tone is suddenly a lot more serious, and it makes me more than a little nervous.

"Like what?" Logan asks, crossing his arms over his chest as he leans back in his seat.

"How about Dr. Hugecox?"

Logan winces.

"That was—"

"Screamed at the staff Christmas party," Frankie reminds him. "We were all there, Logan."

We're a small faculty, and sometimes that means we forget things when it comes to interacting with one another. Lots of us send memes via email, gifs in our group chats, and we talk about our personal lives in great detail. Academia is a strange vocation, and sometimes, it's hard to tell where the line between co-worker ends and friend begins.

"Okay, what else you got?" Logan's confidence has all but returned after his previous humiliation.

Frankie clicks his tongue, rocking back and forth on his heels.

"Baby, sweetheart, or how about *cutie pie!*"

"I've never said cutie pie," Logan replies with a shake of his head. "You're not cute."

Frankie lets out an indignant scoff.

"First of all, I'm adorable. Second, you said it to me last week in a *very important* email."

I've told Logan to be on his best behavior with interdepartmental emails, but when it comes to his friendship with Frankie, I think he views some of their communication as one big joke.

"I didn't know it was gonna go to the Dean!" Logan shouts. "You could have scrolled through Outlook and deleted my reply—"

"I'm not involving myself in mail tampering!" Frankie snaps back. "And besides, you're the idiot who hit reply all!"

He sighs, and as much as I want to laugh, I feel sorry for the guy. Logan's impulse control is about as good as a toddler in a toy store.

"Mail tampering, are you fucking serious?" Logan mutters under his breath, angrily shoving another donut into his mouth. "So I'm the reason for this seminar?"

Little pieces of chocolate fly onto the table with each word, and I can barely make out what he's saying.

"No, but that was a good reminder to Ian that we needed to have one." Frankie puts his hands on the table, staring at all of us. "Look, I know that we're a close faculty, and because of that, sometimes those lines blur. Nobody's in trouble, this is just a reminder."

Logan nods, throwing Frankie a thumbs up, as if giving his permission to continue the seminar.

"Alright," Frankie sighs. "The last and *real* reason why we're here is... workplace relationships."

Oh, fuck.

"As you all know, Emerald Bay University has a zero tolerance policy for faculty-student relationships, and that policy *will* be enforced to its fullest extent. Any faculty member who is caught having an inappropriate relationship with a student will be immediately suspended and face the possibility of termination, following a disciplinary hearing and a full investigation."

I glance around at a sea of uncomfortable looking faces. We all know what happened between Roman and Imogen. Even for the people who didn't know them well, it was impossible not to notice their sudden disappearance from campus. Everyone put two and two together, and eventually Logan and Frankie started talking about it more openly.

"That said, I also want to talk about romantic relationships between co-workers. This can be a tricky topic, but EBU's policy is that if you are not teaching in the same department as the 'object of your affection', you're golden. However, if you *are* in the same department, things get stickier. Romantic relationships in the workplace could lead to favoritism, inappropriate public displays of affection that could make others uncomfortable, distrust amongst fellow faculty, and most importantly, it could impact your performance."

I shift in my seat, and that talk I had with Piper comes rushing back with a vengeance. The plan to ask Logan to be my fake boyfriend just got a lot more dangerous. Should I bail on this reunion? Should I just go by myself, and lie my ass off about my so-called tenure and my amazing new boyfriend with no direct evidence?

"So, hypothetically..." Dr. Barnes chimes in. "What happens if two people in the same department just happen to fall in love?"

Frankie stares at him, stone-faced, and I glance at Logan who's slowly arching a brow. I can tell he wants to say something but I press down hard on his foot.

"One of those professors would have to transfer to a different department or university." Frankie lets out a breath, scanning the room. "Look, as close as we are here, this is still a professional environment and we have to keep it that way. So, *please* don't harass anyone, don't fuck your co-workers— and don't tell Ian I said *fuck* in a professional setting."

"I think he used it in an email last week," I chime in. "You're good on the cursing front."

Frankie smirks at me. I know he'd rather have someone poke his eye out with a stick than be doing this on the last day of the semester.

"Well, good to know I have your blessing, Dr. King." He sets the remote down. "So, anyone else have any questions, or is this all pretty straightforward?"

"Straightforward," we murmur in unison.

Except for Logan.

"I just want to clarify, are we allowed to call the Dean Ian now?"

Frankie claps his hands together loudly, ignoring him completely.

"Excellent! I just want to remind everyone, the budget meeting is at the end of the month. The results of that discussion will be sent out via email to all faculty members—"

"Like, in general?" I ask. "Or only if the cut pertains to our position?"

"Regardless of your position," Frankie replies. "There may be some cuts to classes, some rearranging..."

"It's the damn STEM department," Janine grumbles with a shake of her head. "They get all the money."

"Well, they're important too," Frankie reminds her as he turns off the projector.

"I know, it's just... the humanities matter. I just don't understand why these bureaucrats don't see the bigger picture."

Trust Janine to say the things we've all been thinking out loud.

"Because all they give a shit about is money and prestige. Science is where it's at, as the kids say." Dr. Barnes groans as he stands up. "Lovely meeting as always, Francis. Unfortunately, I have to take my leave. I've got a hot date with the wife."

Logan opens his mouth to say something and I immediately put my hand on his thigh, giving it a firm squeeze. It's so automatic, I don't even realize I'm doing it until I look up at Frankie, his brow raised as he stares *right* at me.

I quickly remove my hand, my cheeks burning with humiliation as Logan stands up, hauling his bag over his shoulder. I don't think he even registered what just happened.

"Dude, I really am sorry if you got in trouble for my dumbass email."

Frankie scoffs, rolling up a cord and tucking it into a nearby desk.

"You didn't get me in trouble. Ian just *gently* asked me to remind everyone of our policies— and honestly, this was overdue with everything that happened."

"Cool. We'll meet you outside and head to the Hi-Dive?" Logan asks.

Frankie grins from ear to ear. With the crushing weight of his HR obligation off his shoulders, he's free to be himself again.

"Sounds good. I just have to lock up— Actually, Abi, do you mind if I talk to you for a second?"

Oh god. It's the thigh thing.

"S–sure. Yeah, that's–" I clear my throat. "Yep."

"I'll wait by the elevator!" Logan calls, already halfway out the door.

I turn to Frankie, who's in the midst of sliding his laptop into his bag. If I can filibuster, I'll get in less trouble... or at the very least I can confuse him so he forgets his original point.

"Frankie, I didn't mean to put my hand—"

"Relax, okay? I'm not a cop. That's the last thing I want to be." He grins, slinging his dark leather messenger bag across his body. "And that's not even what I wanted to talk to you about."

The relief nearly brings me to my knees.

"It's not?"

"No." He clears his throat. "With the budget meeting coming up, I just wanted to let you know that I'm going to do *everything* it takes to keep you here. And if the Gods are merciful, maybe you and I can talk about an adjunct position?"

If the Gods are merciful. The fact that not even Frankie knows my fate makes my stomach churn.

"That sounds great, Frankie. Thanks."

He pats me on the shoulder.

I didn't think my smile was convincing at all, but maybe I'm a better actor than I thought. It's hard to have hope that things are going to work out when everything is beyond your control.

"Perfect. Now, I think I owe Flynn a beer for forcing him to endure that presentation."

"It was a good—"

"Don't bullshit me," he chuckles. "It was the worst thing I've ever done. I'm gonna smack Roman with a pool cue tonight because this is all his fault."

As we head out the door toward the elevators, I spot Logan leaning up against the wall, scrolling through his phone. He's got an especially cute nerdy look going on today, and my conversation with Piper comes roaring back with a vengeance one final time. If I *was* going to pick someone to fake-date, it would definitely be Logan Flynn.

He glances up as we approach, his warm smile lighting up his face.

"You fuckers ready for some karaoke?"

CHAPTER EIGHT

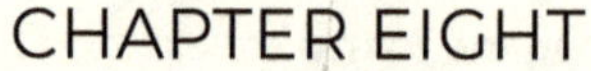

LOGAN

EMERALD BAY UNIVERSITY
PRESENT DAY

Abi's been weird since the seminar.

I mean, it was a weird seminar, but still.

She's been eating lunch alone in her office a lot lately, and I've caught her zoning out mid-conversation. I know sometimes she can have these prolonged periods of introversion, self-imposed in order to work extra hard on something, but this feels... different somehow.

I need to know exactly what's bothering her, hence the bribery; croissants and coffee have always been her buttery, flaky weakness. Superman's got kryptonite, Abigail King has croissants.

"Abi?" I gently knock on the door while balancing the drink tray with one hand. "You in there?"

I've been trying not to call her Shortcake at work since that seminar. Talk about embarrassing.

"One second!"

She flashes me a big smile as she stands in the door to her office, dressed in a sleeveless turtleneck with a long red and black plaid skirt and combat boots, her dark hair all twisted up into a tiny messy bun. She looks happy enough I can clearly see the exhaustion in her eyes.

"Handsome *and* brings pastries? What did I do to get the royal treatment?"

"You existed? Duh."

Her office is smaller than most of ours given her temporary position, but it's so cozy, packed tight with piles of books all over the floor, because the shelves were already overflowing by her second month. Abi hasn't been with the department for long, but her classes are popular, partially due to how generous she is with her opportunities. If there's a chance to publish presented to her, she usually gives it to a graduate student or offers to co-author rather than snatching it up herself. If anyone had doubts about the public opinion surrounding her, the scatter-shot thank-you notes and cards tacked up all over her walls would clarify things the moment you walked in.

"You've been very mysterious this past week," I smile, placing her coffee and croissant on her desk before making my way to my traditional seat in the corner.

She nods, her own smile a little uncertain, but sincere.

"Got a lot on my plate the last few days."

I raise a brow, trying to grab her attention with a playful little tilt of my head.

"Yeah? Like What?"

"Just grading and handling emails," she laughs. "You know, the usual chaos."

She fiddles with her necklace, a little rose gold skull pendant that I got her for Christmas last year. She always plays with it when she seems anxious, or zones out thinking about something. She's stressed so often these days I'm always noticing that little tick; probably why it feels like she never takes it off.

"You rarely disappear like you have this week." I sip my coffee and lean forward. "You can't hide from me."

She blushes and looks back down at her laptop, taking a deep breath and scrunching up her face for a few seconds before she seems to make a decision, slowly spinning it in my direction.

It only takes me a moment to figure out what I'm looking at.

"Ten year high school reunion invite, and it's on Facebook? Jesus Abi, who's still on Facebook?" I look up at her, shaking my head. "And wait, you're 26. That math doesn't math!"

"Graduated early, remember? Perks of being a 'gifted learner,'" She winks at me, sipping her coffee. "But forget that, look who invited me."

I lean forward, clicking on the profile. The woman has long auburn hair and a sugary sweet smile. Is it someone I'm supposed to know? Maybe an old friend she mentioned?

"Oh, Carly Howard? She looks nice."

The second I see Abi's face, I know I've guessed wrong.

"She was the Queen Bee at my high school, made my life a living hell, but that doesn't matter right now! Click through her profile. See any familiar faces?"

I scroll through the wedding photos: dozens and dozens of variations of Carly in her sparkling white gown posed beside a guy with short dark hair and chiseled features. It's not until I see the tagged name that it all clicks: Brendan Howard.

The absolute piece of shit who fucked up my best friend's life.

And technically the guy I owe for ever having met her at all.

"Ah," I mutter. "Good-guy Brendan."

"Ding ding ding!" She leans back in her seat. "I'm surprised you remember, actually. I don't think I've talked about him much and for a second there I thought you were just going to look at me like I was crazy."

"Nah, my memory's basically photographic," I puff my chest out, hoping to diffuse a little bit of the anxious energy. "Nothing gets past this steel-trap of a mind."

"Really?" Abi teases. "What did you have for lunch yesterday?"

I roll my eyes as she takes her computer back.

"So is Brendan the reason you've been holed up in your cave?"

"Partially, yeah," she replies. "My best friend—"

"I'm your best friend."

"My best friend back *home*," she lazily tosses a pen at me, grinning. "Wants me to go to this stupid reunion so I can flaunt my big tenured professor job and my new boyfriend."

"Ah, see, I can help with this! You don't have either of those. Like, at all." I sit up a little straighter, widening my eyes dramatically. "Unless I missed something?"

It's possible but, given how much time we spend together, highly unlikely Abi's gotten a secret promotion without my knowing. Even less likely than a secret boyfriend.

"Okay, it's not *that* far-fetched, Logan!" She laughs. "But besides that… I don't know, sometimes you just want to exaggerate a little."

I give her another shot of my wordless little head-tilt.

"Hey! Don't give me that suspicious look! You know me, I'm not a liar. It's just, I was in a different headspace at the time. Real relaxed, get it?"

I squint my eyes a little.

"Ugh, okay, how about we just say I may have done some… gardening one night, and that helped me calm down a bit too much."

"Abi, what the hell are you talking about? The closest thing you have to a garden is—"

"God, how old even are you?" She giggles, popping a piece of croissant into her mouth. "Can you tell me about the war of 1812? You were there, right?"

"Shut up! I'm hip and cool! I bet you don't even know what rizz is, do you? Well I do, and I didn't even have to google it!"

Abi's laughter turns into a small coughing fit, her eyes watering as she waves her hand in front of her face.

"Okay, no more rizz!" She takes a deep breath and another sip of coffee to calm herself down before lowering her voice a little. "Look, I may have smoked a joint in the middle of a particularly drawn out phone call, and made some very specific statements about where I am in life that I can't back out of."

I snort.

"Why not?"

"I'm not sure if you're aware of this, but information in a small town in Canada travels fast."

"Ah, yes. Small town gossip."

"Exactly. In Blackburn, it's talking shit, tailgate parties, and shopping cart races."

"Shopping cart races?" I raise an inquisitive brow. "Is that a Canadian custom I've never heard about? It sounds prestigious."

"Sometimes I forget where you grew up," she sighs forlornly.

Imogen and I went to a private high school— my mother's idea. We both hated it. Dorky uniforms, tortuous school bus rides, and a hell of a lot of rich kids. But in our neighborhood, it was the thing to do. Regardless, private schoolers from Upstate New-York aren't the most likely to be hooked into the Eastern Canadian shopping cart racing scene.

"A tragedy, I know, but don't leave me hanging."

Abi closes her laptop, pushing it aside.

"It's really not complicated. We'd just have two people in a couple carts at the top of the hill, push them down, and see who won." She pauses, giving her head a little shake. "Obviously you never did shopping cart races, but you had to have done some dumb stuff like that when you were a kid, right?"

"There wasn't time. It was school, after school clubs, band practice— oh, and somehow trying to find the time to download porn onto the family computer, and then hide it really, really well. And then panic delete it at 3AM."

"Jokes aside, sometimes I forget you really are from the ancient times," she grins, her cheeks dusted the most gorgeous shade of pink. "Were your parents paying for the internet per-hour, or..."

"Jesus, Abi, I'm not even that much older than you! But if you must know, I was curating a private collection, well within our monthly bandwidth limit."

She chuckles, and I can see that weight on her shoulders lift ever so slightly.

"So? Are you planning to go back for your reunion?"

"I don't know," she sighs. "I haven't been back home for a while because I've been so busy, but... I lied, Logan. I mean, my ex has a brand new wife and baby. They own a vineyard! Hell, even ignoring them, two of the densest people I graduated with have started their own tech company, and I'm just a loser who might not have a job next year."

I've been desperately trying to push away the fear that she might be forced to leave Emerald Bay, all because some suits think her position has no value. Abi's a brilliant scholar with so much to offer, but even more, she's great with the students. So many professors just ignore the teaching part of their jobs as much as possible, wanting to research and publish over anything else.

I just wish they could see how much better she's made this place.

"I know I shouldn't compare my life to Brendan's, or anyone's really," she murmurs. "But he gets to just start over with the white picket fence, the rich in-laws, and the perfect kid? And all I end up with is existential dread? That's bullshit."

She slumps, defeated in her chair, and lets out her longest sigh yet.

You always feel it in academia. That you're never smart enough, never ahead of the curve, and there's always someone who's a better writer, better lecturer, or who wins more awards. It's a highly competitive industry, but in the end, the race is mostly with yourself.

Even if you think it's not.

"You want to show up there and show him you did well for yourself," I nod, clicking my tongue. "Without him."

"Exactly!" She smacks her desk and her coffee jumps a little. "You get it!"

My own 20 year reunion is lurking around the corner, and the very thought of it makes me shudder. I wasn't popular in high school, and got bullied a lot. I even had a John Waters mustache for two weeks in senior year until my mom made me shave it.

I've put it to bed, though. None of those people matter anymore, so why try to keep up with them, right? But Abi's ten years younger than me; it's still a lot more raw for her.

I watch as she stares down at her closed laptop with a mixture of nostalgia and frustration, probably holding back a desire to flip it open and post some colorful comment on that Facebook page.

"I just won't go. I mean, what if someone looked into my position here and found out I'm not actually a professor? And besides," she chuckles to herself, "where am I going to get a fake boyfriend? Not like you can just buy one online."

"Actually, you can, and they're called male escorts. He'd probably show up shirtless, though. Make a real Magic Mike situation out of the whole thing."

She smiles, rocking back in her chair.

"Magic Mike was strippers, not escorts, Mr. Cinephile, but I'm so proud of you for making a pop culture reference from only a *tiny bit* over a decade ago."

I crank an imaginary Jack-in-the-Box, whistling the music before the reveal: A big fat middle finger just for her.

"That's three old person jokes, Shortcake. You're on thin ice."

"Oh, come on. That was a good one, so it's a freebie!"

Maybe, but I'll never admit it.

"Hey, you know what? If you don't want Magic Mike, you can have *Logan Michael Flynn.*" I stretch out my arms, wrapping each of my words in the gravitas of a professional boxing announcer at a big prize fight. "He's scrawnier than most, and he dances like a Midwestern dad at a barbecue, but he won't cost you... $500 a night!"

She tenses a little, a quick flash of fear in her eyes before she covers it with a giggle. Gotta crank up the charm to keep her from worrying about this whole thing.

"If we're going that far, why don't we just pretend to be married?" She asks with a teasing grin. "Take it all the way?"

"Have you *seen* me at charades? Have you heard me at boring dinner conversations? I'd make one a hell of a fake husband."

I give her my big puppy dog eyes. It always works, so I never use them for evil. Mostly just when I really want her to give me the remote, or order pizza even after we promised we'd stop using Doordash.

"Logan..."

"Hey, it was *your* suggestion! Haven't you ever heard of 'commit to the bit?'"

I stick out my lip in a pout, and Abi reflexively covers her eyes with her hands.

"You can't weaponize those puppy dog eyes like that! You know the rules!"

"Too late, consider them weaponized," I reply, batting my eyelashes. "See? You need the nuclear codes for these babies, and we're at defcon one."

She glowers at me, and I swear I can see a bit of blush creeping into her cheeks, at least before she tears off a piece of her croissant and tosses it at my head.

"Cut it out, you dickhead!"

I mean, why shouldn't we do it? Abi's not interested in me anyway. It would be like we're undercover secret agents. We could come up with a backstory, tell a few elaborate lies, get some free wine, and make classic good guy Brendan Howard look like the absolute piece of shit loser that he is. But, if she's this stressed about it...

"Fine, I'll stop. I promise." I check my watch: ten minutes before I have to get my ass to class. "Look, I gotta go. My advice on this whole reunion thing? Don't sweat it too much. If you want to go, go. If you don't, then don't."

"Thanks, Logan. And thanks for offering, that's sweet of you."

"Hey, anything for my bestie," I reply. "Do the kids still say bestie?"

Abi snickers and raises her coffee.

"Thanks for breakfast, bestie."

"Hey, you wanna do lunch too? We can meet at that new deli that opened on campus."

"Sure," she replies. "That'd be nice."

"It's a date, Shortcake."

I wink at her as I slip out the door.

"Our first official fake date!"

how my heart behaves

LOGAN

EMERALD BAY UNIVERSITY
FALL 2021

"I have an iced pumpkin oat milk latte for Logan!"

I push through the small crowd to grab my drink from the barista, heading out the door with a quick thank you. There's already a bit of a bite, even only a couple weeks into autumn, but I still find myself smiling as I take in the golden leaves on the ground, almost glowing with the glare of the sun cutting through the crisp air.

I have a bit of time before my next class, so I decided to continue a podcast on the history of Sociology I started when I woke up this morning; I got part of the way through an in-depth discussion and analysis of the works of Augustus Comte, all for a little last minute-prep before I had to head out for the day.

I reach into the pocket of my tweed jacket, rooting around for my AirPods.

"Shit."

Empty.

I fish around in my pants, struggling to slurp down some coffee at the same time to get that buzz as soon as possible.

"Dammit, gotta be…"

With my coffee tucked precariously in the crook of my elbow, I continue the hunt in my bag, rummaging around blindly while trying my best not to crash into anyone.

"Come ooon! Where the fuck– oh!"

I'm delighted to feel the smooth rounded edge of the AirPod case, but just before I pull them out, I slam right into someone, soaking myself in iced coffee.

What a great way to start the semester.

"Oh my God! I'm so, so so—"

Her dark hair is styled in waves, tussled by the wind into a perfect mess as she vainly tries to help. She's wearing a black and white striped dress, pointy black boots, and even has little bat earrings to complete the ensemble.

"Abi, is that…?"

She lifts her head, her mouth falling open as her eyes hit mine.

I didn't think I'd see her again. We agreed it would just be that one night in Toronto. There would be no exchanging of numbers, no last names, no divulging of personal information, and *absolutely no* looking each other up on social media after the fact. She said she wasn't looking for a relationship, that everything was lovely, but she was taking the next steps in her life and she didn't want to bother me with any of that.

I swallowed that pill, even if I had to choke a little to get it down. I'd be lying if I said she didn't wander through my mind at least once a week after the fact.

"Logan?! Oh my God— Your jacket, I am *so* fucking sorry. "

"No, it's fine!" I shake my head, holding back a laugh. "Abi, what are you doing here?"

She fiddles with one of her earrings, looking just as surprised as I am.

"Me? I'm– Well, I work here!"

Suddenly my soaked shirt doesn't even matter.

"Work? Here?"

"Yeah! I got a postdoc position here. I mean I guess I don't really technically work here yet, I'm starting today!"

I still can't believe she's right in front of me. I have to admit, I was tempted to look her up online, but I respected our promise not to hunt each other down. Besides, what the hell was I going to search? *Abi comma Hot?*

"Wow, that's quite a move!"

Hopefully she came here alone and not with her ex. I try to see if she's wearing a ring, but her left hand is stuffed in the pocket of her dress.

"Yeah, well, I needed a fresh start, and EBU had an opening."

The way she sucks on her lip makes me want to bite it, but I need self control now more than ever.

"I didn't know you worked here!" She squeaks, still blushing.

"Yeah. Been here for a while now."

"I couldn't really access the faculty portion of the website. Frankie said it's been down."

The faculty website is ancient. I swear, some idiot made it in the early 2000s with some of that good old Angelfire drag-and-drop bullshit, full of the standard slew of dead links and blank pages. Frankie tried to fix it himself but wound up almost tearing his hair out. He's still trying to convince the department that we need to live in the future— or at the very least the recent past.

"That site's about as useless as the G in lasagna."

"Actually, I think the G helps with pronunciation," Abi replies. "Linguistically speaking. Otherwise it would be *lah-sanna*."

I chuckle, nodding my head.

"Alright, point taken. But, hey, Postdoc is great! What department are you in?"

I figure shifting away from what may have been the most stupid comment about lasagna I've ever made is probably a good idea.

"Oh, Sociology! I'm sticking with it no matter what."

Is she serious? More importantly, is the *universe* fucking serious? Frankie didn't tell me anything about a new postdoc starting, but I guess that makes sense. Abi and I won't have a lot of crossover because she's not working under me.

Uh... *with* me.

"Wow! I knew we were looking, but I had to bail from the search committee, and Frankie's not allowed to talk about— I'm rambling, sorry. So, you moved here? All the way from Canada?"

"Yeah. Thank God for dual citizenship, huh?" She chuckles.

"Yeah, no kidding."

This whole thing is surreal. I'd just sort of accepted that I was never going to see her again, and now that she's here I'm struggling to keep myself from going straight for a kiss. Unfortunately, it looks like she may have caught on to the somewhat awkward situation as well.

"So, this is… unexpected."

She tucks a bit of hair behind her ear, shifting on her feet.

"Yeah…"

Wow, Flynn. Profound.

"Listen, I'm late to my next class, but—"

"Oh, gosh! I'm so—"

"No, no! I *like* talking to you." I suck in a deep breath. Just do it. "Do you want to meet up for a drink later and talk about this? There's a bar on campus—"

"The Hi-Dive," Abi replies. "Frankie gave me a tour."

"I'm done teaching around 4:00, so does that work for you? Don't worry, I'm buying!"

"I'm pretty certain I owe *you* a drink, actually." She gestures at my latte-soaked shirt and jacket. "And probably a dry-cleaning bill."

"How about you buy me a beer and we call it even?"

The Hi-Dive is falling apart, and it seems to get worse every year. The lights flicker like a haunted house, the floors seem perpetually sticky no matter how many times I've seen them mopped, and the place has been severely understaffed since the new owners took over, and that had to have been at least 2 years ago now.

But none of that is important. The drinks are cheap, the karaoke is amazing, and they wouldn't dare to charge us to play pool. If the cast of Friends has Central Perk, the EBU faculty have the Hi-Dive. All that to say, If this place ever closes, I'm probably going to have a mental breakdown.

"Hey! You better not have paid for that, we made a deal!"

Abi walks towards me, pointing at my beer as she does. The slight illumination from the only semi-transparent windows gives her an almost ethereal quality, and I find myself taken aback by the sight of her for the second time today.

"I, uh— Well, I mean technically, I spilled a drink on you first, so... you kind of got me back, right?"

"Well, I'll get the next one."

She orders a pint of beer for each of us, and follows me to the back of the bar, sliding into the seat across from me. We stare at each other in a silent standoff as we try to figure out who should start the conversation. I chose the spot tactically; it's probably the most quiet and private spot in the bar during their busier hours, not that there's anyone here to disturb us right now.

"So, this is..."

"Serendipitous?" She asks, her lips curling into an adorable little grin.

"I feel like we've had this conversation before."

"Maybe once."

I stare into my drink, hoping to find some sort of answer written at the bottom.

"So... you wanna talk about the elephant in the room?" I ask.

We might as well rip the bandaid off.

"Yeah. I think that's a good idea. Frankie's informed me of the staff fraternization policy."

I sigh, feeling my shoulders slouch as I deflate. That's what I was afraid of, but it's not unexpected, and it's not like I'm the kind of guy to break the rules or anything. I love my job, and I don't think I could start over at 36.

I tried to wait tables in college to make some extra cash, but it was a disaster. Sure, analyzing Habermas is a piece of cake, but working at Chili's? I was in the trenches. Mixing up orders, dropping full plates of food on the ground, and forgetting absolutely *everything* I'd been told. I lasted about two weeks before they finally fired me.

"I figured as much. Look, I don't want to make you uncomfortable, or make things weird by bringing our... past up out of nowhere."

"Logan, I really like you, and I've thought about that night a *lot*."

I sit up a little straighter.

"You have?"

"Yeah. But, you know…" She twists her drink nervously, chewing on her lip.

I have to crush the urge to reach out and stroke her cheek.

"We can't do what we did again," I finish for her.

"Exactly." She's smiling, but she looks about as bummed out as I feel. "And, if I can be honest?"

"Sure."

"Even if the rules weren't this strict, I… don't think I'm really ready to get into another relationship. Not right now."

Although I've been steeling myself for this conversation for hours now, the words still feel like a knife in the back. I don't want to be one of those guys who doesn't take rejection well, but it doesn't mean I'm not a little crushed.

I'll get over it, though, and I'll move on.

That's what people do, isn't it?

"I get that this is awkward, but the fact of the matter is, I had a fucking awesome time with you that night. And if it's not too weird, I'd really like to be your friend — if you need a friend."

"Yeah, I kind of do," she laughs. "Most of my friends are all the way back in Ontario, so… kind of have to start over."

For the longest time I was never really sure how adults were supposed to make friends. Do you just ask them, or is it better to naturally fall into familiar routines and conversations with people who match your energy? My dad was always so good at it; everywhere he went, he met up with some pal from the old days. I remember the day of his funeral, over 100 people showed up. It was incredible to see how many lives he'd touched.

Abi swallows, looking down at her drink. I can tell she misses home, and I try to fill the silence as best I can.

"I get it. I mean, take me for example: I'm from New York, my whole life was there before I pulled up my roots. Parents, sister, best friends, the whole nine yards. The good part is I think you'll find that this department is pretty tight-knit, and we take care of each other. I think anyone would struggle to find a better group of people to work with, with… maybe a couple exceptions."

"Everyone seems really great so far." She takes a sip of her beer. "I gotta say, I *definitely* didn't expect to run into you today, so my first day has been full of learning *and* unexpected surprises."

"Look, I know we have a bit of an awkward history, but if you ever need to talk, my door's always open — and will *remain* open. When we're both inside. Because of professionalism."

She raises a glass.

"To boundaries, and not freaking out when they're set."

"Hey, boundaries are great! What do you think keeps the zombies out in all of the movies?"

We clink glasses and dive into our drinks, as I resign myself to the fact that the woman I haven't been able to stop thinking about for months is now totally off-limits.

Out of reach again.

"So? Are you enjoying it here?" I ask. "The city, I mean."

At least this time I can still talk to her.

"I am, actually! The mountains are gorgeous, and I managed to get an apartment near Guardian Point. It's kind of small, but all my stuff fits in there. Everything except my books at least."

"I think that's an academic problem," I laugh. "I'm guessing they weighed... thirty, forty pounds a box? Can't imagine having to transport all of mine."

"They're comic books," she says softly, clearly a little embarrassed. "Kinda different."

"You read comics?"

Abi gives an enthusiastic nod.

It's the opposite, of course. It makes her at least twice as cool.

"I like the old horror comics. Twisted Tales, Tales from the Crypt, stuff like that."

This is blatantly unfair. I need to have a discussion with the universal force in charge of my love life because it just feels like I'm being curb stomped into the concrete at this point.

"Oh sure, my dad used to collect those."

"No way!"

"Yeah, he wrote a lot about horror, and its impact on social conscious-ness. You know, stuff like why we love to be scared, how horror influences culture, things like that."

"Is he an academic?"

Hearing him brought up in the present tense stings a little. I still text his number sometimes when I'm feeling down. Stuff like little reviews of movies I watch, papers I've gotten published... *I love you.*

It's my little way of holding on.

"He studied Cultural Anthropology."

"No shit!" Abi laughs. "That's what I got my PhD in!"

"Oh, maybe you've seen one of his papers. Declan Flynn?"

Her jaw drops and she leans in toward me, eyes shining with a newly burning passion.

"I've read five of his books! It's been a while since I dove into any of his work, but I'm pretty certain I remember it all!"

I puff my chest out and grin.

"Seriously, *he's* your dad?"

"Yep."

"Wow, that's amazing! Is he still writing? Or teaching?"

This part always sucks. There are a lot of people who read my dad's stuff and don't know that he's passed. When you Google him, his obituary isn't anywhere near the first result; his work is what floods the search engines.

Thankfully, it's exactly the way he would have wanted it.

"He's uh... he's passed away."

Abi's face pales, and she reaches across the table, putting her hand on the back of mine.

"I'm so sorry."

I fight the urge to reciprocate, to rush over and hold her. It's something I'm going to have to get used to.

"It's okay. He was really sick." I shake my head, a little ashamed that's the first thing I thought to mention. "He lived a good life, and went out on his own terms."

Her eyes widen, and I realize the implications of what I just said.

"You mean, like he..."

"No, not— It was medically assisted death," I tell her, hoping it does at least a little to ease her concerns. "The whole family was there, and the nurse walked us through the process. It was... peaceful."

And gut-wrenching.

That's the part I didn't talk about for such a long time, because it felt selfish to bring up. Who was I to question his decision? To crave his presence for just a little while longer, if all it would do was cause him more pain?

Once he was gone, I had to step up and be the man of the house. I insisted on dealing with lawyers and the paperwork so that mom and Imogen wouldn't have to. I made sure that everyone felt safe in their grief while I swallowed mine whole.

Abi and I sit quietly for a while, both of us staring down at the table, only stealing the occasional glance at each other. When Roman and I talk about this stuff, it's based in theory. I think it's a way for us to deal with our own personal tragedies without having to fully open up.

"So that's what inspires the work you do?" She finally asks, still not fully looking at me.

"Did you look me up?" I laugh.

"When I got back to my office after we met today, yeah," she confesses, somewhat sheepishly. "I just typed in 'Logan' and 'Emerald Bay University,' and all of your papers popped up."

"Ah, I see you had a chance to revel in my genius."

"I guess so," she laughs. "Listen, I was wondering if I could pick your brain about—"

"You can pick my brain any time, Shortcake."

"Shortcake?" she chuckles. "I'm 5'10", that's tall!"

"Not next to me," I reply with a smirk.

She rolls her eyes, kicking me gently under the table.

"Don't worry. You'll have all the time in the world to come up with an even worse name for me."

Really, what a great way to start the semester.

is it over now?

ABI

EMERALD BAY, WASHINGTON
PRESENT DAY

Piper, Imogen, and I are crammed into Emerald Bay's one and only vintage store, *Throwback*. It's a bit of a local hidden gem and I'm kind of obsessed with it. The owners are an old hippy couple, one of whom claims they used to be a fashion editor for Vogue back in the '70s. The two of them hand pick all of their pieces and get stuff from all over the world, which is pretty special for a little town like this.

"Oooh! Abi! Check it out, this would look incredible on you."

Imogen is holding up a gorgeous plum-colored crushed velvet dress that reminds me of an 80s era prom. It's short and a little small, seeming like it might just barely fit over my thigh, but when I tug on the material I can tell it's spandex right away.

One thing I quickly learned about Imogen is that she's got an eclectic style. She'll dress like a 70s rocker girl one day, and a cowgirl the next, and it feels like she could throw nearly anything together and still look amazing.

In contrast, everything I wear to work is stiff and structured, mostly black and white with a pop of color at most. I often find myself in high collars, higher waists, and a little bit of flare in the form of some black pointed boots. My mom's always said she thinks I dress like I'm auditioning for The Crucible.

She's kind of right, but I feel safe in those clothes.

I started the trip today by telling the girls I wanted to branch out; that I wanted something to actually show off my body for a change.

"It would be cute to wear to your high school reunion," Piper offers. "It'll go perfectly with your brand new fake boyfriend!"

I roll my eyes. Piper brought up the situation in our group chat, and neither her nor Imogen have let it go since, so much so that I just ended up RSVPing in the car out of spite.

"I already said I'm not doing the fake boyfriend thing."

"Aw, why not?" Imogen laughs. "What's wrong with my brother?"

They pestered me about it on the entire drive to Throwback.

"Nothing!" I reply, immediately wishing there was somewhere I could escape to. "I— Logan's the best. I just... I don't like having to lie to people. It makes me really uncomfortable."

"Why are you worried about lying to a bunch of people you haven't even seen in years?" Imogen asks.

"It's not just the people I went to high school with, it's..." I sigh. "Look, I told my mom too. So, if I bring Logan, we have to come up with a whole story; my mom will ask a *bunch* of questions, one of us will inevitably slip up, and it'll end up being super awkward for everyone."

I had some time in the car, in between the snark and quips, to come up with this perfectly good explanation. I think I delivered it pretty damn well considering.

Imogen shrugs her shoulders, looking a bit disappointed.

"Well, I'm just saying, you two are cute together— and more importantly you'd be totally believable as a couple."

I match Imogen's wry smile.

As far as anyone else is concerned, Logan and I didn't know each other before I set foot on campus. It's the secret we've both been keeping for years now. We never bring it up, we never acknowledge that night... but I can feel it sitting in the corner every time we're in the same room together.

"Don't start."

"I'm not starting!" Imogen laughs. "Piper, what am I starting?"

"I told her the same shit," Piper sighs, holding up a blue paisley jumpsuit. "But what do we think of this?"

I can always depend on Piper to prioritize shopping over talking boys.

"It's very 70s flower child," Imogen replies. "I love it."

"Yeah?" Piper eyes the jumpsuit with a mixture of suspicion and desire. "I'm afraid it tells people 'whoever wears this literally lives at Burning Man.'"

"We can't afford to go to Burning Man," I chuckle. "Just show them your bank statements and I think you'll be safe, babe."

"Well, I think it'll look cute with that leather belt you bought the other day." Imogen drapes her own bright pink dress over her arm. "As long as you wear some chunky heels."

"Alright, you sold me." Piper carefully places the jumpsuit into her little wicker shopping basket. "Are you ladies ready to try stuff on?"

Imogen thrusts another dress into my hands.

"Hang on, no rushing! This color is gorgeous, it goes so well with your hair."

The beautiful emerald color comes out wonderfully in the crushed velvet fabric, with little rhinestones stitched into the bodice adding an ostentatious flare. It's gaudy and glitzy, maybe even a bit tacky, and I fucking love it. If there's anything I adore in fashion it's camp, and really anything over the top. I think I walk a fine line between a Tim Burton character and Party City. When we finally got to know each other after Logan introduced the two of us, I remember Roman comfortably described me as 'the most confident walking cliche' he'd ever seen.

I took it as a compliment.

"Add it to the pile, I'll give it a whirl!"

The three of us head for the little saloon doors and slide into our change rooms.

I hang my dresses up and shed my clothes, starting with a long-sleeve 70s cocktail dress, sheer-black with white polka dots. At first I'm not sure I'm going to be able to get it up past my hips, but with a deep breath and a hell of a lot of hope, it slides down around my body. I pull my arms through the tiny sleeves and drag them down my shoulders to reveal a hell of a lot of collarbone.

I turn to the side, letting my hands glide over my stomach. It's protruding a little, but I like it, and this thing even makes my ass look good. My opinions aside, I'm still a bit nervous. I might think I look great, but what I think and what's really happening are sometimes two very different things in the fashion department.

I grab my phone in a moment of pique, snapping a picture and shooting it off to Logan for a second opinion.

ME

I need you to be honest. Is this too slutty, too 80s, or both?

Logan's got a very similar fashion sense as me. He's even joined us on a couple girl's days of thrifting, cocktails, and talking about our favorite smutty books.

SUNSHINE

I'm sorry, is this Hollywood's own Molly Ringwald? I thought my friend Abi was texting me. Give me a minute while I spread this all over the internet and I'll get right back to you!

It's hard not to blush. He's just so damn cute, even when he's being a total dork. I set my phone face down on the bench and grab the emerald dress that Imogen picked out. As pretty as it is, I quickly learn it doesn't even come close to getting over my hips.

My eyes light up when I slip on the final one, a certain plum colored dress that glides up my body with ease like it was meant to fit me. There's no tragic second-act to the show either, and it zips up with no extra effort, sitting comfortably against my body.

"Perfect..."

The fabric is almost buttery against my skin, and it still has a faint scent of perfume. Amber and sandalwood. I don't know if it's from all the incense they burn in here, but I love it all the same.

I snap another picture and send it to Logan.

ME

I think I like this one better. Thoughts? Or are you still busy committing crimes?

I would usually defer to Piper and Imogen for a final verdict, but sometimes you just need to go with the wild card. Besides, it's not uncommon for him to text me five different tie options first thing in the morning and demand that I make the decision for him. Time he put in the work.

I swear, our entire message history is just shit like this. No matter the topic, movies, music, or academic rigor, there's always going to be a tidal wave of stupid jokes. One time Logan even narrated his entire morning for me through voice memos. This man just proves the old adage that you really are only as old as you feel.

As I step out of my dressing room I catch sight of Imogen in a pair of tight bell bottoms and a little rainbow tube top, with a leather jacket thrown over it. Piper's off in the corner, checking herself out in the jumpsuit she grabbed, her dark hair cascading down her shoulders as she shifts back and forth in front of a mirror.

"Oh my God! This dress is amazing!" Imogen rushes up to me, immediately buzzing with excitement. "Fuck the green one I gave you, this is it!"

"I liked the green one, but this just feels..."

"It's perfect," Piper cuts in, glancing over from her corner. "It hits you in all the right places, babe. I'm a little jealous, I haven't been so lucky."

I beam, turning back around to stare at myself in the mirror one last time before heading back in and swapping into my street clothes

"Do you want to try on anything else?" I call as I'm climbing back into my jeans.

"Ummm, maybe shoes?" Imogen calls back. "I need something presentable for conferences."

"She means something Barbie-pink!" Piper shouts.

"Okay, and? Is that not presentable? Is it a crime or something?"

"No, just an observation! A very scientific observation based on years of research: You like pink!"

I giggle as I step out of the dressing room and wait for the girls to finish up, pulling out my phone to see if Logan's gotten back to me yet, only to feel the blood drain right out of my face when I see the notification.

BRENDAN HOWARD WANTS TO SEND YOU A
MESSAGE.

I stumble back, just barely landing on the bench behind me instead of heading straight to the floor.

This can't be happening.

Three years of no contact and now he wants to send me a message? I'm shaking with anger and adrenaline, my body cold and clammy as a bead of sweat trickles down the back of my neck. The fucking audacity of this man.

I gnaw on my lip. It might be better to just block him. Don't even read the message, just get it over with right away. What could he even say that would be worth reading? Or I could just not respond, let him think I never saw it. But then that notification will sit there, taunting me the whole time. Eventually, I'd roll over in the middle of the night and open it.

I know I would.

I'd type out some stupid response. Something I'd fire off without even thinking. I wouldn't even feel good about it afterwards.

"Abi, you ready?" Piper shouts from outside, obviously ready to leave.

"Yeah!" I snatch my belongings up off the bench and stand, feeling my phone clenched so tight in my hand I think I might crush it.

Imogen raises her eyebrows as I rush out, both girls exchanging a look.

"You good, babe?" Piper asks.

"Totally fine," I say far too quickly, sounding out of breath despite barely having moved at all. "Why?"

"Because you look like you saw a ghost," she tilts her head. "And your hands are all white, are you sure you're okay?"

I let out my breath, my stomach bubbling as I try to relax. I feel like I could throw up.

"My ex messaged me."

"The dickhead who ghosted you?" Piper gasps.

I nod and Imogen grabs my hand.

"Fuck shoes. We're going to get a drink. We can help you figure out what to do."

"I think it's better to just block him, isn't it?"

She scoffs.

"And give him the satisfaction of winning? Fuck no!"

Before I can even respond, she's dragged me to the cash register and we're working out paying for our items.

"So where are we going?"

"To Simmer Down!" Imogen replies, taking her receipt and rushing me out the door with a wink. "I know a *really* sexy prep cook who'll let us drink for cheap."

Simmer Down isn't far from Throwback, maybe a ten minute walk, and it's a perfect blend of old Italian restaurant and New York deli.

The hostess beams at Imogen as we enter, picking up some menus.

"Hey, Ig!"

"Hey Charlotte, is my man here?"

"He's on his fifteen, hiding away in the back office. Want me to grab him for you?"

Imogen strides right in like she owns the place, but there's no resistance at all. It's clearly a normal thing around here.

"Nah, I can do it myself. Thanks though!"

"You want your usual table near the window?" Charlotte calls after her.

"That'd be great! Thanks, babe!"

Charlotte's curly red hair bounces up and down as she leads us toward a bright and spacious table by the window, with a lovely view of the street. Piper orders a margarita pitcher along with some appetizers for the three of us, and I can feel her gaze on me as Charlotte leaves to get our drinks.

"I should reply, shouldn't I?" I ask, nervously tapping on the back of my face-down phone.

"You do whatever you need to do. Don't let me or Imogen pull you away from what you think is best." She leans over, cupping a hand around the side of her mouth with a whisper. "But personally, I think you should tell him to sit on a chainsaw."

I snort, nodding and flipping my phone over. I shouldn't even be entertaining messaging Brendan back, but I need to see what he has to say for himself.

BRENDAN

Wow, you RSVPd?

I give an indignant scoff. Did he and Carly invite me out of pity? Or obligation?

My fingers linger over the keypad for a few moments, but deep down I know I already made my decision. No point in prolonging it any longer.

ME

Yeah. I did. Figured it'd be nice to see everyone.

I thought about lying, pretending I didn't see who was hosting, maybe that I clicked on it by accident, but that just makes the entire thing even more pathetic. Besides, there's a chance he won't even see the message, or at least won't see it for hours. I can come up with a perfect speech in my own time.

Absolutely tear into him.

But then right as I'm about to flip my phone back over, I see it.

BRENDAN IS TYPING…

"What the fuck?" I whisper.

"What? What's he saying?"

"Shhhh, nothing yet."

I wait for a minute or so, watching the ellipses appear and disappear.

The classic sign of having no damn clue what you're planning to say.

> BRENDAN
>
> Oh, so it wasn't a mistake, then. Cool. I guess I'll
> see you.

I hand Piper my phone and watch as her eyes nearly bug out of her head.

"Is he fucking serious?! I'm gonna crawl into that phone and—"

My heart is racing and my palms are already clammy. She slides out of her seat and into the one next to me, setting the phone down.

"Hey, hey, we don't need to talk about this stuff. You look like you need an Emotional-Support-Piper, at least until we get the margaritas."

"I do," I chuckle, giving her shoulder a gentle squeeze. "Thanks."

But I'm not done with Brendan Howard today. Not by a *long* shot.

> ME
>
> YOU invited ME.

That beautiful ellipses, that tells me he's at the very least a little flustered, appears and disappears a dozen or so times. I stare at it, my phone trembling like a leaf in my hands.

"What's he saying?" Piper asks, trying her best not to read over my shoulder.

"Nothing yet."

When my phone finally buzzes a minute or two later, I nearly jump out of my skin.

> BRENDAN
>
> We had to invite everyone. I think Carly just
> clicked send all or something. I didn't really have
> anything to do with it. I just didn't expect you to
> say yes after everything that went down between
> us. Just kinda surprised me so I thought you
> might have been hacked or something. It's cool
> though, you can come.

"Everything that went *down* between us?!" I hiss. "It's *cool?* Is he fucking serious?"

My rage feels like a volcanic eruption, the aftershocks tingling all the way down to the tips of my toes.

"Tell him—"

"I got it. I got it, don't worry."

My fingers are already flying across the keyboard.

ME

Brendan, I have every right to want to see MY friends and go to MY high school reunion in MY hometown. If you think I need your permission to come, you've got another think coming you deluded prick.

There's another pause, but much faster than the last time I got a reply.

BRENDAN

It's thing.

I blink.

ME

What?

BRENDAN

You said I had another think coming. It's thing.

You know that scene in Return of the Jedi where Luke just beats the shit out of Darth Vader with his lightsaber, and the whole time the Emperor is cackling behind him? I feel like Luke right now, and the little Palpatine on my shoulder is telling me to give Brendan everything I've got.

"Get his ass," Piper murmurs, a malicious sense of glee in her voice.

"Way ahead of you. There's nothing worse than an idiot who thinks they're right about something."

"Careful he doesn't drag you down to his level and beat you with experience," Piper replies as Charlotte brings over our margaritas. "Seems like he's been an idiot since birth."

ME

Brendan, not that any of this matters, but it is
'think.' You should try Googling it, maybe along
with how NOT to end a relationship like a coward.

BRENDAN

Yeah, I knew you'd hold that against me.

ME

I'll see you at the reunion. Right along with my
fiancé. Maybe you can learn how a real man's
supposed to act.

The moment I hit send, that same sense of dread from the other day washes over me. What the fuck did I just do?

"Abi, what the fuck did you—"

I put my head in my hands and shove my phone toward her.

"Take this away from me!"

Fiancé?! What the hell was I thinking?

"Abi, are you alright?" Roman's voice booms from above me. "You look like you're gonna be sick."

I lift my head slowly, gazing up into his warm hazel eyes currently full with concern. He's holding one of those big clear containers, filled to the brim with Diet Coke, a wedge of lime floating on the top.

"Piper, show him the phone," I groan, leaning back in my seat.

Roman's brow creases as he reads over the messages, and Imogen gets up on her tiptoes, covering her mouth as she starts to catch herself up.

Roman's eyes meet mine, his expression serene, maybe even a little amused.

"So?" He asks, sipping his drink. "Who's the lucky guy, and where's he been hiding?"

I swallow the bile that's been creeping up inside me.

"Logan. God dammit, it's gotta be Logan."

It's like the words themselves are burning away at my throat.

pretty boy

LOGAN

EMERALD BAY, WASHINGTON
PRESENT DAY

I lean over my desk, pushing my glasses up the bridge of my nose as I try to decipher my own bullshit. I've re-written this sentence four times and it still doesn't make any sense, even less when I realize everything's looking blurry. I took my contacts out because I swore I was going to bed.

Three hours ago.

"Okay, let's try this again." I sit up straight and massage my temples as I decide to read aloud. I dunno, sometimes it helps. "*'Late modernity posits that individuals are responsible for their own thoughts, their actions, and their own destiny. Therefore, it is assumed that individuals have complete and total power to change the conditions within which they live, if they choose to do so...'* Alright, sure. Sounds fine, but what the *fuck* am I actually talking about?"

The big grandfather clock in my office ticks menacingly in the background, and it's only then that I notice the symphony that was pouring from the record player is silent.

No more Beethoven.

I still have at least two pages worth of edits to finish before my deadline and no idea what the fuck I'm reading. I'm starting to think that pulling these all-nighters isn't helping me the way it used to.

Just as I'm contemplating putting on a pot of coffee, my phone buzzes, rattling against my desk.

ABI CALLING…

I scoop it up immediately. She's usually in bed with a book by 9:00. "Abi?"

"Sunshine!" Her voice crackles over the line, and one word's all it takes to suss out the fact that she's at least a little drunk. *"I need help."*

"What happened?" I get to my feet, already looking for my shoes. "Are you okay?"

"I told Roman and Imogen I'd walk home from—" she hiccups. *"But I can't find my phone!"*

Normally I'd probably be a little annoyed that the two of them left someone alone like this, but it's distressingly likely Abi just snuck out the back to make her way home alone. She can be stubborn after even a couple cocktails, and it sounds like we're definitely into a few more than that.

"How many drinks have you had?" I ask, slipping my hoodie on.

"I don't knooooow! It was sad-drinking. There's no rules with sad-drinking!"

"Sad drinking, why were you sad drinking?" I ask, checking my pockets for my keys.

"Because I'm a big screw up!" She whines. *"And I can't find my phone!"*

I can picture her right now, stomping her foot and doing that little pout she does when she's over tired, annoyed, or too intoxicated for her usual filter.

"Well, I have at least a little bit of good news for you. You found your phone."

"I did?"

Her voice sounds squeaky, like she's playing a cartoon mouse in a show.

"Yep!" I laugh. "Unless I'm mistaken, you're using it right now, aren't you?"

"Wh—" I hear rustling, followed quickly by that boisterous drunken

laughter I'm so familiar with. *"Oh my God! Logaaaan! This is so embarras-siiiiing!"*

"Why don't I come and pick you up? Drop me your location and I'll be there quick."

"Dromywha?"

"You know what? Don't stress it. Just tell me where you are."

"No, I can walk! I can do it! I'm sorry I called you, I'm–"

"You're not walking, and no sorry's necessary. Where are you?"

"Right outside Duffer's Donuts," she sighs. *"I feel sick."*

"I'll take you back to your apartment, and get you all set up to deal with your hangover in the morning."

"Noooo!" She sobs. *"No consequences, only beer!"*

"Ten minutes, alright? Do *not* move from where you are!"

I hang up and slide my slippers on, an adorable pair covered in little bats. Abi got them for me as a Christmas present last year and I wear them all the time. I've even brought them to work a few times, just to have something to relax in when I'm trapped in my office. Frankie wasn't particularly fond of that idea, although to his credit I probably shouldn't have worn them to class.

The second I'm in the car, I drag out my phone to a text from Abi. It's a selfie of the underside of her chin, a bit of text laid out underneath it.

SHORTCAKE

This is me not moving.

"Atta girl," I chuckle, pulling out of the driveway and gingerly dropping the phone into my cup holder.

If she's hammered like this, it means she probably let her anxiety get the best of her. She's not a mean drunk, but she is emotional. Most of the time, she passes out before she can cry all of her makeup off and tell everyone she loves them for the hundredth time. I think a part of her is always worried she's going to lean on substances for comfort just like her dad did, so there's a level of shame there as well. Kinda explains why she always tries to bail at the end of any night that goes this way.

I take a deep breath and push the thought out of my mind as I pull up to Duffer's Donuts. Abi's sitting on the curb, dressed in a gigantic blue hoodie that has to belong to Roman. It's obviously far too big for her, but besides that I know pretty much everything in her wardrobe at this point.

She turns to rifle through her purse, not quite noticing the car yet, just in time for the wind to kick up and spill tubes of lipstick and pens every-where. Her head snaps up from her desperate attempt to regain her loot and she smiles, sticking her arms straight up in the air.

"My hero!"

But of course, she also takes the opportunity to break into song: *My Hero* by the Foo Fighters, except she doesn't seem to know the words, and based on the impression I think she's mixed up Scott Stapp and Dave Grohl.

"Hey, drunkie!" I laugh, climbing out of the car. "What was the drink of choice tonight?"

"Margaritas." She lets out a dorky giggle, swaying from side to side. "I *am* Margaritaville!"

"Jimmy Buffet would be so proud."

"His name is *James Bouffet*," she scoffs, over-enunciating every single part. "Get it right, Mr. Know-It-All!"

"I don't think—" I stop myself. This is *absolutely* not the time to be arguing about the true identity of hit musician James Bouffet. "The margaritas were good, then?"

"They were..." she closes her eyes, pointing dramatically at the sky with one finger as she sings, "amaziiiiing!"

Then, she's on her way over, with all the grace of a newborn foal, trip-ping over the strap of her purse and stumbling right into my arms.

"Whoops! Sorry!" She snorts, looking around. "Wherethefuckis..."

She mimes lifting something up and down a few times, a sad look on her face.

"Purse?"

"Yes!" She pats me on the chest. "You're the smartest giant I've ever met!"

I can't help but laugh. She's like a chaotic gremlin when she's hammered like this.

"Wow, you are *drunk*, dude!"

Abi scrunches her nose up at me and does a full spin, some sort of wordless rebuttal, but she forgets me again immediately when she spots her bag, flailing her arms in the air.

"Found it!"

I follow behind, helping her gather up the mess she's made. Pens, hair clips, candy wrappers, and three pairs of wired headphones that are all tangled into one giant rat king of cords. It's the lipstick that really gets my attention though; she's got at *least* fifteen tubes that I can see, and I know for a fact there's more in her bag.

"How do you have so much of this shit?" I laugh, picking up one of the bullets.

"*Because* I like to coordinate them with my *outfits*, Logan!" She whacks me in the arm. "It's like you don't know me at all!"

"You're right, you're right. I don't know you at all, Shortcake."

She clicks her tongue and makes a little *aww* sound, leaning up against me as I pass her purse over to her.

"I didn't mean that," she sighs. "You're just a bit of a butt, but you know everything! I want to be *mysterious* but you know all my *secrets!*"

I grin. As much as we hang out, there's actually a lot I don't know about her. She keeps her past pretty guarded, and I always figured she'd open up when she was ready. I guess we just never really got there.

"Come on." I help her to her feet and carry her bag. "Let's get you home."

I help her into the car, making sure to put my hand on her head to make sure she doesn't give herself a concussion before jogging to the driver's side. Abi's wasted no time, already mid-way through a fight with her seatbelt by the time my ass hits the seat.

"Hey, chill, this is an old car! You've gotta be gentle with her!"

I fixed this one up about two years ago and she runs like a dream, but Abi's found pretty much the only problem with it: the seatbelt.

"Here, let me."

I gingerly let it retract before slowly pulling it forward again. securing her in with a soft click. She stares at me in complete bewilderment.

"How'd you do that so good?"

"I'm sober," I tease.

She snorts, gently whacking me in the arm as I buckle myself in. The second I pull out of the parking lot she's clearly flagging, and three or four blocks out she's fast asleep, head against the window and clutching her purse as tight as she can.

I smile, watching the gentle rise and fall of her chest in the rearview mirror. The drive is just as quiet on the way back to her apartment as the way out, not a car in sight until I turn down a side street. There are a bunch of cars parked outside of a big house on the corner with a couple of passed out freshmen on the lawn. Them aside, I can identify at least another two people who are having a *much* worse night than Abigail King.

The thumping bass from the house quickly fades into the background as I take the final toward her little building. It's a cute place, and it sort of has a New York brownstone feel to it despite being from the completely wrong place and time. I've always been pretty fond of it, but Abi hates the building. The water pressure is garbage, it's too cold in the winter, a furnace in the summer, and worst of all the handles are always breaking off of her cupboard doors. I swear, we've replaced them at least five times.

I kill the engine, sitting for a few minutes in silence before I lean over and gently shake her awake.

"We're here."

She lifts her head, eyes barely opening as she groans. Her lipstick is smeared across her mouth and she sniffles a couple times before she moves, opening her door and struggling to get out while completely forgetting her seatbelt predicament. Her body jerks forward and back, and back and forward again as she grunts.

"Why am I in car jail?!"

I manage to hold back a snicker until I reach the back of the car, but the challenge becomes significantly harder when I get a full view.

"Logaaaaan!" She bellows from the passenger seat. "Get me out of this prison! This is unconstitutional! I have a Charter of Rights and Freedoms!"

"Do you know what country you're in?" I ask, opening her door.

"*You're* a country," she slurs. "Get me out!"

"Alright, calm down."

I crouch down, reaching over to unbuckle her as she continues to try valiantly to get herself out. When her seatbelt is finally released, she lurches forward right into my arms and we both tumble backward onto the hard pavement. My shoulder hits the ground first and I hiss in pain, hoping for a bruise over a fracture. As if on-cue, Abi's purse smacks me right beneath my eye.

"Ow! Abi!"

She tries to scramble off me, but then I hear a yelp and she falls back down all over again, nearly knocking the wind out of me.

"'M'sorry!" She yelps, rolling off me and onto her side.

I grunt, forcing myself to sit up despite the pain, glancing over at her. Her dark hair is a mess of chaotic frizzy waves around her head, her little bat barrette is barely holding on by a thread.

"I'm too druuuunk," she groans, flopping back onto the ground and nearly falling into a puddle.

"You are, but you're mostly harmless. That bag's got a hell of a right hook, though."

She's unsteady, clinging to me as I lock the car. I swear, the smell of tequila gets more potent as time passes. It's like she swam in it.

"You don't hate me, do you?"

It's hard not to melt when she looks up at me with those big doe eyes... even if one of them is wandering a little because of the alcohol.

And that's when I notice she's missing a shoe.

"I don't hate you." I cup her face in my hands. "You're my favorite person in the world."

Her cheeks heat up against my palms and she reaches all the way around me, letting herself hang off of me like I'm a set of monkey bars.

"You're mine."

Boy, do I wish this was literally any other context. If she asked, I'd go steady with her in a heartbeat, work regulations be-damned. Right now, it's all I can do to keep my mind from wandering to that place. It tends to get stuck, and I know if I let myself indulge in that fantasy too often I could get lost in it forever.

"Let's go."

I walk her up to her apartment— actually, it's more like dragging her up to her apartment. This building doesn't have an elevator and getting her up the stairs is tough.

When I unlock the door, Abi immediately rushes toward the rat cage.

"Hi babies!" She coos, sticking her fingers in and giggling as they lick her. "Oh, I missed you! Here, I'm gonna give you some extra yummies to make up for being gone so so so long."

I grin, grabbing her a big glass of water from the kitchen as she fawns.

I love Wednesday and Lydia. When Abi's out of town, I look after them with Frankie. She doesn't really like moving them much, so we take turns swinging by the apartment to make sure they get enough playtime, and obviously all the food they could want. Sometimes we bring my XBox over and play Halo while the rats use us as a makeshift obstacle course. Wednesday's a little more rambunctious, but Lydia always ends up napping on my shoulder.

"Here." I pass her the glass of water when I finally manage to get her attention away from her little babies. "Drink."

She grabs it with both hands, guzzling it down like she's just run an entire marathon in an hour. Some of the water drips down her chin and onto her tank top; when she's finished, she presents it to me with a big smile.

"Done! What now?"

"Now, we get you into bed."

"Oh, I love bed!" She gushes as I gently guide her toward her room.

Abi's room is honestly the coolest I've ever seen from a working adult. She's got big framed comic book prints, movie posters, and loads of rubber bats hanging from the ceiling that glow under a black light.

I help her pick out a set of comfy pajamas and then head outside while she changes.

"You need to wash up or anything?"

"I've got makeup wipes."

She opens the door dressed in a big silk pajama top with little bats on it, and a pair of matching short shorts that show off the tiny tattoo on her upper thigh. It's a little heart that she gave herself when she was in grad school. I have very distinct memories of tracing it with my tongue that night in Toronto.

She blinks at me, rubbing her eye with a makeup wipe and smearing mascara halfway down her face. Her hair has gotten even messier and she's doing a horrible job of wiping off her eyeliner.

I bet she's long-since forgotten.

"Here, I might be able to help."

I clean up her cheeks, carefully dabbing under and around her eyes. She lets out a frustrated little growl, and it's the third time this evening that it's taken everything in me not to just lean in and kiss her.

"I did something dumb," she murmurs.

"What?"

"I told Brendan you were my fiancé… and that we'd be going to the reunion. I did it to rub it in his stupid ugly face, but I know it was wrong."

The fake fiancé thing?

She's clearly exhausted, slurring her words as her eyes glaze over more and more, but I'm still stuck on that revelation. I thought we were just joking around like we usually do. I didn't mean to plant something in her head.

"You told him we were engaged?"

"Are you mad?" She asks, her voice equal parts apologetic and gravely.

"Of course I'm not mad, but you *definitely* need some sleep. Maybe I can give you a call in the morning and we can talk about this? If you still want to when you wake up at least."

"Okay."

I help her climb into bed, tucking the blankets around her and bracing an extra pillow behind so she doesn't roll onto her back in the middle of the night.

"I'd be your fake fiancé," I murmur. "All you have to do is ask."

CHAPTER TWELVE

LOGAN

EMERALD BAY, WASHINGTON
LATER THAT NIGHT

I turn the engine over and start the short trip back to my place. When I pull into the driveway, I sit and stare at the house. I love this house, but it gets lonely sometimes. Growing up with siblings in a big Irish family, people were always coming and going. Dinner parties, Sunday brunch, birthdays, and at least half the neighborhood would show up when my mom had afternoon tea.

Don't get me wrong, I like my solitude, but there are some nights I go to sleep with an ache realizing I don't have someone to brush my teeth with.

When I get inside, instead of heading back to my laptop to finish up those edits, I find myself in the kitchen, taking out a couple of mixing bowls along with some heavy cream, vanilla, pumpkin puree, pumpkin pie spice, cinnamon sticks, and maple syrup.

Abi adores this pumpkin creamer at Déjà Brew. She goes nuts for it the second fall hits. In fact, she's said she would start a riot for the last drop of it. Apparently it's *that* good. The only problem is, this creamer is seasonal. Thankfully, before the old manager Ashley ran off with that chem professor, I think his name was Chuck? She let me in on the secret recipe. It's just a splash of vanilla.

That's it.

Which is great, because I figure Abi's gonna need a hefty dose of one of her favorite things to help ease her hangover tomorrow.

I start by grabbing a whisk, dumping the ingredients in a big bowl, and putting on some music so I don't feel so crushed by the silence that's been permeating the house since Iggy moved in with Roman. He's the person who really taught me how to cook, long before my sister and him got together, but I've gotten even more into it lately, and I think I've improved a lot. I was always curious, but never thought I had the skill until I finally took the dive and really applied myself. I'm still not anywhere near his level, but I've got a knack for transforming the recipes he provides into my own unique thing.

Admittedly, sometimes it's by burning them, but that's besides the point.

When my sister got diagnosed with ADHD during her bachelor's degree, I thought about getting myself checked out. Imogen and I are alike in a lot of ways. We tend to latch on to certain hyperfixations, and we both often find ourselves so focused on a single thing that everything disappears around us. Normally that would be fine, and sometimes even useful, but it gets a lot more difficult when you forget to do basic things like eat, drink water, or even take a piss until suddenly your body's on high-alert.

Hell, back when I was in high school I was late or nearly late all the time. I just didn't understand how people had so much time in the mornings. How the hell did they get everything done and *still* make it to class? Of course, the answer was just that they weren't getting hung up on every other thing they laid their eyes on.

My tenth grade report card concluded, and I quote, *'Logan is a pleasure to have in class. However, at times he refuses to apply himself, and his antics sometimes distract his classmates,'* which... not so bad, right?

I got off easy.

Imogen was slower to start, more distracted, zoned out a lot— even mid conversation. Ultimately her diagnosis was a blessing, and a good first step toward treatment.

But by the time she got her assessment, I was afraid that the doctors wouldn't take me seriously. After all, I had never really had trouble in school— not the way she did. I never failed a class, I jumped straight into a PhD after my Bachelor's degree and things got a little easier as I got older. I had a great job, I was writing books, teaching courses I loved, and guest lecturing at universities. More than anything, it had just been too long. Besides, I had adapted, so clearly it wasn't a big deal.

The intense bouts of anger for no reason, the disorganization, the time blindness, and the difficulty fitting in socially was all chalked up to my 'genius,' even by me after a while.

And that was a problem: knowing I was different made it so hard to connect with people. I felt like I constantly had to soften my rougher edges, the parts of me that were acceptable at home but weird in public. That's one of the reasons I got rushed into post-secondary. Academia opened up my entire world— socially, emotionally, and psychologically.

I finally found people who got it.

The heat from the stove drags me back into the kitchen, my mind briefly struggling to make the jump, as usual.

I shake my head, grabbing a pot.

I didn't even realize I'd turned it on.

"Jesus, Flynn. Try not to burn the goddamn house down, will ya?"

I pour the creamy mixture into the pot and let it warm up on medium, stirring it a bit every half minute or so to make sure it doesn't get too thick. The last thing Abi needs is lumps in her coffee. Once it's finished, I let it cool for a few minutes before giving it a try.

It tastes like... pumpkin? Which makes sense I guess. It's a little sweet, but not too bad, and after a moment or two the vanilla really does come in with a bit of a bite. It's *almost* as good as the stuff from Déjà Brew, at least as far as my uncultured tongue can tell.

"Not bad, Flynn." I nod to myself as I pour the rest into a thermos. "Not bad at all."

I head down the hall, stripping off my clothes and tossing them into the hamper before changing into a pair of sweatpants and rifling through my closet to pick out my outfit for tomorrow. My bedroom, like every other place in the house, is filled with horror memorabilia. Posters, figurines— I even have an original slate from the Evil Dead movie. It's signed and everything. I paid *way* too much money for it, but it was worth every penny. This, of course, leaves a little less space for the more... practical things one might expect in a bedroom.

Basically, my organization leaves a bit to be desired.

After a while sifting through different drawers and closet space, my eyes finally land on a shirt, specifically the one I wore the night Abi and I first met.

I still blush thinking back on it. The way she moaned beneath me, the softness of her skin, but it's impossible to forget the way she rode me with such reckless abandon.

It was like she was trying to forget.

I knew I was a rebound that night, a balm for her pain. Even if she didn't say anything, it would have been obvious.

I didn't care.

Abi and I had this intense connection, one that bled from that 'one night,' long into the next morning. She was bright and witty, and *so* quick on her feet. She laughed at my shitty jokes, but it never felt like she was laughing *at* me. She got them.

Maybe we were just two people aching for someone to understand us, and maybe it wasn't anything more than that, but I was head over heels after that night, and it was everything I could do to let her go. If I couldn't have Abi as a girlfriend, I still wanted her in my life.

And then she was back, back in my life, and exactly what I wanted, what we both said we wanted, happened. We became friends. The very best of friends.

And it was perfect. Exactly the way it should have been.

But whenever the subject of settling down came up, I got cagey.

Because the only person I ever felt truly comfortable with, the one that no one else can measure up to, is the one the two of us agreed I just can't have.

Because we figured it all out.

Because we're such good friends.

I let out a deep breath, fiddling with my dad's watch hanging slightly loose on my wrist as I think back on his words.

Promise me you'll fall in love.

Promise me that.

Because at the end of the day, when you add everything up, there's nothing else that matters.

"I'm trying, dad."

I tighten the band, re-adjusting it for what has to be the hundredth time.

"I'm trying."

this is me trying

LOGAN

FIVE YEARS AGO
UPSTATE NEW YORK

"You know, they used to make shit that lasts!"

Dad's been shouting mostly random complaints and curses for the last few minutes in his thick Cork accent, waving a broken shovel the entire time.

IMOGEN

So how is he?

ME

Threatening the gardening tools. Other than that? Seems fine.

IMOGEN

Oh, okay. So normal.

"Fuckin' piece of shite!"

ME

Totally.

The chemo's been taking its toll for a while now, and while he hides it pretty well, it's starting to become more and more evident. It seems innocuous, but he's started wearing hats; at first I thought it was just a late-age fashion change until I noticed the clumps of hair in the shower. After that I started paying a lot more attention, probably more than would be considered healthy. He's more exhausted than ever, but if Declan Flynn is anything, above all else, he's stubborn as a mule. He's always insisted he's fine, and that he never needs help with anything, even as his body is completely betraying him.

Some days, I don't think he's fully accepted his diagnosis.

Most days, I'm pretty sure I haven't either.

"I think it might be a user error, dad," I tease, setting a couple beers down on the patio table beside him. "You're really going all-out on those cucumbers."

Thankfully, today is a good day. He's got enough energy to do a little bit of gardening, and complain *very* loudly about the shitty tools that he paid far too much money for.

He puts his hands on his hips, lowering his aviator sunglasses as he glares at me.

"Y'know, Logan, if there were two cunts in this town, you'd be both of 'em."

I start laughing almost immediately; I can't help it, I see so much of my sister in him. They definitely have the same death stare. If there are two things the cancer hasn't managed to tear off of him, it's his quick wit and quicker temper.

"Come and get your drink, old man!"

He waves me off, dismissing the notion as he bends down to retrieve his shovel before trudging back to the shed. He used to be quick on his feet, dancing and jumping on a whim. More than that, though, he loved to run.

The cancer's taken all of that from him. He was diagnosed with glioblastoma three months ago, and the doctors gave him another eighteen, tops. Now he spends his days barely managing the headaches, nausea and dizziness, while pretending nothing's changed.

There's a part of me that's always counting down, constantly reminding me how little time is left, but I took the most cliché advice I'd ever heard, and decided to try to take each day as it comes. It turns out it's not just something people say to you when they don't know what else to say. Some days are better than others, sure, but we watch rugby matches and baseball games, we drink beer and talk about horror and pop culture, and all the while I just keep thinking he might beat this somehow.

He'll get better and he'll be my dad again.

He has to, because the reality of facing a world without him terrifies me.

Nobody talks about the time leading up to that loss. How it's like putting on armor every morning, spending days and weeks and months bracing yourself for a punch that's going to knock you out, no matter how hard you try to keep standing.

Dad told me that he wouldn't let me put my life on hold for him, but I did it anyway. He spent years taking care of me, wiping tears and bandaging skinned knees, and now I spend my days helping with chores around the house, doling out his medication, and making sure there's always at least a little bit of laughter.

Even on the hardest days.

Especially then.

In contrast, Imogen isolated herself. Don't get me wrong, it's not like she's given up. Just earlier today she mentioned looking into an experimental treatment in the UK. Like me, she's hoping for a miracle. The difference is, a phone call is the closest she's managed to get, and every time she gets the courage to ask about him, I can hear her voice crack.

Mom's... Well, at first I thought she was just pretending none of it was happening, but then I caught a glimpse of her out one night, sitting in the backyard and crying into her glass of wine. She's always been private about her grief, never wanting to burden anyone with it.

When I think about it, I don't even think any of their friends ever really saw them apart; Annie and Declan Flynn have been practically attached at the hip for 34 years, and I'm not sure what she's going to do without him.

I rub my eyes, watching him walk toward me, wobbling with each step. The tumor's been messing with his equilibrium and he's been unsteady on his feet for a few weeks now. I move to help him, but he lets out a snarl as he swats me away.

"I'm fine, Logan."

"Okay." I raise both hands, letting him stumble toward the lawn chair and slowly ease himself down into it.

Mom told him he should think about a wheelchair, but he brushed the idea off without a thought. Said he'll walk until it's too hard to take another step.

I pop the cap off his beer and slide it over to him.

That's just who he is.

"Garden looks good."

"Yeah. Those pink roses your sister likes are really taking to this new fertilizer I got."

"Different brand?"

"The dog next door keeps hopping the fence and shitting in the rose bush," he laughs. "I figured he's not destroying them, so what's the harm?"

The two of us clink our bottles together, staring out at the gorgeous summer day. Sometimes I like to sit out here with a good book and just get lost in it all, the words and the breeze and the heat. It reminds me of the first summer I spent at home after college, back when I was still deciding if I wanted to follow in dad's footsteps or not.

I was so anxious about making the right decision that the first thing I did after I parked my car in the driveway was go straight into his office and ask for his opinion.

"It doesn't matter if you choose to be a plumber or get a fuckin' PhD, both are just as necessary. I'll always be proud of you, mo chuisle."

His little name for me. It means *my pulse.*

He calls Imogen mo stórín.

My little treasure.

Of course Mom is mo ghrá.

My love.

"It's a cruel irony, you know..."

I watch as he tears at the edge of the label on his beer, getting most of it off before balling it up between his thumb and forefinger, the same way he's always done when he's anxious about something.

"What is?" I ask.

"Growing all this while I'm dying." He gestures to the gorgeous garden he's spent years creating. "I've only got 15 months, but even then I don't know if I have the energy to live what I have left."

Dad sleeps a lot, more and more in the last few months. Sometimes we catch him dozing off in the middle of dinner, and try our best to pretend we didn't notice when he wakes up. His body's exhausted from fighting; he's both physically and psychologically depleted from the anxiety, the legal bullshit, and everything else that comes along with watching your own life slip away. I can tell he's starting to get fed up with it all; he finds the whole thing humiliating.

"We'll fit in the important stuff," I tell him. "Iggy's coming out soon."

"Yeah." My dad nods. "That'll be nice to have you both under one roof, fightin' and teasin' each other just like old times."

Iggy and I were terrors to each other growing up. You might think I'd be the mature one with a ten-year age difference, but I learned quickly that it's a brother's sworn duty to terrorize his little sister, and I'm never one to shirk when family is involved. She got me back, though, almost as often as I got her.

Maybe even more when she was a teenager.

"I don't want to die."

His words are pinched at the edges, and raw with grief.

"I have so much more—"

I watch his face crumple, tears rushing down his cheeks as he swears under his breath. He rests his head in his hands and I feel myself grip my beer bottle so tight I think it might just shatter.

The cruelest thing about all of this is that there's nothing I can do; anything I say is trite and meaningless. Every night, he goes to bed counting how many days he has left to breathe this air, to see the sun, or to smell those damn pink roses in the garden.

"It's okay, dad."

He shakes his head, tears rushing down his face.

I can only imagine that kind of terror, or how paralyzing it must be.

"I wasn't done raising the two of you. I wasn't done being proud of you. Loving you. I wasn't done watching your mother dance in the kitchen every morning. I wasn't done writing, I wasn't done teaching…"

He collapses into sobs and I'm pulled out of my chair by some invisible force, crouching down in front of him, my hands on his knees.

He looks up at the sky like he wants to curse it, but he doesn't have the strength.

When he was diagnosed, I told God to go fuck himself.

If his faith is right, and there's an all-knowing, all-seeing divine presence that could make this all go away but chooses not to? Chooses to take people like my dad?

That's fucking cruel.

"I just want the two of you to be happy," he whispers. "I want you to find someone who loves every single part of you, even those damn mismatched socks."

My laughter turns to sobs as I press my forehead into his knee. We haven't had many talks like this. For the most part, both of us just pretend none of it is happening when we're around each other.

"Promise me you're gonna be okay. That you'll look after your mum and your sister."

"I promise."

"And I want you to find somebody, to fall in love. Because at the end of the day, there's nothing else that matters."

"I will, dad."

He kisses my forehead, just like he used to do when I was a kid, before he'd 'fight off monsters' that were hiding under my bed.

"You're a good man, Logan. Mum and I did a hell of a job with you."

He gives my cheek a gentle pinch and I chuckle, getting to my feet and heading back to my chair before the two of us settle back into the quiet of the afternoon. The breeze makes a beautiful whooshing sound as it brushes past the trees, and Dad clears his throat, passing me the beer I left abandoned on the edge of the table.

"I've been meaning to talk to you about something," he says softly.

I look over at him, my stomach churning.

"I've been talking to some people in Oregon about…" He pauses for a moment, looking for the right words. "Well, about assistance. You know, for… what's coming."

My heart pounds as I watch him struggle to fully verbalize the thought. It's been happening more often lately, where he'll forget what he's saying as he's saying it, but this isn't exactly that.

"Death?" I ask, a lump forming in my throat. "You're looking into assisted suicide?"

We both wince at the word, but he nods.

"Your mother and I are going to be flying out there next month. We'll be filling out some forms and—"

"Dad, you still have fifteen months."

It's selfish. I know it's selfish, but the scared little kid in me just wants his dad.

"Sure, that's what they said. But that's at the top end, and probably only a handful of those will be good ones," Dad replies, his eyes welling up again. "I know what happens at the end of this. I've seen it. Slurred words, trouble holding a conversation, memory loss, confusion, and that's all before I start shittin' myself and getting the headaches— blindingly *painful* fuckin' headaches. That's all three to six weeks prior, and it just gets worse from there."

I didn't even think about that part. I know I googled it, along with: *cures*, *prognosis*, *clinical trials*, and *transplant*. Maybe I was too focused on the Hail Marys, anything that could give me some hope.

Even then, nothing did.

"I'm fighting a losing battle with something I can't even see, and it wants everything, including my memories." My dad's chin trembles, and that steely expression breaks all over again. "I'm not dying in a hospital bed with no conception of where or who I am. Or who you all are."

He sighs, swallowing his pain and turning back to me with a mischievous glint in his eyes.

"And then there's the hospital food. I wouldn't even feed that shit to a dog."

Even in his darkest moments, he's cracking a fucking joke.

"Does Iggy know?"

"No. I'm gonna break the news to her when she comes up. She'll hate it, but I need you both to know they've assured us it's peaceful. It's *humane*. And I'll be able to call the shots right up until the very end." He snorts. "You know how some people say you can't play God? I just tackled the fucker to the ground."

I don't know much about medically assisted death. What I do know is that I'm terrified to lose him, and I'm still hoping that we can find a way to beat this thing. This late in the game, though, it would take a miracle. When he's gone, I'm not sure I'll know what to do with all this weight. I don't think I have the strength to carry it with me every day.

I'm so angry all the time, but I've been holding it in and staying strong for everyone around me. That's my job. I can work through the pain later, but I refuse to watch this family sink.

The deeper the love, the deeper the grief.

My dad reaches over, giving my arm a gentle squeeze. I've watched these last few months as his hands have become bonier, his skin paper-thin and stained with light purple bruises. It's a hard thing to process.

"Fuck sakes," he sighs. "I hate crying like this."

"You know, the last time I really saw you cry was when Iggy graduated."

"Right, right," he laughs. "How many tattoos is your sister up to now?"

"At least 40," I chuckle.

"Good, good. I saw the Michael Myers one she got. Good taste."

"She got it from you," I reply, grinning at him. "We both did."

Dad smiles, nodding as he looks out at those pink roses.

Iggy's roses.

Imogen's in the city right now, not too far away from here, but she doesn't make it Upstate often with her school schedule. Dad keeps telling her she needs to focus on that, and that he'll be fine. I think they both like to pretend it's true.

It's not like she's completely avoiding him or anything; she emails snippets of her honors thesis chapters so he can look them over and give her feedback. Lately though, he's mostly been framing them to put up in his office.

Even the ones with spelling mistakes.

"Hey, what color's her hair now?"

"Uh, green, I think?"

I take out my phone and pull up her Instagram to show him. There's a picture of her in a black dress with long, emerald green hair that just barely touches her elbows.

"Looks nice," he whispers, leaning back in his chair. "It's a pretty shade."

My sister attempted to have a rebellious phase a couple times growing up, but it never really worked out. Mom and dad figured we'd try to rebel anyway, so why fight it? Communication was a big thing in our house, so the only real rule was that we had to be home for Sunday dinner, and when there's no real rules to break, well.... Iggy was always at that table, even if she was getting shit for getting her tongue pierced at 15.

"You both grew up to be good looking kids," Dad chuckles. "Didn't get that from me, that's for sure."

My dad's got wild jet black hair and dark green eyes didn't really translate to us, my mom's sandy blonde hair and brown eyes pushing to the forefront in our genes. We've both got his long, slightly upturned nose, though.

And his temper.

I take a moment just to breathe, the wind rustling in the trees around us while the birds chirp and sing off in the distance. This would be a perfect day in almost any other scenario.

"Can I ask you something?"

"Sure," he murmurs, paying more attention to the blue jay that just landed on the fence across the yard than anything I'm saying.

"If you decide to go to Oregon to–" I clear my throat. "How will you know when– you know..."

We both watch the bird preen its feathers in silence for a while. I almost wish I didn't have to ask, but it's not something I can ignore.

"I dunno," Dad eventually replies with a shake of his head. "But even if I don't, my body will. I'll keep going until it gets too hard, until I'm forgetting too much, sleeping too long... until I'm not really living, and then. Well, I think it'll be time."

He gives my hand another squeeze.

"It's like you said, we make time for the important stuff."

My own words repeated back wash over me like dread.

The problem is we don't have much time, not for 'the important stuff,' or anything else. Imogen should be here, we should all be here.

Possibly against my better judgement, I whip out my phone again.

ME

You should come out this week instead.

IMOGEN

Did something happen? Is dad okay?

ME

He's fine. I just think you should be here.

I see three bubbles pop up and disappear again and again. She knows something's up. My sister has a weird intuition for this kind of shit.

IMOGEN

I'll talk to my professors. I can submit my final
papers this week. They're basically done anyway.
I'll be there as soon as I can.

ME

Thanks, Ig.

IMOGEN

Are you sure everything's okay?

ME

Everything's fine. I just think we need to be a
family right now.

"Boys?" My mom calls from the back door. "Supper's ready!"

"Oooh! Lasagna!" My dad sings, reaching for me as I get up from my chair. "Come on, Logan. Help your old man up."

I grasp both of his hands, staring at their wrinkles, and the way his wedding ring's ended up slightly too big for his finger. When I pull him to his feet, he stumbles forward and I catch him.

"You okay?"

Dad only grunts, patting me on the shoulder and flashing me a warm smile that almost convinces me nothing's changed.

"I'll be just fine, son. Just fine."

CHAPTER FOURTEEN

paper bag

ABI

EMERALD BAY WASHINGTON
PRESENT DAY

I wake up to the sound of a blaring alarm, my head thumping violently, with the distinct taste of cheap tequila and old lime juice completely coating my tongue.

"*Fuuuuuck* my life..."

I lay there breathing, staring at my phone for some impossible amount of time as it trills happily on the nightstand. It's plugged in; did I do that? Usually it ends up on the floor. One time it ended up in my toilet.

All I remember is bottomless margaritas.

"Why would they betray me?" I groan.

Margaritas are pure happiness in a glass, but somehow I never remember the part that comes after that. The consequences. Why did I drink so many—

Oh.

Right.

I was messaging Brendan.

I shoot up out of bed, my arm flying to my phone and nearly knocking over a half-empty glass of water in the process.

It feels like my fingers can't move fast enough as I punch my password in and pull up the dreaded exchange. The second I see the words *fiancé* I can feel my stomach sink as low as it can go, and all of that tequila and lime juice comes rushing back. I don't even read the rest of it, tossing my phone down, sprinting for the bathroom and just barely making it to the toilet in time to puke my guts out like a civilized person.

Fiancé? I said I had a *fiancé?!*

My stomach takes another turn around the bend and I splash more vomit against the edge of the toilet bowl. And then I keep going, for quite some time, until there's gotta be nothing left. And then I go just that tiny bit more, you know, for extra credit. Finally I manage to flush, my stomach slightly calming as I slump against the bowl, breathing hard as I feel the cold sweat pouring down my face.

I groan into the crook of my arm.

"Fuck you, Roman. I'm *sure* those margaritas were your idea."

I'm really hoping I didn't say or do anything stupid last night, but given the state of things I'm guessing that's off the table.

After what may as well have been an eternity, I test the waters, slowly dragging myself to my feet. Shockingly, standing upright for a minute or so has no negative side-effects, and I'm filled with unearned confidence.

I strip off my pajamas and make for the shower.

I move slowly at first, not wanting to disrupt my stomach again, but soon I'm reveling in the brutal heat as it melts the knots in my shoulders and back. I use my favorite shampoo, the one that I usually just save for nights out, primarily because It's something like $40 a bottle. Today though? We're celebrating my stunning recovery.

I inhale deeply, closing my eyes and lathering up my hair. It smells like the strawberry compote my mom used to make when we had pancakes every Sunday, and once I rinse it out I always feel a little more human.

It's hard to move through the day worrying if someone else can smell the booze you guzzled last night, so sometimes you just need to go those few extra steps to make sure you're not *completely* repellent to your fellow man.

Fully rinsed and clean, I turn off the wonderful, gorgeous, scaldingly perfect water, dry off, and trudge back into my bedroom, carefully bending over to pick up my still lit-up phone.

There's a missed text from Logan, but only from about an hour ago.

SUNSHINE

So how's the hangover, party girl?

ME

Awful. Bring gun, please.

SUNSHINE

How about we don't do violence today and I bring you some coffee and breakfast instead?

ME

Oh thank god, you're actually coming over.

I stare at my phone for a moment, the anxiety starting to seep back in now that I'm away from the perfect mental defence of a hot shower.

SUNSHINE

Do you remember last night?

I try to parse out what I actually remember.
Being pissed at Brendan.
Shopping, with Imogen and Piper?
Roman's suggestion of margaritas—
It fucking *was* him, I knew it!
And then there's waiting in the cool summer air.
Laughter.
Logan's car.
Falling... on top of him.
"Nooo!" I whine, covering my face with my hands. "No, no, no!"

ME

Not really.

SUNSHINE

I think we should talk. I'll be over in ten. Any food preference?

Okay, it's not that bad. He's not mad at me or he wouldn't even be coming over. And if he's not mad at me I must not have done anything *too* idiotic.

ME

No eggs and no tomatoes, please.

SUNSHINE

Yeah, you don't like the texture right? How about
a big New York bagel with lox and some cream
cheese?

ME

That sounds incredible. BTW try not to scream
when you see how haggard I look.

He shoots me a thinking emoji, followed by a picture. It's him with his glasses askew, his eyes crossed, and his hair a complete mess.

ME

Wow, that is SEXY, Flynn. You got an Onlyfans?

SUNSHINE

The ladies love it, but you gotta pay the big bucks
to get the real goods.

Fuck, you know what? Logan would be coming over even if I did something really bad. He's just cool like that. Great, so I still have no clue how awful I was.

SUNSHINE

Make that 20 minutes, this old lady at the front of
the line is acting like she's never ordered food in
her life.

ME

You're a real speed demon, you know that?

I guess he was already out getting food, but I'm not complaining. I send him a heart before tossing my phone onto the bed and digging through my clothes for an outfit. I end up picking out my tattered over-sized U of T sweater and a pair of buttery black leggings, and toss most of my hair into a claw clip, tucking the shorter pieces behind my ear. I look awful, and I feel even worse, but at least I'm not still shuddering on the floor. That said, who knows how long that'll last. My stomach is in knots thinking about what Logan could possibly want to talk to me about.

What did I do? Did I try to kiss him? Was it Aspen all over again?

I can't do this right now. I have to force myself out of the quickly-forming spiral, and step one is to convince myself to focus on feeling less like I want to curl into a ball and die of a hangxiety.

"The rats," I murmur. "They always help."

I head for Wednesday and Lydia's cage, shaking out their morning kibble and giving them both a few quick little tickles. Lydia takes the opportunity to climb up my arm, totally uninterested in her breakfast, while her sister tries to fit as many pieces of food into her tiny mouth as possible before scurrying back into her house.

I give the more adventurous Lydia a little kiss on her head before letting her perch on my shoulder, feeling her go crazy on the tips of my wet hair.

"Thank you, baby," I murmur. "Momma's having a rough morning."

She turns at the sound of my voice, giving me little kisses on my cheek.

I can't help but giggle. She always seems to know when I'm feeling down, whereas Wednesday couldn't really give a shit, especially if there's food to hoard.

Honestly, given the way I feel right now? I can't really blame her.

But then the sudden sound of my buzzer ringing through the house shifts the two of our priorities, sending Lydia into a little panic as she dashes down my outstretched arm back into her cage. She makes her way straight to Wednesday, who's trying even harder than before to keep her food out of sight. I quickly grab a few little munchies and pass them right to Lydia through the gap in the cage, the first time she's noticed the food's existence all morning. Once she's grabbed her fill I leave my sneaky little babies be, quickly head for the door and pressing the little button on the intercom.

"Hello?"

"*Let me iiiinnn!*" Logan whines."*I think I've been out here for a whole minute!*"

"Do you have bagels?"

"*Of course, and coffee, what do you take me for?*"

"My hero!"

I hit the button to unlock the front door, and in only a few seconds I can already hear the soft rhythmic sound of his shoes on the hardwood stairs. Moments later, his familiar knock reverberates through the apartment.

And there he is, a little scraggly but shockingly well put together. He's holding a brown paper bag sitting on top of... two iced coffees and what looks like a little thermos.

"Aww, I get two of you?" I say, taking hold of the drinks without even making eye contact. "What a privilege!"

Logan isn't even phased, fully in-sync with our playful bullshit, and just walks straight past me to the rat's cage. I smile to myself as I watch him gently scritch Lydia, who sticks her nose out to investigate the newcomer. He waves at Wednesday, who completely ignores him as is tradition, before brushing past me, briefly placing a hand on my waist as he moves for the kitchen.

He's dressed casually, as he so often is, in a Tales from the Crypt t-shirt and a pair of black and white striped dress pants which I'm almost certain are ones he bought at a costume shop. His bright green Converse just barely poke out from bottoms, further accentuating what could reasonably be called an already quirky outfit. His unruly dark blond waves are on full display, and he looks so fresh faced I'd swear I was looking at a man who was my age, and not 10 years my senior.

"Here." He hands me my bagel and places the thermos on the counter. "Lox and cream cheese on a plain bagel. No poppy seeds, just in case. For the girls."

When I first got Wednesday and Lydia, Logan researched *everything* there was to know about fancy rats and printed out a binder full of foods that they can and can't eat, both for treats and major meals.

"Honestly, you look great for someone who moved to Margaritaville last night."

"You can blame Roman for the suggestion," I mutter, taking a bite of my bagel and walking over to offer the rats a little piece of salmon. "I know I am."

Logan grins as he sips his coffee, but his eyes are doing that thing they do when he wants to say something, but is still working out how to put the words in the right order. Normally I'd let him take his time, but the way it's been eating at me I know I just have to tear off that band-aid as quickly as I can.

"So, what did you want to talk about?"

He gestures to the thermos sitting on the counter, taking a bite of his own bagel.

"That first."

I roll my eyes. Hangovers make me impatient, and more than a little petulant; I frequently have to remind myself that I'm a 26-year-old woman, and not a high-school student fighting with her mom after stumbling home from a party.

"Logan, please. Just tell me what I did so I can apologize and we can get this weirdness over with!"

He snorts, nearly choking on his food.

"Trust me, it'll make you feel better. Then we can chat, I promise."

"Fine."

I set my bagel down and snatch up the thermos, cracking it open. Immediately I'm hit with the rich scent of pumpkin, mixed with nutmeg and vanilla. The little satisfied groan that slips from my lips is entirely involuntary, but that doesn't make it any less humiliating. That said, I don't give a shit. I fucking *love* pumpkin spice. I don't care what people say, that stuff is pure comfort in a cup.

"It's the pumpkin creamer from Déjà Brew!" I whisper. "Where did you get this?! It's Summer!"

Logan beams, puffing his chest out as he walks a little closer.

"I actually made it from scratch! You remember Ashley?"

"The old manager? Yeah."

"I managed to get in contact before she bailed, and convinced her to send me the recipe! I've got it all saved into my notes app and—" He pauses dipping his head slightly with a smile. "Doesn't matter, Anyway, I figured you might be needing a pick-me-up this morning after how I left you, so I whipped it up last night."

I could actually fucking cry.

"This is so sweet, Logan. Thank you."

This is exactly what I needed this morning, he has no idea.

"No problem." He pours some of the creamer into my coffee and slides it over to me. "Besides, I need the world's harshest pumpkin creamer critic to judge it. I thought it was pretty good when I did the taste-test last night, but things might have changed."

I grin at him, picking up my coffee and giving it a little swirl. The first sip? Heaven. I let out another groan and immediately take a significantly bigger gulp. Somehow it's still perfect. It's almost exactly right, I think it might have just a splash more vanilla.

"This is just what I needed, I actually think I might like this more."

"Well, you're very welcome! That's high praise coming from you. Oh, hey, did you know the biggest pumpkin in the world weighs approximately 2,750 pounds and it's owned by a guy in Minnesota?"

Logan's full of these strange facts, has been since the first night I met him. Even back then when we were just in it for a whirlwind night of sex, he was still telling me tiny little details of things that fascinated him at some point in his life, and then somehow just stuck there in his brain. This is a guy who will scroll through Wikipedia for hours on end and edit sections he knows are wrong. He's come into work furious that some 'moron' rejected his edits, or tried to change them.

I think it's one of the things so many people are attracted to.

I lift the thermos, a little surprised by how full it is. For some reason I just sort of assumed he'd made enough for a couple days or something.

"That's a lot of pumpkin creamer."

"At least a couple months' supply," he replies with a wink. "Well, for you maybe two weeks."

I laugh, taking another long swig of my now-perfect coffee before setting it down, and putting on the most serious face I can muster.

"Okay, you've improved my day ten-fold. Now rip the band-aid off and tell me about the stupid shit I did last night."

Logan sighs.

"You can't keep that anxiety down for even a little bit, can you, Shortcake?"

"Nope." I make a come hither motion with my fingers. "If I had to guess… you're gonna tell me I tried to make out with you, so just tell me so I can promise to do your laundry for a week. Lay it on me."

"First of all, I do my own laundry, thank you. I might be a single man, but I'm *certainly* capable of sorting my darks and lights." He grins, stealing a piece of smoked salmon from my bagel and popping it into his mouth. "Second, it's not something you did so much as something you said. You really don't remember what you told me last night?"

Oh god.

What the hell did margarita-brained me say?

I shake my head slowly and Logan clears his throat.

Even I have no idea what that woman might do.

"Well, you said you had some sort of altercation with Brendan, and that in the end you…told him that I was your fiancé. Probably more importantly, you also told him we would, and I quote, *see him at the reunion.*"

I can feel my entire body tighten up.

"I didn't say that."

"You did."

"There is no fucking way."

"Where are you going?!" Logan yells after me, as I rush back into my room.

I find my phone, snatching it up off the bed, and scrolling back through my messages at lightning speed, my mouth dropping open when I make it back to the last thing I sent.

ME

I'll see you at the reunion. Right along with my fiancé. Maybe you can learn how a real man's supposed to act.

I can feel the room begin to spin, and I sink down into the mattress, my body equal parts hot and cold at the same time. All I can manage is to stare at the words on the screen while my heart thunders away in my chest. I can't even bring myself to look at the rest of the conversation. Is context even important after a finale like that? And.besides that, why the hell don't I remember it? Was I wasted that early? Did I block it out?

"Logan, I think I'm gonna be sick again."

"On it!"

He scurries into the living room as I jam my head between my legs and try to focus on just breathing. I hear him murmuring something to the rats from the other room. Then there's the sink, and the clattering of the cupboard doors before he comes barrelling back in with a damp cloth in his hand.

"Here." He gently hands it over to me. "Iggy does this for panic attacks, she says it helps ground her, and that it gets her nervous system regulated. Or something."

"Where do I put it?" I ask.

Logan bites his lip in thought for a moment, looking a little unsure before he takes a seat beside me. He gently moves my damp hair aside and presses the cloth against the back of my neck. It's such a sweet act, so quiet and soft, a strangely effective balm on my escalating nausea. I exhale slowly, focusing on calming my racing heart.

Logan goes to move his hand, but I shake my head.

"Keep it there?" I ask, briefly looking him in the eyes. "It helps."

He stays completely silent, but he doesn't take his hand away, instead starting to caress my neck with the wet cloth. The slow, repetitive movements help to anchor me, keeping me calm as I begin to bring myself back on my own terms.

I keep breathing. In for four, hold for four, out for four.

Imogen taught me that.

"I am never drinking again," I rasp after a long silence. "That's my new year's resolution."

"Well, you're a little late for that one," he chuckles.

I let out a long, shaky breath.

The worst part is how easy it was for me to slip. Why was my first thought, the minute I had a couple drinks in me, to immediately greenlight the plan we were absolutely mocking just a day or two ago? Maybe part of me really wanted it to be real, even if just in the moment. Even if it was just to show Brendan how bad he fucked up.

"I wouldn't worry too much about all of this, Abi. You're not locked into it or anything, you can just not show up if it makes you feel this way."

I shake my head.

"I can't, or he's going to know I was lying."

"Right, maybe, but like... who cares what he thinks?"

"I do!" I squeak. "I care, because he's an asshole, and I need him to see that he's not better than me!"

"I mean, obviously he's not," Logan chuckles. "Have you seen his Facebook posts?"

"I don't mean as a human being," I grumble. "I mean I want to show up at that reunion and rub my amazing job and awesome fiancé right in his stupid face! I need him to know that he fucked up. That I'm worth something!"

I can practically see it: the defeat in Brendan's eyes when he sees how much taller Logan is than him. How much more handsome he is. How much smarter he is. I want him to squirm when he hears about how many papers each of us have published, and how I'm such a huge asset we are to the school.

I don't want to be a better person than Brendan, I want to crush him like a roach.

I turn to Logan to see him smirking at me.

"What?!" I growl, a little more aggressively than I intended, but he doesn't even flinch.

"So... are you gonna go?" He asks, his eyes practically gleaming.

I stare at him in disbelief. I know that Logan goes out of his way for me sometimes, but this feels like *way* too big of an ask, even for us.

But even still, I ask it anyway.

"Logan, do you... do you wanna be my fake fiancé?"

"Nothing would make me happier, Dr. King."

mastermind

LOGAN

LOGAN
PRESENT DAY

"I needed this," Abi sighs, biting into a surprisingly hefty egg roll. "You really should have let me pay though, I'm the one who got us into this whole thing so I should have bought the apology meal."

It's late in the afternoon, and we've been lounging on Abi's couch with a horror movie on in the background for the last hour or so, a big spread of fried rice, chow mein, and egg rolls sitting in front of us. Abi's been eating like it's her last meal on earth, groaning every so often when she hits a particularly good bite.

"Hey, I'm your fiancé now. It's my job to provide your hangover food, right?"

She chews slowly, her cheeks tinged pink.

"I guess we should start to plan this out, huh?" She asks.

"I suppose." I reach over and grab the remote, turning the TV down. "So, when's the reunion again?"

"June 20th." Her tone is completely flat, and she's staring off into the distance like the reminder just forced her into a PTSD nightmare. "Just four weeks away."

I pull out my phone, taking a brief look at my calendar.

"Well, I don't teach until the fall, and I've got nothing lined up, other than some extra writing, and I'm sure I can get at least something done on the road, so..." I glance up at her. "What would you say to a three week road trip across Canada? A week there, let's say a week in Blackburn Falls, and a week back?"

She blinks.

"You don't want to fly?"

"Hell no, I've only ever been to Toronto! I want to experience the majestic beauty that is Canada. I want to see a moose, and bears scooping big fish out of a lake. I want to watch a hockey player guzzle a bottle of maple syrup like its water and then punch someone in the face!"

"You know, I've always envied your breadth of knowledge," she murmurs, grinning from ear to ear. "But your imagination is even more impressive."

I love the idea of a road trip.

I want my foot on the gas, the windows rolled down, and my favourite music blasting from the speakers. More than that though? I want her in the passenger seat while the two of us talk up a storm. There's a good chance her position may be cut in the coming weeks, so I want to get as much time with her as I can get before things get really hard.

Abi gnaws at her lip, reaching over to take a big gulp of her water.

"You really want to stay in my hometown? For a whole week?"

"Sure! Why not?"

I clear my throat, struggling not to sound *too* enthusiastic.

"I mean, it's nothing special," she chuckles. "Pretty boring actually."

"Well, if you'd like to go to the reunion alone—"

"No, no!" She sighs, running a hand through her dark frizzy hair. "I can text my mom and see if we can hang out with her for a few days. I'm just not really sure how to plan all this out, is all."

"Well, luckily for you, planning is my specialty." I point at her laptop. "Pass it over."

"Are you sure? There's porn on it. Written *and* visual. It's not nearly as finely curated as the Logan Flynn Museum of Pornography."

"Nothing is," I sigh dramatically. "How about we drive?"

"Drive?"

"Sure! We could do a whole touristy thing— oh, we could even go camping!"

"You camp?" Abi asks, her brow raised in legitimate surprise.

I'm mildly offended, how could she think I'm not a camper?

"I love camping! It's one of my all-time favorite pastimes!"

A wide grin spreads across her face, and she rests her chin on her hand.

"Okay, so when's the last time you went camping?"

"Uh… I was 12? I think at least. Iggy was definitely 2, and we were in an RV."

"That's *Glamping*, not camping. You weren't really roughing it."

I roll my eyes. I know she's doing this just to get a rise out of me, but it's working.

"Okay, wilderness expert. What's camping to you?"

"A tent, hot dogs over an open fire. Ghost stories are ideal, but you definitely need a whole lot of stars," she says with a wistful look in her eyes. "I was in Girl Guides when I was a kid, we did that stuff all the time."

"What the heck are Girl Guides? Is that like scouts?"

"Oh, right, you wouldn't have them here. Yeah, we were like Girl Scouts, but our cookie selection wasn't as vast. I got lots of badges though. My mom still has them framed in the living room like I went to war or something."

This is a good start on the path toward learning about Abi's past, and I have a good feeling she'll open up a little more along the way.

So that settles it. The road trip is 100% necessary.

"Did you have Thin Mints?" I ask.

I'm a big Thin Mints guy. There's something about chocolate and mint that's just perfect. Roman thinks it tastes like chocolate toothpaste, but he has a far more discerning palate, whereas I tend to eat like a toddler loose in a candy store. At least that's how he puts it.

"A variation of them, yeah," she chuckles. "I remember one year, my best friend Kat and I sold enough boxes that we got to go on a trip to New York."

"And you didn't visit *me*?!"

"I was 11! You would've been soaring through NYU by then, and I'm sure my pre-teen crush on Jack Skellington wouldn't have been the most interesting conversation starter."

Sometimes I forget about the age gap, but it's more like I forget how old *I* actually am. I've never really felt like I belong in my 30s; most of the time I just feel like a big kid who's allowed to drink. How someone gave me a mortgage, I'll never know.

Abi's angled her laptop between the two of us, and she gestures for me to get closer as she scrolls through a roadmap of the great white north.

"If you want to camp, my suggestion would be to do it in British Columbia, or Alberta at the latest."

We spend the next half hour or so googling campgrounds in the two provinces, sad to discover pretty much all the ones on our potential route are already booked, save for one single campground in a place called Cranbrook.

"Logan!"

I shove my way in front of the computer and quickly mash in my details, paying for the booking before she can make any sort of real fuss.

"First off, it's too late and my credit card's already been accepted, so I'm officially a Canadian now, as per the Rules of the North as I'm sure you are aware... Second, it's like twenty bucks Canadian. That's basically a dollar in real money, so who cares which one of us pays?"

"You should teach economics, you really missed your calling."

"You know, I would, but I'm far too controversial. Just print more money, you idiots!" I put my hands behind my head. "Boom, I just saved the American dream."

Abi giggles, the mood much lighter now that we've taken at least a couple steps toward dealing with her predicament. It's really not that big of a deal, but friends have to have each other's backs, right? Besides, who was her other option, Frankie? That guy's road trip playlist is pretty much just Dashboard Confessional. It's like he never crawled his way out of 2007.

I watch as Abi stretches her legs out on the coffee table, wiggling her bare toes while the rest of the logistics begin to dawn on the two of us.

"We should probably lock in which cities we want to hit to give you the quintessential True North experience."

"You're the expert in all things Canadian, so I'll forego my usual leadership strengths and leave that to you, my liege."

I bow as deeply as I can, but when I look back up her focus is elsewhere.

"Well, you *have* to see Banff... and then you simply *must* experience the glory that is Saskatoon."

"Did you know Saskatoon was named after a wild berry?" I ask, the fact shooting to the front of my mind completely unbidden.

"Did you google that just now?"

"No! I memorized it because I wanted to try every berry *ever!* Anyway, that one's called—"

"Misâskwatôminihk," she finishes for me. "It's Cree."

"Yes!" I squeak, throwing up my hand. "High five me!"

When I found out Abi was Canadian, I went down a rabbit hole of research on the country. I learned how their political system worked, and fun facts about each province... It kind of became my main obsession for a couple weeks. I really wanted to impress her in the early stages of our friendship, and there's no better way to weaponize my ridiculous brain than compartmentalizing obscure information.

"Well, we'll have to get you some Saskatoon berries then. I only went there once when I was a kid. It's mostly pickup trucks, Molson Canadian, and dudes in cowboy hats."

"Sounds like a patented Roman Burke wet dream."

"Nah, I think *that* would involve your sis—"

"Abi!" I hiss, gently reaching over to mess up her hair. "This discussion is quickly turning uncouth, and is *certainly* unbecoming of a lady!"

She cackles, tossing her head back like she's a goddamn cartoon villain.

Over the course of the evening we plan the rest of the trip, ironing out the kinks as I take note of any potential hotel to book along the way. Despite my persistence, she made me promise that we wouldn't be camping the entire time.

About an hour in we finally reach Blackburn Falls on our itinerary, and I can feel Abi suck in a deep, silent breath beside me.

"Can I say something with all the love in my heart?" She asks, wincing slightly at her own words.

My stomach twists a little and I wonder if she's already getting cold feet about the whole thing.

"What's up?"

"Would you mind if we stayed in a hotel when we got there? I'll pay for it. I love my mom, but there are just some... things that happened in that house that I'd like to forget."

I look over at her as she chews on her lip, staring at the word document we've created. It's very organized and color-coded by activity.

Classic Abi.

"Yeah, sure. You don't want to stay with your mom?"

"No, I– I just don't know if I want to sleep with my fake fiancé in my childhood bed—" She cuts herself off, almost immediately at least 3 shades of pink darker. "Sleep *in* the same *bed*. Not with—"

"You're worried the bed will be too small for the two of us, and it'll make for a really uncomfortable couple nights. I get it, say no more."

"No, that's not what I—"

I put my hand up with a grin.

"I got it, Shortcake. I'm just messing with you."

I reach over and squeeze her shoulder as she forces an awkward smile. The worst part about being friends with Abi is... well, it's me. The way I feel about her has never faded, and what's worse? I'm the only one who can deal with that.

Abi takes a deep breath.

"Thank you for understanding. How about I book this last hotel and we give your credit card a break."

"You don't wanna see how fast I can max it out? Not only is it exciting because my livelihood is on the line, but I get a whole bunch of stuff without having to spend *any money!*"

She smiles half-heartedly but doesn't say anything in response, and I give her another gentle shove with my shoulder.

"You okay?"

"Yeah. It's just—" She sighs. "I don't even know why I'm telling you this, but it's... not just Brendan's weird gross energy tainting everything."

She clears her throat, nodding to herself as if to confirm she's ready.

"My dad OD'd in the living room of that house when I was 12. It's...

difficult for me to be in there." Her chin trembles. "I had to give him CPR until the paramedics got there. They said his heart stopped."

Tears slip down her cheeks; I can already tell the hangover might have made her a little softer, and much more vulnerable than I've ever seen her in quite a while. Abi's always been easy to get close to, but only to a point. It feels like she's put up all these walls and guards around the really rough stuff because she thinks it'll make her a burden. Now though, she's offering me a look past all of that, at a piece of herself she's been too afraid to show before.

"What happened after that?" I ask quietly, not wanting to push any of her limits.

She sniffles, taking another sip of her drink and wiping her nose on her sleeve. I know Abi's dad is still alive, I've just never really known what kind of relationship they have. I just assumed it was normal family stuff.

"He never got sober. He *couldn't*." She sighs. "I didn't understand the 'couldn't' part until I started to get into this research, but it really put things into perspective."

Abi told me the vague motivation for her research in the past, but never where it came from. She always used to say she just likes to help people, but this is a big piece of the story, one that I'm only now starting to get a fuller picture of.

"Mom had to kick him out. She said she could raise a kid or take care of his illness, but she couldn't do both, and she wasn't about to abandon me. Not too long later Dad met another woman from town and the two of them moved out."

"Jesus... When's the last time you saw him?"

"I was 14," she replies, her voice pitched a tiny bit higher than normal, but still in control. "It was mom and I against the world after that. She started a business, a little wedding photography studio in Blackburn. She was busier than she'd ever been before and she loved it. I'm pretty sure my dad was holding her back, horrible as it sounds."

I've read everything Abi's ever published, and a good amount of the material she's cited in the process, which is how I know that kids sometimes wind up in a sort of role reversal. They feel responsible for managing a parents' illness, or picking up the slack around the house, and often wind up with far too much responsibility on their shoulders, far too young.

In Abi's case, she applied that responsibility to every aspect of her life going forward.

"I think you might be right," I mutter. "Love isn't always enough, and it doesn't always save people, no matter how much we want it to."

I wish all the love I had for my dad could have actually done something for him in the end. Anything. Instead he slipped away in that little room in Oregon.

"I really wish it did."

I feel a lump forming in my throat as she stares over at me.

"Me too."

I give her another squeeze, planting a quick kiss on the top of her head, and she leans into me for a brief moment before shaking herself off, wiping away the remnants of any tears.

"Okay. Back to business." She reaches for her phone like it's a security blanket. "I'll text some people from back home and let them know we're coming."

Classic Abi, always ready to move on to the next thing on the list.

"I'll pick you up next week from work and we'll head out?"

She nods.

"Thanks for being such a good sport about this."

"Hey, it's the fiancé thing to do!" I chirp.

Abi just smiles, shutting the laptop before grabbing the remote and cranking the volume back up. It's not long before the two of us fall back into our rhythm, snickering and dishing out random bits of movie trivia back and forth, like nothing had happened at all.

And the entire time, my arm never leaves its spot around her shoulder.

i got you, babe

LOGAN

PRESENT DAY
SOMEWHERE ALONG THE CANADIAN BORDER

The week leading up to this trip was only *slightly* chaotic. In between lectures, comforting stressed out students during office hours, *and* grading final papers, we were both scrambling to book campsites and hotel rooms. I felt a little guilty typing in my credit card information while one of my students was in shambles at my desk, but I made her a cup of tea so it kind of makes up for it, right?

Chaos aside, everything worked out for the best.

Abi naps peacefully beside me while I listen to a podcast on navigating the aftermath of neoliberal policies. The border is still about half an hour away after a few hours on the road, reminding me that the worst part about living in Emerald Bay is just how far it is from everything else. It can be isolating, but it's also the place I love most in the world.

When I left New York, I was running from my dad's death; and from the person the grief was turning me into. Having to be strong for everyone *but* myself began to take its toll, and one day I looked in the mirror and simply didn't recognize the man staring back at me anymore.

Dad's passing was both traumatic, and somehow not, at the same time. We were as prepared as anyone could be; the hospice nurses were incredible, extremely empathetic, and we even had a death doula who walked all of us through the process and made everything more manageable.

But even though I could see inevitability in the distance, no amount of support could have prepared me for the day we finally reached it. Watching that man slip away right in front of me shattered my whole world.

I still remember every detail, the way the wind rustled the trees, the birds outside that seemed to be calling him home, the sun beaming through the window... and the sound of my father's raspy voice telling us it was okay to let him go. He was my solace, and then he was gone.

Some days, the grief feels so fresh I swear I've traveled back through time.

Dad died in July, just after his birthday. He insisted on one last blow-out with all of his dearest friends. The house was packed and even though dad was so sick, he still blasted Springsteen and busted out his best dance moves.

The Devil's not taking me until I've had at least twelve hot dogs and watched some fireworks.

We lit up the sky for him that night.

It was magical, and it was the perfect way for Declan Flynn to say goodbye to the people he loved most.

I sip my coffee, hoping my mind might wander onto something else if I give it some mild prompting. I start with to-do lists I've made in my head, books I need to read, papers that need to be graded, and then on to conferences to apply to...

But pretty soon I'm glancing over at Abi again, thinking back to the last trip we went on together: the sociology conference in San Francisco. We only had a couple days, but we made the best of them, finding restaurants with the most incredible food, some key spots from a couple of our favourite movies, and of course riding the trolley.

We even took pictures in front of the Tanner home from *Full House*.

Admittedly, she was a bit embarrassed when I wouldn't stop singing the *Rice-A-Roni* song, but after a few rounds she joined in.

It was one of the best trips I've ever had.

I hope this one beats it.

I stop at a drive-thru close to the border to grab another coffee, and get Abi a little apple pie just in case she's hungry when she wakes up.

The lineup for the border isn't terrible, but I immediately begin to feel nervous. Whenever I go through customs, they always make me feel like I'm doing something wrong— like there are secretly drugs shoved into my car, or up my ass or something.

Or I get paranoid that I've accidentally packed a bomb.

Somehow.

Obviously my anxiety is totally normal.

I always start to over explain things to the border guards, say things they don't care about... it's generally a disaster.

But I rehearsed this time. I have a script.

We're going to a high school reunion and Abi is my Canadian girl-friend. The car is bomb-free, I packed my bags myself, and no officer, I am *not* smuggling drugs.

Except Advil.

Oh, God, can I bring Advil across the border?

I reach over and tap Abi on the thigh.

"Abi," I hiss. "Is it illegal to bring Advil into Canada?"

"What?" She groans, lifting her head. "What are you talking about?"

"There's Advil in my bag. Is that illegal?"

She blinks, struggling to break through her sleep-induced haze.

"No," she grumbles. "Canadians are generally pretty chill, so your *very* hardcore drugs are probably fine."

"Okay, good. Great. I'm just a bit paranoid is all."

"Could it be because you're such a goody two-shoes that you get a buzz just *standing* next to something illegal?"

"Hey, I did the edibles in California!"

"*Did the edibles?*" Abi snorts, finding her bagel and taking a big bite. "Alright, grandpa, I'll talk. You're already sweating, you are *clearly* not cut out for this."

"Sweating?" I tap my forehead. "Dry as a bone."

"Yeah, well I give it ten seconds. You'll be melting down the second the border guard opens his mouth."

I put my hand on my chest, letting out what I intended to be a disgruntled huff, but it somehow comes out more along the lines of a shocked little squeak.

"I forgot how mean you are when you're tired!"

She reaches over and boops my nose and I struggle to keep from blushing.

Abi's reminded me multiple times that the guards' job isn't to laugh at my jokes, and my job isn't to try to charm them, yet as we pull up to the booth I immediately feel compelled to put on a show.

The lady waiting for us, fortunately or otherwise, doesn't seem like she's the type to be easily charmed, and I decide to lay off a bit this time. If I had to describe her from memory all I'd probably be able to say is she was the definition of uptight, just a severe bun on top of a permanent scowl.

The process is simple enough. She asks how long we're traveling for, who we're visiting, the usual. Abi does most of the talking, even giving the guard her mom's address when prompted. She's so together, I think I might have just blanked if the guard asked me anything more complicated than my own name. Even then there's about a 50/50 chance I'd say it was Abi King without a second thought.

Finally, the border guard asks us how we know each other, and without thinking I move into autopilot.

"She's my Canadian girlfriend."

My perfect preparation, coming in clutch.

Abi pinches my thigh so hard I almost lurch out of my seat, but the guard only nods, handing our passports and IDs back through the window.

"Enjoy your trip, folks."

"Thank you for your service!" I chirp.

And with that, a foot on the gas, and a dream, we officially enter Canada.

"It smells different here!"

Abi chuckles, looking very happy to be returning to her bagel.

"Sometimes it still amazes me how much of a dork you are."

"True, but you adore me anyway."

"I do." She grins, licking some peanut butter off of her thumb. "So I'm your Canadian girlfriend now? That official?"

"It depends, I'll have to make sure you're up to snuff first. Don't want to pick the first Canadian I see now that I'm here, you know? I got options."

She rolls her eyes, but I can tell she's grinning as she chows down on the rest of her food. I get it, there's something pretty magical about a road trip, and I'm definitely feeling whatever that is as I pull us into the gas station.

"Well, I've thought it out over a long two minutes, and I've decided it would be an honor to have you be my Canadian girlfriend."

I take her hand, gently kissing her knuckles. Her cheeks blaze and my heart pounds against my ribs.

"Fiancée," she corrects me with a slight rasp stitched into her voice. "Remember?"

It's just pretend.

No big deal.

"My mistake." I give her fingers a gentle squeeze before flicking my head toward the gas station. "Now come on, I wanna buy one of those Coffee Crisp things you were telling me about the other day. You made them sound like God's gift to the sugar junkie."

When we get inside, Abi heads straight for the fridge, grabbing a couple of energy drinks and some Gatorades to keep her going for the drive. Meanwhile, I peruse the... *extremely* distressing candy selection. The Smarties here are... chocolate? And what the hell are Hickory Sticks?

"I don't understand this country," I murmur, grabbing both items regardless.

When it comes to junk food I have a mission to find the best of the best, and you can't rank something if you don't know enough about it, so it's fair to say this is definitely going to be some very important research.

As I'm searching for more novelty snacks, I spot one I recognize on the bottom shelf.

A Ring Pop, apple-green.

Abi's favourite.

And I even think her birthstone might be green. Well, I know it is.

It's kind of serendipitous.

Our favorite word.

I crouch down, picking it up before glancing over at Abi through the aisle. She's busy with her own mission: filling up a giant slushie container with as much sugar as she can legally walk away with. I quickly pull the Ring Pop out of its wrapper, hiding it up my sleeve as I strut over to her.

She notices me just as I lean up against the edge of her little kiosk.

"Hi, beautiful," I purr. "Come here often?"

Abi doesn't miss a fucking beat, no surprise or haughty little huff, just casually sliding into our usual style of banter.

"To the slushie machine?" She gives a small shrug, her face less than impressed. "It depends, who's askin'?"

"Me, and— wait a second... What the hell's behind your ear?"

She's already in the midst of rolling her eyes as I slip the candy into my palm, deftly pulling it out from behind her ear.

"Oh my god!" I gasp. "You said you needed a ring, right? It must be kismet!"

She sips on her slushie, barely reacting as I slowly lower myself down to one knee and hold it up to her. There's a brief moment of confusion, and then she realizes what I'm doing, her eyes widening as she quickly looks around the gas station.

I've committed to the bit.

"Logan..."

"It's too late. I'm already down."

"Logan, you are *not*—"

"Dr. Abigail Autumn King, will you marry me?"

There's a couple beside the register that's giving us a... particular look, and I can see the clerk just past them filming us on his phone. I'm hoping it doesn't go viral, or I might have some explaining to do in a couple weeks.

Abi laughs, a little more nervous than normal, but still clearly amused.

"Logan what are you doing?"

"If you say no I'm not paying for your candy."

She squeaks, her eyes glittering.

"You're making me marry you under duress? You're not even doing a good job of it, anyone else would have gotten up off the floor by now!"

"That's a yes! You said 'making me marry you!' She said yes!"

"There is no possible interpretation of what I said that— *Logan!*"

But I'm already out of reach, doing victory laps around the tiny little store as the cashier cheers me on. Abi can barely hold herself together, but she makes a valiant effort as she lets me finish my celebration. I return to her to find her hand outstretched, waiting for me as the two of us dissolve into laughter.

This is so fucking stupid. I'm a 36-year-old man.

I pay taxes. I have a mortgage.

And now I'm back down on one knee, trying to shove a Ring Pop onto my best friend's finger.

"Well," she huffs, once again struggling to keep a straight face after I've tried and failed for the 5th time to get the ring on. "Thank you *so much* for embarrassing me less than 10 minutes back in my home country. Really, I'm sure we're making an amazing first impression."

"Well, I'm gonna be your husband," I reply, getting to my feet and plucking her slushie from her hand. "Humiliating you is the name of the game, right after stealing all your stuff. Haven't you read the pre-nup?"

As we make our way to the front of the store I grab two bags of gummy worms for the road, and we pay for everything before heading straight out to the car without another word. Inside the vehicle, Abi slips her metallic pentagram off of the small leather cord around her neck, and starts securing the ring pop in its place, tying it carefully around each end before letting it hang loose against her chest.

I smile, popping a gummy worm into my mouth as I start the engine.

"Didn't think you'd actually wear it."

"Well, it's my ring, isn't it?" She asks with a wink. "Gotta show it off somehow."

i was a teenage werewolf

ABI

CRANBROOK, BRITISH COLUMBIA
PRESENT DAY

"Are you ready for it?"

Logan's voice is practically a purr amidst the pitch black of the night.

Thunder rolls above us, and rain begins to batter the tent we just barely threw up before the storm came rushing in. We have our sleeping bags set up next to each other, and a surprising amount of snacks laid out between us which we thankfully thought to snatch from the car.

Logan half-jokingly told me he was ready with all the camp-fire stories we could possibly need, but now that we're effectively locked in this tent for the night, I'm actually looking forward to something spooky before we head to sleep.

I promised to maintain the ambience until he was ready to begin, so it's a little bit more difficult than it would normally be to start gorging myself in the darkness. Luckily, I manage, pawing my way to a bag of ketchup chips and immediately digging in. Logan thinks the chips are disgusting, based on principle alone he says, but that's just because he never had a chance to develop a truly refined Canadian palate like my own.

"I'm ready!" I noisily bite down onto a couple of chips, the rest of my words jumbled with my mouth full. "Spook me, Doctor Flynn!"

A flashlight flicks on, still startling me a little regardless of how prepared I was. He's resting it just underneath his chin, angled to create those harsh shadows that make his already sharp cheekbones look even more pronounced. It looks like he even used my eyeliner to paint on a very recognizable style of mustache in the dark.

"I looked up a *very* special story—"

I'm struggling not to burst out laughing.

"Looked up?! That's cheating!"

"Hey, this is my Vincent Price moment!" He shouts enthusiastically. "You want a story or not?"

I giggle, nodding and chomping down on another potato chip.

Logan flashes me his most sinister grin, leaning forward as he angles the flashlight even more dramatically.

"This story takes place in a campground *a lot* like the one we're in now... *some people* might say it could have happened not too far from here."

When Logan and I wrote our first paper together we would often get lost in our work, only realizing how much time had passed in the early hours of the morning. One particularly stormy night we decided to make the best of the situation by trading ghost ghost stories. It's kind of been a tradition ever since.

"Oooh, sounds spooky!" I rub my hands together in anticipation.

Logan takes a sip of his beer.

"Very spooky, you're quite correct, and like most spooky situations, it was a dark and stormy night. A young couple named Brad and Justine had just arrived at their campsite. They did all the things one does when camping: put up their tent, stoked a big warm fire, cooked dinner–"

"What did they have?"

Logan sighs.

"I don't know, burgers."

"What kind?"

"Abi!" He laughs, shoving me gently in the shoulder. "I'm trying to be a storyteller here!"

"I'm just curious! What if the food really matters to the story?"

"They had regular burgers, okay? Pickles, ketchup, mustard, the whole shebang."

"Okay, I'm satisfied. Please continue."

"Well, satisfying you is what's most important after all—"

The second he says it, I'm almost sure Logan's face turns a deep red, but he quickly shifts the flashlight away for a moment while he regains his composure.

"That is *not* what I meant to say! Is there weed in those ketchup chips you gave me or something? Are all Canadians secret criminals? Is this an evil scheme?"

"It's fine, Logan, I promise. Just keep going." I laugh, resting my hand on his knee. "And don't worry, I'll make sure to let you know if you haven't left me satisfied."

Logan's eyes dart downward, and for a moment I'm worried I may have crossed a line, but he quickly flicks the flashlight back up to his face, looking completely confident once more.

"Okay, where was I?"

"Brad and Justine, they just had burgers."

"Right. So, the lovely couple, watching the sun begin to dip below the horizon, decided it was the perfect time to get some sleep after a long day of travel. At first, everything was perfect, and they slept completely undisturbed. Then, at precisely 3:15am, Justine awoke to the sound of something brushing up against the tent."

He reaches to the side and drags his nails across the nylon, making a strange scratching noise.

"And it sounded... exactly like this!"

I raise my hand to my lips in mock horror, waiting for him to continue.

"Justine made sure not to make a sound, just in case it was an animal that might react poorly to being startled. Instead, she slowly and carefully reached behind her, trying to feel for Brad in the darkness of their tent. But much to her horror... his side of the tent was empty."

"Uh oh!" I whisper "What happened to Brad?"

"Who knows," Logan replies. "Definitely not Justine, so she waited, unsure of what to do as the scratching noises began to surround the entire tent. She was growing more and more terrified, her heart pounding, her head spinning, and as she let her imagination spiral further and further she began to break out into a violently cold sweat."

I'm hanging on every word, shoving chip after chip into my mouth.

"Suddenly, a loud snarling comes from behind her, just beyond the extremely thin layer of tent separating her from the horrifying world outside. She screams, yanking the sleeping bag over her head, thunder clapping just in time for her to catch the briefest flash of lightning illuminating *something* standing outside the tent."

He pauses, raising one arm in a very familiar pose.

"Or should I say... some *one,* and someone with a knife no less, ready to strike! Justine *screams,* scrambling around the tent, still no sign of Brad... at least until she finds his phone near the entrance. With *fresh blood* on it!"

"Oh shit!"

"Oh shit indeed," Logan replies with a practiced, somber nod. "Justine, terrified, doesn't know what to do. She tries to call 9-1-1, but of course there's no service, and then, all at once, she realizes it's quiet outside. The only sound is the thunder rolling away from their campsite, and a light breeze through the trees. Her heart *pounds.* She knows the man with the knife could still be out there, *must* still be out there, but she has to find Brad. So, with all the bravery she can muster, she reaches for the zipper on the tent–"

"No! The murderer's definitely there..." I whisper. "Brad's absolutely worm food, she needs to save herself!"

Logan simply raises a brow, the flashlight still illuminating his face with a haunting glow.

Half of my reaction is just playing into the bit, pretending to be scared, but I really want to know where this story is going. Logan doesn't think he's much of a storyteller, but I disagree wholeheartedly. The flashlight, the facial expressions, the tension building... he really is a regular Vincent Price.

And then, as if on cue, his eyes go wide, and he leans forward until we're barely inches from one another.

"Slowly, she unzips the tent and *crawls* out into *pitch black* of the night. She can't see, and she doesn't dare make a sound. She's desperate, terrified with no idea where to go or what to do, trying her very best not to cry. She walks forward, aimlessly, step after step into the night as she struggles vainly to see anything around her. Finally the fear overtakes her, and she changes her mind, struggling to figure her way back to the tent just as a distant clap of thunder fills the air, leading to the inevitable splash of lightning. At the end of their campsite, standing next to their car, she sees a figure all in silhouette... holding a *knife*!"

I can see the little twinkle in his eyes as I gasp, a tingling sensation starting at the back of my head and slowly dripping down my spine like honey. I love listening to him talk. When he gets intense, his voice gets a little lower, and even kind of gravelly.

"Justine panics, screaming out for Brad, but the only response is the sound of footsteps pounding against the ground. Seeing the man in that brief flash of lightning was enough to stun her, pinning her in place with fright, but it clearly had a far different effect on him. Faster, and faster, and faster still, the footsteps crash into the earth as she can feel the panic consume her."

Logan's smile turns sinister.

"She can't see, completely disoriented by the dark, but she just barely manages to use Brad's phone as a flashlight to find their tent. Then she's running, lurching forward and barely on her feet as she scrambles, afraid she might collapse." He takes a dramatic pause, holding up one hand as his eyes widen even further, almost impossibly so. "And that's when she *knows* he's behind her, his footsteps so close she's sure she'll feel his breath against her neck any second... But all that follows is silence. Silence, and a soft hiss of her name... *Justine*."

I'm utterly captivated, staring into Logan's eyes as he holds my gaze, completely unflinching in his performance.

"She lets out a bloodcurdling scream. Why haven't the other campers rushed out of their tents yet? Surely, there must be *someone* around! But it doesn't matter. The moment she reaches her tent she can feel the man's knife slice through her pajama shirt, violently cutting into her back!"

Logan can't seem to contain the grin that spreads across his face as he watches my horrified expression. We're so close we're practically sitting on each other, huddled together in the glow of our single flashlight.

"Then what? Then what happened?"

"Then?" Logan asks. "She made it back to the tent, obviously. Aren't you paying attention?"

Logan just sits there, smiling in silence for a while before I finally raise a brow.

"That's it?!"

"No, of course it's not it Abi! I was pausing for dramatic effect!" He laughs. "Also, my throat's getting dry. This is self-care."

He takes another sip or two of his beer, dragging things out as long as he can.

"Now," Logan continues. "Like I said, Justine makes it back to the tent *just in time* to turn around, and even zip it shut! But of course, she knows that's not going to stop the man or his knife. His blade pierces straight through the fabric, tearing and shredding the meagre amount of protection she'd found."

Logan pauses, holding my gaze for a few moments until suddenly the flashlight shuts off, making me nearly jump out of my skin before he flicks back on with a big grin.

"Silence," he whispers. "As Justine waits for the inevitable, there's only silence. She waits, and waits, and waits, but there's nothing. No footsteps, no rustling in the distance or closer by... it's just *quiet*. She waits as long as she can, keeping herself awake until she simply can't, falling into an unwilling fitful sleep filled only with the echoing sound of Brad's screams in the night."

He takes in a deep breath, then lets it out, repeating the action a few times, playing it as if he's calming himself down from his own spooky tale before continuing.

"But the dawn comes, as it always does, and Justine wakes the next morning to the feeling of rain dripping down on her. At first she's confused, not quite sure what's happened, but when she fully comes to her senses she can see exactly what's occurred. The cool air blows against her face, the little drops of rain pelting her as she stares out through the gaping hole that man tore into the tent. But she's made it. For whatever reason he's gone and she's made it. Feeling emboldened in the daylight, she decides to crawl toward the front of the tent and carefully unzip it."

He reaches behind him and I hear the distinct sound of the tent's zipper.

"Logan Michael Flynn, you'll let bugs in!"

"Sorry, sorry!" He mutters, quickly shutting it. "Just wanted to add a bit of ambience."

"Finish the story!" I giggle, squeezing his knee.

I realize now that I've never moved my hand from that spot.

Logan doesn't seem to mind.

"When she makes her way out of the tent, her eyes immediately fall on Brad's backpack laying out in front of her. It's open... and as she makes her way toward it she can feel the dread build inside her. Step. By painful step. Toward the inevitable. And when she looks inside?" Suddenly he speeds up, his volume rising to match the new pace. "It's Brad's *severed* head! She screams and screams and screams again, but just before she can get to her feet, someone grabs her, but from where? From *inside* the tent! It's... *the man with the knife!*"

I give him a big, theatrical gasp, and he absolutely eats it up.

"She struggles and thrashes against him, but he's far too powerful, leaning in with all his strength and driving the knife deep into her chest. His face, still obscured by his dark hood is the only thing she can think of in that moment, and with her dying breath Justine reaches up, and pulls it off to see... *Brad!* Staring right back at her!"

He roars, tossing the flashlight aside and tackling me to the ground. I let out a squeal of laughter, what's left of the bag of chips dashed from my hand in the chaos. Logan's all pink-cheeks and smiles as we wrestle around the tent, the dim light of the flashlight barely illuminating that stupid drawn-on mustache. Finally, after what feels like an eternity, he gives up, the two of us rolling over on our backs and struggling to catch our breath.

"So, pretty scary, huh?"

His question is practically a string of gasps for air.

"Yeah... that was really— wait, one second, I thought Brad's head was in the bag?"

"Oh, it was. The guy with the knife... *was his evil twin!* That's all in the prequel though. I'll tell you that one on another trip."

His eyes are wild, his wavy hair tumbling all around his face, and without a second thought, I reach up and brush a bit of it away, my fingers gently grazing his cheek. His skin is warm, even hot to the touch, and for a split second I see him as the man I met in Toronto. All we'd have to do is say 'yes' again. Nothing new, nothing really difficult.

It would be as easy as breathing.

Toronto, our failed double date...

Even Aspen, as completely cursed as that turned out, they all felt right.

I let my fingers dance across his cheekbone and Logan's lips part. My heart leaps into my throat, and I find myself mirroring him.

Nobody needs to know.

*Nobody **would** know.*

The thought isn't just a little rattle in my head, it's pots and pans clanging around together, so loud that it's drowning out everything but the hammering in my heart.

And the wind.

"What's up?" Logan whispers.

And the storm building outside.

We can't do this, and not just because a weird part of my brain keeps expecting Frankie to roll up and catch us in the act. Logan's moved on. He's dating other people and that's healthier for the both of us. What happened between us is in the past, and besides, we're more than that now. We're friends. Best friends.

It would be so stupid to throw that all away.

"I, uh..." I clear my throat, swallowing any number of impulsive urges. "I have some makeup remover for your fake mustache."

Logan's brows furrow.

"What?"

"The one you drew on?"

"Oh!" He laughs, his face suddenly snapping back to its usual brightness. "Right. I forgot. Sorry, I should—"

He shifts his weight, propping himself up before helping me up as well. I root through my bag, hoping I'll find something to use along with any of the common fucking sense I clearly left at the bottom. What the hell was that about? It's like any time I don't have my guard fully up, and there's even a fraction of a spark between us, my head jumps into what could have been. I'm torturing myself, that's what it is, and if I keep this up I'll be torturing him, too.

I spot a small pack of makeup wipes poking out of a little internal pocket and snatch them up.

"Got 'em."

"Thanks, Shortcake." He pulls one out and rubs it over his face, smearing black all over his lips and chin in a complete and total mess.

I snort, completely taken aback.

"What's so funny?"

"Here," I murmur, crawling toward him. "Let me–"

"No, I'm– I got it." His face is bright red again. "I'm good, Abi. Seriously."

Shame hits me hard and fast. Maybe this tent wasn't the best idea after all. We made things weird. Maybe *I* made things weird.

"I'm sorry," I mutter.

"What? Why are you sorry?" Logan asks.

"I... I didn't mean to make things awkward, I'm sorry."

He sighs, tossing the remaining wipes down onto his sleeping bag.

"You didn't. Honestly, I probably shouldn't have tackled you. Or that whole thing with the wrestling." He takes a deep breath. "I kind of wasn't thinking."

I want to tell him I didn't mind.

I want to unspool every single thought, every little desire that has been filling my brain. I wish I could show him that for the past three years, he's the only man I've been thinking about.

But instead, I just shrug.

"Sometimes we get carried away."

Because this is what we promised.

"Yeah," he chuckles, cleaning off the remnants of the eyeliner. "We should get some sleep. Gotta be on the road early tomorrow."

Because this is how we stay friends.

"Logan, I'm sorry–"

He cuts me off, reaching out and grasping my face with both hands.

"Hey. No sorries. I'm told they're illegal in Canada."

"Actually, I think apologizing is our whole thing."

Logan chuckles, pressing his forehead against mine.

"We'll just be a bit more careful from now on, okay?"

I nod, and we each climb into our sleeping bags before I grab my phone and stuff my AirPods into my ears. The plan is to boot up Spotify, put on some soothing whale sounds, and fall asleep, but I can't help myself. I have a problem.

I check my email.

Nothing about the scholarship I applied for, or the three other teaching jobs. I could call it there, but I go to the university's website instead, and start scrolling through the internal postings. I've been hunting through these over the last few months, and not finding much. They're mostly looking for faculty and postdocs in STEM. More than likely that's where the budget is going; the social sciences and humanities are going to have to squeeze their belts even more.

God, I can't even think about what they're doing to the Fine Arts.

Suddenly, in the midst of aimlessly scrolling through page after page, something catches my eye.

ANTHROPOLOGY – ADJUNCT POSITION

It's perfect.

Somehow, I meet all of the criteria. I have a PhD in anthropology, I've been actively publishing, I'm currently conducting research, *and* I have great teaching experience.

I scramble through the process of applying; I even have all my credentials and documents accessible on my phone. Bless you, Google Docs.

All it takes is a few minutes and a couple major tweaks to my cover letter and I'm ready to submit. My finger hovers over the button, every possible mistake or thing I may have missed rushing through my mind, drowning my lungs, and paralyzing me.

I can't. There's no way I'll get it. I'll just be humiliated.

"Sleep tight, Shortcake, and thanks for being the best."

The second the nickname leaves his lips, a wave of relief completely overwhelms anything else I'm feeling. We're fine. Nothing's been ruined.

I smile, still staring at my phone.

Submit Files.

Confirm.

"Night, Sunshine."

she's a rainbow

LOGAN

BANFF, ALBERTA
PRESENT DAY

"This place is gorgeous!"

I shake my head as we stroll down Bear street, taking in all the small-town sights.

Abi wasn't lying when she said it was picturesque, but I'm still shocked by how close we are to the mountains, endless and snow-capped as they stand out against the bright blue sky. It feels like they're everywhere at the same time, like they're embracing us.

"Kind of reminds me of the bay," Abi sighs.

"A little, yeah."

The town itself has dozens of little tourist shops, filled wall-to-wall with maple leaf... *well everything*. Everything is made of— or *smells* like— maple. Maple trees, maple syrup, maple gelato... It's like this town fucked a maple leaf ten years ago and can't let it go.

Abi says I'm wrong, but I'm pretty sure even the money smells like maple syrup. Speaking of the money, we realized pretty quickly that she absolutely needed to give me a crash-course on their coins. Most of them are the same as they are in the States, quarter, nickel, dime. Sure, they don't have any pennies anymore, which is pretty wild, but it's nothing compared to the loonie. And then there's the abomination of metal known only as... the toonie. If there's anything about Canadians that I will never understand, it's their willingness to accept the pure and concentrated evil that is the coin-within-a-coin that replaced the completely reasonable two dollar bill.

I'm still fearfully awaiting the reveal of the Five-y, 5 unholy rings of unique metal bound together and ushering in the end of all things.

Anyway.

We arrived this afternoon after a long, beautiful drive. Really, Abi did most of the driving while I bounced between napping, and trying but failing to get some work done on my laptop. The second I saw a deer on the side of the road it was all over; I was too busy snapping pictures to get anything done. I think my camera roll is probably just 500 pictures of a single deer at this point.

Somewhere buried between the many tourist traps, we found some designer boutiques I recognized. My sister's been a passionate thrifter for years now, always fixated on finding stuff from Prada, Chanel, and vintage Valentino at a really good price. She'd go hunting for *hours* when she lived in New York, for the perfect designer bag or shoes. My sister and I may have a lot in common, but when it comes to fashion my policy is the weirder the better.

When that's your goal, you can find some great stuff anywhere, even in a costume shop.

Maybe especially in a costume shop.

"Come on." Abi tugs on my sleeve, giving me that look I'm more used to seeing from Imogen. "I need shoes."

We amble down the sidewalk, passing store after store until she stops dead in her tracks in front of a large window filled with costume jewelry, fringed leather jackets, and a bunch of kitschy stuff that I'm *pretty* sure my mom would love.

Abi places her hand on the window, leaning forward until her nose is practically smooshed against the glass.

"What are you looking at?" I chuckle.

"That ring." I follow her finger to a small round amethyst surrounded by tiny white diamonds on a gold band. "It looks *just* like one my grandma used to own."

"Oh yeah?"

I can feel the gears start turning. She needs a real engagement ring to pull off this whole fake engagement. I don't think a ring pop is going to cut it when we meet mom.

"I always loved that ring. I thought it was the most beautiful thing I'd ever seen when I was a kid."

Abi nibbles on a painted black fingernail, her eyes misting with tears.

"My grandfather gave it to her. Saved up every dime he had for it, too. Mom insisted that it stay on her finger when she passed." She shakes her head, laughing in disbelief. "It's weird, you know? We land in Canada and I find Baba's ring. I know it sounds silly, I know it can't be hers, but it kinda feels like she's looking out for me."

I didn't know any of this. Abi keeps so much of her past locked up tight that I usually only get little snippets of it in brief moments of vulnerability. Moments like this.

"When did she pass away?"

"A bit before I got my doctorate," she replies, her voice pinched as she tries to keep her composure. "She was so proud. I even gave her a draft of my dissertation; she read one page and told me it was brilliant."

"Well, you are brilliant. Baba's got good taste." I wrap an arm around her and pull her close.

She's getting that ring.

No ifs, ands, or buts about it.

"Sorry for all this," she laughs, gesturing vaguely at her eyes full of tears.

"Hey, I cried at the deep emotional message of a Panera Bread commercial the other day, remember?"

She snorts.

"I thought you said it was just because you were hungry."

We continue our walk down the sidewalk, and I make a mental note of the cross street. Now all I need to do is finesse up a clever little distraction, make sure she has absolutely no idea what I'm doing, and—

"Oh! Shoes!" Abi squeaks. "Right here!"

We're only a few stores down from where she first spotted the ring.

There's no way I'm this lucky. Maybe Abi's Baba *wants* me to buy it. Who am I to deny a ghost? If I did, she might follow us back to Emerald Bay and haunt my basement. I don't need that kind of stress in my life.

I love that goddamn basement.

I take a quick look around and spot a little western shop filled with cowboy boots, big metal belt buckles, and big ass hats, right next to the shoe store Abi's practically jumping to get into.

I grab my phone and take a picture for Roman.

> ME
>
> Is this cowboy heaven?

All I get in response is an eye roll emoji.

And then a cowboy emoji.

I snicker, sliding my phone back into my pocket.

"I wanna check this place out." I gesture toward it. "I need a tie, and maybe I can pick up a souvenir for the ol' Horse Doctor back home."

Abi clicks her tongue, frowning at the storefront.

"I don't think cowboys wear ties. They're rugged, and chew tobacco."

"Well, maybe there's a nice cowboy shirt in there. Cowboys like shirts, right?"

Abi chuckles, opening the door to the shoe store.

"Not our cowboy, the way I've heard your sister tell it, but you do you. Meet back here when you're done?"

"Sure!" I chirp.

I watch as Abi disappears into the shoe store, taking a few perfectly-acted steps towards the cowboy shop before spinning on the ball of my foot and high-tailing it back to the jeweler. When I get inside, I realize it's less of a jeweler and more of a second hand store, narrow alleys between shelves filled with delicate vases and expensive china in every direction.

I keep my arms glued to my body as I make my way to the front where an older woman with a big cherry-red bouffant hairdo sits perched on a stool, filing her long red nails as she watches me approach. She looks like Imogen might in 30 years.

"You look a little terrified," she laughs, setting her nail file down on the counter. "You need a hand?"

"Yeah, I don't want to knock anything over," I reply, glancing around me to make sure I haven't inadvertently elbowed something off the shelf.

"Careful," she warns, pointing at a sign that says *You Break It, You Buy It!*

I wince, but relax as a warm smile spreads across her face.

"What can I help you with?"

"That ring... the amethyst in the window—"

"Oh, I love that ring!" She gushes, her eyes widening as she rounds the counter.

She's much shorter than me, something closer to 5'1", and her jeans make a soft whooshing noise as she struts right past me with all the confidence in the world.

"It is for sale, right?" I ask, suddenly realizing with horror that there's a chance it's just some sort of lure to get suckers like me in the door.

"Honey, everything in this store's up for grabs," she calls, reaching over the window display to pluck out the ring. "Take a look up close, what do you think?"

She holds it up to me, shifting it around a bit to catch the light. She's right to do it; the ring is so much prettier when there's not a thick pane of glass in the way. The purple is richer, glittering as it's set against the large beam of golden light that's streaming in through the window.

"It's perfect," I whisper. "My, uh... my girlfriend was actually looking at it. She said it reminded her of her grandma's ring. She's really sentimental like that."

"Grandma had good taste," the woman replies with a wink. "Or maybe the man who put it on her?"

"Yeah." I reach for my wallet before stopping myself. "How, uh... much is it?"

"Five hundred as is. If you want it resized, I can do it here, but it'll be an extra hundred."

I whistle. That's cheaper than I thought it would be. Thanks, Baba.

"I'll take it at five hundred."

"Sure thing, sugar."

I follow her to the register where she packs the ring into a small box and tucks it into a nondescript black bag with a quick little wink.

Abi's going to love it. I just know she will. Yeah, she'll love... that I just spent 500 dollars on a fake engagement ring. That reminds her of her dead Grandma. I immediately think about canceling the transaction, but before I know it I've forked over my credit card and I'm watching bright red nails tap against the machine.

"So, engagement ring?" She asks, waiting for it to go through.

"Yeah, I wanted to get her something special. The second I saw her staring at it, I knew this was it."

The machine makes that oh-so pleasant beep that means I'm $500 poorer, and she hands me back my card and the bag with a warm smile.

Is this too much? It really is just a cute little joke after all.

So why does this feel so real?

"She's a lucky girl to have a man who notices these kinds of things."

"I'm the lucky one, ma'am. Thank you for your help."

"Pleasure's all mine. Have a wonderful day, sweetheart."

I can feel the back of my neck begin to heat up as I take the bag from her. I guess I'm locked in, so now I just have to figure out when I'm going to give this to Abi. That, and how I'm going to explain my way out of a potential ass kicking. It's not the ring that's going to upset her, it's what I paid for it.

We exchange one final smile before I rush out the door and straight toward the shoe store, hoping I beat Abi there so I don't have to explain myself. But by the time I make it to the window I'm relieved to see her standing in front of a mirror, admiring a pair of bright red leather heels.

I let my gaze wander up and down her body. She's always been the most gorgeous thing in the world to me, with exquisite curves, thick thighs, and an ass I'd like to sink my teeth into, but I'm always doing my best to put all of that aside. We're friends after all, and I'm pretty certain it's seen as a bit weird to think about how much you want to take a bite out of your bestie.

But the thing I love the most about her? It's that little frown she gets when she's trying to make a decision about what she's going to wear. It's adorable to watch her hum and haw over any new addition to her massive shoe collection, often testing out three or four pairs before she's satisfied.

I force myself to tear my eyes away from her before she catches me staring, and make my way back toward the western store. I really *do* need a nice dress shirt to wear to the reunion, and somewhere better to hide this box. Who knows, maybe something will speak to me.

The little bell dings when I push the door open, but what really gets my attention is the smell of old leather mixed with a musk that I can't quite put my finger on. Whatever it is, it hits me the moment I enter the store, and I fear I may never be able to forget it.

I wander around, plucking dress shirt after dress shirt from the racks, holding each one up to my chest, then putting them back with a disappointed sigh. They're all plaid. I love plaid, but plaid is not what I need right now. I need something dressier, and preferably black.

Shockingly, Plaid is neither of those things.

I can tell pretty quickly that everything in this store is very... not me. I wish it was. I wish I looked great in a pair of jeans and a relaxed button-up, but I kind of feel like a muppet at the best of times.

Tall, lanky, and awkward is pretty much my M.O.

I continue my hunt, passing by a surprising number of tourists in golf shorts and polo shirts, until I come across exactly what I'm looking for. The shirt is black, with gold trim around the collar, shoulders, and pockets. The trim itself looks like it had to have been done by hand, even prettier and more detailed up close.

I walk over to the mirror and hold it up in front of me.

I like it, but there's something missing and I can't tell what it is.

"Here," one of the staff members says as he approaches, holding what looks like a piece of leather cord with gold caps on the ends. "Try this."

I only identify it as a bolo tie after I take it in my hand.

It's beautiful, in a sort of strange way, the main feature being the large black oval stone with gold 'cracks' and flecks running through it. It's surrounded by a thin rim of gold with what looks like sun rays etched into it.

"This is... actually kind of incredible."

"Special occasion?" He asks.

"Yeah, my fiancée and I have a high school reunion in Ontario. We made a whole trip of it; we're on the way there now."

"My condolences," the man chuckles. "If it helps, I think you'll probably be the best dressed there if this is what you're going for."

I'm not really sure if I'm being upsold or if he's just really passionate about gold trim and bolo-ties, but I laugh and nod along anyway, holding up the ensemble together just to make sure they really do match up.

Damn. Guess so.

"I think I'll take these."

The man nods, and I follow behind him to the register where he folds my shirt into a small square, sliding it into the bag I offer up from the jewelry store. He puts the bolo tie in its own little box and slips it in as well, setting it on top of my other, much more secret purchase. I already feel a hell of a lot better now that this bag has something else tucked inside.

We call that plausible deniability.

Or something.

When I emerge from the shop, Abi's already waiting outside with two bags in her hands, and a pained expression completely eclipsing her face.

"What's the damage?"

"Like three hundred bucks," she groans. "But they were both *so* nice! I got a pair of red heels and a pair of black ones. I can wear them for conferences, and probably even job interviews. Really it's an investment when you think about it, right?"

"You don't have to justify your spending, Shortcake." I hold up the bag. "Look at me, I got a cool shirt and a bolo tie for the reunion. When else am I gonna use that?"

"Oooh, no that's amazing!"

She reaches for the bag but I panic, jerking away without thinking, in fear that she'd find the little box. I quickly grab the bolo tie box, opening it up and showing it off over-dramatically, in the hope that weirdness will be enough to distract her from my other weirdness.

"Holy shit! This is beautiful, Logan!"

Mission Accomplished.

"The guy in the shop said it would go with my shirt. It's got all this gold trim— I think it's actually hand-stitched!"

I give her a small peak of the fabric, thankful for how much of the bag it's taking up.

"Oh, wow! Very Roman Burke of you, color me surprised!"

"Hey, listen, if I can be half as confident as *that* guy at your reunion, I'll consider this entire trip a success."

I've always looked up to Roman. He's just... cool. I don't even really know why, considering the man is practically allergic to his phone, and groans every time he gets an email or a text message. I guess I just admire him for taking charge of his life. He fought for what he wanted, in spite of all the odds.

"You wanna grab some food?" Abi asks. "The girl at the shoe store told me there's a great burger place down a few blocks. She said you can sit on the patio and get a beautiful view of the mountains."

"Sounds perfect," I chuckle. "And a view of the mountains? Around here? That's gotta be a really special sorta spot."

The two of us walk side by side, and I reflexively reach for her hand, her fingers gently linking with mine for only a second or two before we both pull away just a little. I do my best to make it look like it was an accident, and she seems to do the same. I wonder if she's thinking something similar to me, that it's impossible to ignore the way my nerves light up when we touch.

Either way, I can't deny just how heavy that ring is starting to feel.

wheat kings

LOGAN

SASKATOON, SASKATCHEWAN
PRESENT DAY

"You weren't kidding, this place is flat as shit," I grumble, keeping my foot pressed down on the gas.

It feels like we've driven past nothing but golden wheat fields with a few rolling hills peppered in for some flavor. If we didn't have our phones, it'd be nearly impossible to tell how long I've been driving or where the fuck we even are. The most entertainment we get is when we see some cows in the distance. Abi said it's a cultural tradition in Canada to say 'cows' when you drive past them. I know it's not true, but when we pull over at the next rest stop, I'm googling it just in case.

"My dad used to tell this dumb joke that Saskatchewan is so flat, you could watch your dog run away for a week straight," Abi chuckles.

That sounds like something *my dad* might have said; he would have loved it out here on the open road, though. Dad was a huge fan of these kinds of trips, although I think he preferred the ones where his two kids weren't screaming the entire time. I remember many family vacations crammed in the backseat with Iggy, teaching her how to play whatever game I happened to bring on my Game Boy. I think her favorite was

Kirby's Dream Land, specifically because Kirby was pink. She'd used to get me to beat the really hard levels, and I let her take all the credit, but it wasn't too many trips before she was clearing those little cartridges on her own.

"It is peaceful out here, though," I remark, glancing over at her. "There's a certain charm to that."

She's been knitting for the last few hours, working on something she pulled out about halfway through the trip. She's got these really dorky glasses on too, that apparently keep her from getting car sick. I've never heard of that being a thing, but she's been bopping along to the Beach Boys album the last 20 minutes so they must be working.

"What are you making?"

"A blanket," she murmurs, her words punctuated by the knitting needles clacking together gently. "I'm going to try and knit some little ghosts, too. Maybe some bats if I'm feeling ambitious."

"Where'd you learn how to do that?"

"What, knitting?"

"Yeah."

She shrugs.

"Baba taught me. At first, I just loved listening to the sound of the needles, but eventually I really wanted to learn. So, she put me in her lap, visit after visit, and taught me all the stitches she knew. It took years."

"So she was Canadian?"

"Ukrainian and Canadian," Abi replies with a soft smile. "She'd make me borscht when I was sick and we'd watch Soap Operas together. Her house always smelled *so* good; she was always baking something or trying out a new recipe or other. I'd go back to my mom's with bags of cookies, perogies, stuff like that."

"She sounds pretty cool."

Abi beams, nodding enthusiastically.

"She was. Actually, I'm sure she would have liked you an awful lot." She gently pokes my bicep with her knitting needle. "She'd probably want to put a little more meat on those bones, though. *He's so sickly looking, onuchko! Take better care of him or he will fly away in the wind!*"

"Hey, I'm working out!" I flex one bicep. "You can tell Baba perfection takes time!"

Abi scrunches her nose up at me, sticking out her tongue before diving back into her knitting. The quiet clicks of her needles are an interesting accompaniment to the music, getting me thinking more about her grandma and this whole situation.

What if I crossed a line buying that engagement ring? Her grandmother's ring clearly meant a lot to her, but this isn't that same ring, and I'm not really her fiancé.

Guilt bites down hard, bristling down the back of my neck.

What was I thinking?

Like, what was I *actually* thinking?

That I'd buy her a ring, and she'd fall in love with me and throw her entire career away? Lord knows I've tried to avoid this sort of thing, tried to fall in love with other people, but it never works. I've just never felt the same spark that Abi and I had that night in Toronto.

And I've been chasing it for years.

This hotel looks like a fucking castle got dropped smack dab in the middle of the city. The building itself is a mix of genres, classical European and modern architecture— almost like someone Frankeinstein'd the two styles together.

Light orange brick, black pitched roofs, ornate windows, and some rounded columns that look like they *might* be chimneys. The building sticks out like a sore thumb compared to the other drab structures on this street, but at least it's hard to miss.

"I cannot believe you booked this place," Abi laughs as the doorman helps us with our bags. "We could have just stayed at a motel."

"No offense to your otherwise impeccable taste, but I'm 6'4" and my spine may as well be made of glass at this point. I'm sleeping in a comfortable bed. Plus, I got a good deal on it."

$200 Canadian for a night. Limited time offer. The deal popped up in my email, and that's the kind of thing you can't refuse. Sometimes that Flynn impulsiveness comes in handy.

I told Abi I would take care of at least some of the hotel bookings to ease her financial stress. She's tried to Venmo me a few times, but I've been diligently declining every one. I have money to burn and she's got a lot on her plate.

The lobby is stunning as we enter, with cream and silver marble floors, large ivory pillars, and a massive crimson rug that leads all the way to the front desk. There's a little lounge area for people to relax in, with luxurious-looking charcoal couches and wingback chairs that look like they might devour you if you stayed too long.

The doorman points us toward the front desk and proceeds to take our bags away; Abi looks a little bit panicked, but I do my best to calm her down. She's used to roughing it on the conference circuit, staying at shitty motels and dragging her suitcases up long flights of stairs all by herself. Not today, though. Today, some random guy we don't know gets to carry our bags out of eye-shot while we hope he really works here.

Today, we're living the medium-high life.

"Good afternoon!" The concierge chirps from his spot at the front desk.

"Afternoon!" I hand him my phone with the discount code on it, along with my passport and credit card. "Booking should be under Dr. Logan Flynn."

The man nods, pleasantly typing away on his computer as Abi glances around the lobby.

"Our bags are fine," I laugh. "They're professionals, Abi."

"I know, it's just... you know, there's a lot of people here and we have expensive shit in those bags."

I scoff. She's got nothing to worry about.

"It's Canada, everyone's too nice to steal! And besides, I've heard that in this country, stealing... *is a crime!*"

Abi and the front desk guy exchange a small smirk and she turns back to me, cocking her head to the side.

"Good thing you're not a criminologist, huh?" She quips. "And remember, we're not nice all the time. Some of us are actually kind of passive aggressive."

"It's called a joke, Shortcake," I murmur, reaching over to boop her nose.

It's busy in here, with staff and guests milling all around. I'm a little surprised.

"Is it always this busy?" I ask him.

"This time of year? Absolutely," he laughs.

"Good thing you got that email," Abi mutters.

"Yeah, or you'd have to survive another night of *Logan's Horrifying Tales!*"

The front desk clerk slides a small white envelope across the desk with his beaming customer-service smile.

"You're in room 1205. Enjoy your stay."

"Thanks!" I reply, taking Abi's hand and leading her to the elevator where the doorman is waiting with our bags. "Room 1205!"

He nods, immediately splitting off in a totally different direction, and Abi stammers in shock.

"Wait! There's an elevator right here!"

"It's fine, Abi. They take a different elevator to fit those big luggage carts."

"Oh," she murmurs. "Seriously?"

"Yep!" I guide her toward the guest elevator, and hit the button for the 12th floor. "And also so they don't ruin the ambience of the hotel. I had a friend in college who used to be a concierge at a five-star hotel in Manhattan and he said they had a ton of secret elevators and passage-ways that only staff have access to. It's so that the guests see as little as possible when it comes to the inner workings of the whole thing."

"Like what?" Abi laughs. "Pushing cleaning carts around and running food to rooms?"

"I guess so," I reply, as the elevator doors up to our floor and we step outside. "He said the hotel wanted to maintain a certain magical image. There's also a chance they're letting assassins use their secret tunnels to commit heinous deeds undetected."

"Uh huh," she murmurs, craning her neck and looking down the long hallway.

I spot the doorman standing outside of our room halfway down the hall, the luggage cart already gone. He's either a wizard or extremely fast. Regardless, I tip him 50 bucks and we slip inside.

The room is spacious, with charcoal carpet, cream-colored walls, a large mahogany desk, a balcony, and...

"Logan. Why is there one bed?"

No way.

There's no fucking way.

I dash around the room, scrambling to find some sort of secret pull-out mattress I could banish myself to for the night, but I'm coming up empty.

"Hang on."

I reach into my pocket and grab my phone, pulling up the email confirmation from the hotel, and my stomach sinks to the floor.

Honeymoon Suite, complete with complimentary champagne and a jacuzzi in the bathroom.

I booked a fucking *honeymoon suite*.

Slowly, I turn to Abi, flashing a big charming smile that's absolutely not going to get me off the hook, but it's worth a shot, right? Either way, Roman and Iggy cannot know about this. They'll never let me live it down.

"You're gonna laugh. I *promise* you're gonna laugh."

"Am I gonna kill you after I finish laughing?" She asks, razorwire stitched into her voice. She's really cute when she's mad. Terrifying, but cute.

"If you kill me, there'll be no one to pay for the next hotel!"

Her gaze is steely, and it doesn't look like the old Flynn charm is going to work on her this time. This road trip was supposed to be fun; the main goal was to have a good time and unwind on the way to what will most likely be a pretty stressful destination. It was my job to take care of at least a couple of the hotels, which should have been one of the easiest ways to make things run smoothly. And, of course, it was a job I gave to myself.

"Let me just call the front desk and see if I can deal with this mixup."

I have to force myself not to stammer as I sit down on the bed and pick up the phone, dialing down to the lobby.

"Marriott Hotel, this is Thomas speaking."

"Heeeeyyy, Tommyyyy! What's up, dude?"

My voice cracks like I'm going through puberty, and I make a big show of clearing my throat as Abi moves to stand right in front of me, blocking out the light from the window. She's looming over me, like she's coiling up, ready to strike the moment I'm not able to find a positive outcome. I may not survive the night if I can't fix this.

"Sorry, I must be coming down with something."

"Would you like room service to bring you–"

"No no! Just a quick Q for you. I could have sworn that I booked a room with two beds? My fiancée snores, and—"

Her little pointed boot connects with my shin and I yelp.

"That doesn't even make sense!" She hisses. "And I *do not* snore!"

I mean, she does.

It sounds like a little motor boat, but now is probably not the time.

"Sorry," I laugh. "Um, we just uh... you know, we sleep differently, and I could have sworn I booked two beds."

"Um, no, Mr. Flynn. You booked the honeymoon suite with the honeymoon package. It does include complimentary champagne, which we can bring to you whenever you'd like! And don't forget to enjoy the magnificent view of the Saskatchewan River, it looks absolutely stunning this time of year."

She's going to smother me in my sleep.

Should I even have my PhD at this point? Would anyone have let me into the program after an idiot move like this? My dad would be howling right about now. I can practically hear him.

"Are you sure– Nevermind. Of course, you're sure. Um, we probably can't switch rooms, can we?"

"I'm so sorry, Dr. Flynn. Unfortunately, there's a medical convention in town and the hotel is fully booked out for the next week."

I didn't know that, because I'm not that kind of doctor. I wouldn't be able to save anyone on a flight, but if they needed an emergency primer on Max Weber, I could bore the cabin to death less than an half an hour after departure.

I'm trying not to look at Abi, but she's not making it easy as she stares daggers at me from nearly any direction I manage to shift into.

"Right, yes, of course. Alright, thanks anyway!"

I hang up and give her another cheesy grin, one that I hope at least somewhat shows how sorry I am.

"Logan!" She stomps her foot. "Two beds! That's the most obvious thing in the world, literally the only thing we needed! We could have been in a motel and it would have been fine if we just had *two beds!*"

"I know!" I exclaim, trying my best not to sound angry.

She's the one who deserves to be angry at me. I'm even on her side in that respect, I'm pretty damn furious at myself right now.

"I'm a moron, and I try too hard to be funny, and I'm super impulsive, and now all I'm hoping is my best friend isn't going to punch me in my stupid face."

Abi sighs, leaning into me as she wraps her arms around my waist.

"I'm not going to punch you in your stupid face," she whispers. "But I *am* mad at you."

I let out a big sigh of my own, relief bubbling up as I run my fingers through her hair.

"I know. I'll do everything I can to make this right. I'll sleep on the floor!"

"No, what? If you sleep on the floor, it'll be me driving for the rest of the trip while you moan and groan in the back seat."

She paces around in silence for a few seconds, weighing our options.

"It's just for tonight, right?"

I take a step back, raising a finger as I whip my phone out at lightning-speed. I hop from reservation to reservation, checking each one at least a couple times. All two beds. This is the only one where impulsivity completely screwed me.

"Okay, yep! We're two-bedding it for the rest of the trip, high-five!"

She raises an eyebrow, but otherwise ignores me, returning to her pacing.

"Until we get to my mom's place," she grumbles. "I didn't manage to come up with an excuse that wouldn't screw everything up for that one."

"Right."

Abi bites her lip, nervously twisting the big silver bat ring on her finger.

"I... did tell you that, right?"

If she did, I don't remember. We spent the week scrambling, packing, and booking hotels. It was pretty chaotic, but we didn't have very long to plan for this.

"Yeah," I lie. "At least I think you did."

"Okay. It's fine, I think we should just come up with some rules," Abi says, her voice soft and gentle. "That's the smart thing to do, right?"

"Yeah, that sounds good," I reply, doing my best to allow for all of these changes to wash over me instead of sparking a big ol' panic. "You got a few in mind?"

"Actually, I do!"

She rushes for her bag, pulling out a notebook and a pen before plunking down at the big mahogany desk in the corner of the room.

"Wow, okay! We're making this super official."

"Well, you and I both tend to be... let's just say forgetful," she replies, spinning her pen between her fingers. "Anyway, I think the first rule should be no tongues when we kiss."

I ease myself slowly back down onto the bed, completely blown away.

"We're– uh– we– kissing? We're kissing?"

I have *got* to figure out a way to keep my voice from cracking.

"Oh!" Abi's bright red, her pen hovering above her notebook. "We don't have to be one of those PDA couples, but—"

Right. Of course. Couples kiss. Actually, it would probably be weird if we didn't.

"Do *you...* want to kiss?" I ask.

I feel like I'm suffocating. Play it cool, Logan. It's just Abi. It's just a big game.

But it's *Abi*.

"I mean... I'm okay with kissing." Her voice sounds a little unsure, but she's definitely not in panic-mode. "We've done it before, and if I remember right we were pretty good at it."

"It was so long ago," I sigh. "I almost can't remember anymore."

It's such an obvious lie I can feel my grandma shaking her head at me from the afterlife. Sure, I can barely remember where I left my car keys most of the time, but I remember every single detail of that night. Her smile, her soft skin, even the way she tasted...

You don't forget someone like Abi.

"Oh," she whispers. The blush refusing to fade as she draws nervous little loops on the page. "I do."

"Okay well uh..." I stumble, still trying and failing to play at being Mr. Cool. "What else?"

"Number two is no sex." She scoffs, rolling her eyes. "Obviously."

I give her an awkward thumbs up, and it earns me a little huff of a laugh.

I'll take it.

"Holding hands is fine." I can hear her pen scraping across the page, filling up the silence in the room. "So are general public displays of affection. That'll actually let us avoid makeout sessions without looking like we're having some sort of falling out."

My imagination starts swirling.

"Public displays, like...?"

"Your hand on my waist, pecks on the cheek, stuff like that."

Okay. Yeah. That won't be too bad. I can deal with that.

Abi's still blushing, nervously playing with her pen as she waits for my response. It's kind of a relief because I've definitely got the jitters, similar to when I drink too much coffee.

"That's cool with me too. Good rule."

"Cool," she breathes. "That's all of them, for now at least. We can always add more if we need to, but now they're all written down. Official."

"Perfect," I mutter, looking for anything to distract me from the situation, and I spot a flyer poking out from underneath the hotel phone. "Oh hey, check this out!"

I hold it up in front of her. It's an advertisement for a night market and carnival that's just a stone's throw from the hotel.

"You wanna explore Saskatoon's nightlife?" I ask, my voice hopeful. "Something to get our minds off my complete and total failure as the trip's official planner?"

Abi beams back at me, and I know I'm forgiven.

"You know what? Win me one of those ridiculously huge teddy bears and you've got yourself a deal, Flynn."

try a little tenderness

ABI

SASKATOON, SASKATCHEWAN
PRESENT DAY

"So…" I sip my cherry slushie as we wade through the endless crowds of people. "I guess we should figure out how we met."

"What do you mean?"

The night market was a great idea. So far, we've devoured about three bags of mini donuts, chased each other with bumper cars, and enjoyed gourmet hot dogs— well, Logan said they were gourmet, because he dipped them in Canadian mustard.

"Well, we can't tell the truth."

"Why not?"

"Because!"

I laugh, but I don't really have an answer for him. It just seems kind of absurd that we wouldn't come up with some clever little deception.

"It doesn't exactly look great, especially if we have to admit we met three years ago. My mom would probably flip if she thought I was hiding a relationship for that long! Even a fake one."

"Fair," Logan replies. "Okay, new plan. We met at a department shindig or something. Then a couple months later, I proposed to you at Guardian Point."

"A couple *months*?!" I exclaim. "Damn Flynn, you move fast!"

"Ah yeah, you see, fictional me doesn't like to waste time. He's like real-me, but if I had even an ounce of willpower. No procrastination, only dynamic moves to build toward my best life!"

Logan's a master at procrastination, and he has been as long as I've known him. Similar to his sister, he says he likes to 'race the clock' when it comes to completing deadlines. It gives him a rush, or maybe more accurately it gives him motivation. Too often our brainstorming sessions for papers turn into playing board games, or talking about TV shows, all the way up until the 11th hour.

"Who made the first move?" I ask. "That's a big one we need to figure out."

"Um... okay, so we're at a conference, yeah? We traveled together, found ourselves alone in the hotel bar, and I couldn't stop praising your work." He elbows me gently in the ribs. "Which real-me also loves, by the way. Just want to point that out."

I take another long sip of my slushie, grinning back at him until I get a little bit of brain freeze.

"Okay, the big question: Where was our first date? I'm thinking..." He clicks his tongue, confirming his choice to himself. "How about The Orchid! We went for a nice romantic evening. Oldschool."

"Nice, very fancy. My mom'll love that."

The Orchid is one the most expensive restaurants in Emerald Bay. Alternate universe Logan was definitely on his A game.

"And then I took you to the Hi-Dive, to relax and just see how things would go. We played pool. You won, obviously. Sunk the 8 ball into the center right pocket to end the game. And then, not to be outdone, I brought the house down with a karaoke version of Wanted Dead or Alive by Bon Jovi."

At first I assumed he was just making all this stuff up off the top of his head, but I'm realizing that most of these details are ones he's plucked from different moments in our lives together. We've spent a lot of nights at that bar, shooting pool and talking about philosophy, theory, politics. He took me to that restaurant to congratulate me on an early publication opportunity. He's absolutely belted out Dead or Alive on more than one occasion.

"I'm just a little surprised you're being honest about the pool thing. Isn't Other-Logan also a master shark? You're saying there's actually something he *can't* do?"

Logan grins back at me, and I can't help but let out a loud cackle. He's one of the worst pool players I've ever met. He spends all of his time talking shit rather than actually focusing on playing, which works out great for me.

"Oh, no. No no no. The only thing that's different between me and Other-Logan is I'm even *more* of a gentleman! I don't want you to feel bad when I take away the one thing you have over me, so I let you think you're the superior player!"

I smirk.

"Okay, Flynn. How about we test that theory? There's gotta be a table around here somewhere."

The night is warm, and I shed my leather jacket, slinging it over my shoulder. I chose a pair of skin tight purple leather pants for the night, and a black tank top I picked up at Throwback a few years ago. It looked really cool when I threw it together back at the hotel, but the leather was probably a bad choice. I'm sweating like crazy.

We wander through the crowd, taking in the flashing lights and drooling over the smell of corndogs and mini donuts. It reminds me of being a kid, going to little summer fairs in Blackburn. The carnival would roll in for the weekend and it was a huge deal. I remember practically dragging my mom along with me because all the parents said it wasn't a good idea for the kids to go alone.

"How come we never do anything like this in Emerald Bay?" Logan muses. "There's plenty of farmland available to put up some rides and some food stands… people would love it."

"Well, I mean they do that winter thing sometimes, don't they?"

"Sure, but that's not—"

"And if they did it in the summer some drunk frat boys would absolutely roll up wasted and ruin it all."

"Ah, yes, but then at least Emerald Bay's finest would have something to do."

Neither of us can hold back our laughter at the thought, only interrupted by an even louder cheer up ahead of us.

Logan is instantly curious.

"Tell me what those elf eyes see, Legolas," I tease.

Logan cleans off his glasses, straining his neck as he shifts on the balls of his feet. He's so cute when he squints.

"It's hard to tell. There's a big crowd. Come on."

He takes my hand, leading me toward the commotion as the cheers grow louder. Everyone's packed into the beer garden, and as we get closer I spot a hand waving back and forth erratically above a sea of people. It takes me a moment, but quickly everything comes together.

"It's a mechanical bull!"

We manage to slide into the crowd, pushing our way through until we spot a man hanging on for dear life as the machine bucks and squeals.

"Wow, I haven't seen one of these in years! That guy's doing pretty good too, don't you think?"

Logan doesn't respond, he's too busy staring down the mechanical bull. It almost looks like he's sizing the damn thing up, prepping to go into battle.

Oh, I *have* to see this.

"Okay, we didn't find a pool table, but how about tackling that?" I ask. "In what might be a world's first, I think we've found something you could beat me at."

"I'm considering it."

Logan can't resist trying something he's got no experience in; he likes to find things he's never done before and master them as quickly as possible, taking them apart in his head until he understands just what levers to pull or buttons to press. The funny part is the result ends up the same either way: either he figures it out, masters it and moves on, or he hits a wall, gets bored, and looks for the next thing to catch his attention.

"How long do you think I can hang on for?" He asks, his voice suddenly full of bravado.

"Do you want me to hype you up, or tell the truth?"

He slings his arm around me, squeezing me tight.

"I can take criticism, constructive or otherwise."

I click my tongue, watching as the man tumbles off the creaking machine.

"Hmm, let me do the math. At your height, with your relative strength, combined with your body mass and experience... I'm thinking less than a second."

Logan lets out a loud, bark of a laugh.

"A second?! You don't even think I could last for *one second?*"

"To clarify, I said *less* than a second. Those things are intense, and you already look like one of those wind-sock men at a car dealership on a good day."

Everything around us smells like sweat, sunscreen, and beer, and it seems like the atmosphere's affecting both of us in similar ways.

"Nah, you know what? I'm strong, I'm talented, and I'm brilliant. I give myself at least five seconds."

"Logan, five seconds is insane for your first time!"

Logan's a man on a mission, pushing his way to the front of the crowd much quicker than I initially expected. He puts his hands on his hips, looking around at the other people standing around the bull.

"Is there a line?"

A couple of them snicker, but a guy I think must be around my age with a trucker hat and jeans gestures to the bull.

"No line. You're up, bro."

Logan takes off his glasses, handing them over.

"Hold these for me if you would, gorgeous."

He gets a few laughs from the crowd as he walks up, and it's obvious why. The cardigan, dress pants, and oxfords make him stick out like a sore thumb amidst a sea of cowboy hats and denim; he's basically the poster-boy for adult male nerd. I've always loved his ability to just exist, completely himself, no matter who he's around.

Logan walks toward the bull with confidence, but things get a bit awkward the moment he attempts to get up on it, less climbing on and more throwing himself right at it. I can see his mismatched striped socks peek out as his legs stick almost all the way up into the air. A few more laughs ripple through the crowd, but when the attendant tries to help him, he waves him off.

"It's fine, it's fine. I got it!"

A few more grunts and some awkward flailing and he does manage to get himself upright, turning to look at me with that shit-eating grin he's so fond of. It is, of course, short lived. The moment the bull starts bucking he lets out a screech, seemingly shocked that the bull's doing the thing he just spent a couple minutes watching it do, lurching forward and holding on for dear life.

He kind of reminds me of a muppet.

"Just fall off!" I laugh. "Your pride isn't worth this, Logan!"

"Has it been a second?!" He yelps.

"Almost five!" Someone shouts from the back. "You got this, Longlegs!"

Logan holds on for a couple more seconds before releasing the bull and letting it buck him off, landing on the mat with an undignified thud. He grunts and rolls onto his stomach, hair falling in his eyes, but he's still got that bright, optimistic smile plastered onto his face. He did it, after all.

"That's seven seconds! Not bad for a first-timer!"

At least half the crowd cheers, and a couple people step forward and help him to his feet, patting him on the shoulder.

"Thank you, thank you for watching my complete and utter humiliation!" He turns to me, cheeks flushed and breathing heavily. "You want a drink? I feel like I need some liquor in me after that."

"Sure! I'll grab us a table— unless you want to break your record?"

Logan scoffs, giving it a dismissive wave.

"I think I proved my point. I'll get us the beers and be right back."

He heads for the bar while I slip over to one of the empty picnic tables in the back, and I watch as he makes his way to the front, chatting with the bartender. It's only a few seconds in and he's already making her laugh; she's definitely hitting on him, but I know he's just being his usual charming self.

I'm not jealous. I can't be because I don't have the right.

Logan's not mine.

But ever since this trip's started to ramp up, I can't get the image of him on top of me out of my fucking head. His warm breath on my neck, the way his arms caged me in, the way he moaned my name in my ear when he came all those years ago.

I haven't had sex like that since.

I let out a long, shaky breath, pulling out my phone to distract me from my own thoughts.

"One night," I murmur. "It's just one night."

It'll be fine. We set up those rules to keep things where they need to be. Nothing is going to happen.

"Hey, pretty lady," a deep voice rumbles, the man it belongs to sliding into the seat across from me. "What're we drinkin'?"

He's wearing a backwards snapback, blue and black flannel shirt, and a white t-shirt. He's got a cigarette tucked behind his ear, and a lopsided smirk on his face.

Not to mention the fact that he *reeks* of booze.

"Oh, no thank you," I chuckle. "My friend's on his way—"

"I didn't ask for your life's story," the stranger scoffs. "I asked what we're drinking."

I try to keep up my sweetest smile, struggling as I feel venom swirling together with the bile rising up from my stomach. I glance over to Logan, but he's still laughing with that bartender. I think he's showing her one of his damn coin tricks.

I flip out my phone for a second underneath the table and shoot him a text.

ME

Creep alert.

"Did you hear me, sweetheart?"

The man's voice is still mostly calm, but I can tell he's starting to get agitated, and I figure now's a better time than any to set some clear boundaries.

"Are you too stupid understand what a no is?" My tone shifts into something sharp and confrontational. "Because I'm pretty sure I said that my friend—"

"Is an idiot for leaving you alone." He smirks, looking me up and down. "I wouldn't let you out of my sight for a second. What an asshole."

What is it with men and not knowing when it's time to just pack it in and take the L? It's not exclusive to guys like this, either. I've been at more than a few academic conferences where an attendee gets so drunk they don't even care how handsy they're getting in public. No matter what the setting is, there's always someone who feels entitled to something.

"I said no," I reply firmly, a slight snarl rising in my voice. "My fiancé's at the bar."

"You said he was your friend."

That drunken smirk is really starting to piss me off now.

"I meant—" I take a deep breath. I don't need to justify or explain anything to him. "I said no. I'm waiting for my fiancé, and I—"

"Hey, babe."

Logan puts his hand on my shoulder. I don't know how I missed him walking over here, but I've never been so relieved to see him.

"I got your drink. Who's your friend?"

The stranger across from me leans back in his chair, staring at Logan like he's sizing him up.

"Look, I'm not bothering her." The stranger's eyes lazily float back to me. "We were just having a nice conversation, right?"

Logan doesn't miss a beat, setting our drinks neatly across from each other before leaning over right in the guy's face. There's not even a smidge of fear in his body language; no hesitation, and seemingly no idea that he might actually be about to get his ass kicked.

"Nah, see, you *are* bothering her. I'm guessing she told you she wasn't interested. So now that we know what's what, if you've still got a problem, you get to talk to me."

I'm actually a little taken aback, but this guy isn't intimidated at all, and when he gets to his feet I can see why. He's got to be about two of Logan across, and nearly as tall. He cocks his head to the side, sizing Logan up with a sneer. Nobody else in the beer garden is paying any attention, and why would they? So far nothing's gotten out of hand. Still, we could use a few Saskatchewan cowboys to take this guy out.

"Logan, it's fine." I keep my voice soft as I tug on his shirt. "He just wanted—"

"I don't care what he wants," Logan smiles, staring the stranger down. "I think it might be time for him to head home."

The guy bursts out laughing, errant spittle flying into Logan's face and he breaks, giving the man a hard shove into the edge of the table.

"Did you not hear me, or are you just fucking stupid?" Logan snarls.

Okay... this is bad. His jaw is clenched and I can see a bright pink flush on his cheeks as he tries to control his breathing. I've never seen Logan's temper get the best of him like this, but the man still seems surprisingly calm, licking his lips and chuckling as he straightens.

"Look, buddy, you sure you wanna do this? I don't mind lettin' it go if you just wander on back to the bar."

"How about you get the fuck away from my girl?" Logan snarls.

Before I can even get a word out, a giant, meaty fist comes flying through the air, cracking Logan right in the jaw. I let out a shrill yelp as he staggers back, grunting as I stumble out of my chair toward him.

"Logan!"

He's doubled over, cupping his face with one hand. I only take a moment to check on him before I feel my own senses start to blur into red, spinning back around to the giant dickhead and lunging for him. I'm only a couple steps away when Logan grabs me by the back of the shirt, pulling me backward and putting himself between the two of us.

The rest of the room is starting to take notice as Logan rushes him, taking a swing that actually manages to end up right between the man's beady eyes.

Within seconds he bounces back, clearly a little stunned that he actually took a hit from a guy like Logan. He takes up an extremely messy boxing stance, but that still makes it at least 50% better than whatever Logan's got going on, and I watch in horror as the altercation turns into a full out brawl.

Logan's chest heaves, taking a weighty hit and tumbling backwards, the burning rage briefly visible in his eyes before he snaps himself forward in a shockingly quick motion. Just as it looks like he's about to take a swing he pivots, jutting his leg out at the perfect angle to slam full-force in the man's crotch. I hear something snap and the guy screams, doubling over as he struggles to breathe.

Logan smiles, letting himself breathe for the first time since the fight started, but it isn't over. The drunken asshole straightens up, still wheezing, but despite the agony, he manages to throw another wild punch that connects right in Logan's temple. All I see is blood streaming down his face as he hits the floor, and I can feel my heart stop. I hear someone shout for security, vaguely aware of movement around me, but all I can think is that we have to get the hell out of here. Fast.

I crouch down next to Logan, shaking him to try and get him up, but before I can even get a word out that giant moves in, towering over the two of us with a disgusting grin.

"You don't wanna fight back, huh, pretty boy?" He spits on Logan. "Little bitch."

And that's it.

"You fucking asshole!"

I remember the words, and then some movement. I think I grab my beer and toss it in the man's face. I think he stumbles. The one thing I know is that I take a lesson from watching Logan to heart: When my knee connects with his balls, it's got all my weight behind it.

He lets out a shattered whine before he drops, clutching his crotch for dear life. There's a second where it looks like he might make it back up, but I watch his legs wobble and give out completely, leaving him squirming on the floor. I turn back to Logan, but I'm shocked to see him already on his feet, waving me over. His face is bloodied, and it's already starting to swell around his eyes. I'm pretty sure his nose is broken, or at the very least fractured.

The stranger grunts, squirming on the ground as Logan steps toward him.

"Don't you fucking touch my girl!" He gives him a hard kick to the ribs, spitting some of his own blood back in the man's face. "You fucking hear me this time?!"

I try to pull him away, but he wrenches himself out of my grasp, his jaw ticking as the blood continues to pour down his nose. There's a moment where I think he's going to go back in on the guy, losing himself completely in his anger, but then his shoulders slump.

"I need some air."

"Logan—"

His eyes are wild, his face a mix of fear and disgust.

"Abi, just— I need some space!"

And then he storms through the crowd, out toward the exit.

Leaving me alone in the chaos.

don't go breaking my heart

LOGAN

SASKATOON, SASKATCHEWAN
PRESENT DAY

I'm not a jealous guy.

Really, I'm not.

I just can't stand a man who doesn't understand one of the simplest words in the goddamn language.

I should feel great. I got a few good punches and kicks in, and in the end the two of us left him squirming on the floor; instead, all I feel is overwhelming humiliation for letting my temper get the best of me. I don't have a problem dealing with people like that. What I hate is going from a feeling of calm control to practically losing my mind at the drop of a hat.

And I hate that she was ever in that situation to begin with.

I shouldn't have been talking to that bartender. I should have gotten our drinks and headed straight back to the table. Abi looked so uncomfortable, even terrified as the fight amped up, but all I could think was how pissed I was that some dickhead in a John Deer hat was making a move on her.

Now I'm all fucked up. I can feel the blood still dribbling from my nose, and I'm almost certain I sprained my ankle kicking that guy in the dick.

I wipe my face, weaving carefully through the crowd of people and doing my best to ignore the pain that's been shooting from my skull. I just want to get back to the hotel.

Never see any of these people again.

"Logan!" Abi calls, her voice trailing a little ways behind me. "Logan, slow down!"

I don't even know where I'm walking. All I know is that I need to get as far away from that beer garden as possible.

If I hadn't pushed him, he wouldn't have punched me. We should have just walked away, but I let everything get out of control. When I was younger, my rage felt senseless; directionless but often overpowering, like an all-consuming force that would take over without warning. I hated being like that, so over the years, I'd just mask the anger with pleasant smiles.

It's cool, man!

Don't worry about it!

No problem at all!

All I've ever wanted is to be liked.

No one likes someone who's angry all the time, and can't even tell you why. They want people who are agreeable, easy to be with. Calm and collected and cool. So I pushed every little bit of positivity I had to the forefront. I'd be so pleasant I'd glow like the fucking sun, and everyone would like me.

And the crazy thing was, over time, I was happier. Sure, sometimes it hurt to keep things bottled up, but I found people I could really talk to as well. Just a few, but it was enough to keep from exploding. I'm sure a shrink would tell me the way I found this balance wasn't ideal, that it fucked me up in some not-so-insignificant way, but they couldn't deny the results.

I was calm and collected and cool.

People liked me.

The problem, of course, is when I slip up.

I couldn't get the image of his face out of my head, of the way he was looking at her. It was like she was a piece of meat— and then that smirk when he looked at me? It's like he didn't think it was possible. There was no way someone like me could possibly get a girl like Abi.

But I could.

I could get a girl like Abi.

I *had* Abi.

And I needed him to know.

"Logan, what the hell?"

She grabs my arm, yanking me back with a force I didn't know she had in her.

Her cheeks are flushed and her pupils are all blown out. At first I misread it as anger, but then I realize she's terrified. I don't know if that makes me feel better or worse.

"Your nose is still bleeding—"

"Don't," I turn my head away, wiping the blood off my chin with the back of my hand.

It's worse. It makes me feel worse. I know I need to be soft with her, but there's so much adrenaline pumping through me that it's hard to figure out what's threatening and what's not.

"Logan, what's going on?" She sighs. "What the hell was that back there?"

All that anger comes rushing back to the surface, funneled entirely into a desperate need to explain myself.

"I hated the way that guy was talking to you, how he was fucking *looking* at you! Like he owned you or some shit!"

I slow myself down, my breath shallow and shaky as I suddenly notice how tightly clenched my fists are, swollen and tender as I flex them.

Abi takes another breath, rooting herself to the ground and crossing her arms over her chest. The defiant look in her eye surprises me, but also makes me want to...

Do something really stupid.

"Okay, so why are you getting angry with me?"

Her tone is measured, coated in sugary sweetness, and I instantly feel the guilt start to pour in. She knows that this is what happens when I lose my temper. I lash out at everything and everyone, and people catch strays. I don't deserve this level of patience, not when I should know better. I owe her a real explanation, and an apology.

"I'm... I'm not. I'm angry because you're my friend, and I should have protected you. So, I'm angry at myself, and now my face is all punched in and my ankle hurts, and..." I flail my arms helplessly. "I'm just embarrassed, okay? I made an ass out of myself, and of you. We were having a great time, and I ruined it. So I'm sorry."

She smiles kindly, but I can tell she's doing her best not to laugh. That feeling of humiliation starts to grow some serious teeth, and I feel like I might as well just lay down in the middle of the street instead of letting it devour me whole.

Abi, in all of her sunshine and wisdom, wraps her arms around my waist and pulls me close, resting her head on my chest. I feel panic start to build, my mind shooting in at least 10 different directions all starting with 'we shouldn't,' but I refuse to let it run wild. I can smell the hotel shampoo she used. Pineapple and mint. It's a strange, but oddly soothing combination.

"I appreciate you kicking him in the nuts," she murmurs, rocking us from side to side. "We can live happily ever after knowing he'll never forget that moment."

I snort, immediately regretting it as I feel a bit of blood bubble up in my nose, along with a sharp spike of pain.

"I'm... I'm sorry you had to see that."

"The last time I saw you get mad like that was with Roman," she says softly.

"Yeah. Not my finest moment either time." I sigh. "I must have scared you a bit."

She lifts her head, not saying a word, but she doesn't have to. I know the answer. She's let slip a few things about her dad— mostly about his temper when he was in withdrawal.

"Let's go back to the room."

Changing the subject is Abi's international signal for *I'd rather not talk about this shit anymore*, but she's not angry, slipping her hand into mine and steering me in the direction of the hotel.

It's a few blocks before the noise all begins to fade away, the two of us ending up on a lovely little street, blanketed in silence. I look down at her hand clutching mine, but my eyes are quickly drawn to some specks of blood on her shirt instead.

"I bled on you," I wince. "Sorry, Shortcake."

Abi just shrugs, brushing everything off like it's no big deal.

"I've got a Tide pen in my bag. We'll go back to the hotel, fix that nose up, and I'll order us some more drinks."

"Abi—"

She presses a finger to my lips, shaking her head.

"Shut up and let me do something nice for you. I can afford two twenty-dollar cocktails."

"I mean— That's really nice, but I think they're more like forty."

"God, that's fucking criminal," she mutters, deciding to shift the topic away from the horrors of the hospitality industry in an inflation economy. "I really do have to hand it to you again, Flynn. That dick kick was solid. He went down hard."

"Well, it's like my dad always said, if the guy's bigger than you, go for the eyes. If you can't reach the eyes, it's gotta be balls." I shrug to myself, tilting my head with the ghost of a smile. "You weren't so bad yourself. I saw that knee action."

Abi doesn't lose her temper often, I think I've seen it happen twice since I've known her, so it was actually kind of hot to see her haul off like that. I don't know if I'll ever have the privilege of seeing it again.

Having her beside me helps to soothe my frazzled nerves on the slow walk back. She fusses over me every couple blocks, wiping away the excess blood on my face, adjusting my rumpled shirt, and always taking my hand again each time. When we make it back into the lobby we get a few weird looks, but we manage to slip our way into the elevator without a word to anyone.

I pull the tissue away from my nose.

"Fuck, it's like a faucet," I groan.

"That's what happens when you start a Canadian duel," she chuckles, raising her fists dramatically.

Back in the room Abi heads straight for her bigger suitcase, rooting through it for a small first aid kit that we packed just in case, before walking me into the bathroom. She gets to work fast, soaking a cotton pad in some warm water to clean me up. Her touch is delicate, giving me goosebumps, and she's careful not to press too hard.

"Does that hurt?"

"Only a little."

Her face is screwed up in concentration as she works, continuously checking in with me every 20 seconds or so.

"Sorry," she murmurs, running it over a particularly tender spot that makes me hiss.

"I'm fine."

"Sure you are, tough guy," she purrs. "Just gotta bandage that up and you'll be good as new."

When she turns around to grab a bandage out of the kit, it's a conscious effort not to lean in for a better look at her ass. The thought shoots through me with a shiver of excitement, and I snap my head down, focusing on my mismatched socks instead.

It's the classic problem so many have had before: some days, it feels like we know exactly how to navigate this whole situation, that it's totally natural to be the most platonic friends anyone has ever seen. Then there's the other days, where you find yourself on a road trip to your friend's highschool reunion, where you have to pretend to be her fiancé while not having completely unprofessional, prohibited thoughts at every opportunity.

It's one of my more relatable problems, I'd say.

"It seems like all the blood is coming from the bridge of your nose," she announces, placing a small white bandage over the cut. "I don't think it's broken, but I'm not really qualified to make that call."

"Well, you had *me* fooled, Doctor."

Abi ruffles my hair, letting her hand linger for just a second too long.

"I think you'll end up with some bruising around your eyes. They're already starting to swell a bit, but I have a sleep mask I can pop into the fridge for tonight. Might help take some of that down."

"That'll look great for your reunion," I scoff. "Everyone will know your fiancé's a total badass. Don't fuck with the Flynns."

I was supposed to be her handsome professor fiancé, but it's looking like 'bar fight enthusiast' is a more likely role at this point.

"It does make you look pretty tough." She crouches down, nestling between my legs. "Once Brendan sees those bruises, he's not gonna mess with you."

Abi rests a hand on my forearm as she wipes off the rest of the blood with a wet cotton pad. The hairs on my arms start to stand straight up, and I'm thankful to be wearing a long-sleeve shirt so it's not *quite* so obvious how hard this is for me.

"It's okay. Almost done." She sighs, dabbing my nose a couple more times. "And who says we'd be the Flynns?"

I have to bite down on my lip to keep from kissing her. It doesn't help that this *stupid* soft lighting is making her look particularly angelic. Her eyes flicker like a flame dancing on a candle wick, her soft petal pink lips *so* kissable in the warm evening air.

"I'm still so—"

"No more sorrys," she laughs, leaning over to give me a quick kiss on the forehead. "Get into your pajamas and I'll order those drinks."

Abi heads out of the bathroom, closing the door behind her to give me some privacy, and I immediately get to my feet, limping over to the mirror to get a better look at the damage.

There are still some rust-colored smears on my chin, and a good bunch of the area around my eyes is absolutely swelling up. There's a bruise on my jaw, too, but that one's a little less noticeable. Hopefully it won't be too bad tomorrow. I'm not looking forward to questions or pity from the front desk.

I grab my phone, snapping a picture and sending it straight to Imogen.

ME

Hey, does this make me look tough?

IMOGEN

Broooo! What the fuck happened to you?!

ME

Some creep hit on Abi at a carnival. I sprained my ankle kicking him in the nuts.

There's a good few moments before I get a response, and I have to imagine Iggy struggling to type through the laughter.

IMOGEN

> I'm so sorry, it does look pretty serious, but like…
> dude. You've got that temper.

I sigh. We've talked about this at length, about how my outbursts of anger could be a symptom of ADHD. Imogen's gently urged me to get tested, but I've…

Well, *forgot.*

Hilarious, right?

ME

> Yeah, yeah. I know.

IMOGEN

> Okay, but how's the trip so far? Are you two in
> love yet?

Jesus, not a minute in and she's already back on her bullshit.

ME

> Goodnight, Iggy.

IMOGEN

> Oooh! Avoidance! That was my favorite tactic too!
> By my calculations, you'll be head over heels by
> the time you get home.

ME

> Forgot to give you your last birthday present. You
> like it?

I send her three middle finger emojis.

IMOGEN

> Oh, I love it, but make sure you save some for
> yourself too.

There's another few moments pause, and I can practically feel her forcing herself into sappy-mode.

IMOGEN

Alright, go fuck off and chill with your bestie. Love
you, assclown.

Okay, maybe she's not in full-on sappy-mode.

ME

I love you too.

I slip my phone back into my pocket and step outside to grab my pajamas, finding Abi stretched out on the bed, her back propped up against
the headboard while she scrolls through her phone. She's changed into a
pair of dark purple leggings and a matching tank top.

No bra.

I snatch up my PJs and rush back into the bathroom, changing clothes
and killing as much time as possible as I brush my teeth. Do they make
steel boxer briefs? Because at this point, I think that's the only thing that's
going to prevent me from making an absolute fool of myself.

"You need to get a grip," I mumble, with the toothbrush still stuffed in
my cheek. "Nothing is happening. She just feels bad for you because you
got your ass absolutely handed to you."

I finish up, splashing some cool water on my face and quickly
drying off.

I have to go out there, cool and collected and calm. We're just sharing
a bed. I'm not a horny teenager anymore, this is no big deal.

But *fuck*, we're sharing a bed.

One bed.

But it's only one night. That's all I need to make it through.

I can do this.

When I step back out of the bathroom Abi's shifted around again,
nestling herself underneath the blankets on one side of the bed, sipping
her cosmo as she flips through TV channels. I must have been deep into
my existential crisis, because I didn't even hear room service knock.

She hands me my drink, smirking as I climb down onto the bed
beside her.

"Here. It's the best face-trauma remedy I can muster."

We clink glasses and I take a sip, the alcohol hitting me like a truck and burning my throat.

"Wow, that is boozy!"

"I asked them to put an extra shot in there. Figured it would help take the edge off."

"You're the best doctor I've ever had. Thanks, King."

"No big deal. I know you'd do the same for me."

I smile.

"Yeah, you know what? If you ever get your ass kicked, I'll be right there with bandaids and dad jokes. I'll make sure to absolutely destroy the dude's junk too."

midnight rain

ABI

ASPEN, COLORADO
SEVEN MONTHS AGO

I'm so sure that something is going on with Roman and Imogen. The way they've been looking at each other all weekend, the inside jokes, the obnoxious chemistry and all the closeness... Logan hasn't seemed to notice. Of course, his obliviousness could come down to the many glasses of wine he downed over the course of the night, two and a half hours into Monopoly. Now, with everyone retiring, it's my job to guide him up the stairs like a newborn foal walking for the first time.

Back in college, I lost a friend to alcohol poisoning. She choked on her vomit while she was passed out in our bathtub. The first responders were kind and sympathetic, they let me know it wasn't my fault, but I'll always feel guilty for not checking in on her. I've never left anyone in that condition alone again.

"Ow, fuck!"

Logan hisses at me, nearly tripping up the last step of the landing. I manage to catch him, but awkwardly, barely keeping myself stable in the process. Nobody told me how hard it would be to catch a guy who's nearly a foot taller than you, but here I am with my arm twisted around his waist as he holds onto me for dear life.

"Careful, Sunshine," I laugh, bracing myself as he gets his footing. "You'll break a hip doing that."

He stares at me with glassy, honey-colored eyes and a big, dumb smile.

"Ma'am... I think you saved my life."

"I saved your *knees*," I chuckle. "Come on, let's get you into bed."

"Yoooouuu got it, Doc!"

Logan's clothes for the next day are folded on the desk, resting right beside his laptop and messenger bag. He's meticulous in so many areas of his life, in spite of how chaotic he seems moment-to-moment. I remember once he told me he has to stay organized or he starts to feel like he's drowning, and I've definitely seen it catch up with him when he's stressed out.

Logan stumbles toward the bed and does a full face plant, his long legs sticking straight out off the edge. Hilarious as it is, there's no way he'd manage to actually fall asleep like this. He needs water and painkillers, or he's going to be absolutely awful to deal with tomorrow morning.

"Come on. Under the covers," I mutter, tapping his foot gently.

"I gotta—" He pushes himself up, rolling over onto his back and struggling for a moment before giving up with a pathetic grunt. "I gotta get my pajamas on. I can't sleep in my clothes, it feels weeeeiiiird!"

"Okay, okay. You get changed and I'll grab you some water from the bathroom. I'll knock when I'm about to come back in, alright?"

He rolls off the bed and gets to his feet, stumbling a bit before flashing me finger guns. I chuckle, making my way down the hall to the bathroom. I can hear Roman and Imogen, both of them talking softly enough to be almost inaudible, and it's a struggle not to sneak over and listen in. I'm still so certain they're up to something, but I'm on nurse duty, so I shake off my suspicions and get to it, filling up a glass with cool water, and downing half of it myself before heading back.

The moment I step out of the bathroom I spot Imogen's door closing, and I can't help myself. It's not really being nosey if it's just something you notice on the way back to your room, right?

I peer over the railing, straining my eyes and ears as best I can.

No Roman.

I grin, shaking my head as I stride back into Logan's room. There's no way I'm wrong about this. They're definitely up to something, but before I can think too much more on the topic, I hear Logan's muffled grunts spill out from underneath the door, followed by a dull thud.

"Logan?" I hiss, giving a brisk knock. "Are you alright? And dressed?"

"My dick's not out, if that's what you mean."

"Well, that's a plus," I mutter. "I'm coming in!"

He's lying flat on his back, with his pants around one ankle and his dress shirt discarded in the corner. His long, gangly legs are splayed out and he's breathing hard, like he's just run a marathon.

It's tough not to laugh.

"I tripped," he whines, reaching for me. "Help…"

I put the glass down on the dresser and reach down. Problem is, Logan clearly doesn't know his own strength, and he nearly pulls me down on top of him as he struggles to get to his feet.

I panic, my heart smashing a chaotic rhythm into my ribs. I just have to put him to bed. That's it. And then I go to my own room and it's like this *never* happened.

"Hey, I got you some water, just let me—"

Logan doesn't utter a word, only reaching up to brush a strand of hair away from my face. The touch is so gentle that I feel myself involuntarily shudder, but I don't stop him. He glides his finger further, across my cheekbone as he traces the little freckles in his path.

I've had *just* enough alcohol to think that kissing could feel like anything but what it is: a terrible idea.

"You're flushed," he remarks, his eyes glittering in the moonlight.

Okay, maybe I've had *more* than enough.

"It's probably the booze."

His hand stops its wandering and he cups my cheek, brows pinched together in concentration as he dips his head like he's planning to kiss me. Sometimes, I daydream about what it felt like the first time we met, and the warm glow of knowing I was wanted.

"We shouldn't," I breathe, letting my hands travel on their own, all the way up his waist.

He's been working out, I can feel the slight indents in his abs under his shirt.

"It's wrong," he murmurs, a sheepish grin slipping over his face.

At the start I thought he might have pretended to fall down on purpose, and that he's not nearly as drunk as he lets on, and I'm still not so sure.

"Very wrong."

"We're in Aspen. Frankie's ears are good, but they're not *that* good."

But it's more than just getting caught, it's the risk to our friendship. I know the tension between us spikes from time to time, and that sometimes I find it hard to watch him date, or even scroll through Tinder, but that's a small price to pay for a friend like him.

We drew our lines in the sand a few years ago.

We can't go back.

"You're drunk, Sunshine," I whisper.

"I'm not that drunk."

I want him so bad I can fucking taste it; even before he leans in, my body starts to sing with anticipation. He slides an arm around my waist, pulling me so close I can feel his heart thumping like it's my own.

"It's one weekend, Abi. Nobody needs to know."

His eyes are electric, singing my skin as they dart all over me.

I feel a familiar pressure against my thigh as I find my hands teasing the waistband of his boxers, my fingers brushing across that little happy trail beneath his bellybutton.

"I couldn't stop thinking about you all day," he purrs as he nuzzles against my cheek.

"You couldn't?"

I'm starting to get tunnel vision, only able to focus on the heat of his skin and how fucking good he smells.

"Mmm-mm. It's hard to focus when you're in these tight little jeans. It drove me crazy every time you turned around."

This is drunk Logan, unfiltered Logan; this is the Logan I've been needing, even if it's just for a night. He pulls back, the moonlight turning his eyes to a glowingly soft amber. Fuck it. I want this. If Roman and Imogen can sneak around, we can too.

"One weekend," he purrs.

"One *night*."

"Have it your way, one night. But let's make it count."

"You talk a big game, but I can't help but notice you're just sitting there," I grin.

Logan's eyes blaze to life, and within seconds his mouth is smashing into mine. The kiss is heated and intense, exactly what I've been hoping for, and probably what we've both needed for a while. We stumble toward the bed, like we're being pulled there by an invisible string, neither of us quite in-sync even as we reach our destination. Logan nearly trips over his own pants and a snarl tumbles from the depths of his throat, kicking the traitorous clothing aside.

"Having trouble, Doctor?" I giggle.

He pushes me onto the bed, wasting no time as he climbs on top of me.

"No trouble now. I'm in my element."

When he presses his lips to mine again, I fully give in to him, to this, to everything we shouldn't.

He tastes like sweet wine, with a tiny hint of those little swedish fish candies he loves to nibble on; it's a strangely addicting combination. I let my hands wander even further, totally unafraid as I slip them beneath the waistband of his boxers to give his ass a rough squeeze.

Logan rips his mouth away from mine, snarling as he tears my blouse open in a couple rough motions, and I gasp in shock as some buttons fly across the room.

You'd think I'd be mad, but I know how to sew.

"We're gonna have to be quiet," he purrs, swapping instantaneously back to his much more calm and collected demeanor, ghosting his lips up and down my bare stomach. "Which is a shame because it means I'm gonna miss *all* those gorgeous moans."

My face is flushed, and my back arches involuntarily as he nips at my skin. I feel like I'm on the verge of a moment of revelation or a panic attack. Everything I've wanted is right in front of me.

But only for a night.

Logan makes quick work of my jeans, peeling them off and tossing them aside. His eyes rake over every inch of me. Over my breasts, and the soft curves and bone white stretch marks that adorn my stomach.

"I almost forgot how beautiful you are."

"Happy to remind you," I murmur.

He doesn't waste time, nestling between my thighs and lifting my legs over his shoulders while he places soft kisses along my skin. I'm trying my hardest not to make a sound and to control my breathing. I don't want anything to ruin this, because we may never get another chance again.

I can't believe we're giving in; the fact that it took almost no convincing has me worried. I've always thought our friendship balanced on a razor's edge, and tonight just proves it. All it took was one glance and one brush of his fingers against my cheek and I was wrapped around his finger.

God, his *fucking* fingers. Sometimes I watch them glide down a page as he's reading and think about how good they felt inside me.

And then I try to focus on *anything* else, but it all comes back to Logan.

He's the sun, and so much of me orbits around him.

"You still know where to touch me," I whine.

"How could I forget?" He purrs, teasing me over my panties. "I still remember exactly how to lick your pussy, too. Soft, slow circles and then–"

The sound of Imogen's door shutting down the hall causes both of us to freeze.

We stare at each other, wide-eyed, as we hear someone creeping down the hallway. The floorboards make a soft creaking sound as they get closer, eventually stopping outside the bedroom door.

Logan turns his head, resting it on my thigh, like he's listening.

Even if she catches us, I can play it off as me taking care of him while he's hammered...

Except for the fact that we're both naked.

Okay, maybe this isn't going to go down that well.

In the dark, I listen hard, just waiting for the other shoe to drop and for someone to walk through that door.

But nothing comes.

And the footsteps fade away.

I wait... and wait.

Finally, when we're in the clear, I jostle him a little. Part of me wants to jump right back into what we were just doing. My body clearly hasn't gotten the memo despite the close call.

"Logan!" I hiss, trying to shake him awake.

He groans, a deep snore tumbling from inside him. I look down at him, watching his chest rise and fall steadily with each breath. There's no way in hell I'm falling asleep like this.

"Well, I'm glad you're comfortable, Sunshine."

His snores grow louder and I stare up at the ceiling, tracing the lines in the wood with my gaze. I feel his head turn and I *think* he's starting to drool on my thigh.

This is fucking absurd– so absurd that I start laughing. I have to cover my mouth to keep from making any noise, and my body shaking the bed only makes things worse.

I look down, seeing Logan's face smushed up against my leg, his mouth hanging open. Tears form in my eyes as I struggle to get some semblance of self-control.

I manage to slide out from underneath him, hearing him grunt when his head hits the mattress. I grab one of his t-shirts from his suitcase, slipping it over my head. I at least want *some* layers between us, because there's no way in hell I'm going back to my room. What if Imogen catches me?

Gently, I manage to roll Logan onto his side, which is quite the feat considering his size. I really have to start going to the gym more.

I grab a couple of extra pillows from the closet and tuck them around him to keep him from rolling back over before finally crawling back into bed next to him. It takes a while, but eventually, I fall into a fitful and restless sleep.

It feels like I just closed my eyes when Logan's blaring alarm goes off, bright and early at 7:00am. Both of us groan in response, and I wake up, realizing we've rolled onto our sides. His arm is wound around my waist and his breath is hot on the back of my neck.

"Sorry," he grumbles. "Forgot to turn it off last night."

He sits up in bed and pauses, glancing over at me as he takes stock of the situation. Him in nothing but his boxers, me wearing his t-shirt, the rest of our clothes strewn on the floor...

"Oh, fuck," he whispers, and then catches himself, his eyes widening as he starts to panic. "Did we?! Oh, God, Abi!"

He leaps out of bed, and despite his bloodshot eyes, I don't think I've seen him this manic before.

"Please tell me we didn't. Not that— I mean, if we— it's not you— it's—"

"Logan, it's cool," I chuckle, watching as he fishes his phone out of his pocket to shut off the alarm. "You don't remember what happened last night?"

He presses the heels of his hands into his eye sockets, standing in front of me with a massive case of morning wood. It's hard not to look at it, and even harder to ignore how much my body wants what his is offering. Instead, I do the responsible thing and turn my attention to my chipped nail polish. Anything to keep me from ogling him like a piece of meat.

"Some of it." I hear a belt jingle, and look up just in time to see him tugging his pants over his hips. "Things get a little fuzzy when, uh... did we have sex?"

He whispers the question, a pained expression on his face.

"No." I shake my head, deciding to save him the embarrassment hearing how he fell asleep on my thigh. "We didn't. Just some... heavy petting."

He winces, squeezing his eyes shut.

"Yeah, I'm starting to remember a bit of that, and I said something about your pu–" He shakes his head. "Abi, I'm so so–"

"Shh." I press my finger to his lips. "It's okay. We were both drunk, it happens. We just chalk it up to being cooped up together and we move on, right?"

Logan's eyes trace my face, and he gnaws on his bottom lip like he's holding back.

"Yeah. Yeah, you're right. It was totally not appropriate, sometimes that drunk brain just..." His cheeks flush bright pink. "I am sorry, though."

I reach for his hands, giving a gentle squeeze that seems to reassure him a little.

"You're all good, Sunshine. It never happened."

"Yeah." Logan's throat bobs. "Of course it didn't."

espresso

ABI

SASKATOON, SASKATCHEWAN
PRESENT DAY

I wake up to sunlight cutting through a small break in the curtains, illuminating the last sliver of the cosmo I never managed to finish, and I reach past it, over to my phone in the hopes that I can shut off before any ill-conceived alarm I may have set ruins the morning.

It's resting right next to my ring pop necklace.

I smile and reach for the 'jewelry,' dropping it into my palm and playing with it for a little while. I can feel that same rush of adrenaline I felt back at the start of our trip, when Logan dropped to one knee in that gas station. I knew it was a gag, there was no chance it was anything but, and yet just for that tiny little moment it felt so fucking real.

It might be the first time I've been able to fully admit what I've known deep down for a while: It wasn't just a fluke, we'd be good together.

We *are* good together.

Sure, it's stupid when you think about our jobs, our lives, and just how far we've gone to avoid this very specific situation, but I still can't keep myself from picturing it. I wonder what our new first date would be like. I wonder how long we'd manage to keep things from our friends and co-workers. I wonder what kind of tux Logan would wear to the wedding.

Probably purple.

He loves purple.

And of course, that's when the previous night comes flooding back to knock down my defences even further. The protective way he told that guy off, told him that I was *his girl*. And I swear, he was *so close* to kissing me when I was patching him up.

We've made excuses for our little side glances many times in the past, along with our inside jokes that no one else gets, and the stunningly obvious fact that we're always the first point of contact the other one reaches out to when something goes down.

Best friends.

That's what we are, and that's what we've been since we had that talk at The Hi-Dive.

But over the years, we've definitely almost crossed those lines a few times.

The double-date.

Aspen.

It wasn't that long ago that I tried to put Logan Flynn's drunk ass to bed and wound up making out with him instead.

Probably half a dozen other times if I'm honest.

As I gaze down at the ring pop, I feel his warm body press up against me, followed by his lanky arm wrapping around my waist. I stare at his tattooed fingers unconsciously pawing at me before glancing over to some slight red irritation on his wrist, from his dad's oversized watch being left on overnight.

He groans and pulls me close, and I freeze because the next thing I feel is his still-hard cock pressed against my ass. I hold my breath, squeezing my thighs together and willing myself to stay strong.

Yes, he's gorgeous.

Yes, I'm 99.999% certain I'm in love with him at this point.

But even if I confessed everything I've been thinking, who's to say he won't tell me he's moved on? That I waited too long and things really have changed.

The tip of Logan's nose brushes against the back of my neck and goosebumps prickle up on my skin. My toes curl instinctively, my brain torn between getting out of bed to escape this awkward situation, and staying right here.

I can almost hear his groans, soft but rigorous next to my ear. I want to feel his body pressing down onto mine, his hips rocking as he thrusts deep inside of me.

My heart knows what it wants, but I deny it because I have to, because it's the right thing to do. My back arches as I feel him grind up against me, his soft moan permeating the room. I have to admit, it's getting harder and harder with each passing day.

"Fuck."

I close my eyes, letting that first night together flood back to me in vivid detail. The tiny bit of soft hair on the back of his neck, the way his voice broke when I sunk my nails into him.

I can even feel his hand around my throat.

Fuck, you take me so well.

Okay, this bed is The Bad Place. I need to get the hell out of here and... go for a walk or something.

I could get us some croissants. Logan loves croissants. As long as I slipped out quietly enough it wouldn't even—

The thought is ripped from my head the second his hand slides up my body, and in the moment or two where I could do something about it, I simply don't.

I could just pull my leggings down and let him—

No.

I have to get up, or this is going to get very out of control very quickly.

I hate taking the high road, being a good person who follows the rules. When I die, this better put me at the top of the list.

Did not have stupidly hot morning sex with your best friend.

Logan is still fast asleep, his brows knit together and his fingers extending along the blanket like he's searching for something as I gently move his arm and slip out of bed. I stand there in the silent room for a moment, heart pounding as I take in features: his full lips, the soft dusting of dark blond stubble on his chin, and his slightly upturned nose. What I'm focusing the most on though, is trying to avoid staring at the raging hard-on that's fully visible through the thin blanket.

They couldn't have given us a duvet?

Now I have to think about how I want to straddle him, sinking down onto his perfect cock while he moans praise into my ear.

I slink toward the bathroom, gently shutting the door and running the water as I strip out of my pajamas. The first aid kit is still on the counter, along with the bloodied tissue and gauze that I used to clean up Logan's nose. I'll worry about that stuff later. Right now, I need some fucking release.

The moment I spot the removable shower head, I breathe a sigh of relief.

"At least something's going right this morning."

The water is exactly the right temperature, and I close my eyes as I lean up against the wall, letting one hand wander down my body. My mind replays that first night at the hotel. His mouth on my pussy, the way his fingers sank into my skin like they belonged there all along.

Like Brendan never happened.

I let myself get swept up in it, trying to recall the exact way he touched me, and replicate it all as the sweat starts to gather on my skin. He was so gentle and sweet, practically purring affirmations in my ear, but he brought a certain roughness with him as well.

You're fucking perfect.

Look at how pretty you are with my cock in your mouth.

A whimper escapes my lips as I twist my nipple hard enough to make my toes grip the warm tile. My free hand slips between my legs, finding wetness and heat as I let myself explore. I hear myself whisper his name, ignoring the guilt as I strum my clit with a finger.

By the time this trip is over, I'm going to have to shower in holy water or something. I can hear his voice, I can smell the cologne and the sweat, and I still remember the way his eyes dug into mine.

Look at me when you come.

I reach for the shower head, nearly tearing it off the wall in desperation. It takes me a few seconds to adjust the pressure. Nothing too strong. One time, when I was a teenager, I had it on the highest setting and thought I was going to blast my clit off. I've learned to be patient... not to mention gentler.

With shaking hands, I tilt the shower head so that the stream hits my clit at the perfect angle, and I'm able to relax against the wall. I close my eyes and just let the water do its thing, adjusting my hips ever so slightly until it starts to feel *really* good.

Part of me wants to fill the bathroom with loud, sultry moans in the hopes that he'll wake up, open the door, and find me like this.

And he'd say something like...

If you wanted me, all you had to do was ask, Shortcake.

I swallow my moan as I picture him turning me around and pulling my hips back so that he can take me from behind. Suddenly he's spanking my ass, calling me a good girl, bad girl, and any number of other things that turn me on.

My toes curl against the shower floor, and I continue to play with myself until I'm almost at the brink of climax. I'm so close. So *fucking* close. My breathing picks up and up and up, and just as I'm about to topple over the edge, my eyes snap open and I'm greeted by the sight of a *massive* spider dangling from the ceiling.

The fire in my veins turns to ice in seconds and I let out a blood curdling scream. Without a second thought, I'm hurling the shower head at the spider, which is unfortunately located directly on the glass door. Luckily, it doesn't shatter; unluckily, I miss. The spider swings toward me and I let out another scream, almost certain I can feel it land on me.

"Oh, fuck!"

I'm screeching and flailing, fighting to kill it or at least smack it off of me, and In the chaos, I step on the long metal cord that's attached to the shower head. It scrapes against the tile and I slip, lurching forward and crashing into the glass.

The bathroom door flies open and Logan stumbles inside with a lamp that he ripped off the nightstand held high above his head. From my crumpled spot on the ground he looks like a man possessed, his hair wild and frizzy like he's jammed his whole hand into a light socket.

"Abi what's happening?!" He bellows, ripping the shower door open.

I shriek, wrapping my arms around my body as I try to cover my—

Well, everything.

It's in these moments I wish I had some sort of power or ability, like kids did when they were younger. I wouldn't want super strength, or psychic powers or anything though. The thing I'd want is the power to make the earth open up and swallow this entire hotel on a whim. If we're all dead, I can't live through this embarrassment after all.

Logan freezes, and we both stare at each other in total disbelief until I feel something skitter across my bare foot and let out another terrified scream, leaping out onto the bathmat and right into his arms.

The lamp clatters to the floor as my wet, naked body presses up against him. He doesn't move a muscle, keeping his arms outstretched, clearly unsure of what to do.

I shove him off of me and he immediately spins around, gasping in horror when he realizes he's ended up face to face with the mirror.

"Oh my— Oh, fuck, Abi! I'm sorry!" He jams his eyes shut, blindly reaching for a towel, but smashes his hand into the drawer instead. "Ow, motherfucker!"

It still hasn't occurred to him to just *leave*.

"Logan stop!" I snap, snatching a towel off the rack and wrapping it around my trembling body. "It's— It's fine, you can open your eyes."

I run my fingers through my hair, trying to shake out the total humiliation of what just happened along with the water.

I'm swearing revenge against that spider in particular, for all of time.

Blood feud.

Logan turns back to face me, plucking the lamp from the floor and setting it on the counter. It looks flimsy, like it's made of plastic and spray painted gold. I bet I could find it on Amazon for ten bucks.

"That's your weapon of choice?" I chuckle, gesturing at it. "Not particularly imposing."

He laughs, his eyes still puffy from sleep.

"Hey, look, I woke up to the sound of you shrieking like a banshee, what the hell was I supposed to grab? And I mean, I'm glad to see you're okay, but what even happened?"

I glance around for a moment before honing in on the giant spider that's managed to crawl to safety, sitting in the corner of the shower as the water continues to run.

"Logan—"

I point to it, and Logan immediately nods, brushing past me to turn the shower off and getting his pajama pants soaked in the process.

Despite growing up in the country, I'm not an insect person. I get freaked out if anything has more than four legs and moves really fast. One summer, mom and I were camping up in Quebec and something hit me in the back of the head. I thought it might have been a rock until I felt it moving. It was a cicada. I spent the rest of the trip wearing a hat and my mom had to talk me down from shaving my head.

"It's fine," he chuckles. "Here, get me that glass on the sink, and can you grab me a thick piece of paper? Cardstock is best. I'll let the little dude or dudette outside."

I cannot *believe* this is happening to me; maybe he was too pumped full of adrenaline to notice how flushed I was. For once, I'd really like his obliviousness to work in my favor. I rush around our room, grabbing the glass Logan asked for from our half-kitchen, and manage to find some advertising leaflets from the hotel that are on what seem like at least slightly stiffer than normal paper. When I come back into the bathroom, I watch as he deftly cups the glass around the spider, slipping the leaflet underneath and flipping the makeshift trap upside-down, effectively trapping the spider inside.

"Looks like a wolf spider," he mutters, bringing the glass up close to his face

"Well, he can go be a wolf outside. Please."

"You know, they really are more afraid of you than you are of them."

"Yeah, well, when you're trying to ma— meditate. When you're trying to meditate, it's easy to get surprised!"

"Meditate?" Logan chuckles. "In the shower?"

I can feel my face burning and I start to stammer, completely losing my cool.

"Y— yeah. The, uh... the water he— helps me, uh... focus on my breathing."

Logan quirks a brow, but he doesn't press the subject, only shrugging as he heads out the bathroom door, and leaving me with the sinking feeling that he's not buying any of this. I squeeze my eyes shut and grip my hair, practically tearing it from my scalp in frustration.

Meditate?! A bachelor's, a master's, and a PhD, and *meditate* was the best I could come up with?

I waste as much time alone in the bathroom as I can before trudging outside, spotting Logan out on the balcony, hovering over some potted plants.

"Where are you taking that thing?!" I yelp.

"I'm letting him outside, where you can't drown him," he chuckles, crouching down to release the spider into some shrubs.

"I did not drown him! He attacked me in my own private bathroom!"

"Nah, you totally did! He told me so."

I roll my eyes as Logan slips back inside, locking the door tight before he grabs the rest of his clothes from the bedside: a plain black and white striped t-shirt and a pair of slacks, along with mismatched socks. He told me it was bad luck to wear matching socks, that the last time he did it he crashed his bike into a telephone pole. Probably explains why he's worn that 'pair' on and off since the day I met him.

"I'm gonna grab a quick shower."

He brushes past me before stopping just short of the bathroom, and turning dramatically on the ball of his foot.

"Unless you want to... meditate again."

My whole body feels like it's on fire as I stand there, stammering while he stares me down. I feel the same compulsion I always do in these situations, to give him a good hard elbow in the gut for the shitty joke, but I guess I just forgot how sexy he could look first thing in the morning. I can't even be mad, I just wish I'd stayed in bed at this point.

For more reasons than one.

But I cannot give in. I *will not* give in.

"Nope, I'm all good. Totally done, do whatever you need to, I don't care."

Logan casually bites his lip as he tilts his head, nothing overt, but enough that those familiar feelings come rushing back with a vengeance. At this point, if he asked me, I think I'd do anything.

But he only shrugs.

"Just yell when you're finished changing," he calls before shutting the door, leaving me alone with my thoughts. Those shameful, shameful thoughts.

I let out a sigh, grabbing my suitcase and dragging it up onto the bed. I rifle through my clothes, trying to find something that's going to be cute but comfortable in the heat. It's supposed to get up to 35 today– Celsius, that is.

God, I have a lot of pants... Why did I bring so many pairs of pants?!

After a few more minutes of rummaging, I choose a black mini skirt and a white t-shirt. It'll look cute with my pink Dr. Martens and vampire socks.

I stare at my exhausted reflection in the mirror before grabbing my makeup bag and painting on a few swipes of concealer and some blush. When I was a kid, my mom always said I looked a little sallow; I think it's the black hair and pale skin combination, it washes me out.

"Hey, Shortcake?" Logan calls from the bathroom. "You decent?"

Shit. I didn't even hear the shower turn off.

"Yeah, sorry! You can come out!"

Logan emerges in his slacks, holding the rest of his clothes in his hands, and my heart skips a beat as I struggle to drag my eyes away from his bare chest. Sometimes I forget how much he's changed over the years, his body more toned, and a light golden color from running shirtless in the sun.

It seems like Roman had at least a bit of a positive impact on him.

"You okay?"

"Totally!" I squeak. "I was just thinking that we should get on the road if we want to make it to Manitoba by the end of the day."

"Sounds good to me. You wanna grab some breakfast first?"

When Imogen and Roman tried to stay away from each other, she said it felt like the whole entire universe was trying to push them toward each other, like a kid enthusiastically smashing dolls together for the first time.

It sounded so ridiculous at the time, but now...

"Breakfast would be great."

I don't know.

Maybe some things are meant to happen after all.

CHAPTER TWENTY-FOUR

ahead by a century

LOGAN

MANITOBA
PRESENT DAY

Fuck, I feel terrible.

Abi's shut down. She just keeps staring out the window, silently tearing off little pieces of her muffin, and rolling the pastry between her fingers into a little ball. She eats like this when she's nervous, or embarrassed about something, and it doesn't take a PhD to guess what's on her mind.

I could have knocked this morning, but instead I burst in like the Kool-Aid man with a fucking plastic lamp without thinking. It was pretty obvious what she was doing, it's not like I didn't grow up with a sister who would frequently forget to put the shower head back in its place. Now we're halfway through the day, cruising through the middle of some small town I've never heard of before. A lot of it looks abandoned, and the grey skies above us don't give me much hope for the rest of the drive.

"Hey, um... about earlier—"

She's already turning red. I can see it out of the corner of my eye.

"Logan—"

"I just wanted to say I shouldn't have burst in like that while you were meditating—"

"You're making it worse," she whispers, her cheeks practically fuchsia.

"I just— It's not so bad! We've seen each other naked before, and—"

"Logan!"

My name comes out of her like a half-laugh, half-bark.

"Okay, I'm sorry!" I sigh, offering her a sheepish smile. "I really am sorry, Abi. Seriously."

I don't want things to be weird. It throws off our shtick. I've got kooky antics and she laughs at said antics and eggs me on. That's our thing. It's always been our thing. It's not like I haven't thought about throwing caution to the wind, especially after Roman and Imogen's relationship exploded. That whole thing gave me some hope that Abi and I might actually be able to do it too, if we managed to get so fed up we just said *fuck it,* and ignored all of the reasons it's a terrible idea.

Sure, Roman ended up quitting his job, and my sister transferred schools just so they could be together, but they did it. I mean, they also almost didn't really have a choice of anything but leaving in disgrace, but they got lucky.

So, I guess that's the question: am I willing to give up my job for her?

My mom says that a relationship should enhance your life, but it shouldn't *be* your life— and I think she's probably right about that. I love Emerald Bay University, and I don't know if I have the stomach to leave after all the work I've done and the people I've met.

I know Abi feels the same way.

When my dad died, my sister shut down. She refused to let anyone into her life until she met Roman. Me? I went the opposite direction. I've been wearing my heart on my sleeve, like a badge that screams, *please just fucking love me.*

And I found the one person who might just be able to do that.

She soothes something restless in me, a part deep inside that's been yearning for this kind of connection, of companionship, for most of my adult life. The worst part is, I'm certain I could never find someone like her again, even if I met every single one of the 7 billion people in the world.

"I'm so embarrassed," Abi mutters, her head turned off to the side.

"Hey, look on the bright side: maybe in the next hotel, there'll be a centipede in our room and I can be the one to scream like a girl. I've got a good set of pipes on me, as you well know."

Abi stays silent, staring out the window.

"You're supposed to laugh at that, you know. It's a classic bit! Me screaming like a girl—"

"Maybe we should book separate rooms for tonight."

I keep my eyes on the road, feeling the grin that was so wide on my face falling back into neutral. The suggestion shouldn't hit as hard as it does. Falling asleep next to her has been the highlight of the trip so far, her soft skin, the way she smelled, and even her snore was sort of adorable... until I had to elbow her to get her to stop.

"Sure," I reply. "Of course, whatever you need."

I'm terrified the rest of the drive is going to be like this, mired in an awkward silence, but thankfully she pipes back in after only a minute or so.

"Are you mad?"

"No," I laugh a little awkwardly. "Not at all. If that's what makes you feel comfortable, that's what we'll do. We can re-book two rooms tonight when we get into— where are we ending up, anyway?"

"Swan River," she replies, pulling out her phone.

"Does the river look like a swan? Because if not, I'm complaining to the mayor. I'll write the strongest worded letter a Canadian has ever read."

"Oooh, with swears?" Abi teases.

I lean over, cupping one hand around my mouth.

"The *eff word*," I whisper. "I'm bringing out the big guns."

She snickers, cheeks still a little pink as she scrolls through her phone. If I had a nickel for the amount of times Abi's been blushing around me lately, I'd probably be able to trade them in for one of those godforsaken toonies. I know this whole thing's been humiliating for her, but she's so fucking cute.

"Well, I've never spent the time mapping out the exact shape of the river, but I do know there *is* a giant swan statue. Everyone makes their way over there when they're heading through, so you can take all the goofy pictures you want."

"Only if you're in them with me, Shortcake."

Suddenly, as if on cue, I hear a loud pop from the car, and it feels like we're being yanked off to the side of the road. Abi yelps as I try to regain control over the wheel. I can't accelerate, so I take my foot off the gas and do my best to keep the car straight, hoping that'll be enough to make sure I don't accidentally fucking kill us.

And then I hear that unmistakable sound.

Flap, flap, flap, flap.

"Fuck, did we blow a tire?!" She squeals.

"Hang on!"

My heart is racing as I wrench the wheel hard to the right, trying to pull off to the side of the road. Abi squeaks as she reaches up to clutch the grab handle, her body going rigid as memories of my old drivers test from 20 years ago flash through my head. Despite what Imogen always says about my driving, she's the one who drives like she's a character in a Fast and fucking Furious movie, and this is probably the one time I wish she was at the wheel.

After struggling for the longest few seconds of my life, I spot a small patch of gravel off to the side of the road and manage to stop the car. The two of us let out a collective breath, taking a moment to let our heart rates slow.

"Let me check the trunk. I think there's a spare tire in there."

It's just one more thing to go wrong on this damn road trip.

"I'll help you."

She unbuckles her seatbelt.

"I'm fine, Abi. You can sit tight, I'll—"

"Logan Michael Flynn, if you pull this macho shit I'm going to smack you so hard a blown tire will be the last of your problems," she snaps. "Shut your mouth and let me help."

I blink, too surprised to respond before she hops outside and slams the door.

Out and away from the blessing that is modern air conditioning, it's so humid it's actually hard to breathe; worse, it smells like rain's coming, and my suspicions are confirmed when I look off into the distance and see a particularly sinister cloud formation. I'm so used to the Pacific Northwest, and seeing mountains framing the horizon in most directions, but out here there's nothing but wide open space.

Nothing to slow down the inevitable.

"We've gotta move," she murmurs. "Those things look like they're ready to burst, and I'm pretty sure they're headed this way."

"Agreed."

We rush to the trunk and I drag out the spare tire, while Abi finds the jack and lug wrench. The smell of petrichor ramps up around us, and I kneel down next to the burst tire and get to work. It probably shouldn't surprise me, but we function well as a team, sliding into our roles as I loosen the bolts and she jacks up the car.

My dad taught me everything I know about cars, and I learned how to change to a spare when I was barely 10 years old. He was always in the garage, especially when he needed to think, or take a break from working on a paper. He said that seeing all those parts laid out around him helped put things into perspective. After he got diagnosed with cancer, we spent a lot of time fixing up junkers and pet-projects alike. We didn't talk much about his illness in that garage, in fact we didn't talk about much of anything other than cars. I think he was thankful just to be doing something close to normal at that point.

I finished up the Jaguar after he died.

It was my way of telling him that I would be okay without him.

"Grab me that tire?"

In the distance, I hear the roar of thunder, and I glance over at Abi, reaching out my hand.

"On it."

Abi rolls it over to me, holding it still as I place the bolts and tighten them one by one. Suddenly, with only a couple left to finish. the sky opens up. Abi shrieks, letting out a loud laugh as she tries to keep her grip on the tire; we're immediately drenched, the deluge of warm summer rain completely enveloping everything in seconds.

"Logan, hurry up!"

"I'm trying, just one or two left!"

Water pours down my face and I feel Abi reach over, brushing my hair out of my eyes so I can stay focused. When I finally secure the last bolt we're immediately on our feet, dashing over to toss the old tire back into the trunk. Abi's jet black hair is plastered to her face, and she's soaked from head to toe.

Another clap of thunder echoes through the sky, accompanied by the slam of the trunk as we rush for our doors. The two of us burst out laughing, the adrenaline flowing as the rain continues buffeting the windshield.

I glance over, quickly catching sight of Abi's pebbled nipples sticking out under her soaked t-shirt; it's difficult to fight the urge to lean over and bite down until she squirms.

I didn't expect to see so much of her this morning, and I haven't been able to crush the thoughts that came along with the view. All of those feelings that got brought right to the surface are still swirling around inside me, and now we're here, and I don't know what the fuck to do about them.

I keep thinking about her soft skin, and that little splash of freckles adorning her hip. The ones that I traced with my tongue that first magical night. Thankfully, the only thing drowning out my rising horniness is the extremely irritating sound of the rain, and what I'm shocked to say must be hail, hammering against the roof of the car.

"Earth to Logan." Abi raps gently on my head with her knuckles. "You in there, Sunshine?"

She's staring at me like I have two heads.

"I left a hair tie in the cup holder, have you seen it?"

"Yeah— I— uh... I don't know. Maybe it got thrown out accidentally?"

Abi lets out a groan before climbing into the back seat, giving me a full view of her perfect ass.

"What are you doing?" I ask, carefully adjusting my quickly stiffening cock in my pants, in the vain attempt it won't be incredibly obvious if she just happens to look down.

"I need something to put my hair up. The water dripping down the back of my neck is a fucking sensory—" She grunts as she starts to pry the back seat open, trying to get into the trunk. "Nightmare!"

Her skirt rides up as she struggles, giving me a distressingly good view of her lacy red panties.

Do not look.

Do not think about her like that.

Think about anything other than tearing them off with your teeth.

Maybe baseball?

Do Umpires ever get hit in the nuts accidentally? Why are the beers so expensive at the games? Why does Frankie scream at the TV like he's a deadbeat dad getting divorced when his team's playing?

And why are the games so long? They should have baseball cheerleaders. Abi would look so good in one of those skirts, I bet she'd—

Fuck.

"It's really coming down," I murmur, making sure to look straight ahead.

I hate a full circle moment.

Suddenly, something hits me in the back of my head, and it takes a few seconds of blindly fumbling behind me before I realize it's a t-shirt. Abi crawls back into the front seat, plopping herself down and using the shirt to start wringing out her hair.

"Sorry," she mutters. "Didn't mean to toss it that hard."

I glance over and shrug, watching her for a bit before a giant clap of thunder overhead makes us both jump. It only took a few minutes to get so dark it feels like we skipped the afternoon, almost like night is already descending. Even with my wipers on, the visibility is complete shit. I wouldn't even drive in this in Emerald Bay, much less a city I don't even know.

"How long do you think this is going to last?" I ask.

"Well, the good news is that there are no mountains around here to trap the storm, so normally it would move along quickly." Abi wipes her face, digging out her phone and swiping through it. "The bad news is it seems like the wind patterns are gonna keep it stuck here for another hour at least. You wanna wait it out on the side of the road?"

"Probably should," I mutter, spotting a lightning strike off in the distance.

"I know it's kinda lame, but lightning sorta freaks me out."

Her tone is wavering a little, and she's obviously unnerved.

"We get really bad thunderstorms in Blackburn, and I was always terrified that I'd get struck by lightning whenever I got caught outside."

"Did you know 28 people in the United States die from lightning strikes every year?"

"No," she laughs, whacking me in the arm. "And that's definitely a stat I could have gone *not* knowing, Dr. Flynn."

"Sorry," I mumble, turning on the car radio to distract myself.

From her. From this road trip. From us.

I told myself I agreed to play out this cute little lie to help out a friend, but that's bullshit. I did it because it's the closest I'll get to the real thing. We've both said so many times that we're just friends, and it's all we're ever going to be, so if I want to taste the life I could have had, this is it. This is the only way it's happening.

The rain hammers against the roof of the car, the sound drowning out every last thought in my head, except for one.

"Have you heard of multiverse theory?" I ask.

She glances back at me, looking bewildered.

"Multi-what?"

"You know, multiple universes, that different versions of us exist in. Places where things are... different." I shrug. "Like, say, if you took a different job, or maybe you ended up dating Sebastian Stan—"

She grins.

"Oooh, where's that universe? I want in!"

Now I'm wondering how well alternate-universe Sebastian Stan could fight. Maybe I could beat him if I went for the knees.

"Why are you asking me this, Logan?"

"Have you ever thought about what one of those universes would be like? Say if you hadn't taken the job at EBU, or hadn't gotten a PhD? Maybe one where you didn't leave Blackburn Falls?"

"I think my life would suck," she replies flatly. "Those are three of the best decisions I ever made."

I bite my lip, listening to the soft sigh escape her lips.

"I mean— obviously it probably wouldn't *totally* suck, things would just be different, but..." She pauses for a moment, frowning as she tries to figure out how to say exactly what she wants to say. "Ugh, this is going to sound so stupid."

"Hey, I'm the King of saying dumb shit. You can take pretty much everything I've said today as evidence of that."

She snorts, looking a bit more comfortable after another one of my stupid jokes.

"Well, if I'd stayed in Blackburn, if I'd married Brendan, if I hadn't gone for my PhD... I wouldn't have been happy– not really, I don't think. And I wouldn't have found Emerald Bay. Or any of you."

"And I wouldn't have spilled my drink on you," I snicker. "Sometimes the smallest things make the biggest ripples."

Abi's straight-faced, clutching the t-shirt so tightly in her hands her fingers are almost bone white. Her eyes blaze, piercing into mine with such a vicious intensity that it makes the back of my neck heat up. I can't tell if the rain's picked up even more, thundering against the car, or it's just the blood roaring in my ears.

"Do you believe in fate?" Her voice is barely above a whisper. "Like... that things are meant to happen the way they do?"

Out of the corner of my eye I catch another flash of lightning, but Abi refuses to take her eyes off me.

"Do you?" I ask.

She gnaws on her lip. Is this really happening right now? Are we having this conversation?

"You asked me if I think about alternate universes, and I sorta do. I'm constantly thinking about another place, or maybe it's more like a different road, one that leads to a different future, a place where..."

The hairs on my neck stand up as she trails off.

I want to tell her that she's all I think about.

That if we let it happen, my entire world would revolve around her, that the love I have for her hasn't ever faded, not even a little, just shifted into something I'm trying to outrun.

"Where what?"

I need her to say it.

"A future where what, Abi?"

Her chin quivers and her eyes fill with tears.

"Where we made it."

CHAPTER TWENTY-FIVE

ABI

EMERALD BAY, WASHINGTON
ONE YEAR AGO

I thought double dates were supposed to be fun.

You go out for dinner or a movie with another couple, and hopefully walk away with new friends. But this? This is the worst fucking double date I've ever been on, and it's all Logan's fault.

Him and his stupidly handsome face.

It started when I met Chuck at Déjà Brew last week. Our coffee orders accidentally got mixed up, we got to chatting, and crazy enough I found out he teaches chemistry. I thought he was cute, and he obviously thought the same because he asked me if I wanted to go out for dinner this weekend.

Perfect.

I figured I'd take a chance on love for once.

After all, what could possibly go wrong?

When I texted Logan about the date, he told me he was planning on going to dinner with Ashley that same night. She'd been managing Déjà Brew pretty much the entire time we'd been frequenting it, but he never made a move. In the end, what it took was spilling his coffee all over his laptop; when she offered to make him a new drink her phone number was etched onto the cup.

Classic.

Anything that got him back in the dating pool had to be a good thing.

Anyway, we figured since we all met over different sets of tiny catastrophes at the coffee shop, it would be an easy thing to bond over.

And it was! it was a great plan!

Except that the only bonding that's been going on all evening is between Chuck and Ashley; somehow both Logan and I ended up as third-wheels on our own dates.

It started sometime around when the appetizers got here, when Chuck mentioned that he used to tour with a bunch of rock stars when he was younger. Aerosmith, Pink Floyd, Fleetwood Mac, those were the ones he was most proud of.

I have to admit, it was a cool little factoid, but looking at how Ashley reacted you'd have thought it was the greatest thing she had ever heard in her life. Now it's only half an hour later and they're already a little too friendly, taking bites of food off of each other's plates and laughing at the stupidest jokes.

"Oh my God, stop!" Ashley giggles, leaning over and touching Chuck's forearm.

"Hey, it's true! I'd never lie to a pretty lady!"

"You were not a roadie for The Rolling Stones! There's no way, they're like my favorite band!"

"I was!" He laughs. "I swear. I've got the VIP passes and everything at home. I could show you if you don't believe me!"

"That is so cool," Ashley gushes, artfully ignoring the little hint he left for her.

I swallow the bile that's creeping up my throat while Logan and I exchange an enthusiastic roll of the eyes before he picks up his phone. He looks good tonight, his sandy hair neatly combed off to the side and those retro half-frame glasses that I adore on him. He's toned down the Halloween look, at least a little, opting instead to dress like he stepped right off the set of Mad Men with a black dress shirt, a purple cardigan, and a matching tie. His watch is too big for his wrist, so he wears it on the outside of his shirt sleeve. He told me it used to belong to his dad. I still find it endearing that he's never bothered to get it resized.

Logan flicks his head toward his phone and I frown, confused for a moment before I realize what he's asking. I pull my own phone carefully out of my purse, putting it on my lap and flicking over to our chat history.

SUNSHINE

She told me her favorite band was N*SYNC.

I want to laugh, but it's hard given the situation. I really liked Chuck and now he's totally into someone else... but maybe I can still fix this.

I turn to him, ready with a perfect question to get him talking to me again, only to find he's actually shifted his body completely away from me. I clench my teeth, and my cheeks heat up with humiliation; it's like they've formed their own little fort just for them.

No Abi's allowed.

My phone buzzes in my lap and I glance down, a little irritated.

SUNSHINE

Bathroom?

No! I mouth, trying my best to look unamused.

Logan rolls his eyes, tapping away on his phone while I glance back over at Chuck and Ashley. They're sharing food, leaning in so closely they may as well be feeding it to each other.

Another buzz.

SUNSHINE

Come on, we gotta come up with a game plan.

Ugh. He just won't stop.

ME

It's going to look super weird!

SUNSHINE

Oh, please, they're so into each other they aren't
even paying attention to us.

I glare at him and he grins. He knows I know he's right.

SUNSHINE

They're playing footsies under the table.

I roll my eyes, shaking my head at him. There's no way they're that brazen.

His grin widens, and he flicks his head ever so slightly, daring me to look under the table. I sigh. I may as well give him what he wants. At the very least it might make him lay off a little bit, until I can figure out how to get back in the driver's seat in this situation.

I lean back in my chair and glance down, trying to remain somewhat inconspicuous. Ashley's high heel lays discarded on the ground, and any hope that I might have had in regard to the evening is out the window. I watch her while she massages Chuck's calf with the ball of her foot, holding back the urge to gag.

I give Logan a look he's seen too many times: half astounded, half offended. How can two people be so blissfully unaware of the fact that their dates are sitting right next to them? And I mean, if they are aware? That's worse!

It's just rude.

Logan motions toward the back of the restaurant where the bathrooms are located, and at this point I know there's no way I'm getting out of this. I set my napkin down, slip out of my seat, and quietly excuse myself. I'm not angry that they're into each other, I'm angry that I feel cast aside. It's embarrassing to know you're not wanted.

"Abi!" Logan's sharp whisper catches me off guard and he grasps my wrist, spinning me around just before we reach the bathrooms.

I scowl at him but he just smiles back. Logan Flynn is the King of laughing off humiliation. I, on the other hand, am not.

He takes off his glasses and cleans them on his tie.

"Are you okay?"

"No." I think my scowl is going to become permanent at this point. "This sucks, it's *not* funny, and it's your fault!"

"My fault? How is this my fault?"

"That guy's a hottie, Logan, and I really liked him! He's barely said a word to me since *your* coffee shop girl floated in here!"

"Hey, look, it's not like I did it on purpose! Besides, she's clearly not *my* coffee shop girl anymore. I'm pretty sure she's ten minutes away from dry humping him in his seat."

Logan flashes me a dazzling smile. If he weren't so handsome, I'd want to smack it off him.

"Did you see him turn his whole chair away from me?!" I ask. "I look away for 30 seconds and he's locked them into their own little zone. It's not fair, I never even had a chance!"

"Yeah, I saw it," Logan chuckles as he puts his glasses back on, pushing his hair out of his face.

"God, of course the first time I try dating since Brendan it's a complete disaster."

He glances down at me, grinning from ear to ear. It's not smug, and there's no hurt in his eyes. He's probably psyched that he has someone to commiserate with, but I don't want to commiserate. I want to get laid.

He reaches down, sliding his fingers beneath my chin. My heart thunders, and I'm not quite sure why.

"Come on, Abi. If you can't laugh at this, when can you laugh?"

"They're going to sleep together and I'm gonna be sleeping with a hangover, all alone," I grumble. "And don't you forget, neither of us can go to that coffee shop again! Imagine how humiliating it would be!"

"Abi, I'm not embarrassed, and you shouldn't be either. So what if you run into one of them again? You barely know each other. Don't let something like this ruin your best coffee spot."

Logan's never embarrassed, and I've always admired that about him. He says humiliation is a useless emotion that keeps us from being our authentic selves. Not that I disagree, but knowing something and acting on it are two completely different things.

"You're right."

I hate that he's right.

"I mean, we both know I'm always right, but listen: they're clearly having way more fun than we are, and I for one am not interested in watching them escalate to sucking face for the next hour. How about we pay for our dinner up front and just leave them be?" He boops me on the nose. "I'll take you to The Eclipse. They're doing a 10pm screening of Friday the 13th."

"I don't know," I sigh.

It sounds better than suffering through this. I could lie to Chuck; tell him I feel sick or something and Logan has to take me to the ER.

No, that's too dramatic. But we can't just—

I rise up onto my tiptoes, shifting back and forth until I manage to get a clean sightline to the table. Chuck is on his feet, glancing around carefully as he helps Ashley with her coat before tossing some cash down.

"Looks like Chuck and Ashley have the same idea."

"This is hilarious," Logan snickers, leaning in behind me as we both watch them walk toward the front door.

"It's not hilarious! They might be saddling us with the bill! I don't think he put down enough cash."

Logan cuts me off, grasping my shoulders, his expression soft and sweet.

"I'll cover whatever's left, okay? Then we go to see that movie and have a nice rest of the evening. We should salvage this night instead of being bummed out about it."

A deep sigh escapes my lips and I stare at the space where Chuck and Ashley used to be. It's not the worst idea, and I could definitely go for a blood-soaked palate cleanser.

Logan's phone chimes and he snorts.

"What? What is it?"

He flashes me the text, head tilted playfully as I squint through the screen's glow.

"It's Ashley. She said, and I quote: 'hey, I had a great time, but I don't think this is going to work out.'"

I check my phone and sure enough, there's one from my date as well.

CHUCK

> Had a great time, but I just don't think we're a match. You and Logan seem really into each other. Figured I didn't stand a chance.

I stare up at Logan in total disbelief.

"Into each other?! You and me?"

"Calm down, Shortcake. He doesn't know us that well, and probably reads our friendship as something more than it is." He gives me another shrug. "It happens, right?"

Are Logan and I putting out the wrong signals? I mean, sure, we see each other every day at work... and most days after work. But that's just for a bit, little walks or coffee or whatever. We're not even that close! Well, we are, but just— not in that way.

We set up our hardline boundaries, and we've stuck to them.

We're friends. Nothing more, and nothing less.

"Ugh! This is so shitty!"

"Story of my life," he chuckles. "But come on, it's not so bad. At least we have each other."

He reaches over to ruffle my hair, but I swat his hand away.

"Watch it! These curls weren't easy to get!" I duck out of his reach when he tries it again, doing my best to stay serious. "Logan, cut it out!"

Of course, I'm failing miserably, my growing grin is impossible to hide. He just knows how to get me in a good mood, no matter how glum I'm feeling.

"Well, I can't deny I've done some serious damage to your delicate curls. How about I buy you dessert as an apology? They have an amazing double fudge raspberry cake, if I remember correctly."

Logan knows chocolate is my weakness. He knows all of my weaknesses.

"Come on, let me make it up to you. Please?"

He's tilted his head in that sad little way he always does, flashing me those puppy dog eyes. I hate when men know how cute they are.

"I think that look you give should be illegal in all fifty states," I grumble.

"You know what? I agree, but I'd be a fool not to use it before they lock me up, right?!"

I roll my eyes for what feels like the umpteenth time tonight, and we make our way back to our table. Our food's cold, but it was expensive, so we both wordlessly decide to dig back in. Logan glances up at me as he stabs at his potatoes.

"Really though, you have to admit this whole thing was really funny."

"You're such a child!" I grin, opening my mouth and sticking out my tongue, revealing a mountain of chewed food. "I bet you think that's funny too, right?"

He grins.

"Hysterical."

Dating always feels like putting on a mask, one that's simultaneously calm and cool, but that's also silently screaming *please like me* over and over.

It's a huge relief to know I don't have to do that around Logan.

"I was about to clear those," our waitress chuckles as she approaches, a few beads of sweat evident on her forehead. "I thought you guys dined and dashed."

"No, our dates just ditched us," Logan replies, taking a massive bite of his salmon.

"Sure, tell everyone," I mutter.

"I'll cover all of this," he adds, as if he didn't hear me at all. "Oh, and could we get two of those double fudge chocolate cakes to go?"

"Sure thing," she replies.

"Logan, I'm paying for my meal."

"Nope." He turns to the waitress, who's working on clearing the other plates. "Miss, this is a matter of life and death. Do not split that bill."

The server shoots him a cute little smile before she heads off, and I glower at Logan. He's far too generous for his own good, especially where I'm concerned.

"Alright, you win but at least let me tip."

"They already left a tip," Logan replies, motioning to the pile of cash.

"Logan—"

"Look." He dabs at his mouth with a napkin and reaches for my hand. "You seemed really bummed out about Chuck, and I don't want this to ruin your night, okay? Let me fix it."

I sigh.

Let me fix it.

That's Logan Flynn in a nutshell. Always jumping in to lend a hand, always trying to make the best out of a bad situation. I don't know where he got his eternal optimism, but I can't deny it's saved me from a few spirals since I've met him.

"Okay. Alright. You know what? I'm gonna buy you coffee tomorrow morning. You have to let me do that, at the very least."

"Coffee? My drug of choice? You've got yourself a deal, Shortcake."

We finish dinner and Logan pays as promised, refusing to show me the bill, and leaving a substantial tip of his own before we head out toward The Eclipse Theatre. The air smells fresh, and there's a slight chill to it, enough to make me shiver after a couple blocks.

"Here," Logan murmurs, sliding out of his jacket and draping it across my shoulders. "You're freezing."

It smells like his cologne, sweet yet spicy.

Kind of like him.

"Won't you be cold?"

"I'm from New York. Cold, cold winters. I'm pretty used to it by now."

"You know, I think Blackburn is colder than New York. I bet you couldn't handle it up there."

"Oh, yeah?" He asks, recognition of a challenge sparkling in his eyes.

"Minus 40 in the winter. We'd have to walk to school in three feet of snow."

He whistles and smirks at me.

"Uphill both ways?"

"You're such a little shit," I giggle, bumping him with my shoulder.

"Nah, you adore me."

If things had been different, or if I'd gotten a job in a different department, we could have given this a shot.

We'd be so good together.

We walk in silence, and I link my pinky finger with his.

Logan smiles down at me, giving it a little squeeze.

He's right, I *do* adore him.

And I always will.

CHAPTER TWENTY-SIX

do i wanna know?

ABI

SOMEWHERE ON THE WAY TO MANITOBA
PRESENT DAY

Do you ever wish you could press rewind?

Our entire friendship has been a series of close calls, and almosts, and I'm getting so tired of 'almost' being the furthest I ever get.

It sounds stupid but I've dreamed about a wedding in the Irish countryside, because once he off-handedly told me he'd like to get married in the same place his parents did. I've thought about having kids with him, and how cute they'd be with all that chaotic curly hair. I've dreamed about quiet mornings on a back porch, watching the sun come up while we sipped our coffee.

The truth is, I *have* thought about throwing it all away for a future with him, it's just that I'm evenly torn between my love for Logan and my love for my job. I never would have been able to admit this stuff so openly before, but now that we're stuck together on this road trip it's gotten so much harder to say no, and to keep telling myself that it's all a bad idea.

"Abi," Logan whispers, pulling me back to the present as his hand brushes against my cheek. "Did you hear me?"

"Huh?"

No, of course not. I totally missed it. I got so lost in my own anxiety that— Fuck, I feel like I'm suffocating.

"I asked you what you meant by that." His voice is so soft, it nearly gets swallowed up by the sound of the rain. "When you said you'd imagined another future. One where we made it."

"Oh, that, It was nothing, I was just—" I trail off, unsure exactly how to let the both of us down as lightly as possible. To lie.

"No." Logan shakes his head. "You're not going to tell me you didn't mean it. I know you, Abi, and I think well enough to know when you're being honest with me."

After this morning, something shifted in his demeanor. He's more determined, and it's impossible *not* to feel it. Me though? If I say what I want to say, there's no taking it back. I'm floundering, stammering, and drawing a blank.

"Abi..."

His voice is pinched with desperation as another clatter of thunder rumbles above us.

My head is buzzing and I find it impossible to tear my gaze away from his. It's hard for me to look a lot of people in the eye. It makes me feel like they'll be able to see past me, to some horrific hidden quality even I'm not fully aware of.

But with him? He makes me feel safe. I could stare into those eyes for hours.

"I do think about it." I clear my throat. "Sometimes."

All the time. I think about it *all* the time.

"Okay, yeah. Good," he rasps. "I think about it too. Probably more than I should."

The urge to scream the truth has been slowly creeping up the back of my throat the entire afternoon.

I love you. This is killing me.

My skin begins to prickle as I feel the sweat forming on my forehead.

"This morning, I felt you... *all* of you," I confess.

I swallow, pushing the rest of the words out of my mouth.

"And I liked it."

His face flushes bright red, but he doesn't look away.

This time, I don't want to snatch the words back. This time, I let my confession hang in the air between us. It's not a love confession, at least not in the way I really want it to be, but it's close enough.

Logan is stock-still, his eyes darting around my face the way they always do when he's trying to make sure I'm not fucking with him.

"All of me? Like—"

"Jesus, you know what I mean, Logan. You were pressed up against me, and I…"

I'm floundering again, but before I can turn away and get my bearings, he slides his fingers underneath my chin to hold me in place.

"Did you touch yourself?"

Logan licks his lips as I nod, letting out a soft hiss.

"So that's what I walked in on?"

Another nod.

"I was thinking about Toronto."

Blood roars in my ears and I stare at him, not knowing what to do. I stroke his cheek, his warm skin the perfect contrast to my chilled, trembling fingers.

Logan leans forward, his nose brushing up against mine.

You could hear a pin drop, at least in between the rumbles of thunder.

"You have no idea how many times I replay that night in my head."

His voice has some grit to it despite its softness, and I can feel the hairs on my arms start to stand on end. I try to speak, but it feels like I can barely breathe, much less think of something to say.

His kiss is exactly like I remember, tender and sweet, but with so much passion hidden inside it. As much as the logical part of my brain is desperate to pull away, and run through the list all the ways this is a bad fucking idea, every other part of me can't get enough of him.

Without thinking, I climb onto his lap, rolling my hips and grinding down on him. My body is desperate for the release I was so cruelly denied this morning, and his deep, sultry groan makes me shiver in anticipation. Logan rests his hand firmly on my waist, rocking me back and forth. It's all clicking teeth and tangled tongues as we finally give in to what we've both craved for far too fucking long.

And it's fucking delicious.

A particularly loud clap of thunder forces the two of us to stop, but Logan only smirks.

"We keep doing this," he mutters.

I steel myself, drawing in a deep breath as I utter the words I've wanted to say since the hotel.

"You're right, we do. Maybe we need to get it out of our systems."

I'm tired of pretending I don't want him. Sure, it won't end up meaning anything, but we can spend this week fucking each other's brains out and then go back to the way things used to be. It'll be hard, but no harder than staying in denial the entire time.

In the end, we'll have some manner of relief, as well as another filthy little secret.

"Now?" He asks, his voice trembling slightly.

"Why not?" The way he's looking at me gives me a huge boost of confidence, like I could do anything. "The last time we got this close, it was *your* idea."

Logan's impulsivity is often his downfall, but right now, I can tell he's trying to work out every possible outcome. He doesn't want to fuck things up.

"I don't have a condom," he murmurs as he slowly begins to tease my nipples through my shirt.

"Does that mean you don't want me?"

He chuckles at me as he gives one of my nipples a firm tug.

"You think you're funny, don't you?"

My back arches and an involuntary whine slips out.

"Funnier than you, at least."

Logan's eyes soften for a moment, ignoring my snide comment as he presses another kiss to my lips, pulling away again with a whisper.

"Shortcake, I've wanted you for a long time."

His hands slide beneath my tank top, the sensation of his skin against mine and sending sparks shooting down my spine; I let out the most pathetic and sinful sound I've ever heard myself make.

"You kept grinding that perfect ass against me this morning," he whispers.

"You were awake," I moan, rocking my hips faster. "I knew it."

I want his fingers, his mouth, his cock, *fucking anything* to relieve this ache.

"Knowing you were just in the other room with that shower head between your legs... I started trying to take care of my own little problem."

I whimper.

If I had known that I might have stayed, and we could have had this conversation hours ago in a sea of cozy blankets and warm kisses, instead of in the middle of a thunderstorm.

Hindsight's a real bitch sometimes.

Logan pulls my shirt up, exposing my breasts and letting out a deep moan before taking one of my nipples into his mouth. He teases it with his tongue, swirling and flicking until I find my body moving with a kind of desperation I haven't felt in quite a long time. If this is what it feels like to give in, I think I might become addicted.

At this point our groans and ragged breath sound almost as loud as the surrounding storm. I'm grinding down harder, feeling his cock stiffen beneath me. Feeling his hands, his mouth, his—

An overwhelmingly loud blare of sound catches us both off guard and I let out a shriek, my mind suddenly hurtling back down to earth as I try to figure out what happened.

"What the fuck was that?!"

"I think... your butt might have hit the horn."

I glance behind me to find that he's right: I've somehow managed to bump the steering wheel with my ass.

"Oh my god." I bury my face into his shoulder, stifling nervous laughter. "That scared the shit out of me!"

"You okay?" Logan chuckles.

I lift my head to get a better look at him in the low glow of the interior lights.

I feel his hands slip underneath my skirt, and I spot the little dimple on his left cheek that he gets when his smile is just a bit too big for his face.

"I want to watch you ride my fingers, and then you're going to lick them clean like a good girl. You understand?"

"Yes."

I didn't even hesitate.

"That's my girl." He explores my skin with fervor, licking his lips like a man starved. "I've thought about this every day."

"Every day?"

He teases my clit through my panties, each word emphasized by a particularly heavy movement.

"Every. *Fucking*. Day."

My body moves like it has a mind of its own, craving nothing but the bliss that's coursing through me.

"You're blushing. Do my fingers feel that good?"

Logan is chaotic, oftentimes forgetful, and flighty as hell… except when he's in the bedroom. It's like a totally different side of him comes out, and I can't get enough of it. I'm trying to commit every touch to memory because I know I won't be able to hold onto this forever.

"Use your words," he growls, his strokes speeding up as my own pace begins to quicken.

"So good," I gasp.

My fingernails dig into his shoulders, and all I can see is the lust in his eyes.

"Atta girl. God, you're so wet."

He glides his mouth down my neck, the dull feeling of his teeth nipping lightly at my skin lighting me up. He doesn't waste time, shoving my panties aside and pushing two fingers inside of me.

I've always loved his hands. The veins in them, the ring he wears on his pinky, and now I'm being reminded how good his nimble fingers feel when he starts to make that come hither motion inside of me.

"That's it. Ride my fucking fingers like a good little slut."

I have no control over my body, or the moans that spill from my mouth anymore. This man has zero shame, and no qualms about tossing in a pinch of degradation. Desire and pleasure start to build in the pit of my stomach and spread down my legs. I'm embarrassingly close in such a short period of time, but it's been so long since someone's touched me like this.

And it's fine, because it's just for the trip.

It's not real.

"Who's the last man to make you come?" He groans against my neck.

Logan Flynn, always trying to beat the competition. Even that's kind of hot, honestly.

"You," I choke out. "In Toronto."

He freezes, staring up at me, his eyes wide.

"Are you serious?"

"Yes."

I haven't been with anyone else since. I've been too focused on doing my own thing, and my few attempts at dating barely went anywhere.

"You haven't been fucked in three years?" He asks.

I shake my head, and then Logan's thrusts get harder– deeper– and he kisses me again and again. Every time his fingers graze my G-spot, the hunger grows deep in my belly. I need more. I need all of him.

His hands mapping out our secret all over my body.

His mouth on the forbidden places I've only allowed myself to fantasize about in fragments, and in my weakest moments.

We were supposed to be friends.

We swore we'd never cross this line again.

But we almost have, at so many times and in so many different ways.

Drunken collisions of mouths, whispered half confessions that slipped out in our most intimate moments.

I think about our failed double date and the way he looked at me at the end of that night, like he might want to kiss me.

I think about Aspen, about how ready we were to break our rules, even if it was only there, and just once.

My head is fuzzy, like I've had a bit too much to drink, and even if someone pounded on the car window I don't think I could stop. All my body craves is him, and this time, the only thing I refuse is to deny myself.

With one final stroke of his fingers I come undone, sparks shooting down my skin and leaving goosebumps in their wake. My body shudders, hips rutting against the heel of his hand as wave after wave of euphoria crashes against me.

And then I feel his other hand gently squeeze my throat.

"Keep those eyes on me," he rumbles. "Don't look away."

My eyes pop open as the final wave of my climax hits me, in time to see Logan's wicked grin. I shiver and quake, the current still working its way through my nerve endings while my stomach churns with a swarm of butterflies.

I'm not done, and neither is he.

I go to unzip his pants, but he snatches my wrist and shakes his head.

"That can wait… I'm not finished with you."

He slides his fingers out of me, pushing them past my lips so that I taste myself, sharp and tangy.

"Clean them," he orders, his cock throbbing beneath me.

He watches me closely as he thrusts them in and out of my mouth like I'm sucking his cock. I ride that high as hard as I can, swirling my tongue around to eat up every last drop, and the whole time Logan doesn't take his eyes off of me. When I'm finally done he rewards me with a tender kiss, his eyes glittering in the cracks of sunlight just barely making it through the clouds, and in through the car window.

"Look at that, still gorgeous after it's all said and done."

He covers my face with messy kisses as I glide my fingers through his hair, relishing the peace of the afterglow, but the abrupt snarling of my stomach interrupts our little moment.

"Sorry," I giggle. "It really picks the worst times to get hungry."

Logan only smiles, not a hint of anything but joy on his face.

"Will you look at that, the rain's let up. Come on, let's grab some food and I'll fuck your brains out."

And just like that, he's back to himself.

All smiles and crass jokes, with not a care in the world.

"Show me what you've got, Sunshine."

dirty diana

LOGAN

SWAN RIVER, MANITOBA
PRESENT DAY

"Sir, we don't accept Party City rewards cards as a form of payment."

I blink.

"What?"

Abi squeezes my thigh as the kid at the drive-thru window hands my card back. She's been doing it the entire drive, and how I've managed not to crash this car yet is something that should be studied by scientists. Looks like my grade school teachers were wrong. I absolutely can multitask.

But more importantly, we broke our rules.

Every single one.

"Here." She thrusts out her credit card into the employee's open hand. "I got it."

Just as I'm about to protest, she cuts me off with a peck on the cheek.

"No arguing."

I sigh.

"Yes, ma'am."

"So I booked us a hotel about two blocks from here," she tells me as the kid at the window runs her card. "Cable, two beds– but I guess we won't be needing the second one anymore..."

"Do they have a microwave?" I ask with a smirk. "Because with the way you've been today, the food's probably gonna get cold."

She giggles, brushing her nose against mine. I'm head over heels for this woman, and even knowing none of it will mean anything after this trip, I'm going to soak up every second I get with her.

Once we get our food, I set off toward the hotel, with Abi diligently acting as my navigator with her phone.

"You wanna make a right up on Main," she tells me. "It's— oh, Main Street! Right there!"

She points to it like an excited kid and I step on the gas, eager to get her into that bed. The drive feels like it takes an eternity, and the cars clogging up the roads don't help to mitigate that feeling much.

"Is everyone out for a drive today? Don't these people work or go to school or something? It's like 1:00 in the afternoon!"

Abi eyes me with a smirk.

"You know what they say, Sunshine: patience is a virtue."

"Not to me it isn't," I growl, gritting my teeth and leaning on the horn as a station wagon sits for a little too long. "The light's green, dude!"

Abi cheers as the car lurches forward and I immediately speed up to maneuver around it. It's only another few blocks after that when she nods, slipping her phone into her pocket and pointing just a bit further down the street.

"There it is. See? Patience wins again."

"Yeah, yeah."

I pull into the parking lot and kill the engine, sitting still and staring at the frosted glass door that leads into the motel lobby.

The second I touch her, I'm not going to be able to go back to normal. We got interrupted before, but this time? There's nobody to screw that up.

"Logan?"

Not even ourselves.

I turn to her, never more sure of anything in my life. Even the potential of ruining my entire career for this woman doesn't even make me flinch. The kiss we share in that moment contains everything I can't say, all of my secrets and *I love yous* poured into one tiny little thing, and when we both finally pull apart I can see that she looks just as lovestruck as I feel.

"I'm ready if you are," I rasp.

"Definitely."

The check-in process takes a while and the clerk is *far* too chatty for my tastes. I just want that damn key. Abi seems to sense my impatience and takes over, her effortlessly warm demeanor coming out in full force as she chats with the clerk. They touch on everything: the weather, the road trip, Emerald Bay, and even the baseball game that's playing over the radio. Turns out Abi actually does like baseball, which is one of the more unexpected things I've found out lately.

The second we get our keys, I'm practically yanking her across the parking lot toward our room. My hands tremble as I slide the key card in, and it takes a couple of tries before the door finally pops open.

The room is relatively simple, with a large king size bed, a dresser, and a cracked mirror off in the corner.

"Isn't that seven years of bad luck?" Abi asks.

"I think it only counts if *you* break it."

"Right."

We stare at each other, and I find my eyes tracing her full lips, her high cheekbones, and her beautifully arched brows that knit together for just a moment, before her mouth curves up into a gentle smile.

"So. Sex. We're gonna have sex," she breathes.

"Again."

"Yeah." Her cheeks blaze red as she puts her hand on my chest. The gesture feels oddly intimate, cutting through a tension so thick it was begging to explode. "I want you to take control. Just like you did in the car."

I feel like I'm about to pass out.

"Take... control?"

She looks angelic, lit by a beam of sunlight cutting through the gap in the curtains. Her once rain-soaked shirt has dried, her perfect nipples still visibly stiff as her chest heaves up and down.

"Make me yours, Logan."

The first time we fucked I was blessed to have alcohol raising my confidence, because just *looking* at her made everything feel fuzzy. It still does, if I'm being honest. I don't believe in God, which I think might be a crime for an Irishman, but I believe in Abigail King.

Abi's breath catches as I dip my head, ghosting my lips along her jaw. She digs her nails into my chest, pulling a feral sound from the depths of my throat.

"Kneel for me?"

I want to start this gently and then show her all the ways I can take control.

"Only because you asked so nicely," she purrs, lowering herself to the ground in front of me.

I run my fingers through her slightly tangled hair, taking some of it into a closed fist. Abi's eyes volley between my face and my hard cock, and I can't help but smirk.

"Well, I'm very polite."

Her lips part and she goes to reach for my belt buckle, but I tug on her hair, pulling her back.

"What do you say?"

"Please?" She asks.

The way the light hits her cheekbones makes her look like she's carved out of marble, but there are no sharp edges to Abi. There never have been. I can even make out the soft, slightly faded freckles that dust the bridge of her nose.

"Please what?"

"Please let me suck your cock."

Those soft words, spoken so sweetly, nearly bring *me* to my fucking knees. I let out a whoosh of breath, trying to cover everything up and make it look like I'm still in charge, but Abi's already giving me a run for my money.

"That's a good girl. Now, I want you to follow my instructions to the *letter*. Do you understand?"

She nods, sliding the leather out of my belt buckle with expert precision.

"Teach me what you like."

The slow extended sound of my zipper is almost deafening in the otherwise silent room, and Abi frees my cock, pulling my pants and underwear down past my hips.

"Gentle licks to start," I command. "I want us both to savor this."

She obeys, her silky tongue moving in delicate circles around the crown of my cock. Soon, I'm gripping her hair with both hands, trying to keep myself in control.

"That's it," I whisper, feeling myself throb in her mouth. "Pull your shirt up. Let me see everything."

Abi pulls away, releasing me with a pop.

"How about I do you one better and just take it off?"

"Now, there's an idea."

I help her peel off her tank top, tossing it all the way across the room before she wraps her lips around me again. My hips start to move like they have a mind of their own, and soon I'm pushing deeper into her mouth, my ever-heightening moans filling the room.

"Look at what a good girl you are, taking every inch. Can you fit all of me down that pretty little throat of yours?"

She gives me a look that tells me she won't be needing words to answer my questions. My cock throbs as she swallows, that pulsing sensation deepening as she engulfs me completely.

"Oh, *fuck*, look at you. You were made for this."

I'm amazed my brain can form words with the way she's sucking me off, anything articulate being immediately tossed out the window. Deep shudders ripple through my body, pleasure ringing through each and every nerve.

I can't believe this is happening.

We didn't even make it a week.

Sweat trickles down the back of my neck, and my legs begin to feel like jelly. Just as I reach the point of no return I gently pull her off of me, watching her take in a deep breath. She's every single one of my carnal desires personified, drool slipping down her chin as tear-stains cover her cheeks.

"Strip for me, then get on the bed."

Abi shakily gets to her feet, but I grasp her wrist when she moves to wipe the spittle from her lips.

"No. I like you messy."

Abi blinks, pausing for a moment before regaining her composure and pushing her skirt and panties past her hips.

"Is that all?" She taunts, smirking at me and sauntering toward the bed, sitting with her hands on her thighs.

I smile right back, slowly peeling my own clothes off piece by piece. When I'm done I quickly close the gap between us, running my fingers through her hair before pulling her head back again, the same as I did when she was on her knees.

"Careful now, don't push me too hard."

"I think you secretly like it, Doctor."

Abi scoots backward, propping herself up against the pillows as she stares at me, wild-eyed and hungry. A deep ache pulses through me and I can feel my cock twitch in response. It's getting more and more difficult to maintain control with each passing moment.

"Spread your legs for me."

She reaches down, and I'm greeted with the sight of her glistening pussy as she glides her fingers between her lips.

"Like this?"

Her voice is a gentle purr, and combined with the view of that delicious cunt, it takes no time at all for my mouth to start watering.

"Don't hold back," I tell her. "I want a noise complaint by the time we check out."

Her cheeks are bright red and she lets out a giggle, beginning to circle her clit lazily with a single finger.

"Then get over here and make that dream come true."

No matter how much I'd love to, I want to play with her first. Tease her. Watch her wriggle and bend. I want her so worked up that by the time I get to taste her, she's only seconds away from complete collapse.

"Where's that ring pop? I feel like dessert before dinner."

She raises a brow, still waiting for me.

"In my purse."

I quickly root it out, unwrapping it from the plastic before crawling onto the bed, ring pop in hand. I position myself on my stomach, nestled between her thighs, and she breathes heavily as I press the candy to her lips.

"Suck. You're good at that, aren't you? I want it nice and wet."

Abi's eyes shine with expectation, and she wraps her lips around the candy, sucking gently as she lets out a little moan. I pull the ring pop out of her mouth after a bit under a minute, grinning as a thin line of spit connects it to her plump lips.

"That's my girl."

I feel like I'm standing in front of a painting, trying to memorize the details before I move on to the next one. But I don't want to move on from her. In fact, I'm starting to think I may end up barely remembering parts of my life before her. In my head, she's always been here.

What's life even worth if she hasn't always been mine?

I force myself back into the moment, circling both of her nipples with the ring pop, and then slowly licking up the sweet remnants. My breathing is rapid and shallow, my hand practically shaking. Abi alternates between whimpers, giggles, and moans as I work my way down her soft stomach, tracing her little bone-white stretch marks with the sweet treat, followed by my own greedy tongue. I'm obsessed with the soft curve of her stomach, worshiping it, groaning as I glide my tongue over each mark.

She's like sand slipping through the gaps in my fingers; I only have her for a short time and I want to savor every second. I start tracing shapes along her thigh with the candy, listening to the quiet, aching repetitions of my name in a chorus, timed along with every shift and slip of her heels against the sheets.

Swirls, hearts, circles...

And then my name, on her lips and on her skin.

Her eyes burn into me as I replace the candy with my tongue, tracing each letter as Abi's fingers hover over her pussy, nearly twitching in anticipation. I repeat the action, slowly writing my name all over again while she quivers. I like to watch the build up, it's the best part of sex for me. Turning someone on and knowing that I'm the one who's making them beg for it is even better than my own release.

"How often do you think about me when you touch yourself?" I ask, drawing a heart on her inner thigh.

"More than I should."

The confession is raspy, almost strangled, like she doesn't want to admit it to herself.

"Touch yourself," I whisper. "Finish what you started in the shower."

She lets her fingers glide along her pussy lips, her clit nestled firmly between them. Hips roll like a wave, and I feel the bed shift as she moves, pushing her heels down into my lower back and locking me in place between her legs.

As if I'm fucking going anywhere.

She begins to circle her clit slowly again, trembling more and more with each stroke. I lick my lips, mouth watering with each gentle strum of her fingers. A ravenous need begins to build inside of me just as Abi slides a finger into her pussy, letting out a sweet moan.

"Logan," she sighs. "Please. Fuck me."

"I will," I whisper. "But we're gonna see how wet you can get before I taste you."

She whimpers, thrusting her finger in and out a few times more before bringing it back up to play with her clit. I feel like I could watch her do this all day, holding myself back as I practically foam at the mouth to get my hands on her, but we can't just sit here forever.

"Good girl. Use your fingers and show me how to lick you."

"You know how," she purrs. "Don't pretend you forgot."

I do.

Of course I do.

I just want to watch her pleasure herself with only me in mind. I want to know every single fantasy she's ever had about me. I want to hear it from her like it's the last time I ever will.

"Tell me more about this morning," I breathe, placing a gentle kiss on her thigh. "What were you thinking about while you were grinding your ass against my cock?"

Abi continues the gentle strums on and around her clit, her eyes filling with a vulnerability I'm not quite prepared for. I'm not usually *this* dominant during sex. I'll talk a girl through it, sure, but Abi gives me the space to really lean into it. She gives me confidence, and I feel comfortable enough with her to really indulge.

"I woke up and you were *so* hard... All I could think about was sliding my leggings down and letting you—" She's cut off by her own moan as she pushes two fingers inside of her and rocks her hips. "Oh, fuck!"

"I would have if you asked me," I groan, slipping the ring pop onto my finger for safe keeping. "I'd have fucked you like you're mine."

"I am," she rasps. "Yours. All yours, for as long as we're out here."

I shiver at her words, words I've longed to hear for three years. But even in the midst of desire, the caveat hangs in the air: She's only mine until we get home.

And then it's back to normal.

Back to almost.

Abi's breath hitches and she spreads herself, giving me the perfect opportunity to let my tongue glide effortlessly along her clit. Even with a featherlight touch I can feel it throb, and her hips buck along to the tune of her groans.

I repeat the action, rewarded with the feeling of her heels pressing further into my back.

"Good boy," she groans. "Just like that, baby."

Slow licks turn to hungry lashes, and when I finally end up pushing my two fingers into her cunt Abi immediately lets out a high-pitched keen. She pounds one hand against the mattress and tugs viciously on my hair with the other.

"Logan!" She gasps. "Right there!"

I push my fingers right up against her G-spot, making little come-hither motions as another sinful moan is pulled from deep inside of her. She's trembling like a leaf, and the heat radiating from her skin nearly scorches mine as she spasms into me. When she tries to lift her hips off the mattress, moving to get a bit more control over the situation, I pin her down with one arm.

And that's all it takes.

"I'm coming!" She cries. "Logan!"

I suck hard on her clit, listening to her scream my name one more time before she goes limp. Her legs relax, heels sliding down my back as she lets out a deep, satisfied groan. When I lift my head, her jaw is slack and she stares at the ceiling, taking in heavy breaths.

I slide out from between her legs, getting to my feet just as Abi recovers enough to lift herself up onto her forearms.

"You need a break?" I ask, grabbing a condom out of my bag and tearing it open with my teeth in preparation.

She shakes her head, her eyes still brimming with that same desire I've seen throughout our little vacation, as she beckons me over with a finger.

CHAPTER TWENTY-EIGHT

ABI

SWAN RIVER, MANITOBA
PRESENT DAY

He's exquisite. Wild-eyes, bitten-red lips, and my slick glistening on his chin as he crawls toward me like an animal. Taut ropes of muscle flex with each of his movements, and I'm practically drooling at the sight of him.

Logan glides the tip of his nose along my jaw before tugging on my earlobe with his teeth. I shiver, warm breath scorching my already flushed skin as I press my forehead against his. He offers me a bashful smile, cheeks flushed and his nose crinkling a little, the way it does when he's really happy.

"I can't believe we're doing this," he whispers.

"Neither can I. I've wanted you since—"

"I know." He lets out a rush of breath. "Kiss me? Please?"

"Anything you want."

"That's a dangerous sentence, Shortcake."

I know this is stupid. It undermines every boundary we've put in place. But I'm too overwhelmed to care about the rules right now. I guess we could say it's something like international waters, and the rules don't mean shit out here. I push away the fears of what's going to change when we get home, and focus on him. On us. On this. On what we have right now.

I reach between my thighs, dipping inside my pussy and presenting my glistening fingers to him before sliding them across his plump lips.

"You want another taste?"

"Yes, ma'am."

He wraps his mouth around two fingers, sucking greedily as I close my eyes and let out a satisfied sigh. I want to see what Logan looks like when he's completely given in to the desire I know is burning deep within him.

"That's a good boy," I purr, pumping them in and out of his mouth. "I think you deserve a reward."

It's been three years since I've had sex or even let another man do anything more than kiss me. Mostly, I've been content with vibrators, decent porn, and my imagination.

Part of me was hoping for a night like this for a while now, where I could finally throw all of my boundaries aside and fully give in to everything I've been denying myself. I just didn't think for a second he felt the same way, until this little road trip.

Logan doesn't take his eyes off me as I wrap my fingers around his cock, guiding it toward my pussy. I sink down inch by inch, letting out a moan so deep it practically vibrates the bed.

"You were already so greedy," he growls. "And now you want more?"

"Always."

He's thick, and that delightful stretch and light stinging sensation makes my toes curl. I've always liked a little dash of pain with sex, and this is the *perfect* blend.

"Atta girl." His fingers snake around my throat and he applies a bit of pressure, cutting off some of the blood flow. "Be a good little slut and take *every* inch."

It makes me dizzy, and I gasp for air as Logan gives my ass a rough smack before he finally releases my throat, and lets all of the blood rush back to my head.

Before long, the room is filled with our cacophony of moans and skin slapping against skin. He grips me so tight I know I'll have bruises tomorrow, but I don't care. The only thing that matters in that moment is that feeling of my pleasure building, each stroke of his cock hitting my G-spot as he uses me like a toy.

Something about this entire thing is so intoxicating.

I want to see where he's marked me up, and how much.

I want to see how long all of them will last.

I know that my memories will fade. I'll end up missing the details, like the little flecks of gold in those eyes. Or the way being alone like this with me makes him look softer and more vulnerable than I've ever seen him before.

"You're so beautiful, Abi."

But I won't forget the way he says my name.

Not my nickname.

My *name*.

Butterflies flood my stomach as his hand slides softly up the side of my neck, coming to rest on my cheek. My skin feels like it's made out of pure electricity as I press my forehead against his, dangling right on the precipice of my climax.

I've needed this for so long, and he can tell.

"Come for me," he begs, his voice breaking. "I know you want to."

I can feel his thighs trembling beneath mine; almost hear his thundering heart.

Or is that mine?

His cheeks are rosy pink, his eyes fluttering as beads of sweat form on his forehead.

He's so *fucking* pretty.

"Tell me everything you want to do to me," I groan.

I need it now, to hear it all. Every fantasy he's kept to himself for the last three years. Knowing Logan, he's probably gotten quite creative.

"I'm gonna fuck you every hour, until you can't even *walk*. I'm gonna eat your pussy from behind, finger your tight little asshole... God, there's so much to do; we've got a lot to catch up on, don't we?"

I forgot how much his dirty talk turns me on.

"So much for all our rules," I moan.

Logan chuckles, nuzzling against me.

"They don't matter here."

I shudder violently against him, letting my climax hit me over and over again.

He keeps fucking me harder.

"You're going to be my pretty little fuckdoll," he moans. "I want my cum dripping down those thighs."

I wish we didn't have that thin layer of latex between us, but I get it. We only have a couple of weeks, and unlike me, Logan hasn't been celibate for the last three years. Better not to ruin both of our lives over nothing.

I wrap my legs around his waist, smiling from ear to ear as he whimpers. His voice breaks and our pace becomes chaotic; the headboard slams into the wall over and over, and even wrapped up in the middle of this moment I'm pretty sure we're going to have to pay for a new one by the time we leave. With one final slam I cry out, and he lets out a loud groan of his own, trembling beneath me as he comes.

I feel him wrap his arms around me and hold me tight, nuzzling up in the afterglow.

"I forgot how hot your dirty talk was," I laugh.

Logan's all bashful now, the red in his cheeks deepening by the second. It will never surprise me how fast this man goes from sweet, unassuming nerd to an absolute animal in the bedroom, and back again.

"I read a few romance books in college. Picked up some tips."

"A few?" I laugh.

"Okay, *more* than a few. Romance is the most popular literature genre after all, right above fantasy and true crime!"

"Well, God bless your love of literacy."

"It's humanity's greatest treasure!"

Logan grins and the two of us giggle, exchanging sweet little lovers' kisses. I run my fingers through his hair and sigh as he gazes right back into my eyes. This kind of direct intimacy, so soft and quiet and unassuming, it makes it nearly impossible to keep my thoughts to myself. I just want to blurt it out.

This feels right.

I love you.

No. It's just hormones. They'll fade into the background eventually, and hopefully sooner than later if I'm going to find a way to stay sane after this trip. I climb off of him and he unrolls the condom, flinging it into the trash as I roll over and collapse next to him.

"You need help with that, Doctor?" I ask, noticing his still-hard cock standing at attention.

"Not right now," he sighs. "I don't think I have another one in me, even if this dude is ready for round two... the perks of being young and full of vigor, huh?"

"Well, since we've discovered that you're not, in fact, as ancient as the tides... there's always later. In the shower, on the desk, on the floor—"

"Right up against the window, even," he finishes with a smirk.

"Wow, you're kind of a kinky one, aren't you Flynn?"

"What can I say? I like to be a little possessive." He flashes me a charming half-smile. "And maybe use a few toys here and there."

"Oh, I remember," I laugh.

In particular, I remember when he purred in my ear about a butt plug while I was bent over the bathroom counter in Toronto. This man is so sweet and gentle with everyone in his life, so of course he's a freak in the sheets. I've learned to always watch out for the nerdy ones. They're full of surprises.

"You need water or anything?" He asks.

"Nope. Just you."

I snuggle up next to him, resting my head on his chest. His body tenses a bit underneath me, and I wonder if I've crossed a line. It just felt so natural, listening to the sound of his heart and feeling his skin against mine, especially after he gave me one of the best orgasms I've had in years. In fact, he's responsible for the top two, now that he's just dethroned himself.

To my surprise, Logan wraps his arm around me, pulling me a little closer. He turns on the TV, flipping through the channels until we find an old episode of Buffy the Vampire Slayer.

"Ooooh, it looks like a marathon!" He coos. "You wanna order food and spend the rest of the day in bed?"

"Definitely." I grin. "I'm glad we did this."

"What, sex?" He asks.

"No!" I cackle. "It's not all about sex!"

"Abi! Me and my penis are offended!"

I snicker, burying my face in his shoulder. He makes me feel like I'm a lovesick teenage girl again.

"Look, the sex is fantastic, but also the fake fiancé thing is working out pretty great. It's still kind of crazy how smooth it's gone."

"It's totally wild," Logan laughs. "But it's better than you being alone with that asshole who broke your heart."

He's smiling, but I can see the venom in his eyes. I knew Logan didn't like Brendan because of what he did to me, but this anger is a little deeper. It's clearly something he's been holding in for a while.

We watch Buffy Summers kick the shit out of vampires for a while in silence, the two of us seemingly slipping back into our own little worlds, until Logan pipes up, punctuated by a particularly audacious back-flip kick to a monster's face.

"So, tell me about where you grew up. Blackburn Falls."

I snort.

"You know everything there is to know, it's just a small town in Canada."

"Sure, but I want details! You actually don't talk about home much. I feel like Iggy and I are always yapping about New York, and it takes an hour and three drinks to get you to mention something as trivial as a street name."

"I don't know. It's a small town, there's not that much to talk about."

"Come on, who were your friends?"

I hear my phone buzz from across the room and move for it, but Logan pulls me back.

"No, stay!" He pleads.

"Logan, I need to get that!" I giggle, half-heartedly struggling against his grip.

"Yeah, but you're waaaarm, Abi!"

I manage to wriggle free and stumble toward my bag. I stand still for a moment, staring at the screen and trying to figure out exactly what I'm looking at. It doesn't take long though. If the 10 missed calls and twenty-six individual text messages weren't enough of an indicator, the most recent message, all in bold text with at least a dozen angry-face emojis, would have been the obvious giveaway.

MOM

ENGAGED?! ABIGAIL KING YOU CALL ME
RIGHT NOW!

My first thought? I can't believe I forgot to call my mom and warn her about this whole thing with Logan.

My second thought is that I know exactly who's responsible for me getting this text, and there's no setting the record straight on this one now. Of course he would run his mouth all over town, and *of course* it would get back to my mother. All people do in Blackburn is talk.

Fucking Brendan.

I swallow hard, glancing up at Logan, who quirks a brow.

"Everything good?"

"I sort of forgot to tell my mom about, um… everything?" I wince. "And I think Brendan beat me to the punch."

Logan's— is he fucking smiling?

"Logan, this is not funny."

I put my hands on my hips.

"I get to fake-propose to you in a gas station, fuck your brains out, *and* smooth things over with your mom using my devilish charm? What are the words to O Canada? Because I'm about to start belting it out."

Before I can retort, my phone starts to vibrate in my hand.

MOM CALLING...

"Fuck!" My heart drops all the way past my stomach, and I answer it without really knowing what I'm going to say. "Heeeeey, momma!"

"Abigail Autumn King, what the hell is going on? Engaged?! You didn't even call—"

Shit. Middle-named. I might as well lay down and die.

"It just happened!" I lie. "We just got caught up in—"

"Too caught up to tell your mother?!"

And then I realize she's laughing.

Why is she laughing? Is it relief? Or something else? Has this finally sent her over the edge? My stomach knots as Logan sits up in bed, stretching out his hand.

"Give me the phone."

"Absolutely not!" I hiss, partially covering it with my hand. "Mom, I'm sorry I didn't tell you. It all just happened so fast."

"Oh my God, Abi! This is the best news! A promotion and an engagement! Is he good to you? Does he have money? Is he cute?"

The questions are being thrown at me way too fast, and I'm struggling to keep everything straight in my head. I barely have time to process any of it.

Logan continues to make grabby hands at the phone, batting those thick dark lashes of his. He's so pretty it pisses me off sometimes. Mostly because it makes it really fucking hard to say no to him.

"Please?" He mouths, sticking out his bottom lip.

Fine, I mouth back.

Those damn puppy dog eyes really are my kryptonite.

"Mom, do you want to talk to him?"

"Hi, Mrs. King!" Logan shouts.

"Is that him? Oh, is it– Larry? Leonard? You know, the cute professor with the mismatched socks. The one you had a crush on!"

Logan's shit-eating grin just gets bigger.

She might as well be on speakerphone because she's talking so loud.

"You had a crush on me?"

I try to cover the mouth piece with my palm.

"You just put your dick in me and you want to have this conversation?" I hiss.

"Yes? Obviously?"

"No!"

He smirks.

"Liar."

"Abi!" My mother barks. *"Are you there? Where's this mystery man? Let me speak to him!"*

I thrust the phone out toward him, rolling my eyes. Over the years, I've learned it's just better to give my mom what she wants than to try and make excuses. He snatches it out of my hand with glee, leaning back against the headboard with one arm tucked behind him.

"Hi, Mrs. King. Yes, I *am* Abi's fiancé! So nice to meet you over the phone!"

Of course when she's talking to someone else she speaks like a human with her inside voice, pretty much impossible to make out as I strain to listen. Hopefully that devilish charm *will* smooth things over.

"I'm so sorry we didn't tell you. It kind of happened on a whim, actually." I can hear my mom chirping away on the phone as Logan's smile gets wider. "Yes, well, I love Abi very much."

Did he mean that?

My veins feel like they're filled with ice water. Sure we're into each other, but love? No, it's just a bit. Obviously he's putting on a show.

"Abi actually wanted to surprise you, but I guess she let it slip to the wrong person."

I put my head in my hands as he chuckles, nodding along with the phone crooked against his ear. They chat for way too long, enough that I've climbed back into bed well before the call is over. The lies just seem to flow effortlessly from Logan's lips, but either way things are clearly going great. According to him, he proposed to me while we were stargazing by the bay.

I glance down at my barren finger, wishing I'd bought that ring back in Banff.

This whole thing makes me wish it was real.

"Alright, Sherri. We'll see you in a few days. Yep, I'll let Abi know. Okay, bye now."

He hangs up the phone and hands it to me.

"She's very proud of you, and she's *very* excited to see the ring."

"The ring. Of course. You had to get me back for the fake fiancé thing, huh?"

"There's nothing to get you back for, Shortcake!" He laughs. "I want to meet your mom and I want to know everything about you. You're not mad, are you?"

"No," I sigh, tossing my phone down. Logan wraps his arms around me and I rest my head on his chest. "I just can't believe this is happening."

Logan kisses the top of my head.

"It's kind of fun to pretend," he confesses. "It's like we're spies who fuck."

fishin' in the dark

LOGAN

WINNIPEG, MANITOBA
PRESENT DAY

We're at a little hole in the wall country bar in Winnipeg, stuffing our faces with greasy cheeseburgers before we head back to the hotel for the night. I've gotta say, one of the biggest perks about sleeping with your road trip buddy? One bed is a hell of a lot less pricey than two.

Abi's hair is swept up into a messy half-ponytail with some curly strands framing her face. She's in an oversized dress shirt that's covered in little cartoon ghosts. All she's got on her face is some red lipstick, but even in the shitty bar lighting, she glows; the only thing dimming her shine is the contemplative look in her eyes.

"You're quiet," I murmur. "You alright?"

"Yeah... I'm just thinking."

"Would you like to tell the class?"

She rolls her eyes, dragging her french fry through a mountain of ketchup on her plate. Putting ketchup on everything is definitely her worst quality. It's simply vile, but I adore her, so I put up with it.

"I feel inadequate."

Her chin trembles.

"What do you mean?"

"I keep thinking about the reunion, and everyone's getting married and having kids. They've started their lives, and I—"

"Have a PhD, do cool research, and let's not forget you have a great job with a handsome and brilliant colleague." I gesture at her with my burger. "Your fiancé, I might add."

That ring I bought in Banff is burning a hole in my pocket, but it's not the right time.

"Okay, fair. But let's be honest, I'm not making the same kind of money as the rest of the faculty."

Academia is surprisingly competitive and demanding for how little it pays. To get ahead, you have to give some things up: sometimes it's marriage, or kids, and let's not forget your social life. It makes sense for her to be a little bitter about losing out on those things.

While everyone else is growing and changing, you feel like you're stuck at the starting line. After a while, the work becomes your solace, more like a vocation than just a job. The issue is you need that passion or it completely drains you.

"I guess I just thought I'd be further ahead by now," she sighs.

"You graduated high school, what, ten years ago?"

"Yeah."

"You know what I was doing ten years after high school graduation?"

"Writing policies and presenting findings on resources for unhoused people in New York. You know I've googled you, Logan."

I'm a little bit taken aback. I guess underselling my own achievements isn't in the cards when Abi's involved.

"Make sure you keep that Not Safe for Work search on when you do that," I joke. "That's a deep dark history you're diving into when you look into Logan Flynn."

It gets a laugh out of her despite the somber look in her eyes.

"I'm not trying to be ungrateful, but everything just seemed so clear back then. I was supposed to get married to someone I thought I really loved, and then suddenly my whole life was upended and I had to start over. Sometimes I think about all the lives I could have lived, like that multiverse theory, you know?"

"Yeah, me too."

I have so many imagined futures, but the only one I want is with her.

Except the one where I'm Batman, it's all me in that universe, baby.

"You know if you need anything..." I reach over, giving her hand a squeeze. "I'm always here."

"You've already gone above and beyond," she laughs, squeezing my hand back. "But thank you."

This is just the kind of shit we do for each other. When I landed on her doorstep the night I got stood up, she could have told me she was busy, but she dropped everything just for me. I hope she knows I'd do the same thing for her in a heartbeat.

"So, tell me more things about home." I sip my soda water. "Were you cool in high school? Maybe one of those edgy kids on the fringes?"

"God no!" She laughs. "I was a big nerd, hung out with the kids who played Dungeons and Dragons, and spent almost all my time in the library. I got picked on a lot."

"I got picked on too," I chuckle. "Any notable bullies? Mine were ridiculous."

"There were two. Carly Reynolds and Melissa Walsh. Carly started in on me when I wore the same dress as her to some stupid school dance in grade 8, and then it got worse when Brendan, who was kind of this outcast bad boy, asked me to grad."

"Grad? Like you guys brought dates to your graduation?"

"No, grad is like prom. Carly got Melissa to write *slut* on my locker, and all her little goons filled it with tampons covered in ketchup, shit like that. Then she found out about my dad's drug problem and started calling me *Junkie*. You know, as a cute little nickname."

"What a bitch."

I knew some teenage girls could be vicious, but that's going the extra mile.

"Yeah," she sighs, twisting her pint glass until it makes a ring on the table. "And now she's married to my ex."

She shrugs, biting into another fry. I wish I could say something to comfort her, but I wouldn't even know where to start. Her past is the only part of her I've never had a real connection to.

"What about you? Who was your biggest high school bully?"

"Jackson Pierce."

"Jesus, what a name. He already sounds like a prick," Abi chuckles.

"He was a football player, and like four of me across. I truly have no idea why he didn't like me, it feels like one day he just decided I was the one he was going to torment for the entirety of senior year. One day we were in gym class, last period before the end of the day. Jackson and a bunch of his buddies tackled me, stripped me naked, and filmed themselves kicking the crap out of me. They sent it to everyone at school. And I mean *everyone*."

As the words come out, I realize how much of this stuff I've pushed down over the years. I guess I'm not as well-adjusted and carefree about my past as I thought. I can still feel the sharp kicks to my ribs, and taste the grainy dirt from the football field as it clung to the blood in my mouth. I was humiliated, but I covered it up by making it all one big joke.

"Your bullies sound like they walked right out of a John Hughes movie."

"They kind of do, huh," I laugh. "I remember after that, Amanda Lisbon, who was like *the coolest* girl in school, Cheerleader, blonde, pretty and popular... the whole package. Well, Jackson dared her to ask me out, like as a joke, in front of the entire school cafeteria. It kind of crushed me. I almost didn't even go to prom after that."

"But you did, right?"

These are the moments when I wish I'd known Abi all my life. I definitely would have taken her to prom— I mean, if she wasn't ten years younger than me, and we lived in the same country.

"I ended up going though, with my friend Samantha. We were in the chess club together. Dressed up like Wizards."

She leans back in her seat, crossing her arms as nods.

"Yeah, you know what, I can see it! You do seem like a chess club sorta nerd."

"Hey!" I chuckle. "You don't get to act all holier than thou. Our high school selves were absolutely cut from the same geeky cloth."

"True, true," she sighs, starting to get that far off look in her eyes again.

I prod her under the table with my foot.

"Hey, no moping. Tell me more stuff about home."

"Why do you want to know so much?"

"Because I like learning new things, especially when they're about my favorite person."

She fiddles with her necklace, unable to keep herself from beaming. It would be so easy to cross the line. There's a part of me that wants to throw caution to the wind, be totally reckless— I mean more reckless than I'm already being. That part of me wants to say I don't give a shit about my job, I don't give a shit what the department thinks, I just want this.

But the problem is, I do care.

And that's what makes this so hard.

"Um... well, when we get there, it'll probably be hot as hell outside, but the falls cool everything down a bit." Abi smiles. "I used to spend a lot of time out there swimming with Kat, it's beautiful."

"Well, it's a good thing I packed my booty shorts, then."

"No short shorts at the reunion! That's an ass-free zone."

I put my hand on my chest, mouth agape in faux-shock.

"Even *my* ass? You would deny the world that? You've seen it in person! I'm bringing the cake!"

Abi rests her chin on her hands, shaking her head with a groan.

"Are you thinking about my ass?"

"No, you dork," she cackles, smacking me in the arm. "I'm just thinking."

She plucks one of the last fries from her plate and tears it half before popping a bit of it in her mouth.

"I was just thinking about how this whole thing's played out."

"You mean the sex? That we had together? Last night?"

As I reach over to give her hand another gentle squeeze, I notice a small crowd of people making their way onto the dance floor. Some music begins to play, a lot louder than the twangy country that had been the accompaniment to our conversation.

Abi gasps as she realizes, her eyes lighting up while she taps her fingers on the table. And then, the crowd starts to dance. All of them, dropping into form and following each other's lead.

"Is this a flash mob or something?" I shout over the music. "Do people even do those anymore?"

"I don't know!" She laughs. "But this song is great!"

She leans forward, almost like she's being pulled in that direction

"I don't know it."

"It's called Fishin' in the Dark! It's a classic!"

Abi keeps tapping on the table, bobbing her head with that cute little grin, and I can't take it anymore. This woman clearly wants to dance, and goddammit, I'll humiliate myself in front of all these people if that's what it takes.

I get to my feet.

"What are you doing?"

"You wanna dance with a mega dork who doesn't have a country bone in his body?"

"Seriously?"

"Let's boogie."

Abi lets out a little squeal, taking my hand and leading me out onto the dance floor.

She moves slowly at first, teaching me step by step. A whole PhD and I still fuck up my lefts and rights. My dad used to say I was about as coordinated as a newborn foal on ice... but then again, I had to get my dancing genes from *someone*. Let's just say this is a man who thought every song called for The Running Man.

I kind of feel like it's my first school dance, with the girl I've had a crush on for ages. You would think those teenage nerves fade over the years, but she makes me feel like that stupid, gangly kid all over again.

That's another reason it's hard to date other women, none of them make me feel the way she does. With almost everyone else, I'm putting on a front and pretending to be someone I'm not. It's taken me years to figure out the best way to live your life is spending it with your people, the ones who give you the freedom to be yourself, nerves and all.

Abi grasps my wrists, smiling up at me.

"Alright, training wheels off. Put your hands on my hips."

I let her guide me, swaying to the music as she flashes me an approving smile. It's a lot better than tripping over my own feet.

"Atta boy."

Those two words send me into a tailspin, and before I can think my lips are on hers.

Kissing Abi feels like watching the fireworks on the Fourth of July, my body fully lit up, stomach swarming with butterflies. I know to some extent this is just make-believe, but lost in this moment I just don't care.

"Sorry," she laughs as we pull apart, gliding her thumb across my lips. "I don't own any transfer-proof lipstick."

"I like it," I lean forward, nipping at her ear and slipping into my new favorite role. "But I like it even better when it's on my cock."

Abi barks out a nervous laugh, squeezing my ass almost reflexively.

"You're the Devil, Flynn."

"Don't let my Irish ancestors hear that. They hate the guy."

Suddenly, Abi gasps, cupping my face in her hands. Her eyes dance with excitement as the dance floor explodes with whoops and hollers.

"I *fucking love* Shania Twain!" Abi squeals.

"This isn't that *let's go girls* song, is it?" I ask. "Because that's the only one I know."

"No, this is better! It's called *No One Needs to Know*!"

I watch in awe as nearly the entire bar mills onto the dance floor, each and every one of them falling in line.

"Just follow everyone else's feet!" She shouts over the music. "It's easy!"

"Easy?!" I yelp, watching people tap their toes against the floor in some manner of rhythm I can't quite grasp. "Reading *Das Kapital* is easy. This is..."

"Okay, then follow *my* lead! I got this!"

She pulls me next to her as everyone moves to the side, crossing one foot over the other as they walk. Abi picks it up well, but I'm so off-beat it would be devastating in anyone else's company.

But with her?

The more I unravel about Abi, the deeper I fall for her.

But the deeper the fall, the more painful the landing.

CHAPTER THIRTY

magic dance

ABI

WINNIPEG, MANITOBA
PRESENT DAY

An hour and ten songs later, Logan and I are stumbling out the bar door, covered in sweat. I haven't had that much fun in a while, and it would be a lie to say I'm not tempted to rush back in as the music blares behind us.

"Hot damn, those cowboys know how to party! This is the shit I was looking for back in Saskatoon!"

He digs his keys out of his pocket, his cheeks bright pink as he tries to slow his breathing down to a normal rate.

"Yeah, and you didn't get punched in the face this time!" I reach over, lightly tracing one of the bruises on his cheek. "You're healing up nicely, by the way."

"Well, I had an excellent nurse."

The desire in his gaze is a little too potent, and I have to force myself to look away or risk doing something that's guaranteed to get us arrested. Luckily, the moment is quickly cut off by a series of little snapping and hissing noises at my feet. I jump back, doubly surprised to see the tiniest, *dirtiest* baby possum I've ever seen crawl out from underneath our car.

"Oh my goodness!" I stumble back a bit further as the creature hisses at me again, holding its ground like a little soldier.

Logan chuckles, crouching down to get a closer look.

"Look how cu— oh shit!" The possum lunges at him and he falls onto his ass, laughter bubbling up from his throat. "Feisty little thing, huh?"

"It's cute, but... what if it has rabies?"

"Oh, fun fact," Logan chirps as he gets back to his feet. "Possums actually have a much lower body temperature than most mammals, and it pretty much makes them immune to rabies!"

I stare at him in disbelief.

"Somehow, I'm both surprised and not surprised that you know that. It's a very confusing feeling."

He takes a few steps forward and the little guy retreats back under the car, Logan following as he crouches down to investigate.

"Where's your mom, hmm? We're not a daycare, you know. This is more of a mobile home, not great for lil' guys like you."

He slips off his shirt, carefully moving bit by bit until he's able to scoop the animal up in one quick motion. He makes a little possum-burrito, bundling it up and holding it close to his chest to keep it from struggling too much; he beams, rocking the animal from side to side as it makes its screeching protests known.

"Can you head back into the bar and see if they have a box that we can put this little pumpkin in— yes, that's you! You're the little pumpkin!" He gushes at the furious creature, who's continued to snap at him the whole time. "Yes, you're absolutely *ferocious*!"

"Sure, but I think I'm gonna poke around for the mom first. She might still be close by."

"Good idea. I'll wait here with Jr."

I rush around the small parking lot, getting down on my hands and knees to look under car after filthy car. I even trudge through some bushes at the edge with the hopes we'll find a frantic mother possum looking for her baby. Unfortunately, they're empty, which means Logan's little pumpkin might be all alone.

As I emerge, I watch him bouncing the possum up and down like a baby all while he makes dumb faces at it. I pull my phone from my bag as quickly as I can, eager to capture the moment, and snap a photo that gets sent straight to the group chat.

ME

Logan made a little friend!

ROMAN

Do the parents know this strange man has their
child? Is there an Amber Alert out?

FRANKIE

Why's he shirtless? Abi, I have a lot of concerns
right now.

ME

It's a baby possum. We just found her!

IMOGEN

CUUUUTE! Show me more pictures!!

ME

She's pretty spicy. Hissing a lot, too. Actually, I'm
not sure if this little noodle is a boy or a girl.

FRANKIE

If she's hissing at Logan, she's definitely a
woman.

IMOGEN

GOT'EM!

ROMAN

Hahahaha!

"Abi, can you go find a box?" Logan yelps. "She's wiggling!"

"Yep! Sorry!" I stuff my phone back into my pocket and run inside, heading straight for the bar.

The blonde behind the counter smiles brightly, her head whipping around fielding orders as I drum my fingers on the sticky wood, patiently waiting my turn.

"Forget something, sugar?" She asks with a smile, sliding some shots across the bar.

"I was wondering if you had a cardboard box lying around? We found this little possum out by our car and we want to... I don't know, take her somewhere? Like a vet or something?"

"Oh! Give me two seconds," she replies, rushing into the back.

I pull my phone back out while I wait, googling *what to do when you find a baby possum.*

I grumble, scrolling past the Ai-generated garbage until I get to some real results.

There we go: what to feed baby possums.

Egg yolks, yeast... goat's milk? God, this formula looks complicated, where the hell are we going to get any of this tonight? There's got to be a wildlife sanctuary close by.

"Here you go!" The bartender rushes back out, a little out of breath as she puts a small box on the counter. "Is that big enough?"

"Yes! That's perfect, thank you so much!"

I snatch the box up and quickly make my way out of the bar, googling any place we could possibly drop the baby off as I maneuver through the crush of the dance floor.

There's a local vet open 24 hours. They'll know what to do.

I step outside to find Logan is sitting in the passenger seat of the car with the possum still bundled up in his shirt. When he turns to me he's nothing but sweetness, his warm smile looking like it was right out of a movie.

And it's then I realize just how fucked I really am.

I'm in love. It's not just a fling. Well, it is, because it has to be. But I don't want that. Do I? Could it be more than that? No. We made a deal. When the trip's over, we're back to normal. We both agreed, that's the way it has to be.

I swallow everything, forcing a smile as I climb into the driver's seat.

"This might be the angriest thing I've ever held— aside from when Iggy was a baby." He holds the animal up, with only its little head poking out of his shirt. "I named her George."

"A perfect name for a perfect possum," I reply with a wry smile.

"Yeah, we thought so too." He scrunches up his nose and lets the possum grip his finger with its tiny paws. "Isn't that right, Georgie?"

"I think we should probably take *George* to a vet. There's one about 30 minutes from here and it's open 24 hours."

Logan nods, letting out a long sigh.

"Alright Georgie, you got any music requests before we're so unfairly torn from each other's arms?"

"Maybe soft jazz? Chill her out a little?"

The possum snaps at his fingers again and he chuckles, booping it on the nose.

"Jazz it is."

We arrive back at the hotel sans Logan's shirt. Turns out, George got even angrier when we tried to take her out of it, so he just let the vets keep it. I think he was happy leaving a little keepsake, but it did mean we got a few weird looks on the drive back to the motel. And another as we walked past the front office.

"What a night," he sighs, shutting the door behind us. "Line dancing and possum-napping... Canada's pretty amazing."

"Not bad for a bunch of hockey freaks who apologize all the time, eh?" I elbow him in the ribs, a little harder than usual.

Logan chuckles, wrapping his arms around me and pressing his forehead against mine. A wayward curl falls in front of his face and I brush it away. I don't want anything to keep me from seeing those eyes.

"I'm gonna take a shower." He slides his fingers underneath my shirt, gently grazing my skin until I feel goosebumps forming. "You in, King?"

"Yep! I mean... I would love that, yeah."

My heart races, eyes trailing up and down his body. He's less lean than when we first met, especially since he started developing some real muscle lifting weights with Frankie.

I lick my lips, slowly stripping off my own tank top and leggings.

It's been so long since I've wanted someone to really drink me in like this.

"You like what you see?"

He's blushing furiously, holding up his fingers in the shape of a camera.

"Fucking gorgeous," he purrs, clicking the imaginary shutter.

I grin, shimmying out of my panties and toss my bra somewhere behind me as I strut toward him. His arm winds around my waist and he pulls me close, brushing a strand of hair away from my eyes just like I did for him.

"I mean that, you know. You're stunning. It's hard not to look at you someti—"

I kiss him before he can finish, my eagerness overwhelming me. These little slivers of honesty are almost too much for my brain to handle. I need him. Now.

He leads me to the shower, making sure the water is hot enough before stripping off the rest of his clothes. I follow him in, still holding his hand, and we dissolve into more sweet kisses as the water washes over us. His soft hands roam all over my body, mapping out each of the spots on my skin that make me gasp or giggle. At this point I don't think it'll be long before he's memorized them all.

His mouth is all smoothness and warmth; when he uses his teeth, it's only to tease. He kisses the way I've always wanted to be kissed: slow, sensual, and fiery. His cock stiffens against my thigh as he tears his mouth away from mine, only to let it ghost down my neck and along my collarbone. Kisses trail down to my nipples, and I have to lean against the wall for support as he stops to suck and tease until I'm a squirming mess. It feels like everything this man does makes my knees wobble.

Logan pulls back, his chest heaving as the steam curls around us like smoke. I start to press my own soft kisses against his chest, working my way all the way down to hips.

His breath stutters, cock straining next to me as his fingers swim through my hair.

"You're a little tease," he groans.

I slip my tongue along the indent in his hips, batting my eyelashes as I gaze up at him. Water drips off the tips of his hair, trickling down his shoulders. He's nearly angelic, but the look in his eyes is pure filth.

"Don't tell me you don't like it, Sunshine," I purr before wrapping my hand around the base of his cock and giving it a firm squeeze.

His eyes roll, his head rocking backward, as I start to stroke him. Slow. Teasing. Flicking out my tongue to lick the crown.

"I do. Oh, fuck, I really do."

He's pulsing in my hand, soft moans spilling from his inner depths. He's so beautiful like this, and even more knowing he's completely at my mercy. I didn't think I had a dominant streak in me, but there's something about Logan that makes me feel safe enough to try taking control.

I push myself up higher, letting a string of saliva dribble from my mouth and onto the head of his cock, and he lets out a deep and husky groan that sends a warm tingle down my spine. I give him a few more languid strokes, turning my hand in a slight corkscrew motion as I work. I can tell he likes this move a lot, particularly by the way his grip on my hair is tightening by the second.

"You want me to suck your cock?" I ask, my voice coming out raspy and low.

Logan nods and I wrap my hand around him more firmly, giving him a squeeze.

"Be a good boy and ask nicely."

"Please." His voice breaks halfway through the word and he sucks in another breath. "Let me fuck your mouth."

I giggle, spitting on his cock one more time and watching it drip onto the shower floor.

"Good boy. All you had to do was ask."

The flush in his cheeks is creeping into his neck and down his chest. When Logan blushes, his whole body turns red. I think it might be the thing I love most about having sex with him... other than his filthy mouth. And maybe a couple other key elements.

I circle the crown with the tip of my tongue before sucking gently on it like a lollipop. Tiny, little pulses that make him shiver above me.

"Can I try something?" Logan asks, his chest heaving. "Not that I'm not having a great time, I just got an idea."

I release him, arching a brow as I look up from my spot, kneeling on the floor.

"I'm listening."

"Put your arms over your head?"

I raise them and he immediately pins them to the wall behind me, fingers wrapped tightly around both wrists without an ounce of hesitation. He guides his cock up to my lips and slowly pushes himself into my mouth. I choke a little and he stops, using one hand to stroke my face as he studies me.

"Just relax for me, okay? I'm gonna be so good to you, Shortcake."

It's the most romantic thing a man has ever said to me with his dick in my mouth, which I know isn't a high bar, but still. I groan as he pushes a little deeper, hitting the back of my throat. It's hard to relax and breathe through it when my cunt aches for attention. I need to be touched.

Fucked.

Hard.

Saliva dribbles down my chin, tears already gathering in my eyes, but I don't dare look away from him. He's quite the sight, water glistening off his skin in the low light, accentuating the muscles he's been working so hard on.

"You like this?" He groans. "When I use you like a toy?"

A choked moan is the only response I can manage, goosebumps covering my body. I don't know if it's his cock jammed down my throat or the way he's talking to me that's turning me on more.

His hips move faster, the pace growing more frenzied by the second.

"I'm gonna come— shit!" He pulls himself all the way out and starts to stroke his cock hard and fast. "Open your mouth and stick out your tongue."

I do as I'm told, a mixture of water and sweat rushing down my face as Logan's twists up in ecstasy. I love the way he looks when he's just about to come, darkened eyes and apple red cheeks, all surrounded by the messy hair that's stuck to his face.

I watch him stroke himself, the veins in his forearm beginning to pop as he picks up the pace. I want to touch myself so badly it hurts, but I'm doing as I'm told.

All I can do is dig my nails into my palms as my body begs for release.

With a final grunt of my name, hot ropes of cum land on my cheek and my tongue, but Logan barely takes the time to enjoy his climax before he hauls me to my feet and slides a hand between my thighs. My back arches the second his fingers slip inside of me, curling and stroking my G-spot. I'm in fucking heaven as he stretches me wider, digging my nails into his back as he goes. He glides his lips along my jaw, licking his own cum off my face before crashing his mouth against mine. Everything about this is frenzied, horribly messy yet tender.

Heat begins to build in my stomach and hips, slowly wrapping around me as it cascades down my legs. My body feels like jelly, but Logan holds me up straight, only tearing his mouth away from mine to nip at my ear.

"Come for me," he purrs, sliding a third finger inside of me. "Be a good girl, and I'll spend the rest of the night making you scream."

The sound I let out is pathetic, jumbled words with his name thrown somewhere in there. At least, I think that's what I'm saying. My head is so fuzzy, it's hard to think about anything else besides how it all feels. Every touch, every kiss, just like that first night.

Until I'm a panting, quivering mess.

CHAPTER THIRTY-ONE

space oddity

ABI

EMERALD BAY UNIVERSITY

FALL, 2021

He teaches here.

The guy I haven't been able to stop thinking about *teaches here*.

You know that episode of Friends where Ross keeps repeating he's fine, but he's really not fine? That's what I'm going through right now.

I'm Ross.

Back when we met we agreed on first names only, and we didn't talk much about our personal lives. Even promised we wouldn't look for each other online.

And now... I really thought that drink with Logan was going to clear my head, but all it did was make things more complicated. I'm totally fine with being friends, I just... Having to tell him that we couldn't be anything more made me feel a little nauseous, but I really need this fresh start.

And now I have to pick myself up and be peppy and upbeat. It's the mask I put on, and I've been doing it my whole life: smile, even when you're falling apart. I think I probably picked it up from my mom.

I check my watch. The meeting to officially sign my contract starts in 5 minutes, and then I get to sit in on my first ever department meeting at EBU. No way I'm gonna be late for that.

The lobby is a big, open space, with sunshine pouring over the students making their way to and from classes, or huddled together at a couple small tables in the corner, working on assignments. It kind of reminds me of my days at U of T, working late into the night on papers and group projects with other researchers who were just as passionate as me.

I turn and head for the elevators, hoping to reach Dr. Hughes' office with approximately two minutes to spare, but as I'm striding toward them the doors begin to close.

"Oh! Hold it, please!" I squeak, making a mad dash.

These fucking boots were a terrible choice; my feet are aching with every step, but I manage to catch the doors just before they close and slip inside. There's only one other person in the elevator with me. The man is around Logan's height, but much bigger, with a long straight nose, salt and pepper hair, and a matching beard. He's dressed in a tight navy t-shirt that shows off some tattoos, distressed black jeans, and cowboy boots.

"Sorry," he murmurs, briefly giving me the once-over. "I didn't see you."

"No, it's my fault. It's my first day, I'm still kind of figuring out the campus."

"Ah," he replies softly. "You're the postdoc?"

"How did you know?"

"Because I was on the search committee." He extends his hand, grinning from ear to ear. "Roman Burke. Pleasure to meet you."

"Abi King!" I chirp, grasping his hand and shaking it a little too enthusiastically. "But you... probably already knew that."

Roman chuckles as we both awkwardly pull our hands away, and he leans over to press the button for the Sociology floor.

"How's your first week treating you?" He asks.

"Pretty good so far! I accidentally spilled coffee on Dr. Flynn on my first day visiting, though."

He snorts.

"Well, I'm sure it wasn't entirely your fault. Dr. Gumby might be a sociology whiz, but his spatial awareness needs serious work." He sighs. "General awareness, actually. He almost got run over by a cyclist last week."

"Thank God it wasn't me."

"Well, it could have been worse," He laughs, leaning up against the wall.

I can feel an awkward silence coming on, and I figure it's as good a time as any to step out of my comfort zone. How else am I going to become more outgoing?

"How long have you worked here?"

"A long time," he replies with a curt smile.

There's a sadness in his eyes that I can't quite figure out, but before I can think about it any deeper, the elevator dings for our floor.

"I'll walk you to Frankie's office. It's right next to mine."

"Oh, thank you!"

I follow Roman down the hall, keeping close like a kid on their first day of school. I know I've only known him for approximately two minutes, but I kind of like him. At the bare minimum, he's not talking down to me.

"So, you're an anthropologist?"

"Yeah— well, I was. I did my MA in sociology, though."

"I know," Roman replies. "I read your stuff."

"You did?"

"Sure," he chuckles. "You've got a lot of ambition, and a good amount of talent to back it up."

Before I can say anything else, we've stopped in front of a closed door near the end of the hall, and he offers me his hand again.

"It was great to meet you, Dr. King."

"You can call me Abi," I murmur.

"You can call me Roman."

His shake is firm, but there's some real tenderness to it as well. I have a feeling this guy's a big softie underneath it all. Sometimes I just get a good read on people.

Like I did with Logan.

Shit, no time for that right now.

Roman gives me a quick wave as he disappears into his office, leaving me alone in the hall. I glance at Dr. Hughes' door, noticing after about a minute of waiting that it's actually slightly cracked. I draw in a deep breath and give a gentle enough knock not to accidentally shove it open.

"Come in!"

I push the door open, and immediately spot Dr. Hughes at his desk, hunched over and typing madly on his phone. It's another minute or two before he glances up, his eyes sparkling when he sees me.

"Hey, Dr. King! Sorry about the wait, recently I've found myself pretty easily distracted."

"Dr. Hughes, hi–"

He raises his hand, cutting me off.

"Call me Frankie, Dr. Hughes makes me feel like I'm a hundred years old, now come in, come in!"

His phone chimes and he returns to it briefly, snorting with derision before stashing it in his desk drawer.

"Sorry. Department stuff. You want coffee or anything? I don't have a machine, but I'm not above breaking into Dr. Burke's office to use his Keurig."

I really like Frankie— actually, I like everyone I've met at EBU so far. They're professional and warm, which is rare to find in the workplace these days. Everyone's so obsessed with productivity in this capitalist hellscape, it's nice to get a breath of fresh air every once in a while.

"Oh, no. I'm staying away from coffee. I accidentally spilled Dr. Flynn's on him last time we had a chat. So... Red Bulls only."

God, why do I keep bringing him up?

"Oh, you got to meet the human tornado that is Logan Flynn," Frankie laughs, leaning back in his seat. "And what's the verdict?"

My face goes hot *immediately*. I don't want to say anything that could compromise my contract, or get Logan in trouble. This whole thing with us could be a big conflict of interest and I'd rather just pretend it never happened.

"Well, I was very apologetic and he doesn't seem to hate me," I reply, trying not to make my anxiety too obvious.

I've gotten good at hiding it over the years, primarily behind a big, forced smile.

Yeah, I can do that extra work.

No, everything's just fine at home.

Seriously. It's all fine.

"Well, that's good. Logan's good people. I'm sure you'll get used to his antics in a few months." He slides a file folder across his desk. "Anyway, this is your teaching contract, your postdoc research contract, your salary contract— I tried to negotiate for something a little higher but the budget committee is…"

Frankie rolls his eyes.

"Red tape," I mutter. "I understand."

My salary isn't great, but it'll keep a roof over my head, food in my belly, and give me a few extra dollars to thrift some clothes. It's not like I have kids or a mortgage to pay or anything. There's a part of me that wishes it actually was more of an issue, that I had a bit more going on, but I try not to think about it too much as my pen glides across each page.

After a few minutes of signatures, and another fruitless couple pretending to read the fine print of the contracts, I slide the papers into the folder and pass it back to Frankie.

"Perfect!" He checks his watch, nodding to himself. "Well, why don't I show you your office. Sorry if it's a little cluttered. I told Dr. Barnes to get his shit out of there, but he's taking his time."

"Oh, it's really no trouble. I actually expected to share space with the PhD students."

"If you're going to teach a class, you're not holding office hours in a shared space," he replies firmly.

To tell the truth, I didn't think I'd even *have* an office, but one of Frankie's emails said there was a small, quiet space available for me to work out of, and I'd be lying if I said I wasn't excited as I follow him out of the room and down a long hallway.

"You're right down the hall from Dr. Flynn," Frankie informs me, sliding the key into the lock and pushing the door open. "And right next to Dr. Janine Rogers."

"Domestic violence research, correct?"

Frankie grins.

"You looked into us?"

"As many of you as I could," I reply. "I like to know the people I'm working with."

"Well, that's great, because you'll get the chance to tell the department all about yourself at the meeting." He pauses, reigning himself in. "Actually, sorry to spring that on you. It's just that the timing's pretty perfect, so I figured..."

"Don't worry, I kind of assumed you'd be pulling out the icebreaker," I laugh as we step inside the office.

Frankie was right, it's small, but it's kind of perfect. Dr. Barnes even left a couple of plants hanging by the window, and there's an empty bookshelf or two waiting to be filled. I'm already itching to cover my brand new desk with a bunch of my kitschy knick knacks, all the stuff that keeps my brain on-task while I'm trying to read or write.

"It's not much, but it's quiet, and most importantly you'll be able to actually have confidential meetings with students."

I take a moment to breathe it all in.

A brand new job, and a brand new space just for me.

"Thanks, Frankie. This is really kind of you."

"You know, I was just about to bring up how we're a family here? But then I remembered how much I hated it when they said that shit at some of my old jobs." He leans forward, grinning. "That said... we *are* kind of a family here. In a weird, really dysfunctional sort of way."

He checks his watch.

"Ah, shit. The meeting's starting in a few minutes. You sure you don't want a coffee or anything?"

"I'm really okay."

"Alright, let's keep this train rollin'!"

Roman is already seated, cradling a book in his hands as we step into the conference room. And right next to him? Logan fucking Flynn.

My heart leaps into my throat, my body seemingly anticipating a shitload of awkwardness. We had a good talk earlier, played some pool, and I walked away with a budding friendship. I should feel good about that, if only I could get the butterflies in my stomach to calm down whenever I look at him.

"Hey, Abi!" He chirps, waving me over.

"Hey!" I manage to squeak out, raising both hands. "No coffee to spill on you today, sorry."

Roman snickers, briefly giving me a wave before returning to his book.

I glance around the room, noting the only real furniture is a small-ish table and a few scattered chairs surrounding it.

Logan pulls one closer to him, gesturing to it.

"Here. Now you can sit with the cool kids."

His eyes are a little puffy, the dark circles only slightly obscured by his horn-rimmed glasses, and combined with his chaotic sandy blond hair it makes him look like he's just rolled out of bed.

One of the things that first drew me to Logan was the fact that he dresses like an accountant, running straight to a second not-so-secret job at Spirit Halloween. It shouldn't work, but he makes it look effortless.

"So, how was your first week?"

Frankie is busying himself setting up for the meeting while some of the other faculty come strolling in, so there can't be any harm in chatting a little bit.

"Not half bad. I got an office!" I clear my throat, trying not to blush. "Right, uh... next to yours, actually."

"I'll make sure not to blast my late night party tunes too loud."

"Why, do you listen to death metal or something?" I snicker.

"Nothing that refined. I'm down in the pits with some Beethoven."

"Alright," Frankie announces. "Can I have everyone's attention please?"

"Unlikely," Roman replies flatly, flipping the page in his book.

"Thank you, Dr. Asshole," Frankie quips, not missing a beat. "Abi, I don't know if you've met our local ray of sunshine, Dr. Roman Burke?"

Roman rolls his eyes, leaning toward me.

"Frankie has a condition where everything he says sounds sarcastic." He nods, his tone somber. "Don't pay too much attention to him."

"Okay, can we focus?!" Frankie snaps, clapping his hands. "We've got a lot to get through a lot today. First off, I want to introduce our brand new postdoc, Dr. Abigail King. She's come all the way from Blackburn Falls, Ontario to join us."

There's a small round of applause from the other faculty members; it makes me feel like I'm at a restaurant and my mom just told the staff it was my birthday.

"Abi, why don't you introduce yourself to the department?"

I clear my throat, getting to my feet.

"Hi, I'm Abi. I went to the University of Toronto for my master's in sociology and my PhD in anthropology. I did most of my doctoral work at a safe injection site near Belleville, Ontario."

"Any particular reason?" Roman asks, the book he was reading now resting against his chest as he looks up at me.

"It's been the topic of a lot of controversy, so I wanted to get up close and personal with the people who work there. The goal of my research was to look at communities who have been hit hard by the opioid crisis and to see what kind of access they had to long-term harm reduction facilities like safe injection sites. I found that neighborhoods that didn't have access saw higher overdose, arrest, and death rates. Right now we don't treat drug users as people, we treat them as something to be discarded, and what we really need are long-term, community-focused solutions."

I take a deep breath, slowly letting it out as I survey the room. Whenever I talk about my research, I get emotional. I thought that going into this field would help me better understand my father's struggles; I spent so long being angry with him but over the course of my life, my work made me more empathetic.

Even if that empathy hurts sometimes.

"Right on," Frankie murmurs, scribbling something in his notebook. "Was this participatory research?"

"Yes. I volunteered at the center and drew my sample size from there. I had about twenty people who were willing to sit down and talk to me."

"We could use work like that out here. Seattle's getting hit hard and it's tough to watch," Logan chimes in.

"Yeah, actually I, uh, I was looking into overdose rates. The number of deaths in King County alone has grown significantly in the last few years."

Frankie stares at me, and I swear I see a hint of pride in his face—either that or I'm projecting my massive need for approval.

"Anyway, I'm really looking forward to getting to know everyone and, uh, teaching as well. I'm—" I blush, my nerves kicking in full-force. "Uh, thank you."

There's another, shorter round of applause as I take my seat again, and Logan glances over at me, that bright smile of his not even slightly faded.

"I'd love to pick your brain on your methodology," he murmurs. "Maybe tomorrow over lunch?"

I can't.

I shouldn't.

"That sounds great."

paper rings

ABI

BLACKBURN FALLS, ONTARIO
PRESENT DAY

We decided I would drive this morning. After all, I know the way to Blackburn Falls like the back of my own hand, which has the added benefit of letting me take the scenic route. Logan gets to sleep, but more importantly, I get to think.

Think about how my mother is going to meet my fake fiancé.

How my *friends* are going to meet my fake fiancé.

How my ex is going to—

No, we're not going there right now.

As I burn past the *Welcome to Blackburn Falls* sign, a knot begins to form in my stomach. Just like Emerald Bay, it takes about 40 minutes to walk from one end of town to the other. It's filled with white picket fences, manicured lawns, and little shops that are straight out of a Hallmark movie, but coming back still somehow always feels like a funeral. I grew up in this place, had the best and worst days of my life here, and seeing it all again feels like I'm gonna be pretty much forced into reminiscing.

I spot my mom's house at the edge of Prior Street, a little green and white rancher with an emerald lawn that shines like a jewel. The sun spilling down adds to the picturesque look, which contrasts with some of my less than perfect memories.

"Sunshine," I kill the engine, giving him a quick shake. "We're here."

Logan lifts his head, rubbing his eyes as he tries to figure out exactly where he is.

"God, I feel like I just went to sleep."

"You've been out for a couple of hours, it's—"

The front door of my mom's house slams open and she's already on her way down the steps towards us. She looks gorgeous, dressed up in a flowing blue and white floral skirt that's draped all the way down to her ankles, and a tank top that shows off the little tattoo she got for me when I earned my PhD. It's a rose with *Dr. Abigail King* written in the banner below it. I'll never get tired of that.

"Baby!" My mom shrieks, practically launching herself at the car.

The second I lift myself out she's on me, kissing every inch of my face until I can't help but laugh.

"It's good to see you, momma!"

"Oh, it's so good to see you too! You look so *beautiful!*" She steps back, gripping my shoulders tightly as she glances down at my barren hand. The left one. "Where's the ring?"

Have you ever been so afraid your whole body clenches and could swear your asshole might just whistle?

Because that's me right now.

We forgot to get a fucking ring.

"Oh, that's my bad!" Logan calls out, dragging our suitcases up the driveway. "I've been holding onto it!"

When I turn around he's already searching his pockets, his eyes gleaming with mischief as he reaches behind my ear with one swift motion.

"I put it here for safe keeping."

I have to hold back my gasp when he opens his palm. It's the ring I pointed out all the way back in Banff. He went back for it.

"We had to get it resized and polished, and I guess we just forgot to put it back where it belongs."

He smiles at me, with a look that practically screams *now don't mess this up*, but there's more weight to it than that.

"Sorry, my love. I totally forgot to remind you."

"No, it's my fault, I forgot to ask," I chuckle, still a little bit nervous.

"That looks just like Baba's ring," my mom gasps. "Is that amethyst?"

I've never seen Logan this proud of himself before, at least if we don't count the time he took a flying tackle at Frankie during a 'friendly' game of touch football.

Well, it was supposed to be touch football.

"Yes, ma'am. Abi said she didn't want diamonds, and who am I to deny a woman in love?" He winks at me, sliding it onto my finger. "Look at that, a perfect fit."

At this point I think Baba *must* be working some magic from beyond the grave, because that ring looks like it belongs on my hand.

"You have impeccable taste, Doctor Flynn," my mom grins, patting him on the shoulder.

"Doctor was my dad's name," he beams. "You can call me Logan."

"Well, you're free to call me mom if you'd like, since you're marrying my little girl and all."

She has that little warble in her voice that tells me she's about to cry, and I realize for the first time how painful this lie might end up being, but for now he doesn't even hesitate.

"You got it, ma."

Brendan never called her mom. In fact, he didn't seem to like my mother much. I think he resented our closeness, just like he resented my career, my accomplishments, my ambition...

All this time it's been a knife, sitting deep in my chest, just waiting to twist.

"Okay, let's get you kids settled into the guest house. I've got dinner in the oven."

"Sounds good!" Logan chirps, picking up our bags with ease before my mom leads us around the back of the house.

The yard is beautiful, brimming with big pink and white rose bushes, gorgeous blue hydrangeas, a pool, and my mom's big fluffy calico lounging next to it. Good thing I stocked up on allergy pills before we got here.

"Holy shit," Logan murmurs. "This is amazing, Mrs. King! And who's that beautiful beast by the pool?"

"That's Joan. I named her after—"

"Joan Jett?" Logan asks with a hopeful gasp.

"Joan Didion, actually," my mom laughs. "She's my favorite writer."

"Oh, just as cool! I think I must have read *The White Album* at least ten times when I was a teenager."

"Alright Abi," my mom smiles, leading us to the guest house. "This one's a keeper."

The building's about the size of a one bedroom apartment, tucked into the very back of the yard. For a couple of years before I graduated high school, mom actually let me move in as a kind of dress rehearsal for getting my own place.

As we reach the door, my mom digs two sets of keys out of her pocket, presenting them to us.

"You're welcome to stay as long as you want, but I don't expect you to spend all your time with little old me. Tonight though, I'm calling mom-dibs. Now if you'll excuse me, I've gotta pull the pot roast out of the oven and get started on the veggies."

"You need help in the kitchen, ma?" Logan calls back to her, hauling our suitcases inside the guest house.

Even though he's just putting on a show, it still makes my heart flutter. I glance at my mother who has her hand on her chest, looking very charmed.

"Why don't you two get settled, and then maybe Logan could help me chop up some of the veggies for the salad?"

"You got it, I'll be back in two shakes!"

She gives my shoulders a squeeze.

"He's gorgeous, he's polite, and he wants to help out in the kitchen?"

"He's a pretty good cook, too," I mutter.

My mom's smile just gets wider. She knows he's ticking all the boxes.

"Well, maybe we can strong arm him into making dinner for us one night."

"I don't think you need to strong arm Logan into anything," I laugh. "I'm pretty sure he'd clean your whole house just to impress you."

"You know, that could actually be relaxing." She gently boops my nose. "But for now, you two focus on getting settled. Oh, before I forget, I found your old swimsuit when I was cleaning the guest house. The red one with the white polka dots."

I don't think I've worn that thing since I was 21. I found it at a thrift store in Kingston and fell in love with it immediately. It was the bathing suit that made me realize I could both look good and *feel* good in a two-piece.

"It's still here?"

"You know I never throw anything of yours away." She kisses me on each cheek. "It's so good to have you home, baby."

"It's good to be home."

Mom struts toward the house, leaving me standing in front of our temporary home, just as Logan pokes his head outside, grinning from ear to ear.

"What're you smiling about?"

"Nothing, I just heard all those nice things your mom had to say about me." His smile grows wider. "Gorgeous *and* polite?"

"Never heard her string those two together in a sentence before, and I don't know... looking at you now? Maybe her eyesight's getting a little bad in her old age."

"Oh, you're fucking hilarious, King. Now come check out this house!"

It's just as small as I remember, but the interior's gotten slightly more modern since the last time I stayed here. A king size bed has replaced my old shitty twin and the sheets are a soft silky material that feels like butter on my palm.

The walls are filled with pictures of me and mom, me and Kat, and even a few pictures of my mom and dad. My chest tightens, but before I can feel an ounce of grief, Logan squeezes my shoulders.

"So... I saw the bikini," he purrs.

I roll my eyes. This man's libido is through the roof.

"Oh, you did, did you?"

He grabs my swimsuit off the dresser and holds it up to me, his eyes glittering with mischief. I forgot how tiny those triangles were; I don't know if they'll hold my boobs anymore.

"Can I say something crass?"

"Hit me with it."

He wraps one arm around my waist.

"I really can't wait to fuck you in this thing."

"Behave yourself."

"When have I ever done that?" He asks, playfully tossing the bathing suit back on top of the dresser.

We take in the rest of the guest house together as we start to unpack.

All my posters are gone, mostly replaced with paintings and photographs of the main Blackburn attractions. The Silver Oaks trail, the old berry farm, the pumpkin patch, and of course the falls themselves, surrounded by lush trees.

The only remnant of my past still present is a Nosferatu poster that my mom bought for my 15th birthday. It's hanging above the bed, only now it's been upgraded with a slick black frame.

"The last time I was here, that poster was barely hanging on for dear life. I think it may be the only thing that survived my youth other than my Metallica t-shirt."

Logan gives me a quick kiss on my temple.

"You know why we became best friends?" He asks.

"Are you going to say it's because I own a Nosferatu poster? Because that's kind of weird."

"The poster helps, but no," he chuckles. "It's because when I'm with you, I feel like I've known you for like 30 years. It felt that from moment-one."

"I feel it too," I whisper.

Sometimes when I'm telling him a story about something stupid that happened in high school, I catch myself before I say, *'Come on, you remember,'* but of course, he couldn't. Some people are so ingrained in our souls that it feels like they've just always been there.

Logan looks down at me, and this time I can tell there's something forlorn behind his eyes. I wonder how many different futures he has planned for us in different universes. I wish I could see them all.

"What's wrong?" I ask.

"Nothing," he murmurs. "Just... sometimes I forget that this isn't real."

"It's real for the rest of this trip." I reach up and cup his cheek. "Okay?"

The sunlight hits my ring, the glittering gem catching my eye, and I stop to stare at it for a moment. I can't believe he actually bought it.

"So, you went back to that store to buy me the ring?"

"Of course I did. It means a lot to you." His eyes dance around my face, blinking rapidly the way he does when his nerves start getting the best of him. "You can return it if you want. I kept the receipt."

"Why would I want to do that?" I ask, placing my hand on his chest. "You did something incredibly sweet, Logan."

I can feel his hummingbird heartbeat begin to slow a little.

"Just trying to be a good friend."

"How about you let me pay for half of it when we get back?"

In an instant, the anxiety on his face melts away.

"I accept Visa, Venmo, and blowjobs."

"Oh!" I laugh, shoving him backward. "You do, do you, asshole?"

In seconds Logan's pinned me to the mattress, peppering kisses up and down my neck. I squeal with laughter, kicking my legs as I try to escape his iron grip. For a skinny dude, he's shockingly strong.

"You adore me! Admit it!"

"No!" I howl as he tickles my sides, my body reflexively trying to curl in on itself. "You're a menace!"

I'm laughing to the point of tears as Logan alternates between assaulting my ribs and kissing my neck, which of course *also* tickles. I haven't laughed like this in years: loud, riotous, and totally unrestrained.

"All you have to do is say iiiit!" He sings.

"Never!"

I try to get the advantage, sliding out from underneath him, but he grasps me by the waist and rolls onto his side. In an instant, we're falling off the bed, each of us letting out a loud yelp as we come crashing down. Luckily for me, I end up on top of Logan, and manage to scramble upright first, straddling his hips as our chests heave in unison.

"Admit it," he rasps.

It doesn't look like he's joking anymore. I can't tell if my heart is pounding because of our play fighting, or something else.

"I adore you."

He lets out a growl, pulling me back down on top of him and into a fiery kiss.

"You promised you'd help my mom with dinner," I murmur as he begins to suck on my earlobe.

"And I never break my promises, but I'm 100% sure I can make you come in three minutes or less."

I raise a brow.

"Prove it, tough guy."

That cocky grin returns as his hands slip up and rest on my hips.

"Your clit has 10,281 nerve endings and I know exactly how you like to be licked."

I grind down on his cock just to make him squirm.

"Unfortunately, I think those 10,281 nerve endings are going to have to wait until after dinner."

His face twists up in only partially feigned agony, and I can't help but giggle.

"Fine, but I can't do dinner with a raging hard on," he laughs, rolling us onto our sides. "Get your cute ass off me."

Logan changes into a tight black t-shirt that does nothing to quell my less-than-pure thoughts toward him. He's always been self conscious of his lanky frame, dressing in layers to look more filled out than he actually is. But I've always liked men who are lean, tall, and at least a little gangly. I could look at him all day, from that perfectly messy hair all the way down to my favorite part of him:

His hands.

They drive me crazy. The tattoos on his knuckles, his pinky ring, and his *fingers*? My god. I don't know how many times I used to imagine them touching me in all the places I know they shouldn't.

"Whatcha lookin' at?" Logan teases. "I usually charge per hour."

"Nothing special," I mutter. "Just your hands."

"Hmm." He glances down, stretching out his fingers as he admires them. "I should probably put them to good use, huh?"

I strut over to him, getting right up in his face as I begin to play with the button on his jeans. We might have a little extra time after all.

"Maybe you should."

"Yeah..." He breathes, his voice as deep and sultry as it can get. "By chopping veggies, right?"

I roll my eyes and Logan lets out a howl of laughter.

"Awww, look who doesn't like the taste of her own medicine!"

I feign a few playful jabs to his gut and he doubles over, holding his stomach as he staggers backward with all the drama of community-theatre Shakespeare.

"Oh Shortcake, you're in trouble now."

Then, he's off like a bullet, darting out of the house as I chase after him.

"Mrs. King! Mrs. King! Abi's bullying me!"

no one needs to know

LOGAN

BLACKBURN FALLS, ONTARIO
PRESENT DAY

"Logan, honey, could you pass me the ladle beside you— Abigail Autumn King, don't you *dare* touch that gravy!"

Sherri nearly sloshes her wine onto the counter as she tries to grab the pot away from her daughter.

"It's burning!" Abi laughs, giving the gravy a rebellious stir.

Her mom bumps her with her hip, pointing at the kitchen table.

"Stop getting in the way and sit down! When you want to move back in, then you can help out in the kitchen, but for now you're a guest in this house."

Roman would be horrified at the level of disorganization, but to me, it feels pretty close to home. Sherri reminds me a lot of my mom, right down to the absolute chaos occurring both on and around the stove. Flecks of gravy spattered like paint, remnants of chopped onion, carrot, and the discarded skins of garlic litter the space.

I'm trying my hardest to clean as I go, in between chopping veggies for the salad, handing her things, and listening to forks and spoons hit the floor with a loud clang.

"Why is Logan helping then?" Abi counters, putting her hands on her hips.

"Because he volunteered. Besides, I still remember the Thanksgiving incident, missy."

I turn around just in time to catch Abi rolling her eyes as she sinks into her chair.

"That was *one* Thanksgiving, and technically? It was your fault, mom."

"What happened?" I ask, dumping some carrot tops into the compost bin.

"I read the temperature in the recipe wrong, and set the oven to celsius instead of Fahrenheit. Mom even checked it and she said—"

"That's perfect, dear!" Sherri chimes in, snickering into her wine glass as the two reminisce.

"Let's just say we hit 9:00 o'clock and the bird was practically charcoal, so we ordered sushi. By our powers combined, we ruined Thanksgiving."

"We didn't *totally* ruin Thanksgiving!" Sherri exclaims as she spoons the gravy into a boat. "We still had the stuffing, candied yams, and green beans! It was just a little less traditional. Don't forget, that tuna sashimi was to die for."

Abi fiddles with a fork while her mom takes the pot roast out of the oven.

"We're almost ready to eat!" Sherri announces. "Logan, how's— Oh! The salad looks amazing! What's in it?"

"Arugula I found in the fridge, some candied walnuts from the pantry, goat cheese, cucumber for a little bit of freshness, dried cranberries, and some very thinly sliced carrots and radish."

Roman first taught me about how to throw a salad together when he found out that, up until we met, I had basically been existing off of coffee, diet coke, and sour patch kids. In my defense, it was my first year teaching a full course load and I was drowning in a sea of last minute essays and exams. In *his* defence, it was still pretty disgusting.

Sherri pats me on the shoulder.

"Excellent work, sweetheart."

"Thanks, ma!"

We plate everything, quickly settling into our seats for the first bite of pot roast.

"Holy shit, mom, this gravy is incredible," Abi mutters, licking some off of her thumb.

"Baba's recipe is timeless," Sherri replies, cutting into her meat. "So's her ring, apparently. I still can't believe you two found one just like it."

I can't help but feel a little proud of myself that I went back to that store.

"So, Logan, Abi's told me you lecture at universities across the country, *and* you publish books?"

"Yes, ma'am," I mumble through a mouth full of food.

"He's done a Ted Talk too."

"But you're so young! When did you graduate high school?"

"Oh, I was 15," I reply.

"Brilliant," I catch Sherri whisper to herself. "Abi was out early too, at 16. You must have been made for each other."

I take a sip of my wine, willing the heat rising up my neck to stay down.

Most of the time, I don't feel particularly smart— or even that accomplished. Regardless of how many milestones I clear, or things I get published, imposter syndrome haunts me on an hourly basis. There are people in this field who have CVs miles longer than mine, after all.

"Logan's a methodology wizard. There isn't a question he can't answer."

"And Abi's a theory Queen, so we work well together."

"And what does your work revolve around?" Sherri asks.

"Medically assisted death. Stigma, taboo, and everything that goes into it," I reply.

"Wow, that's... a weighty topic."

"Originally I was going to do big longitudinal study with unhoused youth, and then my dad got brain cancer. It changed the entire trajectory of my life."

It's gotten much easier to talk about my dad over the years, through the lens of academia. I can distance myself, operationalize concepts and compartmentalize the pain. But for some reason, every time he comes up in casual conversation, my throat tightens.

Grief never leaves us, it just changes form; it mutates. Some days, it's a butterfly fluttering nearby, lightly reminding me of its presence. Other days, it's a monster that's tearing away at me, trying to upend everything I've built. So I've learned to give it space, to let it breathe, and to acknowledge it without trying to crush it down, because it will always come back twice as strong.

"I wanted to do something positive with all that grief. My dad would have liked that. He wasn't a big fan of crying. I think it's the Irish in him."

Sherri chuckles, nodding.

"My dad was Ukrainian. I get it."

We clink wine glasses, and I take another long drink as Sherri's eyes twinkle with mischief, already prepared to shift the mood back in a more positive direction.

"So, how did you two meet?! I want to know all the juicy details—"

"Nope," Abi laughs. "You don't."

"Okay, I want the *romantic* details, unless that's worse?"

Abi lifts a brow as we lock eyes. I know the story we rehearsed. We met at a conference and saw each other from across the room, blah blah blah, love at first sight, happily ever whatever.

But I don't want to tell that story.

While this whole engagement is fake, the connection that Abi and I have isn't. For years, I thought the way my heart raced when she walked into a room would fade, and I'd find someone else to have a devastating crush on. Maybe I just haven't given myself enough time away from her and our hilariously complicated situation, but even with that knowledge, a single fact remains in my mind: Without Abi, my life would be lacking.

"We met at a bar in Toronto."

Lacking in joy, lacking in passion, and lacking in the little spark she adds to everything she touches.

Abi's face pales as she realizes the story I'm about to tell, and I wait for her to stop me, but she doesn't.

"I was in town for a conference and saw her dancing with her friend, Kat I think? Abi had this bright red lipstick on. It was actually the thing that caught my eye first, and I was totally smitten. I had to work up the courage to talk to her because she was so beautiful."

Sherri reaches over and tucks a strand of hair behind Abi's ear.

"And then you accidentally dumped a drink on me," she finishes with a playful little smile.

"It was love at first spill," I chuckle.

Sherri puts her hand over her chest.

"That is so romantic. When was this?"

"About three years ago," I reply as I take a bite of my pot roast. "This is really good, Sherri."

"Abi, I can't believe you hid him from me for this long. Why didn't you tell me?"

Abi takes a deep breath, but before she can answer, I'm already on the case.

"She got hired at EBU after we met at that bar. There's a whole thing about professors not being able to date unless they fill out a bunch of paperwork first and disclose their relationship."

I wish that were actually the case for this department. Unfortunately, our choices would be transfer or termination.

"We didn't want our relationship to affect her position, so we kept things under wraps until it was safe."

Abi nods, poking at her food.

"I didn't want anyone to think that Logan was the reason I got the job."

"And I wasn't," I laugh. "Your daughter's a brilliant scholar and she's... my whole world."

Sherri's eyes well with tears and she sniffles, grabbing her napkin and dabbing at her face.

"Logan, you're gonna ruin my makeup."

"Well, you'll still look gorgeous— you're Abi's sister, right?" I tease with a grin.

Sherri reaches over, swatting me on the arm.

"You've got quite the charmer, pumpkin."

Abi rests her chin on her hand, gazing at me with pure adoration.

"Yeah, I really do."

After dinner, Sherri busts out the cheesecake and we move to the back patio to watch the sunset, alongside more wine of course.

The evening is full to the brim with tales of teenaged Abi, complete with embarrassing photos. The one where she's dressed as PeeWee Herman for Halloween is my favourite. Apparently she was bummed because nobody got it; they thought she was a ventriloquist's dummy. I can relate. One year, I dressed up as Sherlock Holmes and everyone just thought I wasn't wearing a costume at all. The curse of being stylish, I suppose.

Abi stretches her legs out in front of her. She's wearing that *fucking* bikini, and I've been doing my best not to ogle her like I'm some creepy cartoon character.

"It's beautiful out here. I've missed these sunsets."

"I bet you get some gorgeous ones on the west coast though," Sherri replies, interrupting my extremely sinful thoughts. "Right up against those mountains? That's gotta look like heaven."

"Yeah, they're really stunning on the good days," Abi agrees. "When I first moved there, I sat out on my balcony watching the sunset every night for weeks. Then the rain hit."

I did the same thing. New York sunsets are beautiful, but there's nothing quite like watching the sky turn pink and gold over the bay.

Abi and her mom slip into some more personal conversation, and I take the opportunity to flip out my phone and check my messages. Surprisingly, my out of office notification is keeping most people at bay. But I do see a text from Roman that I missed during dinner.

> ROMAN
>
> How's it going?

I frown and tap out a message.

> ME
>
> Fine? Why are you being weird?

> ROMAN
>
> I'm not being weird.

ME

In the history of our friendship, you have never randomly texted me "how's it going?" Are you and my sister eloping? Did you rob a bank?

ROMAN

Wow, you make me sound like a real asshole.

ME

I'm just saying, usually it's a picture of Mitzy or a question like: "What ever happened to Chumbawamba?"

ROMAN

Okay, fine. I'm here in my capacity as an informant for Imogen.

ME

And what doth Her Majesty request?

ROMAN

She wants to know if you and Abi are in love yet.

ME

We're just friends.

ROMAN

I know how that goes, pal.

I stare at the screen for a while, not quite sure what to say in my defense.

ROMAN

Imogen says "You're so in love it's disgusting. Get over yourself."

"Well, I'm gonna hit the hay," Sherri sighs, looking up at the gorgeous blend of deep reds and oranges in the sky. "I'll be up early. There's a farmer's market and if you get there right when they open, they have the freshest strawberries. No pesticides, no chemicals, just delicious."

"I don't think that's true, mom," Abi chuckles.

"Well, it's true for me."

"That's—"

"That's postmodernism," I quip. "Very elevated thinking."

Abi rolls her eyes, but Sherri just ruffles her hair.

"The fridge is stocked with food, so you two can fend for yourselves until I get home at around 2:00 tomorrow."

"Damn, that's quite the farmer's market," I chime in.

"Well, I'm *also* going to Boozy Book Club." Sherri puffs out her chest. "We always go for brunch and the mimosas are half off on Saturdays."

"Book club?" I ask. "What kind of book club?"

"Take a wild guess."

I tilt my head.

"Did you know romance is the best selling book genre?" I ask. "Must be popular for a reason, right?"

"Well, the world needs a little more love in it, don't you think?" Sherri smiles at us. "Night, you two. Be good!"

"Night, mom!" Abi calls.

"Night, ma!"

She glances over her shoulder and smiles at me one last time before heading back into the house. And then it's just Abi and me, and the wind rustling through the trees. Neither of us say a word, only drinking in the warmth of the calm and quiet night.

She looks totally relaxed at home, like a weight's been lifted off of her. There's a bit of mascara under her eyes from the humidity, and the moonlight illuminates her high cheekbones and makes her whole face glow. I'm not sure if I've ever seen her look more beautiful than she does right now.

"I think I'm gonna go for a swim."

Abi sets her drink down and gets to her feet, stopping just long enough to give me a good look at that teenie bikini. The bottoms are shockingly high cut, digging into her hips and ass. I can see the light discoloration of her stretch marks on the sides of her waist as she shimmers in the dying sunlight, the red and white polka dot top doing barely anything to hide her tits. They look like they're spilling out of it... and I kind of wish they would.

"You wanna swim?" She asks.

I want to prolong this as much as possible, but I *really* want to see that bathing suit in action.

"In a minute." I sip my drink. "Let me finish this."

She saunters toward the end of the diving board, hopping once before springing off the edge in a graceful dive.

"Very nice, very nice. Perfect ten, or whatever it is they give divers."

She swims back toward me, holding her hands out.

"Pretty please come and swim?"

I get to my feet, strutting toward her and stopping at the edge, wine still in hand. I've got one sip left and I decide to really milk it just to amp up the anticipation.

As I lift the glass to my lips I feel her hand on my other wrist, and the next thing I know I'm head over heels, with a loud splash.

the new romantics

LOGAN

BLACKBURN FALLS, ONTARIO
PRESENT DAY

"Goddammit, Abi! I'm still wearing socks!"

I do a quick, albeit, blurry scan of the pool before I realize I can't see shit.

"Looking for these?" Abi asks, slipping up behind me and dangling my glasses right in front of my face.

I grumble under my breath, snatching them up.

"Thanks for that, by the way."

She circles me like a shark, her smile shimmering and her eyes warm.

I pull my wallet out of my pants and hold it up, frowning as water pours out of it. Abi follows me, grinning ear to ear as I swim to the edge of the pool and toss it out onto the ground.

"And thanks for this, too."

"Cash dries, right?"

"I didn't have cash, but yeah, everything in there will dry." I tilt my head, grinning at her. "What's gotten into you?"

She reaches behind me, pressing her hand down on something on the pool's wall, and the lights go dim. It takes my eyes a few seconds to adjust, but soon I catch sight of her swimming away from me, still smirking.

"Follow me. I want to show you something."

"What?"

"Just come here!" She laughs as she leans up against the edge of the pool, arms spread out and her breasts bobbing just above the water.

I don't even remember making the decision to start swimming, but the second I reach her, my arms are already wrapped up around her waist. The hair sticking to the back of my neck, my wet socks, and soaked wallet are all in the past.

Water under the bridge.

She tastes like the same merlot she's been nursing all night, with a hint of peach from her lip gloss on top. I groan, desperate to push her up against the wall, but before I can make my move she's already torn her lips away from mine.

"I said I wanted to show you something."

"You could show me what's under that suit."

Her dark hair plastered to her face, the mascara smeared beneath her eyes, and the rosy tip of her nose all combine to make her look wild and hungry in a way I've never seen from her before. She turns me around, and I can feel my heart racing as she pushes me up against the side of the pool. Her mom didn't go to bed that long ago, what if she left something out here and comes looking?

"You wanna see more?" Abi purrs, pulling the two flimsy triangles of fabric aside to reveal her voluptuous tits.

"Your mom's in the house," I laugh nervously, my eyes flicking toward the back door.

"My mom takes a weed gummy every night to fall asleep, and she has a white noise machine for good measure. She's never gonna know."

"Have you had sex in this pool before?" I ask.

"Not with you," she replies, caging me in with both arms. "And like I said, I have something I want to show you."

"Besides your tits?" I murmur. "Because you're doing a great job showing those off already."

"You know, Sunshine, I could always make you put that smart mouth to good use."

I can feel my anxiety flare up again, but even as I strain my ears as hard as I can, all I can hear is the wind and the light splash of the water as it laps up against the pool's edge. No one's around. No harm, no foul.

"Name the time and place."

Abi giggles, floating back just a bit and raking her fingernails down my damp shirt as she goes. Fuck, she's so cute. Even in the silvery moonlight, I can see those little freckles she always gets during the summer, dusted across the bridge of her nose and cheeks. Before this trip is over, I want to make it my mission to kiss every single one of them.

She drifts in close again, slowly working the button on my pants, tugging my zipper down and reaching in to tease my cock. I groan, tipping my head back as she starts to stroke me. Her hand works slowly, thumb gliding over the tip and making me shiver. I don't know if it's water, or the fear of getting caught, but this feels fucking incredible.

"Did I ever tell you about my special talent?" She purrs.

Abi's got a lot of talents, including going from the cutest nerd I've ever met to a fucking siren in a split second.

"Logan," she sings. "Are you listening? Or are you looking at my tits?"

"I can do two things."

She grins, releasing my cock and pushing herself away from me again. I ache at her absence, but before I can ask another question, I hear a splash and she's disappeared under the water. It's only moments before I feel the tug of her fingers hooking into my pants, dragging them down past my hips as a tiny burst of bubbles hit the surface, and I feel her mouth on my cock.

Warm and soft.

"Oh my fucking *God*," I whisper, my cheeks heating up.

Her tongue swirls around the head before she takes me *all* the way down her throat, my hands curling into fists as I suppress a moan. How the fuck is she holding her breath like this? I twitch and groan as she bobs up and down on my dick. It's pure fucking bliss.

The buildup is my favorite part of sex, when all that delicious heat rises beneath your skin just before you reach your peak. The feeling of teetering on the brink of climax is one I'll chase for the rest of my life.

Abi nearly gets me there in a matter of seconds and I have to grab her hair to control the pace. I don't want to come yet.

"Slower, Shortcake," I manage to choke out, hoping somehow she'll get the message.

She takes me down her throat one final time, and I let out another groan, staring up at the stars twinkling in the sky but managing to hold on.

"Good girl," I sigh. "Good fucking girl."

When she emerges from the water, she immediately gasps for breath, her face pink and her hair messily covering her eyes. I help her push it back, cupping her cheeks gently as I move in for a kiss.

"That's a hell of a talent," I whisper.

I can't stop myself from kissing her, reaching around to untie the small knot that's barely keeping her top on. The fabric falls into the water, leaving her gorgeous half-naked body exposed to the night air.

I capture her nipple with my teeth, biting and sucking until she's crying out my name. She wraps her hand around my cock, stroking me as she straddles my thigh, and I bury my face in her shoulder, moaning while she begins to roll her hips and grind her pussy against me.

"That's my girl," I whisper as she continues to stroke me. "Make us both feel good."

The most primal part of my brain is screaming at me to pull those little bikini bottoms to the side and slip right into her. Abi keens, her body moving faster as she wraps her arms around the back of my neck and sinks those sharp nails into my skin. I slide my mouth up and down her throat before nipping at that fleshy spot just above her collarbone.

Her voice breaks and she bucks against my thigh.

"You wanna come for me?" I whisper, trying to keep my voice as low as I can.

I'm throbbing in her hand, just a few strokes away from my own release.

"Yes!" She moans. "I'm so close."

I love that I can work her up just as quickly as she can me; that she's putty in my hands the second my fingers brush her skin.

"Atta girl. Ride that thigh like a dirty little slut."

Abi rips her hand away from my cock, gripping my shoulders as her face twists up in the most beautiful agony. She's a fucking goddess, lit only by the moon and stars that hang above us.

I reach up, wrapping one hand around her throat and putting pressure on the sides as I force her to meet my gaze.

"Look at me," I rasp.

I'm in love with her.

Her eyes don't leave mine for a second as she comes undone, lashes fluttering as her lips part in orgasmic bliss. She shivers, hips rolling with desperation as I move in for a kiss, the rest of her climax rippling through her while our lips crash together. When I finally tear my mouth away from hers, she gasps for breath, relaxing for only a moment before diving back underneath the water. I feel her lips wrap around my cock, one hand on the base as she recreates that same suction from before, clearly determined to make me come.

I'm shivering, the pleasure building until I'm practically clawing at the edges of the pool. The pace is frantic and my heart is fucking pounding. I'm so close... *so* fucking close.

"Oh, *fuck.*"

My throat is dry and my head feels fuzzy, a beautiful ache forming in the pit of my stomach, wrapping all the way around my lower back and shooting down to my toes.

And then I'm coming. Fireworks burst along my skin, and I shudder as I fill her mouth.

She comes up for air for the second time of the night, mascara running down her cheeks, and a little bit of my cum dribbling down to her chin. I can't help myself, grabbing her face and pressing another fiery kiss against her lips. I can taste myself on her tongue, and it ignites a deep and intense curiosity that makes me shiver. I think being with her is unlocking new kinks I didn't know I had.

Abi groans, fingers swimming in my hair as she kisses back.

And I can only think of one thing:

I can't let this go back to normal when we get home.

I wake up the next morning with the sun streaking through the windows and the birds chirping outside. The smell of fresh summer air washes over me and I sit up, pushing my mess of hair out of my face.

Unfortunately, it turns out fresh air's not the only thing you need to deal with a hangover: the moment the blood starts rushing I can already tell that I'm going to feel like absolute shit in a minute or less. My head starts throbbing immediately after the realization, and I feel like my mouth is as dry as a desert.

The worst part about getting older is waking up and realizing you can't really bounce back from a few glasses of wine the same way you used to. I fumble around for my glasses, finding them along with a note on my nightstand, and a bottle of Gatorade plus two painkillers.

> Thought you might need this after the merlot last night.
> I'm making breakfast.
> XO(XO, Gossip Girl)
> PS. Thanks for the ride.

"Oh, you are *more* than welcome, Doctor King."

I pop the painkillers before ripping the cap off the Gatorade, and guzzling it like my life depends on it. Because now that I'm in my 30s, it kind of does.

"Oh my god, I can feel the hydration," I groan as some of it drips down my chin.

When I'm finished, I grab a pair of grey sweatpants from my suitcase along with a black t-shirt with a little ghost pattern on it. I slip it over my head and begin to head out the door, before thinking better of it and giving myself a once over in the mirror.

The dark circles under my eyes have only gotten worse with time and age, and I'm even spotting the faint beginning of crow's feet in the corners. Every day, more and more of my dad's features come through. I used to want to get out from under his shadow, but now that he's gone, I find myself longing to stay here, with even the smallest little connection to him, for just a little while longer.

With a sigh, I head out toward the main house. The back door is already wide open, with only the secondary screen door closed to keep the bugs out, and I can hear ABBA blaring from the kitchen.

Abi has her back turned, hips swaying from side to side as she dances and sings along to her playlist. She's in a little blue and white sundress, her messy hair bouncing to the beat of the music. Every time her hips move, the fabric shifts, revealing just a hint of her lacy white panties.

My morning wood comes in late, but strong and I walk up behind her, clearing my throat so that she knows I'm here. She pauses, glancing over her shoulder as she scoops up some batter with her finger and sucks it clean.

"You know I can see what's under that dress, you little slut."

I gently cup her breasts, teasing her nipples as we rock from side to side.

"Well, good morning to you too."

"Maybe I should tear these off of you." I slide one hand between her thighs, teasing her through the thin lace. "Have my way with you *right here.*"

"Don't tempt me, Doctor."

I place gentle kisses up and down her neck, taking my time, and listening to the soft sighs that slip from her lips. I wish we could do this every day. Not just the sex, *this*. Making breakfast in the morning, dancing in the kitchen, teasing each other...

The fantasy of fucking her over the counter is quickly replaced by something much more potent; it would be so easy to open my mouth and let the words come pouring out.

I love you.

I've loved you since the second I spilled that drink on you, and it feels like my soul's known yours for more than just one lifetime—

Okay, that last bit is a little much, but the sentiment is there.

Abi looks up at me, a hint of concern in those beautiful green eyes.

"You good?"

Tell her.

The pressure at the base of my throat increases, like the words are trying to burst out of me but I'm choking them back. The hardest lesson I ever had to learn was how to leave something I love so deeply, without digging my claws into it before I let it go, and I've had to re-learn it again and again and again.

With people who never really understood me.

When I had to let go of my dad.

With Abi.

But just because I *can* release it doesn't mean I want to.

"Knock knock!" A voice calls from the front of the house.

"Shit," Abi whispers. "I forgot to tell you, Kat and Marcus are coming over for breakfast."

"That's great!" I chirp, thankful to be thinking about anything else.

This is good.

Meeting her friends is good.

It's something, at least.

Something to distract me from uttering the three words that could destroy our entire relationship.

the prophecy

ABI

BLACKBURN FALLS, ONTARIO
PRESENT DAY

Kat was there when my mom left my dad, she was there when Brendan decided the right thing to do was to end our almost decade-long relationship without a single word, and she's here now.

"Abigail King, you are a *fucking* babe!" She squeals, wrapping me up in a tight hug the moment I answer the door.

"So are you," I laugh. "I've missed you so much."

She's always been effortlessly beautiful, with warm brown eyes, and long dark hair that flows down her shoulders in elegant waves. She's dressed in a pair of faded blue jeans and a white tank top that perfectly contrasts her light brown skin. She was like this even back when we were teenagers; I embraced my inner goth while Kat leaned into cheerleading. We were opposites, but I think that's part of what brought us together.

"I missed you too, babe! But hey, someone wants to say hi to his auntie A."

She pulls back as the front door opens and I spot Marcus, with baby Dylan balanced on his hip. I guess baby's not quite right anymore. He's two now, and he looks just like his mom, with puppy dog eyes that could rival Logan's.

"Oh my god, he's huge!" I gush.

Marcus hands him off to me, giving me a kiss on the cheek in the pass-off.

"You look great, Abi," He says with a bright smile. "And congratulations on the engagement!"

"Thank you," I chuckle, gently bouncing Dylan up and down. "You're gonna be a giant when you get older, you know!"

"Speaking of giants, are your fiancé's parents Ents or something?"

Kat's staring past me, and I glance over my shoulder to find Logan leaning up against the doorframe. He holds out his hand, striding toward the two of them with the utmost confidence.

"I'm Logan. To address your question, yes, my parents are both Ents. They were actually extras in the Lord of the Rings films, as well as experts for all tree-related material."

"And funny, too! Abi, you hit the jackpot!"

There's that hollow feeling in my chest again. I hate that playing pretend is so effortless; the words 'my fiancé' come out far too easily, and that should worry me, but at the same time it feels like a forbidden treat, a taste of something I can't have.

Logan and Marcus shake hands as Kat eyes the ring on my finger.

"Your man's got excellent taste. It's so vintage, and so you."

"Yeah, Logan's got quite the eye," I laugh, trying to force down the surge of anxiety. "But come on, let's eat, I've got pancakes to make! You want pancakes, Dylan?"

He grabs my nose and pinches it until my eyes water.

"Ow! Jesus, kiddo!"

"Sorry, babe!" Kat laughs, prying him off of me. "Dylan, baby, soft hands, okay?"

Dylan bursts into tears and Kat clicks her tongue. Marcus just looks tired.

"He thinks he hurt you," he murmurs. "He's at this stage where he's hypersensitive to that sort of thing, and we're trying to teach him to be gentle."

"Aww, I'm fine, baby, I promise!"

I gently boop Dylan's nose, but it only seems to make things worse.

"Marcus, can you grab his bear from the car?"

Marcus winces.

"It's at home."

"Guys, can I try something?" Logan asks, slipping his dad's watch off his wrist and concealing it in his palm.

"Go nuts," Kat sighs, over the sound of piercing screams.

"Hi, Dylan!" Logan coos, crouching down as he approaches. He glances at Marcus and Kat. "Is it okay if I hold him?"

The two seem curious, both nodding silently in response. I pass Dylan off to Logan, watching as he cradles the kid gently in his arms, bouncing him from side to side. My heart swells at his gentleness. He's always been comfortable around kids; it probably helps that he's just a big one himself.

Out of the corner of my eye, I catch Kat beaming at me and my chest aches even more. It's like a pang of jealousy for the fictional version of me that gets to have all of this with Logan Flynn, the version of me that's not just pretending.

Logan reaches behind Dylan's ear, looking like he's searching for something.

"Dylan, I think you've got…" He gasps, revealing his watch. "Whooooaaa! What's that?"

Dylan's eyes grow wide with curiosity as he lets out a soft hiccup in favor of another piercing shriek, and he starts to laugh, cooing as Logan places it in his chubby little hands.

"Holy shit," Marcus laughs. "Do you babysit? You could make a killing from us alone."

"Don't say 'shit' in front of the baby!" Kat laughs. "He's going to pick that up!"

"The other day you called a lawn mower the c word," Marcus reminds her with a raised brow.

"Hey, he was down for a nap. The cursing is free if he's unconscious."

We head in toward the kitchen, that minor disaster averted.

"I hope your watch isn't expensive," Marcus chimes in, pulling out a chair. "He'll probably try to put it in his mouth."

"Family heirloom," Logan replies with a shrug, watching closely as Dylan continues to be enthralled by his watch. "But if it was able to handle my dad falling into the Hudson, it can probably survive this little guy."

Logan takes Dylan straight to the back window, and I watch as he gleefully points out clouds, birds, and anything else that might be interesting for a two-year-old. He's completely calmed down, the only evidence of his tantrum are the tear-stains on his chubby little cheeks.

"You guys want some coffee?"

"I'm off that stuff," Marcus replies. "High blood pressure."

"I think my mom's got some peppermint tea if you— wait, high blood pressure? Aren't you like 28?"

"Yeah," he chuckles. "Time really has a way of grabbing you by the balls and—"

"Marcus!" Kat hisses.

He sighs, rubbing his eyes.

"Balls is not a bad word! He doesn't have the context!"

The next few minutes is a whirlwind of activity as different drinks are divvied out, ending with Logan and Marcus outside along with Dylan, while Kat and I watch through the window.

"He's great with kids. He's gonna be a good dad— I mean, if that's what the two of you want."

"You sound like my mom," I snicker.

I actually do want kids, at least eventually. It was the thing Brendan and I argued about the most. He wanted them immediately, but we were so young, and I wasn't ready. I still had my whole life ahead of me, still had to figure out exactly who I was. In hindsight though, if I'm being truly honest with myself, I think the real problem was I wanted kids, I just didn't want them with him.

"This is all so exciting! I have so many questions. How did you meet? How long have you two been together?" She frowns. "Okay, apparently I have two questions."

"He was actually that guy who spilled that drink on me back in Toronto. You remember the night after—"

Kat gasps.

"Are you serious?! So, what, you guys hooked up and— wait, you kept him a secret for that long?"

"It wasn't a secret," I laugh. "It just took us a while to figure things out. There's a whole departmental thing at EBU... it's a lot of paperwork."

The more complicated the lie gets, the more there is to keep track of. The worst thing about weaving a web like this is remembering which strings could cause it to collapse.

"Okay, so that explains why I didn't know about him until a few months ago, but how come you never told me you were engaged? You were the first person I called when I got pregnant!"

She was holed up in a drug store bathroom when I got the call. We both started screaming out of panic *and* joy.

"It was a spur of the moment thing while we were driving here. He just... popped the question, and I said yes."

"Just like that? Nothing special planned? No song and dance? No flash mob?" Kat elbows me in the ribs and I bump her with my hip in return.

"If he organized a flash mob proposal, I'd have to bury a body *and* face my ex-fiancé at the reunion," I laugh. "That's not the kind of summer vacation I was hoping for."

Kat chuckles, and I hear Dylan squeal from outside. Logan and Marcus look like they're pretending to be dinosaurs, chasing him around the backyard while they let out mighty roars.

Marcus and Kat have been inseparable since that same night in Toronto, when she finally decided to work up the courage to dance with him. Three years later, they have a beautiful little boy and a gorgeous house. He works in real estate and Kat's his assistant. Their pictures are on billboards all over Blackburn.

"Are you nervous about seeing Brendan?"

We're both looking out the window when she asks me, but I don't need to see her face to tell she immediately feels a little awkward about the question.

"Not really," I lie, watching Logan scoop Dylan up, the two men tickling him like crazy. "Is Marcus still friends with him?"

"What? Hell no."

I try not to sound too surprised.

Or happy.

"What happened?"

Kat takes a deep breath, turning back to me as she sips her coffee.

"Can you keep a secret?"

I flash her an incredulous look.

"Remember when we used to steal those menthols out of your grand-ma's purse when we were 13? If I'm taking that to the grave, imagine what other horrible secrets I've kept."

Kat chuckles, leaning up against the counter and clutching her mug close to her chest. This feels like old times, when we used to get together for a little glass of wine and a big gossip session. I swear, it was better than therapy.

"We were playing darts at the Black Bear after closing one night. It was just after Dylan was born and I was still *really* sensitive, you know? I'd just pushed a nine pound kid out of me, and my hormones were totally out of control." She runs her hand through her hair. "Marcus and I got into an argument over something stupid, and he went to the bar to get another drink."

She glances back out the window, reflexively checking to make sure he's still outside before lowering her voice to continue.

"Brendan reaches out, puts his *hand* on my *thigh* and says, *if you ever need a real man, you give me a call.*"

She scoffs at the memory.

"Now, he was wasted, mind you, but still—"

"Doesn't he have a baby? With Carly? That had to have already happened by then."

I'd be shocked, but nothing I hear about Brendan surprises me anymore.

"Yes! That's the *truly* fucked up part! And when I told her what her perfect husband had done? She called me a liar! To my face!" She picks a strawberry out of our assorted fruit bowl and pops it into her mouth. "It became a whole thing. Brendan texted me and told me he was drunk that night and he was just joking around, blah blah blah. Fuck him– fuck both of them, actually."

I wonder why I didn't see the signs. How many times did he pull something like that while we were together and I just never knew? How many other red flags did I miss?

Logan slides in through the door with a big smile on his face. His grey sweats are covered in grass stains, and I watch as he drags his hand through his messy hair.

"God, that kid's got a lot of energy!" He chuckles. "Either that or I'm already too old for this shit."

Outside, Dylan is still tearing around the backyard, with Marcus lumbering after him.

"Could be a bit of both," Kat laughs. "I think the two of us have aged about ten years since he was born."

My phone buzzes on the counter and I flip it over, everything else suddenly fading into the background.

Email notification.

Scholarship application status.

My heart is racing. Maybe I won. Maybe I can go to this reunion relaxed and secure in my postdoc position. Maybe I won't have to lie about all this shit after all.

Dear Dr. King,

Please.

We regret to inform you…

I don't even get past that first line. I can't bring myself to do it.

I can cry later.

I *will* cry later, but not now.

I pour Logan a cup of coffee, bringing it over to him.

"Oh, thank you!" He brushes my hand before taking the cup, sipping at it as I wrap my arms around him and burying my face in his chest.

A tidal wave of grief washes over me as I breathe him in. If my contract at EBU ends, I don't know what I'm going to do. I'll have to get a job somewhere else, find another postdoc if I can. That could take me anywhere in the country, maybe even back to Canada.

He dips his head a little, pressing a kiss into the top of my head.

"Are you okay?" He asks, reading my mood perfectly, and keeping his voice low.

But I can't tell him right now. I can't tell anyone. I have to swallow this.

"Yeah. I'm good."

I'd give myself an A for effort, but my voice still has that little shake which always gives me away. It feels like Logan's about to say something, but Kat's voice pierces our little bubble before we can get any further into the pity party I'm trying my best to avoid.

"Oh, I forgot to ask you guys! We were going to go to The Black Bear tonight for pool and karaoke. Marcus has gotta cook the books anyway, and I figured we'd do a pre-celebration before the reunion this weekend. Drinks are on the house…"

All I want to do is collapse into the guest house and cry, but I have to keep up appearances. I take a few deep breaths and put on my game face as Logan wraps his arms around my waist, holding me close.

"What time?"

"8:00 sharp!" Kat chirps.

"At night?" Logan asks. "You know, someone really needs to do something about you damn kids holding events after 6:00pm."

"Calm down, old man," I laugh.

I'm a failure.

I can't do anything right.

"Count us in!"

At least it'll help numb the pain.

CHAPTER THIRTY-SIX

changes

ABI

BLACKBURN FALLS, ONTARIO
AUGUST 2021

Since Brendan left, it feels like every piece of my life has fallen apart.

My mom told me I could move back in with her and stay in my childhood bedroom, but I declined. There are too many tainted memories that come attached with it: my first kiss with Brendan, the first time we had sex, the first time we said I love you...

A fresh coat of paint and some new furniture can't erase the moments I've experienced in that bedroom.

Instead, I've been living on Kat's couch and working at The Black Bear, a little pub that her dad owns. Just a few months back, Brendan and I were taking the final steps to move into a gorgeous apartment in downtown Toronto. Maybe it's a small blessing we didn't get far enough to take that dive before it all ended.

I haven't seen him since that day, but that hasn't stopped me from getting a lot of pity from patrons.

It's such a shame, you know? You two were great together.

Do you think there's any way to make it work?

This town is small, and word travels fast, especially when you're the two main lovebirds who've been dating since high school. I've been keeping to myself though, pretty much not saying anything to anyone except for Kat, and our conversations tend to just focus on what a piece of shit Brendan is.

Whenever I'm not doing that, though, I go to work, sling drinks, and come home to sleep. Rinse and repeat, with some semi-enthusiastic job-hunting on the side.

I published six papers during my PhD, and wrote two chapters for a professor's book as well. I have multiple years of both teaching and research experience, and I volunteered in the community; even after all that, my inbox is crickets.

The job market is so bad, I even started applying for postdoc positions wherever they crop up. My mom told me to use my dual citizenship to my advantage, but so far, it's not really working out for me, no matter how many positions I apply to state-side.

I'm starting to feel like I'll be stuck in that bar for the rest of my life.

"How's the hunt?" Kat asks, finishing up her breakfast and forcing me to contend with the fact that I've barely started on mine.

I don't really have much of an appetite anymore. I've poured all of my focus into building a better life for myself. Well, that and moping.

"I've filled out so many applications that I'm dreaming about it. I think last night my resume had to go to war against some filing cabinets, so that's where I'm at."

Every day I wish I was somewhere other than slinging drinks and mopping floors, and every day I'm reminded that some people just don't get to do what they love.

"You'll get something, babe. You've just gotta keep your head up."

"I hope so," I sigh. "I've been keeping my head up for so long my neck's getting sore."

"Look, I know it's not ideal and it's not what you signed up for. But the job's a means to an end, right? It puts food in your stomach and it pays your bills."

It *barely* pays my bills, but I nod regardless.

I'm just thankful she's not charging me rent, but I can kind of tell she expected me to be out of here faster. Truthfully, so did I. I'm watching everyone's careers advance around me while I'm still stuck in the same place wondering if any of the choices I made were right.

"Okay, gotta go." She kisses the top of my head. "One more chance: are you sure you don't want to come hiking with us?"

Kat was never really the outdoorsy type until her and Marcus started dating a few months back, but she's really embraced it. She's dressed in a brand new pair of hiking boots, denim shorts, and a tank top. She's even got one of those little fanny pack things around her waist.

Me? I'm more of an indoor cat.

"I'm good, I need to re-work my resume. I think maybe that's the problem. If I crack the code the job offers will just come rolling in."

Kat offers me a warm smile in response, probably happy to see me doing something other than wallow. Honestly, I think *I'm* the problem at this point, but you can only be so negative before your friends start to turn sour, and I'm in no position to lose anyone else.

"Whatever you need to do, okay? Maybe we can go for dinner tonight? Somewhere nice?"

I shrug.

"Yeah, sure. I get off at 8:00."

I wave at her as she slips out the door, locking it behind her before I take my plate of eggs and retire to the couch. I switch on the TV and flip my laptop back open, ready to 'fix' my resume for the fiftieth time in two months. It's time to analyze every punctuation mark, every bolded word, every line break. There has to be *something* in here, something I can point to as the reason I'm not getting hired.

Something aside from a ridiculously competitive job market, with people who are a hell of a lot more qualified than I am, of course.

I always thought I was smart until I got into grad school, and then I was suddenly the smallest of small fish in a massive pond. Except the other fish were geniuses. Genius fish? Whatever. I felt out of my depth, but I kept working and working and working, because if there's one thing I don't do, it's quit. And hey, it paid off.

Up until now at least.

Hours pass, and I think I manage to change exactly one bit of punctuation on my resume. Then, just as I'm about to undo a new formatting decision for the 12th time, I see an email notification that I've somehow missed.

I open my email to find a message from Emerald Bay University, way out in Washington State.

My entire demeanor shifts in an instant, heart pounding as I start to shake. Even if it's a rejection, it's something. The first real something I've gotten from any of the schools I've reached out to.

I hold my breath as I open the message.

FROM: Dr. Francis Hughes

TO: Dr. Abigail King

And the subject.

Postdoc Interview Request

"Oh my god!" I leap up off the couch and flip the entire plate of eggs onto the floor. "Fuck! Oh fuck! What do I do?!"

My brain moves in a chaotic circle for a few seconds, my body half bent as I stand paralyzed, before deciding the email that could change everything might be a little more important than some eggs on the floor.

I can clean up later, this is my life.

Good Morning (or maybe afternoon?) Dr. King,

I looked over your CV and application package, and was very impressed.

Would you be available for a screening interview tomorrow at around 1:00pm on Zoom? If not, we can find a time that better fits your schedule.

Let me know!

Frankie

I let out a scream that almost certainly gets heard by the neighbors, jumping up and down with joy before I realize I've accidentally smashed my cheesy scrambled eggs into Kat's nice hardwood floor.

Shit.

I rush to the hallway closet to grab a broom, texting her along the way.

ME

I GOT AN INTERVIEW!

KAT

OH MY GOD! I TOLD YOU THINGS WOULD WORK!! WHERE IS IT?!

ME

Emerald Bay University out in Washington!

She doesn't text back for a minute, and I realize that I've basically just told her I might not just be moving out, but moving entire countries. I know she was hoping I'd find some place close by in Ontario.

KAT

That's great, babe! I'm super happy for you.
When's the interview?

I can feel the relief wash over me. Even though I know Kat would be upset if I left Blackburn, she's always wanted the best for me. That's just who she is.

ME

Tomorrow afternoon! It's a zoom call so I don't
have to worry about going in person or anything.

KAT

Hey! More importantly, it means you don't have to
wear pants. Live the dream!

ME

Shit, I forgot to throw together an outfit.

I've been applying to jobs for so long with no hits that I completely spaced on the fact that I might have to look presentable when I actually got an interview.

KAT

Don't worry. I have this cute black and white top
in my closet you can borrow. Very goth and very
you, but also professional as fuck. You're going to
nail this.

I smile at the text, hope sprouting up through the cracks in my fractured heart. My mom used to say that when the universe closes a door, it opens a window, and if this is that window, there's no way I'm letting it close again.

build me up buttercup

LOGAN

BLACKBURN FALLS, ONTARIO
PRESENT DAY

I'm exhausted after a full day of entertaining a toddler, and talking Star Trek with a dad, but we agreed to go out tonight and so help me, I do not break my promises. So now, I'm standing in front of a mirror, smoothing out my extremely cool sweater vest, and making sure my tie doesn't look like an absolute mess.

My hair is still ridiculous, the humidity in Ontario doing little to keep me from looking like a mad scientist. I take a bit of pomade that Abi bought me and push it back, trying to sculpt it into some semblance of a recognizable style. Just when I think I've succeeded, a thick curl bounces back and falls into my eyes.

"Now I understand why my mom used to put gel in my hair for school picture day."

"Okay, I'm ready!" Abi calls from the bathroom.

I watch as she emerges, dressed in a pair of black cutoff jean shorts that leave little to the imagination, and a red crop top that shows off just a sliver of her stomach. Her lipstick is vibrant, perfectly matching her shirt, and she's got a pair of black & white checkerboard creepers on her feet to bring the whole ensemble together.

"What do you think?" She asks, doing a little spin.

"I think you're trying to kill me," I chuckle, gesturing to her shorts. "Those can't be legal, not in a decent country like this one."

"Is it too much? It's just really hot out, and I don't feel like sweating more than I have to in a packed bar."

"Yeah, it's definitely hot… because you're here."

She groans, pretending to gag, but I ignore it.

"Your ass looks incredible in those things."

"Well, thank you for the approval, Dr. Flynn," she giggles.

I kiss the tip of her nose before wrapping my arms around her, holding on as tightly as I can. It's so distressingly easy to fall back into this with her over and over again, continuing to blur these lines without even thinking.

Not that I spend much time thinking when it comes to her.

That deep ache radiates out from my chest like a gong, but I keep kissing her in the hopes that it'll push the feelings back down.

That somehow, this will all be totally fine.

We'll make it.

We *do* make it.

Multiverse theory says so, after all.

I step back, letting her free as I stroke her cheek with the back of my hand, gazing into those gorgeous green eyes. Her dark brows are pinched, her slightly crooked nose scrunched up as well. I can see the flash of fear in her eyes, and I wonder if I've somehow transferred my own anxieties onto her, like some kind of depressed amoeba.

"What's wrong?"

It's a defence mechanism. I'm asking so she can't ask me first.

"I'm scared."

I can feel my heart start to pound.

"What about?"

Tears start to pool in her eyes and she sniffles, trying her best to hold back the inevitable deluge.

"I didn't win that scholarship. I got the response this morning."

My heart cracks.

Frankie was counting on her winning, to help solidify Abi's position and make it easier to justify keeping her on.

"Oh, Abi..."

Why the hell does everything always have to be about cutting costs?

"I know, I'm a fucking loser."

"Hey, no." I shake my head. "You're not a loser, Shortcake."

"Oh yeah? Then why are all of the people going to the reunion doing better than I am? Houses, kids, real fucking jobs..."

Her hollow laughter echoes through the house as the dam breaks, and tears begin rushing down her cheeks.

"Look, Abi, you're going through some really rough stuff right now, but I *promise* it's going to be okay. I've always got your back, and there's no way I'm going to let everything just fall apart."

She smiles. I can tell she doesn't believe me, but she wants to.

"And I've always got yours."

She wants to believe it so very badly.

"Then that's all we need," I grin. "Now come on, I've gotta keep impressing your friends. Time to kick all your asses at pool."

She rolls her eyes, giving me a gentle shove backward, the energy in the room shifting so fast it leaves me with a bit of whiplash.

"In your *dreams*, nerd."

"Nerd? I'll show you a nerd!"

I try to lift her up and haul her over my shoulder but fail miserably. Instead of looking like a superhero, I'm stumbling backward and almost tripping over my own feet. Abi shrieks and I struggle to regain my balance as I let her go, gasping for breath.

"Yeah, okay, maybe you have a point there. I gotta get back in the gym when we get home. Work on these guns."

She rolls her eyes, tapping me on the cheek before heading outside.

"Come on, Gumby! We're gonna be late."

I follow her through the backyard and out the front gate. As we reach the sidewalk I give her ass a rough slap, just in time to come face to face with an older couple out walking their dog. Both of them stand stock-still, looking slightly bemused for a few moments before moving on without a word. Abi blushes furiously, tucking her hair behind her ear.

"Those are mom's neighbors."

"Well, now they know what we like to do in the bedroo—" She hits me in the gut and I double over, feigning a horrendous amount of pain. "Oh no! My kidneys!"

"Those are closer to your back, *doctor*," she laughs. "You really do just live to rile me up, don't you?"

I straighten up, quick as a flash, shooting her a big goofy smile.

"I *really* fucking do."

Should we be doing this? What are the rules? Are there rules anymore? I push away the anxious knot in my gut and try to focus on the good stuff. Because it's her. *She's* the good stuff, and I'd do anything in my power to keep her.

Abi takes my hand and we walk on in silence, taking in the peaceful atmosphere. Her mood seems to have picked up a little; her smile is fully genuine this time, and I think overall she really is happy to be back. At the very least, she's trying her best to make the most of it.

"And there it is, the illustrious Black Bear."

She points up ahead, gesturing toward a building that looks less like a bar, and more like a big log cabin. I spot a few picnic tables along with a small fire pit with some large wooden chairs laid out. A few people are already sat, sipping pints of ice-cold beer around a lightly crackling fire.

"Wait, so they just... hang out around a campfire and drink? That's the bar?"

"There's some seating inside too, genius, but sure."

"That's so cool," I whisper.

"Yeah, this part was my favorite thing about the place. Although sometimes, when it got busy, I'd totally forget to check out here for people's drinks."

"You worked here?"

"For a while before I got the job at EBU. Kat's dad used to own it, but he's retired now. Her and Marcus technically run it, along with their real estate company."

"Jesus, that's a lot of work," I mutter as we swing the door open and step inside.

My initial, moment-one impression is that the place looks like something out of Twin Peaks: dark wood, lots of dimly lit corners to sit in, a pool table, a dart board, and a cigarette vending machine that looks like it's been fully repaired from the ground up at least 5 times before I was born.

It's the epitome of a small town bar, but unlike the Hi-Dive in Emerald Bay, it's not in massive need of repair. I love that place, but it's becoming a safety hazard at this point.

The next thing I notice is that Karaoke is in full swing, with some old guy belting out the lyrics to *Piano Man* as a few people in the audience cheer him on.

Abi takes my hand, leading me right up to the bar where a short older woman with a head of dark, tightly coiled curls is pouring drinks. Every movement feels deliberate, and even someone as un-informed on the topic as I am can tell she's pretty damn good at flipping a bottle.

I always wanted to bartend in college, but I've got butterfingers and a shitty short-term memory. I once smashed an entire bottle of Belvedere on the floor of a liquor store because I was trying to show off in front of Frankie.

It was a pretty impressive trick, I made a whole lot of money disappear.

"Hey, Maggie!" Abi chirps.

Maggie's face lights up and she flashes us a big smile.

"Abi! It's good to see you, kiddo! Are you back for the reunion?"

"Yes, ma'am!"

"We've missed you around these parts, you know. Always felt a little sad you had to go off and become a big fancy professor." Maggie's eyes land on me as she finishes cleaning a glass, taking a pause to look me up and down. "And this must be your fiancé. I've heard... well, nothing about you other than the fact that you exist."

"I certainly do!" I chirp, sticking out my hand to shake hers. "Logan Flynn, actual factual human being. How the heck are ya?"

"Very well, thank you! Now what can I get the two of you to drink? First one's on the house, but don't you worry, that's just a trick to keep you coming back."

"I'll take a beer. Logan?"

"Same here," I reply.

"Oh, and two shots of whiskey!" Abi calls after the bartender. "Put it on my tab!"

"You planning on taking advantage of me tonight, Doctor?" I ask with the most charming grin I can muster.

She turns to me, fingers tugging on the hem of my sweater vest.

"You *did* wear those glasses tonight, and you know what they do to me."

"I actually don't," I laugh. "Would you care to elaborate?"

Her cheeks flush and she clears her throat, staring down at the bar before taking a deep breath. This doesn't feel like the preparation for another dumb joke, it's like she's about to—

"Hey, Abi!" Kat calls out from a darkened corner, cutting into our conversation.

"We'll be there in a second!"

Maggie comes back with our drinks and Abi slides a shot glass toward me.

"Do one with me."

"You got it, Shortcake."

We tap our little glasses on the bar, one, two, three times, and toss them back, both of us wincing at the taste for a moment before grabbing our beers and heading over to Kat's table.

"I thought you'd be in the back room playing poker," Abi chuckles. "Didn't expect you out here with the common-folk."

"Poker?" I ask, sliding into a seat. "You guys gamble in here?"

"Duh," Kat laughs. "It's a bar. We used to play poker in the back room a lot after closing. My dad had Sunday morning tournaments with his friends, too. I'm surprised he didn't use the damn place as collateral. Anyway, we used to play for candy when we were teenagers and eventually that turned into quarters, then— Abi, something wrong?"

I look over to see Abi's fists clenched, right along with her jaw. Her eyes are fixed on the front of the bar, and I tell a storm's stirring up inside her.

Kat turns around in her chair and scoffs.

"Oh, that's all. Don't waste your time worrying about Melissa Walsh. She's not worth it."

"Melissa Walsh," I murmur. "Why do I know that name?"

"She was Carly's little minion," Abi practically snarls.

"Still is," Kat grumbles. "Some people never grow out of being mean girls."

I follow Abi's gaze to find our subject, my eyes landing on a woman in a pair of loose fitting blue jeans and a black crop top. She's lean and wiry, like a model, and pretty in that same slightly too put together way. At the very least I can see why she would have been the popular girl in school.

Melissa seems to notice Kat first, recognition flashing in her eyes, but little else until she sees Abi. It takes her a moment to be sure, but when she's figured out just who she's looking at, she immediately turns to me with a seductive smirk. I give her a deadpan stare in response. She's doing this to get a rise, that much is obvious, but I think if Abi starts glaring any harder, laser beams are going to come out of her eyeballs and burn a hole right through that woman.

"How about we play pool?" I ask, pointing to a table in the corner.

I need to find a way out of this situation, fast.

"Diiiid someone say pool?"

Marcus approaches the table, drink in hand.

"You summoned him," Kat chuckles, already moving on from Melissa.

Abi, on the other hand, seems like she isn't letting things go that easily.

"Why so glum, Abs?" Marcus asks.

She flicks her head toward the back of the bar where Melissa's taken her seat. and Marcus immediately lets out a groan.

"Oh, the royalty's here." He rolls his eyes. "Would you guess she lives in LA now? Runs a celebrity gossip blog called Little Miss Petty, acting like she's some kind of secret inside source. It's absolute trash, but it must be making her a shitload of money based on all the expensive shit she posts on her socials. I don't know if she even does a lick of her own work, I've heard she gets thousands of people submitting bullshit every day."

"So, pretty much the same things she did in high school," Abi grumbles. "Great."

"Sure, but who gives a shit? Are we playing pool, or what?" Kat asks. "Because I gotta say, I've had just about enough of looking at her."

I grab my phone, quickly punching *Little Miss Petty* into Google. What comes up is... well, shocking. An Instagram account with 70 million followers, a website, *and* a podcast that's sitting right near the top of the charts.

Yikes.

"Well, her blog looks stupid as shit," I mutter, locking my phone before Abi can see anything. "Enough of that, let's play."

Abi takes the lead, setting up the table while the three of us chat. The game's always been a comfort for her, at least for as long as we've known each other. When she's stuck on a paper, or needs to blow off some steam, she goes to The Hi-Dive to play by herself. It's not even really practice, she always says it's more meditative than anything, but either way, she's gotten really good over the years.

Table completely set up, Abi passes out our cues.

"Alright, looking good. I'm assuming you and Logan are a team?"

Kat looks surprisingly excited to play for someone who not only owns a pool table, but also the bar it's located in.

"Sounds good!" I chirp, with Abi nodding alongside me.

After briefly deciding who goes first, Abi breaks, sinking a stripe and following it up with two more before she misses. As Marcus and Kat make their way over to figure out the best angle for their first shot, I take a moment, gently grasping Abi's chin and running my thumb along her lips.

"You okay?"

"I didn't like the way Melissa smiled at you, that's all."

I can see the shame flooding her face as she's forced to grapple with her own words.

"And hearing it out loud, I know that makes me sound crazy and jealous and all of that shit, but everything was just starting to get a little bit better and then—"

I lean in and kiss her forehead, pulling back again to hold her gaze.

"You've got nothing to worry about, Abi."

She smiles looking a little bashful.

"Tonight I'm all yours."

CHAPTER THIRTY-EIGHT

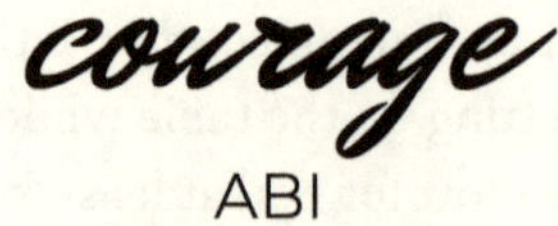

ABI

THE BLACK BEAR PUB
PRESENT DAY

Melissa is sipping a glass of white wine, tapping away at her phone, and doing her best to look nonchalant while she sits at the bar. Every so often she glances over at us, quickly typing something out before going back to scrolling.

Probably texting Carly.

They say time heals all wounds, but I've never really found that to be true. The tampons covered in fake blood and shoved into my locker, their merciless mockery of my dad's addiction, or the giggling and whispering about me when we'd get changed for gym class... I felt unsafe, unwanted, and powerless. Even though I've grown up, those feelings haven't gone away.

They just got buried.

"Shortcake!" Logan calls. "You're up!"

I like to take my first shot at a very particular angle, ever since I sunk three right off the break one time; I'm convinced it's good luck.

I can feel eyes on me as I breathe, readying the shot, and I glance over to find Melissa strolling right for us with her phone in hand. It's probably nothing, she's just heading to the bathroom. All I have to do is focus on the shot, and—

"Hey, Abi."

My guard flies up, and I'm that pathetic 15-year-old again.

"Uh– h– hey." I clear my throat and straighten up. "What's up?"

"Nothing, just out for a glass of wine. I didn't know you were back in town!"

Her smile is sweet, but there's something about it that puts me off... maybe the years of untreated trauma?

"Yeah. Just for the reunion."

"That's great!" Her eyes aren't even on me as she says it, tapping away on her phone for a few seconds before slipping it into her purse and flashing me a dazzling smile. "Sorry, I've still got so much work stuff, even in my free time. Social media is fucking insane sometimes. I feel like I'm *drowning* in messages."

She rolls her eyes before letting out a distressingly familiar laugh.

"But you get it, right? Anyway, what have you been up to?"

I doubt Melissa has changed much since high school, still a second-string mean girl who's nice to your face, just so she can report back to her friends with gossip.

"I'm teaching Sociology."

"That's cool." She's pulled her phone out again. "Like, high school kids, or something?"

"Uh, no. Like at a university. In Washington State."

"Oh! Cool!" It looks like that got her attention, and she leans in a little with a lowered voice. "Listen, can we talk for a second?"

I'm so uncomfortable that the beer in my stomach is starting to creep its way back up, but I nod anyway, and the two of us move away from the pool table.

"All that stuff that happened in high school... it's, like— you know, we were just being stupid. It was nothing personal."

I arch a brow, but say nothing as Melissa tucks a strand of hair behind her ear. What the hell is she doing? Does she actually feel guilty, or is this a trick?

Best to just let her talk.

"It's just water under the bridge, right?"

I'm not sure when *I* was consulted on this whole water under the bridge thing, but I think I must have nodded because she keeps going.

"I mean... we were just kids, right?" She laughs. "It didn't mean anything. I saw Carly and Brendan extended the invitation to the reunion as an olive branch to you, so I thought I'd..."

She shrugs, clearly unsure how an apology is supposed to work.

It's all bullshit. I don't trust Melissa now, and I never have. The few times she was nice to me, it ended up just being to fuel some joke at my expense.

I remember how often I came home from school in tears, being afraid to go to a teacher or the principal because it would inevitably make things worse. I'd fake stomach aches so that I could have *one day* of relief knowing I wouldn't have to face gym class with Carly and Melissa.

I could tell her that her dismissal of the pain she caused makes me want to punch her square in the face. Even better, I could take the swing right now.

But instead, I smile through it.

"Well, it was *great* to see you, but I think I have to get back to the game."

Like you're supposed to.

"Yeah, you too!" Melissa replies, not put off at all by the abrupt end to the conversation. "I'll see you at the reunion, then?"

"Yeah. See you there."

She's probably just glad she doesn't have to twist even further around herself, figuring out how *not* to ever say 'I'm sorry' in her grand apology.

"Pretty ring, by the way." She motions to the stone, and I find myself glancing down at it, still not quite used to it being there. "Super vintage."

"Oh, yeah. Thanks."

She gives a final wave to the group, and blows me a kiss before sauntering back to the bar.

"What was that about?" Kat asks.

"She, uh, wanted to put the past behind us. I mean, I *think* that's what she wanted. There was a lot of bullshit to shovel through."

Kat's eyes narrow as she stares the woman down.

"Yeah, I'll bet she did. Probably just gathering intel."

"You make it sound like she's a fucking spy," Marcus chuckles. "What *intel* would she need on someone she knew in highschool? Is she gonna put a sociology professor in her gossip column?"

"Well, those two are sneaky!" Kat retorts. "They always were. You just don't get it, you never had to deal with any of the mean girls."

I'm not naive. I always knew that if I got any closure, it wouldn't feel the way it does in the movies. But to have everything just brushed aside in a minute? My entire teenage years felt like a study in invisibility, where any time I stood out I was punished for it, and now I'm basically in the same spot.

I want to take this pool cue and... I don't know, hit something with it? But that's not what an adult would do. Everyone knows these problems barely matter, after all. It was just highschool.

Water under the bridge.

"Whatever, let's play."

Logan strides toward me, his arm winding around my waist as he pulls me into him.

"You sure you're good?"

The second I look into his eyes, all the newly wound up tension begins to unwind.

"Totally. I just don't want to think about this high school shit anymore. I'm over it."

He smiles, rubbing his nose against mine.

"I know what you could think about instead."

"What?"

"Me. Bending you over this table."

A shiver rushes down my spine, and I bite my lip to keep from making an obvious noise. Melissa doesn't matter, Carly doesn't matter, Brendan doesn't matter, the scholarship doesn't matter, the lies don't matter...

"Are you thinking about it?" He purrs. "About how good my—"

"Hey, it's still Abi's shot!" Kat barks. "You two can canoodle on your own time!"

Logan crosses his arms.

"I don't know what part of the gutter *your* mind is in, Kat, but we were just discussing important fiancé things."

"Really? Because it looked like you guys were about to start sucking face."

He gives a little shrug, a devilish glint lingering in his eye.

I don't know if it's him specifically, or if it's just finally having a second person who's in my corner now that we're back here, but I'm suddenly flooded with confidence.

I face the table again, line up my shot, and exhale as I connect with the cue ball. The rack explodes, sending different colors every which way. The red solid sails toward the corner pocket, dropping in with a dull thunk and Logan raises his hands in the air.

"Fuck yeah!" He grabs me by the waist, pressing his lips to my ear. "If you're a very good girl and win this game, I brought that little toy I picked up earlier."

My mind shoots back a couple days, just before we hit Ontario. We found a burger joint right across the parking lot from an adult store, and while I went to scope out a table, Logan sauntered into the shop. He never told me what he bought, he just said it was a surprise, but I do remember him coming out with a swagger that made it look like he owned the place.

Marcus curses, leaning over as he surveys the table.

"She plays pool all the time back in Emerald Bay," Logan says, taking the cue from me. "She's turned into a regular shark."

"I am not a shark!" I cackle. "Pool just helps me think."

He leans over, clearly trying to shoot for getting the purple ball into the center pocket, but even before the cue connects, I can tell it's a miss. The ball speeds forward, wide of his target, and bounces off of the bumper before rolling to a stop right in the middle of the table.

"You should have angled it about half an inch to the left," I giggle, sipping my drink.

It's actually kind of impressive to miss every single ball this early in the game, even by accident.

"Well, get ready to have your ass handed to you, King," Marcus takes aim, sinking his target with ease. "Because I get a hell of a lot of practice these days."

"Yeah, when you should be working," Kat snickers into her beer.

Marcus just rolls his eyes and hands her the cue.

"Your turn, gorgeous."

Kat has, apparently, taken lessons from her husband over the years because she doesn't hesitate, leaning over and shooting in one fluid motion, ricocheting a green striped ball into one of the middle pockets.

Logan whistles.

"Damn, you got some tight competition, King... Maybe it wasn't the best day to bring an anchor as your partner."

I stick my tongue out at him.

"Well, if you'd paid attention in those lessons I gave you, we'd probably be dominating this table right now."

Logan's lips brush right up against my ear again.

"There's only one thing I care about dominating on this table."

I can feel my stomach flip, but luckily the tension between Logan and I is broken by the game's, as Marcus takes another shot. The four of us watch with bated breath as the cue ball slowly inches toward a stripe that's sticking to the table by a thread.

It feels like an obnoxious metaphor for my life.

"Come on," Marcus groans. "Just a tap, that's all I need."

"That's what she said," I murmur.

Marcus's cue slips, bumping another ball as he starts to laugh.

"That was a dirty trick, King."

"She's a dirty—"

"Logan!" I hiss.

"Nope, inappropriate. Nevermind."

The last two days have been a ritual of sinking into the familiarity of home, realizing how much I miss it, and then slowly solidifying the real reason why I never came back. One of the most important people in my life left me with nothing but bad memories of this place. I've spent the last three years making excuses as to why I couldn't return home, but really I just couldn't bear to see the remnants of the life I had, and I let them taint all of the good things as well.

Watching Logan joke and laugh with my childhood friends like he's known them for years almost brings a tear to my eye. My mom once told me that the person you choose to spend the rest of your life with should be a reflection of the qualities you're trying to nurture in yourself.

That way, you can grow together.

"Whose turn is it?" Marcus laughs.

"I can't even remember anymore, dude." Logan holds out the cue to me. "You wanna take a crack at it, Shortcake?"

I smile, covering his hand with mine and getting up on my tiptoes for a kiss.

It turns out Logan and I have done a lot of growing together.

Hours later and the games have devolved into a 1v1, me versus Logan, while Kat and Marcus clean up the empty bar, counting the cash and wiping things down for the evening.

I'm perfectly tipsy, tucked right into that blissful little place where everything is funny, but nothing makes me cry. At least not yet. The alcohol's also made me bolder, and right this moment Logan's looking so fucking cute I can barely help myself, bent over a pool table with a strand of sandy hair tumbling down in front of one eye.

"Remind me what's on the line for this game?" He asks, looking up from his shot for what has to be the 6th time in a minute.

I grin, my drunken brain hurtling through a dozen terrible jokes, and a hundred even more terrible ideas as I sidle up next to him.

"How about... you get to do whatever you want to me when we're done."

He licks his lips, nodding his head before taking the shot, and effortlessly sinking his second to last stripe.

"I have a couple of ideas," he purrs.

"Color me curious, Doctor."

"Hey, uh, lovebirds?" Kat calls, swinging her keys around her finger. "You wanna head out with us, or you good locking up?"

"We can lock up!" Logan chirps.

Kat chuckles, slinging her purse over her shoulder as her eyes fall on me. Subtlety has never really been one of Logan's strong suits, but luckily the others are just as deep into their cups as we are.

"You still remember the alarm code?"

"One three... one four?"

"Abi!" Logan cackles. "You're not supposed to say it out loud!"

"Why?" Marcus asks, grinning from ear to ear. "You planning to rob us, Logan?"

"Yeah, exactly." Logan nods. "Being a professor is only my day job. By night, I'm a famous cat burglar— and I'm not one of those wannabes, either. I dress up like a real cat."

"Oh yeah, what's your criminal-name then if you're so famous?"

"Cat... Man. I'm Cat Man!"

I snort so hard I scratch, completely missing the cue ball, and Logan thrusts his hands in the air.

"Yeah! Eat it, King!"

"You fucker!"

I rush around the table, tickling his ribs until he collapses. He grabs my hands, pulling me close, and the butterflies in my stomach stir back to life as his eyes bore into mine. While I'm all hazy and fuzzy around the edges, Logan feels like pure fire. It's those damn eyes; that honey-brown looking particularly stormy in this light.

"Abi, I'm leaving you the keys!" Kat calls, setting them on the bar. "Feel free to have another drink, just don't clean us out, and don't burn anything down!"

"You got it!" Logan calls back, licking his lips while refusing to take his eyes off me.

I give Kat a wave as the two of them walk out the door, letting it slam behind them. Logan and I stare at each other in silence for a moment before he turns, striding to the entrance.

"Can't have any interruptions," he murmurs, flipping the lock. "How do you control the lights in this place?"

I lean up against the pool table, grinning at him.

"Behind the bar. What do you have in mind?"

Logan doesn't say a word, grinning as he flicks the switch and everything dims, leaving only a few ambient lights remaining. He walks toward me, reaching into his pocket before revealing his hand, concealing something closed in a fist.

I tilt my head, curiosity gnawing at me.

"What's that?"

"Close your eyes and hold out your hand."

I let my eyes slide shut and turn my palm upward, feeling Logan place something down into it. I rub my thumb across the object: small, almost tear-drop shaped, it's soft, squishy, and probably made of silicone.

My lips curl into a smile as I feel Logan behind me, pressing his body into mine.

"Open them."

Arousal licks at my skin, sending tingles shooting through every nerve ending as I look down at the small turquoise butt plug sitting in the palm of my hand.

We stand in silence for a moment, the two of us reveling in the thickening tension before he finally wraps his arms around me, his voice low and full of longing as I feel his words prickle up the back of my neck.

"I wanna play a new game."

head over feet

ABI

THE BLACK BEAR PUB
PRESENT DAY

Logan seems oddly confident— way more confident than me at least.

"We need lube, don't we?" I ask.

My heart's pounding as I stare at him, and I try to keep my nervous giggles at bay.

"You think I came unprepared?" He spins me around, pushing me up against the pool table with a grunt. "I'm just getting you warmed up."

I'm fully aware that Kat and Marcus could come back at any moment and bust this whole thing wide open. But I also like the idea of getting caught. It's dangerous, not to mention stupid, but being with Logan has brought out a different kind of animal in me.

He reaches around the front of my body, kissing up and down my neck as he slowly unzips my shorts and slides his hand inside.

"No panties."

"I figured they were a waste of time," I purr.

"You're right about that."

He takes his time, teasing me with slow circles around my clit, and I can't help myself from grinding my ass against his cock. Logan's gentle laughter and little growls are giving me the surge of confidence that I need, but just before we really start to get into it he removes his hand and drops to his knees, pulling my shorts down as he goes. I feel a sharp sting on my backside as the slap rings out through the empty room, and I let out a yelp.

"Can I try something?" He asks.

I glance over my shoulder to see him gazing up at me, a smile on his face.

"You've got carte blanche. Show me what you've got."

He makes sure my asscheeks are spread before he starts to lick me all the way from my pussy to my asshole; I cry out, pushing the pool balls away as I struggle to hold myself up. Everything feels heightened as he swirls his tongue around, the new sensation lighting my nerves on fire. I can't stop shuddering against the table, wondering what he's going to do next.

He continues tormenting me for a while, alternating between his tongue and sliding his fingers deep inside of me. I shove my hips back, silently begging for more, but he denies me, pulling his fingers out and leaving me feeling empty.

He loves to keep me on my toes.

"Fuck, Logan, just put it in!" I half laugh, half moan. "Please?"

I feel him get to his feet, resting both hands on my hips.

"There we go, Shortcake. And all you had to do was beg me for it."

I feel something cool dripping on my ass, gasping as he slides one finger inside for the first time.

"Tell me how it feels."

My eyelids flutter, feeling that familiar ache of desire as he thrusts his finger in and out of me.

"Feels like I want more," I groan.

"Greedy, hmm?"

"Please," I rasp. "I'll be such a good girl."

He adds another finger, thrusting it inside until I'm shaking. My stomach is hot and twisted up as the throbbing between my legs gets worse. All I have to do is reach down and relieve it, but the build up is what's making this feel so fucking good. The anticipation of being completely filled up is something I've never experienced before, and I want to hold onto this.

"Look at you, taking my fingers so well." He groans. "You want more?"

"Please!"

I barely manage to choke the word out before I feel that soft squishy silicone plug press right up against me, but he takes his time, lubing it up and teasing my asshole as I wait with bated breath. Finally he places one hand on my hip, steadying me. Logically, I know what's about to happen, but I'm bracing myself for how it's going to feel.

"We'll go slow. You say stop and we stop."

With just a few simple words he puts me at ease, my heart still pounding, but now from pure adrenaline. I want more. I *need* more. If we only get to fuck each other's brains out for two weeks, I want every second of it etched into my memory.

"Put it in," I rasp, keeping my eyes fixed on the front of the pub.

I barely have time to wrestle with the fear of Kat and Marcus returning unannounced before Logan's pushing the plug inside of me.

"Good girl, just relax for me, okay?"

I breathe, nice and steady. It's not painful, it's just... different. It takes me a bit to adjust before I drop my head and slowly begin moving my hips.

"That's it," he carefully pushes the plug in until it's buried inside me. "You're doing so good."

I let out a groan and he slides his cock along my pussy lips, forcing a whine from my mouth.

"You want more?"

Just as I'm about to glance over my shoulder, Logan snatches me by the waist and spins me around. I don't even have time to utter a word before he's lifted me onto the pool table, and dropped back down to his knees. I try to speak, but I'm cut off as his lips wrap around my clit, sucking on it in gentle pulses.

"Oh my god..."

God bless this man's beautiful mouth. He puts it to *such* good use. I can feel my clit throbbing on his tongue, my body so desperate for him to push me past the edge with a few gentle licks, but I don't want to come just yet. I want that build up. I want an explosion. I want what's left of me to be a fire that consumes him.

He flattens his tongue and I whimper, my body deciding to betray me as I squirm against his mouth. I keep trying to speak, but all I can manage is moaning his name over and over again. Then, just as he pushes me right to the edge, my pleasure comes to a halt, replaced by a cruel ache.

Logan rises to his feet, licking his lips like a ravenous beast.

"You're fucking exquisite."

I bite down on my lip as he stares, thinking about how I can prolong the feeling that's pooling inside of me. I need to be fucked, I'm *hungry* for it, but I don't want it hard and quick. I want to savor it like you would a delicious meal.

I want both of us to work each other up until we can't take it anymore.

"You like games, Sunshine?"

He grins, his eyes dancing with desire.

"You know I do. What did you have in mind?"

"Have you ever played *just the tip*?"

He stays silent, those eyes burning into me, dark and dangerous as he reaches down to give his cock a stroke. I think if you looked up the word feral in the dictionary right now, there's a reasonable chance you'd see a picture of Logan Flynn.

"It's fun." I reach down, spreading my pussy lips for him. "See, you take that big, gorgeous cock of yours and put the tip inside me– *just* the tip. And then we see how long you can last."

He reaches into his pocket slowly, pulling out a condom. I grasp his wrist, shaking my head.

"Abi..." His voice is timid, almost pinched with worry. "Are you sure?"

"I've tested negative. Haven't been with anyone else since you," I whisper.

It feels like all his bravado is sucked out of the room and he's back to the other side of him, the charming, awkward nerd I've known for so many years.

"Oh, me too! I can show you, I have the results on my phone!"

I giggle, covering my mouth, but he still looks a little nervous.

"I figured as much. Don't worry, I trust you, Logan."

We're crossing yet another line, but I don't care. This is the most we've ever given in, and I want to get completely lost in him until it's time for us to stop playing pretend.

The pain will come, but it'll come later, and we can handle it.

We've done it before.

"Are you... on birth control?"

I nod, pointing to the little scar underneath my arm.

"Got an implant last year." I gently pluck the condom from his fingers, tossing it away. "So none of this. I want to feel *all* of you."

Logan unzips his pants, spitting on his palm before wrapping his fingers around his cock. All I can focus on is the way it looks, pulsing in his hand as he glides the tip against my pussy lips. Feeling him without that thin barrier of latex I'm used to only makes me more eager.

"Fu—*uck*!" He groans.

The plug inside me is only satiating a fraction of my hunger. I need to know what it's like to be filled. Entirely. Pleasure begins to slowly consume me, like I'm sinking into a pool, and I drink in the sound of his heavy breathing in turn. I can tell he's starting to spin out of control.

It's all in the tremor in his voice.

"We've barely started the game." I tilt my head to the side. "You gonna come already?"

Logan lets out a snarl, ever so slowly pushing inside me but stopping just past the tip. Holy *shit*. I can feel the head of his cock pulsing already, and I can tell the longer we stay like this, the more I'm gonna want him to ram all the way inside me.

I reach for his hand, linking my fingers with his and squeezing tight.

"So, we know what I get if I win, but what happens if I lose?"

His voice is shaky and he squeezes my hand a little tighter.

"I haven't decided yet," I grin.

I reach down to gently strum my clit, but it feels so good that even the slightest amount of pressure is almost too much. The plug buried inside of me is basically multiplying the sensations that I'm accustomed to, and making things much more difficult.

"You want me to show you how wet I can get?" I ask, trying to keep the tremor out of my voice.

"Y— yes." He shudders. "Please?"

I let out a breath, guiding his hand down to my clit to show him how I want to be touched. He seems happy enough to follow along, letting me guide him every step of the way.

"No need to be nervous," I murmur. "You already know what you're doing."

He nods to himself, flashing me a megawatt smile, and I can physically see the change take him over. He draws himself up a little higher and his gaze becomes more focused. He's determined.

My hips start to rock like my body has a mind of its own, and Logan moves in response, pushing his tip inside before carefully slipping it out over and over again as I teeter on a razor's edge.

My body feels like a tightly coiled spring, trying to maintain what little control I have before finally giving in. I'm so close, I can taste it.

"All you have to do is say the word and I'll be *all* the way inside you."

He pulls out, forcing an agonized groan to slip out from deep inside me. I grit my teeth and he grins before pushing inside me one more time, refusing to give either of us what we really want.

"I want to win," I whimper, trying to keep my cool.

"You never said *what* you'd win."

"I never thought that far ahead."

The confession slips out more as a gasp than as words, but Logan only chuckles, wrapping one hand around my throat and gently squeezing the sides.

"How about you let me come inside you?" He rasps. "Fill you up until you're dripping."

All logic has sprinted out the door, leaving me with nothing but an aching want that can only be soothed by him.

"Yes." I cup his cheek, nodding as I stare into his eyes. "Fuck me."

He sinks himself all the way in, and I wrap my legs around his waist, the combination of his cock and the little silicone plug tearing a sharp gasp from my lips. I stare into his eyes as the hand around my throat slowly slides up to caress my burning cheek.

"That's my girl."

My girl. I'd do anything for him to call me that again.

And again and again.

"What's it like?" He asks.

I swear I can feel every little detail: the way the plug sits inside me, the small ridges and veins on his cock as he gently pushes himself all the way to the hilt.

"It's fucking magic."

Sweat trickles down the back of my neck and I tremble like a leaf as he places a tender kiss on my forehead.

"Can I show you something?"

"Yes."

Logan reaches into his pocket, pulling out a small remote.

"I didn't tell you about the extra features our new toy has."

"What—"

With the click of a button, the plug inside me comes to life. While it's true every part so far has been new to me, I've *definitely* never felt anything like this before. Intense heat shoots through my body and I let out a shriek, grabbing him by the collar of his shirt and forcing my mouth onto his. I need something to focus on, to keep my mind off the fact that my climax is building so quickly I'm afraid I might lose control.

I'm falling fast and I can't stop.

Logan tears his mouth away from mine after a long kiss, his hips slamming into me with brutal force, ruining any chance I have of staying focused.

"I can feel it," he groans. "Oh, fuck. Can I turn it up?"

I don't hesitate. I think I'm on autopilot at this point.

"Please! Please please please, baby!"

Logan's gaze stays locked with mine as he clicks the button another step up, increasing the intensity of the vibrations. My voice breaks as I rock my head back, crying out into the darkness of the empty bar.

"Fuck me like you own me," I moan.

It's all the permission he needs, and he snatches me up by the hips; I cry out, screaming his name along with each feverish thrust, my head starting to spin in circles. All I can think about is him. All I *need* is him.

The table creaks beneath me, rocking with the weight of our bodies as what's left of the balls clatter and clack around, most of them ending up in some pocket or the other. I cling to him like my life depends on it, sinking my nails deep into his arms.

I never want this to end.

"Open your mouth."

He grips my chin tightly, a wad of spit landing on my tongue and dribbling down my chin.

"Swallow."

The moment I obey I'm engulfed in a hungry kiss, followed immediately by him turning the vibration up one more level. I'm falling apart. I have to tear my mouth away from his, and bury my face into his shoulder to keep sane as wave upon wave of pleasure crashes against me. I'm a mess, sweat-logged and ravenous for more of him. More of this. More of us.

Logan keeps his feverish pace until finally, after what feels like an eternity of bliss, he lets out a raspy groan. His body stills and his cock twitches inside me as the two of us catch our breath. Mercifully, he has the sense to turn the vibrations off before we collapse, my muscles feeling more and more like jelly with each passing second.

"That was incredible," he murmurs. "I wish I had a better word for it."

I'm finding it tough not to just sit here, smiling like an idiot, when everything I've ever wanted is right here in front of me.

"You did better than me, I think half the stuff I said tonight was gibberish."

He chuckles, brushing my hair away from my face as his expression grows slightly pained, bringing me back down to earth with him.

"What is it?"

"Nothing. I just don't think I've ever seen you look more beautiful."

I can't keep falling in love with him, I think it'll kill me.

Luckily, as always, he knows *just* how to break the tension.

"I've gotta wash this."

Logan pulls out of me, gingerly removing the butt plug in turn.

"I can do it, it's been in *my*–"

He cuts me off with a kiss.

"You relax. Let me do the work, okay?"

I want to insist, and maybe I would have a week or two ago, but now...

"Sure."

He disappears into a bathroom in the back while I wet a cloth and try to mop up the mess we made on the pool table. Nobody needs to know, and it'll be dry by morning.

Hopefully.

I can hear Logan whistling a song from the other room: Shania Twain. It's gotta be the same one we danced to in Manitoba.

I pull out my phone, bobbing my head as I make sure there aren't any new texts from Kat or my mom. Finding nothing, I move quickly on to clear any new work e-mails that might have slipped past my 'out of the office' alert.

INTERVIEW REQUEST FOR ADJUNCT POSITION

My jaw nearly drops to the floor.

Is this for real?

I blink, reading the subject line over and over again to make sure it says what I think it says, and finally, with shaking hands, I open it.

Dear Dr. King,

We've reviewed your application package and would be thrilled to have the chance to chat with you about the adjunct position. I'm currently in New Zealand, finishing up a project, so the interview will have to be on Zoom, but I've attached a calendar with the date and time of the interview to make things easier.

Warm regards,

Allister Paxton, PhD.

Anthropology Department Head

Emerald Bay University

This is it. If I get this job, I can have all of it.

Everything.

Including–

"Hey, Sunshine! I'm gonna text Kat and see if it's cool if we grab one of these bottles of champagne! We can go out to the falls to celebrate!"

Logan wanders out of the bathroom, drying the plug off with a very perplexed look on his face.

"You know I'm always down for a party, but I don't know if a butt plug calls for a celebration. Is this a Canadian tradition I'm unaware of? Does the Prime Minister know?"

My first impulse is to snark back, but with everything going so right, I can only beam.

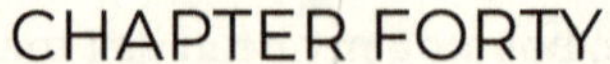

CHAPTER FORTY

bobcaygeon

LOGAN

BLACKBURN FALLS, ONTARIO
PRESENT DAY

I don't know what's better: the enormous rushing waterfall illuminated by moonlight, or the sight of Abi's frustrated half-smile as she tries with all of her might to rip the champagne cork out of the bottle.

I've been waiting for this moment for years, and the excitement that's bubbling in the air is about as intoxicating as the booze she's holding in her hands. It might be pre-emptive to celebrate, but if she gets this position, we could actually have a shot at being... us. If she still wants to, at least.

The champagne foams over the lip of the bottle as she finally wrenches the cork out, and she squeals with laughter, at first unsure what to do before trying to cut off the flow with her mouth. It starts to dribble down her chin which makes her laugh even harder.

I can't help myself, slipping out my phone to snap a picture of her.

"Logan!" She yelps, tearing her mouth away as the champagne flow begins to slow. "You can't just whip out a camera whenever you want!"

I chuckle, making the picture my wallpaper before flashing the screen at her.

"I've just never seen someone try to shotgun a bottle of champagne before, is all. Anyways, you're immortalized now, no take backs."

She sticks out her tongue, pouring me a drink.

"I hope yours has *extra* spit in it."

"I licked your asshole less than an hour ago, Shortcake. This does *not* faze me."

I raise my cup to the sky.

"Cheers to butt stuff!"

"And to job interviews!" Abi laughs. "But the butt stuff is probably more important."

We clink glasses and each take a sip, the roaring waterfall in front of us providing a beautiful accompaniment to the excitement already lingering in the air.

Abi stretches her legs out, kicking off her shoes and pulling her phone from her pocket as she starts to scroll through her Spotify. I always loved her taste, mostly because it's so different from mine, but not in a way that makes my ears want to turn in on themselves. I've always been more into 80s pop, classical, jazz and even those pre-bottled Halloween sound-tracks. I don't tend to listen to a ton of 'new' stuff; maybe it's my age, or maybe I'm just stuck in my ways, but it's usually a struggle to get me onto something that came out anytime after the mid-90s.

Abi's tastes forced me to branch out, and I've always loved that about her.

"When I was a kid, I used to come out here and listen to The Tragically Hip. I don't know why, but this place just kinda *feels* like their music."

"I don't think I've ever heard of them."

"Makes sense, they're more of a Canadian thing. I think you'll like them. It's what I listen to whenever I miss home."

The first thing I'm hit with is the sound of a soft acoustic guitar and the near-instantaneous feeling of comfort that comes along with it, main-tained even after the other instruments come in and the music begins to build.

Even though I'm sure this band's not some hidden gem, it still feels like something she's kept all to herself. It makes me want to know what else I've never seen; I want her secrets, all the things she wants to say but never does... I just know they'll make me love her even more.

"So, the lead singer for the Tragically Hip was Gord Downie. Dude was *the* Canadian poet. He wrote a lot about our history, even the dark parts that very few public facing personalities wanted to acknowledge, let alone put down on paper. I always liked that."

"You said he *was?*" I ask.

"Yeah, he died in 2017. Brain cancer."

I can feel my body tense a little, and Abi clearly notices, giving me a sad smile and resting her hand on my knee.

"The band did a huge goodbye concert. It was in Kingston, not too far from here. I went with my mom and we bawled our eyes out."

Tears gather in my eyes and I blink them away. His voice is powerful, but with a slightly haunting quality to it that makes me miss those summer nights, sitting out with my dad on the patio and counting the stars.

"What's this song called?"

"Bobcaygeon," she whispers.

"Bobwhat?" I ask, suddenly incredulous in the face of such a strange sounding name. "Who's Bob and why's he in a cage?"

"Bobcaygeon," she laughs. "It's a little town in Ontario. Also happens to be one of my favorite Hip songs."

"Well, I can see why."

She leans up against me, gazing up at the stars with a venerable smile, like she's thanking the universe for something. Sometimes being around Abi makes me feel like I'm experiencing turbulence despite being on the ground, and other times it's like this: calm and tranquil flying.

"So, when's the interview?" I ask, only willing to let the silence sit for so long.

"Friday at 3:00. I already put it in my calendar."

"It's gonna suck not having you in the same department anymore. No more meeting shenanigans. Maybe we can create interdepartmental shenanigans instead!"

"Well, I'll probably have to avoid causing some sort of inter-faculty war for at least a couple months in my new role, so you'll have to give me the lowdown via text. That is if I even get it."

"You'll get it."

"It's just an interview, and even if I'm one of the only candidates it could take months to get hired."

"You know, after my dad died, I was *so* pessimistic."

"You?" She laughs. "Pessimistic? That seems far-fetched."

She didn't know me back then. I think if she had, we might not have hit it off the way we did, and she definitely wouldn't have landed on 'Sunshine' for my nickname either way. The optimism and faith I have now was reasonably hard-won, and sometimes I think I use my joy as a shield.

If I can radiate warmth, nothing bad can touch me again.

"There was a while in my life when I felt hopeless, and I was anxious *all* the time. It felt like nobody cared about my grief. The people I thought were my friends didn't show up for me when I needed them. The silence was devastating, and it made me so fucking *bitter*. I was just carting this resentment around and it was bleeding into my grief. On some level I knew it was my responsibility to dig myself out of that pit, but I didn't know how. Then, one weekend I was in Vegas for this conference and I walked by this little psychic—"

"You? Went to a psychic?" She laughs. "Okay, now you're just spinning yarn."

"I think that's spinning *a* yarn, Shortcake."

She frowns.

"Why would it be singular?"

"It's a nautical idiom. When sailors would have to repair rope, they'd tell each other really long stories to pass the time. Hence, spinning a yarn."

"That would be spinning a rope—"

"Can I just tell the story?" I laugh. "And I promise, this is anything but a yarn."

"Okay, okay," she chuckles. "Full steam ahead, aye aye Captain, or whatever the sailors say."

I snort into my cup, doing my best not to burst into laughter.

I've never told anyone this story other than Imogen, who immediately pulled out four different decks of Tarot cards and asked me why I'd never gotten a reading from her. I quickly reminded her that she picked up that hobby for all of two weeks before giving up. She didn't take too kindly to that.

"So I walk in to see this psychic, and I end up getting a card reading. I don't know if it was the free mimosas I had at the casino beforehand that made me kind of loopy, but I went in with a completely open mind. She hit on everything: Dad's death, my sabbatical, and my growing depression and pessimism. It was all laid out in front of me; everything I'd been running from was shoved in my face." I shake my head, my stomach replicating the same discomfort I felt that night sitting across from The Great Madame Mavis. "I wanted to get up, tell her she was a great psychic, and that I didn't need to hear any more."

"Did you?"

"No. Crazily enough, I stayed."

Abi grins, nudging me with her elbow.

"Of course you did, because you're a nice person."

"Sometimes," I laugh. "But then she told me I needed to take more risks, and that our mindsets shape our view of the world around us. Even the things that happen to us. She said I needed to confront the universe and say, *'Show me how good it gets.'* I'll admit, I thought it was pretty stupid, but when I got back to the hotel I couldn't stop thinking about it. So, I went out on the balcony and yelled it out, real loud, right into the night sky. I felt like a total idiot, but pretty soon I was saying it every day. I hate to admit it, but she was right. I felt better, and once I really started embracing it, things shifted."

"What do you mean shifted?" Abi asks, on the edge of her seat.

"I felt that spark for life again. I found a new research topic almost immediately, and dove in with both feet... and more importantly, I wound up at a shitty nightclub in Toronto and spilled a drink on a beautiful woman. Before that, my grief felt like some sort of freezing-cold straight jacket, wrapping me up endlessly, with no way out. The experience helped me reach for that hope, and made me realize it's always there, you just have to manage to keep hold of it."

"Kind of like Dorothy's ruby slippers. You know, when she has the power inside of her the whole time or something?"

"You might be onto something with that."

"I usually am. As you know, I'm very smart."

She smiles, seemingly content, but it only takes staring at the waterfall for a few minutes for that familiar forlorn expression to reach across her face, and I feel like I'm losing her all over again.

Seeing her this anxious breaks my heart.

She needs a win, because right now, the only other concrete thing she has left to bank on is the upcoming budget meeting, and I don't think that's going to swing in her favor. As hopeful as I am, I also know when things are taking a turn, and lately our department's been looking to make any cuts they can. Contract workers like Abi tend to be the first ones on the chopping block when times are tough.

So I pull myself up off the ground, and hold out my hand.

"Come on. On your feet."

"What? Logan, no! I like sitting, sitting is good!"

"It'll only be for a second."

Abi laughs, letting out a pathetic little whine and playing up her resistance.

"Just trust me?" I ask, doing that puppy dog thing with my eyes.

Is it manipulative? Yes.

But will I stop?

Would you ask a master painter to stop painting? Of course not.

Abi groans, rolling her eyes dramatically as she lets me haul her to her feet.

"Okay, what are we doing?"

I breathe in the night air, the smell of dirt and soil that's pungent and sweet, mixed with the mist from the fresh rushing water. It really is stunning out here when you take the time to appreciate it.

"We're going to ask the universe to show us how good it gets."

She does that little scowl that always makes me laugh, looking like an angry little kitten; it's the cutest damn thing in the world.

"Come on! I know it feels dumb, but I promise, it'll change your life."

"Will I have to pay you a hundred dollars too?"

"Actually, I think that reading was more like $250, so…"

"Logan!" She whacks me on the arm, trying to look annoyed but laughing through it. "That's a terrible financial decision!"

"What?! I was in a vulnerable place and my credit card had a lot of room on it!" I yelp, grabbing her hand. I can feel the amethyst from her engagement ring dig into my finger and I smile. "We'll yell it together. Are you ready?"

She sighs, dragging in a breath, almost like she's steeling herself for battle. I think Abi is a hell of a lot like me, using her sunny nature to hide her anxiety, and how much pain she's still carrying with her even now. Like me, joy is her shield, but I know how exhausting that can get. She doesn't have to keep it up, not here, not with me. I want all of it, the tears, the anger, the bad days along with the good. I don't love her despite it all...

"I'm ready," she breathes.

I love her because of it.

"Okay. On three. One... two... three! *Show me how good it gets!*" I bellow, lifting our linked arms toward the empty sky.

I have a picture in my mind, a picture of us. We're sitting in the back-yard on a Sunday morning, drinking coffee and reading the paper together. Then we're off to a pumpkin patch, laughing at kids when they try to climb around on everything and fall on their asses.

Decorating the house for Halloween.

Christmas.

Painting the walls of a nursery.

But here and now, Abi is silent, standing next to me with that pained expression I know so well.

I nudge her gently, getting right up into her face.

"Abi you have to say it."

"Showmehowgooditgets," She mumbles. "Okay are we good? Can we sit now?"

"You have to say it and mean it!"

That only earns me another eye roll.

"Fine, but if I do this, you have to do my thing afterward."

"What's your thing?"

"I'm not telling you until you agree to it," she replies, a bit of that devilish sparkle returning to her eyes.

I fucking love it when she gets that sparkle.

"Fine. But remember, it only counts if you scream it and you mean it."

"Okay." She shakes her body out like she's getting ready for an Olympic event, taking a big breath before staring up at the sky. "Show me how good it gets!"

It's barely a shout, and it doesn't even come close to a scream.

"Nope," I laugh. "Do it again. You have to *mean it!*"

"Logan, this is—"

I grab her face, pressing my lips to hers, and she bursts into giggles after a moment of shock.

"Are you kissing me to shut me up?"

I pull back, feigning my own shock as I put a hand on my chest.

"Me? I would *never.*"

Abi gives me a gentle shove before clapping her hands together, and bouncing from one foot to the other like a boxer before a big fight. I wonder why this is so hard for her. I expected her to take to it like a duck to water.

Or a Canadian to ice hockey.

"Okay." She turns to me with her shoulders pinned back and a bright smile. "I'll mean it this time."

The water roars on ahead as Abi holds both arms out to her sides, screaming at the top of her lungs.

"Show me how *fucking* good it gets! Come on, you fucker! Show me!"

"That's great, Abi, but I'm not sure if you're supposed to threaten the universe."

"Hey, don't tell me how to manifest!" She retorts, thrusting out a finger and poking me in the chest.

I raise my arms in mock-defense.

"Alright, alright. Just don't hurt me!"

"Okay, but how was it?" She asks. "Did I do good?"

I pull her in close, kissing her softly on the cheek.

"You did *great.*"

Abi grins, rubbing her nose against mine.

"Okay, awesome, my thing now?"

"What's your—"

I can't even finish the sentence before she's slipping off her shirt and sliding her shorts down past her hips. I drink her in as she kicks them aside, her pale skin glowing in the moonlight.

"You like skinny-dipping, Sunshine?"

"I might make a habit of it if you can guarantee a view like this."

I can't get out of my clothes fast enough, nearly tripping over my pants as I rip them off, leaving everything in a chaotic pile on a rock. Abi doesn't even wait for me, taking a running start and leaping into the water with total abandon; I fall in behind her with a big clumsy splash. It's cold, but luckily not so cold that it's a true shock to my system.

When we make it up for air, she whips her hair back, letting out a loud laugh before she starts splashing me.

"What the hell, King?!"

She cackles, swimming away without a word. Abi's a good swimmer, and fast, too, speeding toward the waterfall much more quickly than I can manage myself. I haven't done this in years, and within seconds my arms and legs are burning, but as she slows to a casual pace I manage to just barely creep up on her, reaching out and grabbing her ankle to drag her back toward me.

"You can't escape!" I bellow, wrapping her in a big bear hug.

She laughs until she's breathless, eventually going limp in my arms as she gazes up at the sky.

"Do you think I'll get this job?"

I can't tell if she's asking me or the stars, but either way the answer is automatic. This is the closest we've ever been to something real, and I refuse to let a single negative thought enter my head right now.

"Yes. There's not a doubt in my mind."

Show me how good it gets.

stop crying your heart out

ABI

BLACKBURN FALLS, ONTARIO
PRESENT DAY

Logan's been spending the early part of the afternoon outside, in the pool with Dylan, Marcus, and Kat while mom and I fix up some lunch. I watch through the window as he's got Dylan perched high on his shoulders, the two of them sneaking up on Kat while Marcus distracts her. There's a big splash, followed quickly by Kat's giddy screams, raucous laughter echoing through the yard.

I grin as I slice up some strawberries.

"It's been a long time since I've seen you smile like that," mom says softly. "I can't help noticing he's good with the kid, too."

My mother's never exactly been subtle.

"Is that something you're talking about?" She asks. "As a couple, I mean."

"Mom, we just got engaged. Like, a few days ago."

Maybe it was a mistake coming here.

What happens when mom wants to visit us in Emerald Bay? What happens at Christmas? Easter? Are Logan and I going to put on a big show every time she or my friends show up at my door? Initially I just figured I could come up with some excuse; if they never really got to know him I could just say it fell apart, or work got in the way, or any number of other things. Now, though... I don't think she'll rest until she discovers why we 'broke up.' There's no way Logan gets out of this unscathed.

I wish I had gotten over this whole reunion thing; if I did, we could have quietly pined over each other back home with no consequences whatsoever.

"Are you alright, sweetheart?" Mom asks. "You've been a little cold all day."

Sometimes it's hard to pinpoint when my anxiety swoops in, and takes every ounce of my personality with it's arrival. Logan says it looks like a scene straight out of Invasion of the Body Snatchers, but I rarely even notice.

I flash her my biggest, brightest, and most reassuring smile.

"Totally fine. I'm just anxious about the reunion tomorrow. Seeing Brendan, and everyone else again? It's been a long time."

My mom scoffs, shaking her head. She made it extremely clear how much she hated Brendan, after how much we fought toward the end. Every tearful phone call, every sombre, silent afternoon after a message she never got to see; she *loathed* him for what he did to me.

"You know, he *still* won't even look me in the eye? He parades around town with that horrible bitch, but whenever he sees me he—" She shakes her head, catching herself in her little spiral. "You know, the one I actually feel sorry for is that baby."

She slices the carrots with a kind of anger that makes me flinch.

"To tell you the truth, I'm surprised you agreed to the whole thing."

"To tell *you* the truth, so am I."

She sets the knife down, leaning up against the counter, her green eyes honed in on me. I probably should have let Logan take my place when she asked for some help. He's a lot better at keeping up the façade than I am.

"So, why did you come here?"

"What? I told you, for the reunion."

"You hated high school, and you shot out of this town like a bat out of hell the second you got that job in Washington. I'm not trying to make you feel guilty, Abigail, but you ran from a whole lot of pain. Why wander back into all of that?"

"Because Brendan couldn't give me an answer about why he left. I wanted closure back then, and I still do now. I want... I want to stop wondering if it's actually me. If I'm the fucking problem."

"Honey, it's not that complicated. He's a goddamn loser who didn't know how good he had it with you. I'm not saying you don't deserve closure, but I do need you to know that this isn't your fault." She cups my face in her hands and I can smell the dirt from the garden on her palms. "And I want you to know how proud I am of you, sweetheart."

My phone starts to buzz on the counter, and my stomach sinks.

FRANKIE CALLING...

"Hang on, mom. I gotta take this."

I rush out of the kitchen and head for the bathroom, locking the door behind me. My hands are shaking so bad it takes a few swipes for me to actually accept the call.

"Hello?"

"Hey, Abi. Sorry to bug you."

"You didn't," I reply, trying to keep the tremor out of my voice. "Are Wednesday and Lydia okay?"

"The ladies are fine. I actually crashed on your couch last night because we were hanging out watching a movie."

He sounds anxious, but no matter how bad I want to ask what's going on, I decide to stay quiet until he breaks. It's an interview technique that Logan taught me: hold on to the pauses, and people will fill them with the truth.

"The budget committee came back with their findings from the audit, and uh... well, they decided that they're cutting your contract at the end of December."

"Okay."

The words are crushing, but it's not a surprise.

"Unless you managed to get that scholarship...?"

"I didn't."

"Ah, shit. I'm really sorry, Abi. I can work on finding you another position right away. Maybe a research assistant? I know Dr. Barnes needs someone—"

"Yeah, *that's* not happening," I manage to chuckle.

I don't need to be reporting 'accidental' ass grabs, or inappropriate comments about the depth of my cleavage, no matter how much Frankie would probably appreciate the ammunition to use against Barnes.

"Figured as much."

"Actually, um..." I bite my lip. "I may have found another position."

"Really?!"

Frankie sounds a lot more shocked than I'm assuming he intended, because he immediately clears his throat, resetting his tone to be much more supportive.

"Abi, that's great! Where is it? I'll give you a reference if you need it."

"It's actually not too far." I grin. "You might even say it's in the same building."

"Seriously?! What department?"

"Anthropology. It's an adjunct position— the pay is *slightly* shittier, but..." I laugh. "It means I won't have to leave."

Frankie is quiet for a while, and I can practically see the gears spinning in his head before he finally speaks up again.

"Let me talk to the department head. I bet I can get you a leg up on the competition."

"No!"

I practically shout it out. I want to get this job on my *own* merit, to have my experience do the talking.

"Frankie, it's— it's really okay. Besides, I actually think that's pretty unethical."

"Yeah, well, rich parents try to bribe us to bump their kids' grades up, so I figure we deserve a go at it once in a while too."

"Uh huh, but what about our integrity?"

The line is silent for a moment, followed by the longest sigh I've ever heard from him.

"Alright, alright, integrity wins out again. I won't say anything, but I am going to write you a hell of a recommendation letter. I hate that we're letting you go right before the winter season. It's gonna be Christmas."

I laugh, tears rolling down my face as the anxiety fills me up, ping ponging all around. Pounding heart, clammy palms, swirling stomach; my body doesn't know whether to be happy of stressed the fuck out.

"It's just how these things go sometimes, right?"

"It is. But you're part of the family, and we don't let go of our own that easily."

"Thanks, Frankie."

"No problem. But hey, how's Flynn? Not driving you too crazy, I hope."

My mind flashes back to Logan on the phone with my mom.

I love Abi very much.

Maybe he's always meant it, or maybe it's all part of the lie. It's impossible to know.

"No, he's great," I laugh. "He's always great."

I want to tell him the truth. All of it. I want to lay it bare.

"Well, just make sure he doesn't hog the stereo on the trip back. Nobody wants to listen to elevator music or Halloween sound effects for 17 hours straight."

"Thanks, I'll do my best."

"So when's your interview?"

"Tomorrow."

"Well, your reference letter will be in your inbox before the hour's up. If there's anything you need me to change, just let me know."

"Frankie," I whisper through tears.

He's always been *so* kind to me, all the way back to moment one.

"It's the least I can do— and since you won't let me meddle, I bestow you with the horrible honor of copy editing it. My love be with you!"

"Thanks, Frankie. Really. I'll let you know if anything needs to be changed."

"No problem at all, King. Now, sorry to do this, but I've gotta go make some other calls I don't want to make. Talk soon, okay? Let me know how the interview goes."

"I will."

I end the call, and stand alone in the unbearable silence, staring at myself in the mirror. This is the woman who has to go out there and pretend things are fine as her world falls apart, who'll have to suffer through seeing her ex again, smiling through gritted teeth while she lies about how great her life is, all while it sits in limbo.

It's hard not to grow bitter about that.

I grab some toilet paper and dab at the tears in my eyes before heading back into the kitchen, but the second mom turns and sees my face, I know she's clocked me.

"Abi? Are you okay?"

I can't lie anymore. Not to her, at least. It's too much to carry, along with the fake engagement, the interview... I just need to come clean about *something*.

"My contract's up at the end of the year," I blurt out. "And I don't know what I'm going to do."

Her brows knit together, her eyes filling with confusion.

"I thought you had... that T word."

"Tenure." I nod. "Yeah, I—"

"Doesn't that mean you're a permanent employee?"

Lying to my mom never felt good, but I did it. Lying to Kat never felt good, but I did it. The problem is, the deeper Logan and I spiral into this fiction, the harder it is for me to navigate through it all.

It feels so real, so close I can *taste* it.

"Abigail..."

Her voice is a warning. and I know the second I open that door, there's gonna be no going back. But it's too late to worry about that. I've got to come clean or I'm going to be crushed under the weight of it all.

"I never had tenure, mom."

I blurt it out, all at once, and just as expected the rest starts to go along with it.

"The, uh... Okay, so I do have a job teaching at the university, but I'm not a professor, so— Fuck, this is so hard to explain."

Shame stings my throat.

"Basically, I got a postdoc at EBU. It's, um, it's sort of a researcher-slash-teaching position, but it's a contracted position. And like every-where else right now, money's tight at the university, so *because* it's a contract, it can be cut."

Mom puts her hand on her chest. Immediately, I find myself gravitating toward her to soothe the wound I just made.

"It's okay! I'm— I'm okay! I'm interviewing for an adjunct position, same school and everything—"

"What's adjunct mean?" Mom asks, still visibly confused. "You guys have all these weird job titles and I have to admit, I don't really know what you're really saying half the time."

"Adjunct is like... It's a part-time teaching position. I can still publish and do research, it's pretty much the same job I already have, just a little bit different, and in another department— but that's if I get it. It's still in Emerald Bay, so I wouldn't have to move. It's not tenure, but it's... something."

Mom's eyes narrow, and she folds her arms over her chest.

"So why lie?"

I've been trying to figure out the answer to that question for a week now. Not the one I tell myself every day, the real answer.

"I don't know mom, I was just— I was scrolling through the attendance list for the reunion, diving into everyone's profiles, and they're all so... happy? Successful? Like, look at Kat and Marcus: they've got Dylan, the bar, their real estate thing..." I trail off, biting my lip to keep the rest of the truth from tumbling out of my mouth.

I know social media is just us putting our best foot forward and capturing our happiest moments. Nobody shows you the mess behind the perfectly framed photograph. The thing is knowing all of that doesn't mean you won't fall for it.

I look out the window at Kat, watching her laugh as she holds Dylan up above the water. I love my work, but there's a part of me that wants the rest as well. The kids, the house, the white picket fence. It all feels so far away, like a dream I keep being torn from. Because of something *I* did wrong, all those years ago.

"I just didn't want to come home a loser, mom.".

She blinks, silent for a moment before she grasps my face, staring me dead in the eye.

"Abigail Autumn King, I did not raise a loser. You graduated at the top of your class *two years* early. You got straight A's, you won scholarships all through college, you paved your own way—"

"I could have published more, I could have put out a better application. I could have applied myself more, and worked so much harder. Do you know what usually happens to gifted kids? They end up fucking *mediocre.*"

I feel myself shaking, struggling to speak through clenched teeth.

"I can't even keep a postdoc position, not even a real—"

"Abi, budget cuts happen! It's not your fault!"

I squeeze my eyes shut, hot tears rushing down my cheeks, and it takes everything in me not to sob into her chest.

"Do you know how many people actually get a PhD?" She asks. "Abi, I looked it up. Two percent of Americans. *Two!* That is *not* mediocre, and you are *not* a loser. All those things that other people have, marriage, kids... it can all still happen for you if you want it. You're only 26, and you're engaged to a man who *obviously* adores you. I can see it in his eyes."

I can't imagine what she'd say if she found out we were faking *that*, too.

"Mom—"

She cuts me off with a wave of her hand.

"You've *always* been hardest on yourself, but I know you. You're a King! If there's a door that slams in your face, you take a battering ram to it. And if things ever get too hard, or you can't make it through on your own, you've got tons of people who would be so happy to help. All you have to do is ask."

Mom and I have cried together like this so many times... about boys and about school, about bullies, and about the uncertain future.

Through it all, she's always been my rock.

"I'm sorry I lied to you, mom."

It stings so badly that I have to keep doing it too.

"Baby, I don't care about the *lie,* I care about why you felt you *had to tell it.*" She wraps me in her arms, holding me tight. "Everything is going to work out, and you'll land on your feet. You always do."

We hold each other for a long time, mom rocking me from side to side and humming a song I vaguely recognize.

"You know, ever since your dad walked out, it's been you and I against the world," my mom murmurs, kissing my temple.

I look up at her, blinking away tears.

"Wouldn't have it any other way."

"Me neither." Mom brushes her nose against mine. "You're the one thing I know I did right."

perfect

LOGAN

BLACKBURN FALLS, ONTARIO
PRESENT DAY

"Have you ever seen her this nervous before?"

Sherri and I are watering the rose bushes that line the yard, trying our best not to meddle as we watch Abi pacing inside, circling the kitchen table as she gnaws on her fingernail like she's going to take it right off.

"Not since she defended her dissertation," Sherri replies, tutting in frustration when she notices the watering can is empty. "Logan, honey, can you fill this up for me?"

"Of course, leave it to me."

I keep my eye on Abi as I walk to the shed to grab the hose.

Her makeup is minimal, with just a pop of bright red lipstick that stands out as she wrings her hands. My gaze drops to her long legs and perfect ass as she paces in front of the open screen door. Even when she's a wreck, she's beautiful.

God, my fake fiancée's a fox.

I feel something splash against my ankle, and look down to discover I've overfilled the watering can. One of my leather shoes is drenched, but it'll survive. The wet sock thing, though? That's gonna be a real problem.

"Great job, genius."

"Logan, honey?" Sherri calls. "I think you're being summoned."

I grimace, turning off the hose and shaking my foot out in time to see Abi frantically waving at me from the window, a pained expression on her face.

I head straight for the back door, my sock squishing with each step, water seeping out from between my toes. I don't know what it is about the sensation, but the feeling of a wet sock is like the tenth circle of hell for me. I'd rather walk through broken glass.

As I open the door I find Abi shaking out her arms in a panic.

"Sorry, I just... I need someone here with me." She winces. "Is that sad? Usually I can interview by myself, but I don't know, today..."

"It's not sad," I chuckle, pulling out a chair for her. "Here, sit down."

"No, I want to pace."

My eyes land on the sweat clinging to her forehead, and I grab some paper towel to dab it up.

"Fuck, I'm so sweaty. Why am I so sweaty?"

"Probably has something to do with the polyester blouse, the fact that it's like 90 degrees in here, and you stomping around like a horse on steroids."

Abi halts mid-stride, transitioning into bouncing on the balls of her feet. She's wearing black heeled boots that give her an extra inch, but make the entire process significantly more stressful to watch.

"Ooohhh..." she wrings her hands, her cheeks flushed. "There's so much to be nervous about."

I check my watch.

"Really, Abi, why don't you sit down and I'll get you a glass of water? Because your call's starting in exactly two minutes, and I feel like you might want a bit of a cool down period after that marathon of pacing."

"Oh my god!" She yelps, scrambling for her laptop before collapsing into her seat. "I wasn't looking at the time! Why wasn't I looking at the time?!"

I lean over her, giving her a little peck on the temple.

"That's what I'm here for, Shortcake."

I head to the cupboards, grabbing a glass and filling it up with some ice, but before I can pull out the jug of water, I hear Abi let out a small confused noise.

"What's up?"

"I just... I'm logged on, but something's wrong. The date for the interview is for yesterday."

"That's weird," I reply, running the tap. "Some of these websites are really glitchy."

She shoots up out of her seat, turning to me with a horrified expression.

"Oh my god, *Logan!*"

I look down at the jug. Am I supposed to be using different water?

"What'd I do?"

Abi's clutching her laptop, her eyes practically bugging out of her head.

"The interview was set for *New Zealand time*! Not Eastern Time! I'm a day late!"

I watch her spiral begin, totally helpless to step in now that it's started. Surely missing a single interview isn't the end of the world, but I can't be flippant about this. What she's feeling is entirely real, and the last thing I want to do is make her feel like she's crazy.

She can fix this. It's possible all it will take is an email, but that won't matter if she can't get to a place where she believes it.

I set the water down and walk toward her.

"Listen to me, okay, Shortcake? I want you to slow down, just listen to my voice for a minute, okay? Just breathe along with me."

She starts to take deep, shuddering breaths, looking up at me like she's waiting to hear something that's going to fix everything all at once.

"Okay, great. You're doing great. Now, once you're feeling better again, I want you to send him an email. Just apologize for the mixup, and ask to reschedule. If you want to, you can even say you had some sort of family emergency. Don't worry about details, just reach out and let them know you're still interested."

"Logan, he's probably moved on to—"

"Send him—" I pause, kissing her softly. "An email, Abi. That's all you need to do."

Abi's problem is that she never wants to advocate for herself, even when it's important. She'll fight for other people until she's blue in the face, but her own needs? Those get pushed to the wayside, especially if she thinks she's responsible for whatever situation she's in.

"You want this job, right? I mean, it's something you really want right now?"

"Of course I do!"

I place my hand on her cheek. relishing the way she heats up under my palm.

"Then go get it. Everyone makes mistakes, and people reschedule all the damn time. Trust me, as someone who's missed more than his fair share of appointments. It's going to be okay."

She nods, and I ease her back into her seat before grabbing an apple and fetching that water. As I settle down next to her, I can see she's already gotten to work— typing and backspacing over and over again. I watch her the whole time, captivated by her intensity and focus, until she finally slumps back in her seat after about half an hour.

"I think that's good. Can you look it over?"

She looks like she's run a marathon.

"Sure. You eat and hydrate, I'll edit."

I grab her laptop, adjusting my glasses as I lean forward.

`Dr. Paxton,`

`I sincerely apologize for missing the interview. To be completely honest, I didn't realize the Zoom call was scheduled for New Zealand Time and not Eastern. I know you're extremely busy, and I'm sure you have other candidates, but would you be open to rescheduling? I'd love the chance to sit down and talk about my goals for the position.`

`Warmest Regards,`

`Dr. Abigail King`

`Postdoc, Emerald Bay Sociology Department`

"Is it too desperate?"

"No, I think it reads as confident. I'd be psyched to get an email like that, you sound like you're already invested."

"Can you send it for me?" She asks with a mouth full of apple. "I can't bring myself to look at it anymore."

I chuckle, scanning it one more time for any spelling mistakes, but when I go to hit send, she snatches up my wrist.

"Wait!"

Abi stares at me and I raise a brow, but she only shakes her head, smiling to herself.

"No, it's okay," she exhales. "Just do it."

I smile back at her, and hit send.

"No take backs."

"No take backs," she whispers.

I close her laptop and scoot my chair toward her, resting my hands on her thighs.

"He's going to email you back and say, *'Abi, I'd love to reschedule with you. Because you're fucking brilliant, and a real fox.'* I might even have to beat him up for that last bit, *very* unprofessional.'"

She laughs, tears rolling down her cheeks.

"You're such a bad liar."

I stare at her for a moment, watching her face crumple as she sobs and I wrap her up in my arms. At first I thought they were happy tears, but it looks like she's still wound up about the whole thing. It feels like we're two steps forward and three steps back, as out of the corner of my eye I see Sherri striding toward the house in full mother-bear mode.

"What's going on?" She asks, the back door creaking violently as she shoves it open.

"I messed up the time zone," Abi sniffles. "He was in New Zealand, I think for research or something, but when I got the Zoom invitation I didn't even check the date."

She slams a fist into the table, starting to shake.

"God, all I had to do was check the date!"

Sherri walks over, carefully putting a hand on Abi's shoulder as she sobs.

"Oh, baby, it's not the end of the world. I'm sure you can reschedule!"

She flashes me a sad smile and I nod, passing Abi some tissues.

"Yep, and she's already done it, so there's nothing else to worry about."

"Well, then!" Sherri puts her hands on her hips, her smile bright and genuine. "There you go! I'm sure he'll get back to you, right? These things happen all the time!"

"He will," I assure her, rubbing her back. "I promise you, he will."

CHAPTER FORTY-THREE

LOGAN

REYNOLDS VINEYARD
PRESENT DAY

I have to admit, for as much of a shitbag as Abi's ex is, the vineyard he lucked into is pretty fucking cool. The main house is a large blue and white colonial, sitting right next to another brick building with stained glass windows and rustic hand-carved doors. At least, that's what the website says. I'm not particularly interested in the tour, so I'll have to take their word for it.

The sun hangs low in the sky, with servers bustling around removing empty glasses and refilling drinks; what would a winery be without plenty of alcohol? When we arrived, we were each given a glass of sparkling wine with a little bow tied on the stem. Abi rolled her eyes, but I think it was kind of a nice touch. I'd never say it out loud, though, because she's clearly in a mood and I'd rather keep my sex privileges.

I scoff into my glass, making a show of how little I care for the drink.

"Man, this stuff is shit. Looks like they can't even throw a good party."

"It's not," she sighs. "It's actually pretty good... and the vineyard is really beautiful this time of year. Fuck! I was hoping he'd end up a loser who plays video games in his mom's basement, and now I have to look at all of this?"

She's gesturing to… well, everything: starting with the swaths of her classmates all looking content, mired in conversation within the near-endless field of vines and grapes stretching off in front of us. My job here is to be supportive, but my secret mission is to keep Abi calm, and make sure she doesn't drink too much and end up saying something she'll regret. She's still shaken from the interview, and throwing her ex-fiancé into the mix isn't going to help with that at all.

"How about we go and find Kat and Marcus, and maybe grab a hot dog or something?"

"I'm fine here," she mumbles. "I don't know if I want to find another even more beautiful sight around the corner."

We've been milling around close to the front gate for something like 10 minutes, and Abi's body's been coiled like a spring the entire time. I'm afraid her mood is going to continue to dip over the course of the night, and while staying here would probably keep her far away from Brendan, I don't want her to be miserable.

I draw in a breath, wrapping my arm around her waist, but she barely moves. She's so tense, I swear she could be made of stone.

"Hey, we don't have to do this. Do you want to just—"

She turns to me, eyes blazing.

"What, just leave? Then what was the point? This entire trip would be for nothing!"

The words hit a lot harder than I expected. Nothing about the trip has felt meaningless, not meeting her mom, her friends, and obviously not waking up next to her every morning.

"I don't know, I felt like things were pretty… great, at least up until now."

"I didn't mean it like—" She takes a deep breath, gazing up at me. "I'm sorry, I'm not in a great headspace. I just meant the story we came up with, and the reason why we're here, I—"

I pull her toward me, placing a kiss on the top of her head.

"It's okay. I get it."

"I'm sorry," she murmurs, burying her face in my chest. "I'm so sorry, Logan."

It feels like she's apologizing for something deeper, like she's already preparing herself for our worst case scenario.

"Hey, it's okay. We're okay."

What Abi and I have is fragile, but more than that, it has an expiry date. And she's right, it's something that only happened because it was a convenient way to get her some closure, but it's hard to ignore the strong foundation we built our little lie on top of.

"Come on," I urge, trying my best to get her out of her funk. "Let's grab something to eat."

"Logan, I'm just— I'm not hungry right now. You can go, I don't—"

"Okay, great! You can come watch me eat. You know, I've been told I'm a very elegant eater."

She chuckles as I link my fingers with hers, and begrudgingly lets me lead her toward the gigantic row of tables. I grab a plate and start to fill it up while Abi glances around, nervously sipping her wine. Just as I'm stacking the third slider onto my plate, I can see her face pale. It kind of looks like that scene in Jurassic Park where the little girl sees the raptors while she's eating Jello.

I could go for some Jello right now.

"You okay?" I ask.

Abi doesn't have time to answer before a razor sharp voice slices through the chatter.

"Abigail?"

Abigail?

I glance over in the direction of the voice, spotting a woman with long strawberry blonde hair striding toward us. She has a baby balanced on her hip, and a big saccharine smile that looks like it was plastered on her face early this morning, one that's started to sag just the *tiniest* bit.

Carly Reynolds.

"Abigail, it is you! Hiiii!" She extends the last vowel like it's the finale of a brand new hit single as she approaches. "I didn't think you'd make it!"

Abi looks visibly shaken, but Carly just flashes her another sugary smile, bouncing her son on her hip. He's cute, chubby cheeks, button nose, and big brown eyes.

Right, with him in the picture I guess it's Carly Howard now.

Instinctively, I grasp Abi by the waist, pulling her toward me in what's probably a little too protective of a gesture, but I've never really seen her speechless like this before.

"Yeah, well, I wasn't sure—"

"I just thought, you know, with your and Brendan's history, and with you all the way out in Seattle, not to mention your *very* prestigious job, that you would be..." She shrugs. "Busier."

I eye the champagne flute that's clutched in Abi's hand, wondering if I should take it. It's a shockingly easy thing to snap one in half, and then she'd have a weapon. God, what a ridiculous thought; I think I just watch too many horror movies.

But then again...

"I get the summers off," Abi manages to grind out through gritted teeth.

"Oh, lucky!" Carly gushes. "It must be so nice to have all that free time!"

You know what? I came here ready to give pretty much everyone a fair shake, but all it took was 30 seconds and I already *hate* this woman. The crazy part is that I don't really hate anyone; I'm a pretty friendly guy. I always try to see the best in people, even people I fundamentally disagree with. But there's just something about the way she's looking at Abi, an undercurrent of poison flowing beneath friendly gestures, that really pisses me off.

"It is nice, yeah." Abi mutters. "Thanks for inviting us."

Carly shifts her attention to me, like she was waiting for the perfect opportunity to do her little introductory schtick and blow me away.

"Carly Reynolds— Oop! I guess it's *Howard!*" She laughs. "Sorry, I'm still getting used to that."

She's just flaunting it at this point.

"Dr. Logan Flynn," I reply, shaking her hand as pleasantly as I can manage. "And didn't you get married two years ago? Long time to get tripped up on a name."

"Excuse me?"

"Sorry, I couldn't help but snoop through your profile," I chuckle, giving her an equally saccharine smile right back. "I'm a researcher! Tough habit to break."

Carly's Stepford-Wife expression falters ever-so-slightly, and for the briefest of moments I feel like she's considering taking my head off. Is she worried we're going to reveal how sordid the beginning of their relationship was? Did she not think plastering her entire life on social media would unravel her dirty little secret? No, that can't be it. I think she's just surprised that someone is actually standing up to her for once.

"Actually, I only recently changed my name," Carly replies, her gaze turning icy. "I thought I'd keep my own for a long time, but you know what they say: Love finds a way!"

"Of course!" I grin, completely unfazed. "I couldn't agree more!"

Abi looks like she wants to die as an awkward silence falls over the three of us, Carly obviously unprepared for the more competitive dynamic. It's like she wants one of us to back down first, but I stand firm, my smile never faltering even for a moment, until finally she clears her throat.

"Well, it was nice to see you again, Abigail." She flashes me another smile. "And it was *lovely* to meet you, Larry."

She turns on a toe and heads back toward the house in a hurry, but I make sure to give her a big wave as she goes.

"It was nice to meet you, too, Clarice! Thanks for the wine!"

I half-expect Abi to chew me out, or snap at me for making things more awkward with Carly, but instead I just feel her carefully wind an arm around my waist.

"Thanks for stepping in." She sighs. "For some reason I didn't expect her to actually talk to me. Caught me completely off guard."

I grin.

"Yeah, well, nobody messes with my girl."

CHAPTER FORTY-FOUR

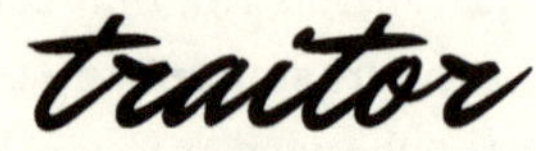

ABI

REYNOLDS VINEYARD
PRESENT DAY

It didn't take long before we found Kat and Marcus sitting at one of the picnic tables near the kid's play area, with Dylan sat down in a little tent alongside a bunch of other toddlers happily playing with blocks.

"Watch. He'll try to get up, and— well, you'll see," Kat chuckles.

Like clockwork, Dylan tries to place another block on his tower, but can't quite reach. So, he rolls over and struggles to his feet before clumsily lumbering toward his masterpiece. Just as he places the block on the top, he loses his balance and lands right on his butt. I brace myself for tears, but he just lets out an unamused *harumph* and grabs another block. His chubby little face is twisted up with determination.

"Marcus has to clear out my phone once a month because I don't have enough storage to take pictures for the real estate company."

I chuckle, sipping my wine as I watch Kat obsessively follow him with her phone camera, taking video as she smiles from ear to ear. We're waiting for Logan and Marcus to return from their mission of loading up on free grub. I can see them off on the other end of the grounds, laughing about something as they playfully elbow each other. It's amazing how well Logan vibes with everyone around him.

"They seem to be getting along well," Kat remarks. "Marcus is a big fan."

"Well, Logan gets along with pretty much everyone."

"He's a real sweetheart," Kat replies. "And you guys have a great vibe. I know I've never seen you this happy with someone before."

"He makes it easy," I laugh.

And it's true, everything is always easy with Logan. It was easy to fall for him, and even easier to fake this entire mirror-life together, pretending any and all of it was real. I want to tell Kat the truth so badly, but instead I'm munching on a cracker, taking in the beauty of this stupid fucking vinyard.

I hate that this place is so gorgeous, and I hate having to admit that Carly did pretty well pulling off the event. Old classmates have been mingling and chatting with each other like they've been hanging out for years. Maybe the real problem is the part of me that's been longing for a place I haven't been able to return to since I left for Emerald Bay. It leaves a bitter taste in my mouth knowing that there are people who got to stay here, to live here without any of the baggage that got forced on me. Maybe it means I'm grieving what could have been had things been different.

I think about what Logan said the other night at the falls, about carting around his resentment. Being on this trip has brought back so many feelings of inadequacy. I should have my shit together.

Show me how good it gets.

"Hey, you okay?" Kat asks.

"Yeah." I turn to her, forcing a smile as I swirl my wine. "Totally fine, just a little overwhelmed is all."

"You sure? You seem pretty on edge. I saw you talking to Carly, did she do something?"

"She was fine," I mutter. "Pretty nice, I guess."

"What did she say to you?"

"Nothing." I wave my hand. "Just pleasantries. It was…"

"Abi. Come on."

I thought this lie Logan and I had crafted would make me feel better about being here. It was supposed to be my armor against highschool pettiness, a tool to make everyone think I had everything together. Now that I'm here, though, I just feel like the biggest loser on the planet. The weight of missing the interview, our uncertainty about the future, and my never-endingly complex feelings about Logan are just making things worse.

"Do you ever feel like you're not enough?" I ask.

"What do you mean?"

What I mean is it feels like everyone can see through this cardboard-cutout version of myself we put together for tonight, and when everyone finds out how deep the lies go, I'll never be able to come home again. But of course, I can't tell her that.

"You know, like, you and Marcus have the Black Bear, and your real estate company, but do you ever feel like you're not where you *should* be in life when you look at everyone else?"

"All the time!" Kat laughs.

I'm a little shocked, I have to admit.

"Really?"

"Yes! Dude, believe me when I tell you this, it doesn't matter what you have or where you are in life, the grass always looks greener."

It's juvenile, but I always thought that once I reached a certain stage in life, I'd stop feeling the way I do right now. Instead of fueling my passion, academia put me in a kind of prolonged fugue state. I'm always off balance, reaching for something more, trying to get somewhere that's crowded with so many people all grasping for the same few opportunities. I guess some people like to chase that feeling, but me? I'd like to have some job security for once.

"Is that what you're feeling?" Kat asks. "Disappointed in how your life turned out?"

"I guess a little, yeah. I just... I thought I'd have, I don't know, something I could be proud of."

"Abi, the only person you need to impress here is you." She clears her throat and takes a breath, twisting her hair between her fingers as she chooses her next words very carefully. "Look, you know my mom and I don't have the best relationship, right?"

I nod. Kat's mom is highly strung and quite demanding. She ruled over their house with an iron fist, and constantly clashed with Kat's more laid back nature.

"When Marcus and I started the real estate company, we had a big celebratory dinner for our one year anniversary. We were *so* proud, so happy that we'd made it through our first year. Most businesses don't even survive even that long, so we knew it was a big deal. Anyway, we decorated the pub, even had some new tables brought in, but when mom showed up, *all* she could do was criticize the changes we'd made." Kat scoffs, shaking her head. "Everything was wrong, she said the additions were ridiculous and would ruin the pub; the crazy thing was she didn't even have anything negative to say about the real-estate stuff, the whole point of the evening. She just latched on to the first thing she could criticize and went all-in on it."

"I had no idea," I whisper.

Over the years, I've been the person Kat's leaned on the most for support, and she's never been shy about her opinions on her mom, but I never knew it was this bad.

"I was so ashamed. My whole life, all I've ever wanted to do is make my mom proud of me, and all she ever does is criticize every move I make." She sighs. "So, after that? I cut her off. She made me feel so fucking small, and I'd had enough."

"When was this?"

"Couple of years ago now. I still talk to dad, but not very often."

"Why didn't you tell me? I feel so terrible I never knew!"

Kat keeps her eyes fixed on the picnic table.

"You just seemed really busy in Washington, and happy too. I didn't want to dump all my baggage onto you— but honestly, at first? It wasn't really a big deal. I was pissed at her, sure, but I don't know when that twisted into me feeling like absolute shit..." She reaches over and grasps my hand, squeezing my fingers gently. "But that doesn't matter now, I just want you to know I've been there before. I think most of us have."

I can feel the weight building on my chest, pushing down and making it harder to breathe as I fight back my tears.

"Then why do I feel so alone?"

She shrugs, giving me a halfhearted smile.

"Because we don't want to admit that we can be vulnerable, that we might be weak sometimes. Even the people who look like they have it all together feel like they're missing something, they just never say it."

Out of the corner of my eye, I spot Brendan handing Carly a glass of wine while she bounces their baby on her hip. They're surrounded by people, everyone all smiles.

"Do you think they're happy?"

"Who, Brendan and Carly? Fuck if I know. Facebook and Instagram sure seem to say they are, but... well, if you buy into whatever people are selling there, I've got a great deal on some swamp land for you."

I watch Brendan for a little longer; he's laughing with a couple of his old football buddies. In the briefest second, with the sun shining down and hitting him just right, I can see the boy I first fell in love with. But I'm not really sure what he saw in me anymore. Stability, maybe? He was flunking two classes when we got together, and I got his GPA up to the point where he could actually apply for graduation. Was that all it was?

But then, he missed out on a football scholarship because of his grades, and I think he might have quietly resented me for not doing a better job of tutoring him. The problem is, it's hard to dig someone out of a hole that deep. They really have to want it, and he just... didn't. Not that much.

Maybe that's where the resentment started. He wanted me to stay home, cook and clean like his mom did, pumping out babies and congratulating him on a day's work well done when all he did was make it home every night. Meanwhile, I had dreams, goals that I wasn't willing to give up.

Not for him, even if I loved him.

If I even really loved him.

Kat taps me on the hand, dragging me back to the present.

"Can I ask you something?"

"Wh– Yeah. Sure."

"When I texted you about the reunion, I was convinced that you weren't going to show up."

"Really?"

Kat smiles.

"Don't *really* me, Abi. No one thought you'd be back, you haven't been for years. So why did you?"

"Closure."

I glance over at Brendan, jealousy starting to gnaw away at my insides again. The researcher in me wants to sit back and observe, as if I could glean something I don't already know, finally solving the mystery of the asshole fiancé, but I'm not even sure if this is even about him anymore.

"How?"

"What?"

"How are you going to get your closure?" She asks.

The problem is, even this far into the trip, and after all our planning, I didn't really think that part through. There's always been a juvenile part of me that was... I don't know, hoping the moment he saw me he'd feel guilty?

"I haven't thought it out."

Was I crazy coming here? What was I actually trying to prove?

"Excuse me!" Carly's voice rings through the vineyard. "Hi, everyone! Hi! Over here!"

She sticks her hand in the air, flitting it around to get everyone's attention.

"I'm going to be starting tours of both the cellar *and* the winery-proper, which as you all know is the crown jewel of the location, so if people want to come along to the tasting room..."

She turns on her heel, heading toward the main building with a few of our classmates in tow. It looks like Brendan's staying behind for this one, and his eyes lock with mine for a brief second before he quickly casts his gaze downward, pulling out his phone and trying to look busy.

The bastard can't even look at me.

Maybe it's the booze, but a new determination washes over me. A sense of righteousness.

"I deserve it."

"What?" Kat asks. "Abi, what are you doing?"

"Closure!" I shout back, making a b-line toward Brendan.

I want to hear the reason why he left, and I want to hear it straight from his mouth. I want Brendan Howard to look me in the fucking eye and tell me *why* he left me. I've carried that pain and that grief for too long, and I deserve better. Better than those sleepless nights where all I did was lay in bed, staring at the ceiling wondering what was so broken, so terrible, so monstrous about me that he didn't want me anymore.

I hear Kat call for Logan, but my spite has already taken control, and there's no way anyone could talk me out of it. Still, just before I reach the halfway point to Brendan, a familiar hand grabs me by the wrist and drags me backward.

I slam into him, his cheeks pink and his eyes wild with panic.

"What are you doing?"

"I'm going to have a talk with Brendan, that's all."

Logan flashes me a worried look, and I can feel my heart rate pick up.

"I'm not sure that's a good idea."

"Why not?"

He sighs, pulling me off to the side, and away from the crowd. I can already tell that he's walking on eggshells around me, and for some reason that makes me even more determined, not to mention a little bit mad.

"Okay, look. I know the whole point of this trip was to show off and prove a point, and maybe get some closure about this thing with your ex, but… I don't know, Abi. I just think you're in a bad headspace right now, with the interview and the job, and…" He looks down at the glass of wine in my hand. "You've been drinking on an empty stomach. Kind of a lot."

Since when is he keeping track of how many drinks I've had? I'm not a child.

"I'm not judging you," he says quickly, obviously sensing my growing irritation. "I just know that when I make impulsive decisions that deep in, they're pretty much always bad ones."

The little needles of annoyance that had been prodding me grow into a full-fledged dagger in my chest. This is my past. I deserve to confront it. Who is he to tell me otherwise?

"You think I'm going to cause a scene, don't you? Worried I'll embarrass you?"

A few people glance over at us, but I don't care. My cheeks are flushed and my blood is already boiling. No turning back.

"Well, if I didn't before…" he mutters.

I glance back over my shoulder at Brendan, still absently scrolling through his phone.

"People never leave for no reason, Logan. I have to know why."

"No, Abi. Trust me. Sometimes there really isn't some big revelatory reason for stuff like this. Sometimes people are just assholes."

"I don't believe that," I grind out through clenched teeth. "It had to have been something about me, or something we could have done differently."

His eyes flash with a sudden streak of anger, and I can see that protectiveness he has warping into something a little different through his frustration.

"Why are you so stuck in the past?" He asks. "What even is there that would be worth it, to lie about your job, about me..."

"First of all, I'm not stuck in the past."

Logan's sudden laughter is filled to the brim with an incredulous venom.

"Yes, Abi, you are! You've spent so much time on this trip calling yourself a loser that you can't see everything you've won!"

"Like what? A failed interview? No scholarship? Unemployment? Because from where I'm standing it seems like everything I touch turns to shit!"

"I'm not talking about any of that." I swear I feel the earth stand still under the heat of his gaze. "I'm talking about me, and *us*. I've been in front of you for three goddamn years! We've had so many missed connections, so many moments where this could—"

My heart pounds. Is he going to say what I think he is?

Here?

"You're my compass, Abi. Whenever anything goes wrong, you're the first person I go to; when I wake up in the morning, you're the first person I think about. I'd do *anything* for you, and I think— no, I know you feel the same way."

He's right. Of course he is. But I want us to be able to start fresh, and for that I need this wound to be sewn up for good. I want to be able to run my fingers over the scar and know I survived it, not to wonder if it might ever open up again and take even more from me.

I take Logan's hands, grasping them tightly.

"Please don't leave. I promise I'll be right back but just, please." My voice trembles as I struggle to keep my composure. "I don't think I could survive it."

Logan's demeanor softens, the crease between his brow smoothing out as he makes those gorgeous puppy dog eyes at me.

"I'm always here." He rubs his nose against mine. "Not going anywhere."

"You get it, right? Why I have to do this?"

Logan chuckles, already accepting defeat.

"I was pretty sure there was no convincing you otherwise, but Kat did ask me to, after all. I think I made a pretty valiant effort."

I love Logan, that much is clearer to me than anything else in my life. I just want to put the final nail in this coffin before I move on.

"I'm going to come right back, and when I do... I'd like to have a talk, okay?"

He kisses me again, and I grin.

"I'll be here."

And of course, he's right.

He always has been.

the smallest man who ever lived

ABI

TORONTO, ONTARIO
MAY 2021

"Okay!" Kat sighs as we push open the door to my apartment and step inside. "Brendan! Come and check out how hot your fiancé looks!"

She was sweet enough to pay for me to go and see a stylist in Toronto who could do my hair up just right for the engagement party tonight. I feel like a princess, but more importantly, I *look* like one-- minus the skeleton sweatpants, no makeup, and my fiancé's oversized hoodie that pretty much hangs off of me.

"Where is he?" Kat grumbles, tossing her long blonde braids over her shoulder.

"I don't know. Maybe he went out to grab something."

The apartment is eerily quiet. Usually, I'd come home around now and find Brendan watching football, playing video games, or just killing time on his phone.

"Well, we leave in an hour."

"I'll try texting him again."

I tried sending him pictures of the shoes I picked earlier, but it seemed like they weren't going through. My phone doesn't have the best reception, it's old and needs an update, but I figure it's worth another shot.

ME

> Hey! We're at home, going to start getting ready to head out. Where are you?

Not delivered.

Same message as last time.

"Still not going through…"

"Try restarting your phone. I'll text Marcus, maybe they went to pregame or something."

I reboot it, wandering into the bedroom so that I can start on my makeup, but only a couple steps in and my stomach drops. The whole room looks like it's been ransacked. Dresser drawers are hanging open, clothes are strewn around the floor, and the bed is a complete mess. It even looks like half the closet's been cleared out. The only thing hanging right in the middle is my dress, still in the bag I got from the boutique.

Either this is the start of a horror movie, or something's happened with Brendan.

ME

> Are you okay? What happened to the bedroom?

Not delivered.

My hands are freezing, but the rest of my body is white hot, adrenaline pumping through me. I try calling him, but after three loud beeps, it just disconnects.

"Kat!" I shout, my voice breaking slightly.

"What's up?"

She's already stumbled into the bedroom, her jaw dropping as she sees the mess.

"Did someone break in?"

"Unless they broke in and only took Brendan's shit…" I show her my phone. "I can't call him either."

Kat's already tapping away on her phone, her brows shooting up her forehead.

"And now mine aren't going through."

"Maybe it's the building," I murmur.

She flashes me her signature, *you've got to be fucking kidding me* look. I spent weeks trying to get a reservation at the restaurant, planning every last detail and making sure that I included all of Brendan's favorite things.

Maybe he had different ideas.

Kat is already in damage control mode as I sit on the edge of the bed, staring off into nothing. I swallow, trying my best to keep the bile in my gut from rising up as I wipe my sweaty palms on my pants.

"Hey, Marcus? Have you been able to get a hold of Brendan?" Kat asks, not wasting any time as the call connects. "No, we've both texted him and it says 'not delivered'. Abi said she couldn't call him either. Yeah, let me know as soon as you hear from him. Okay, talk soon."

She hangs up and takes a few long, soothing breaths before taking a seat next to me.

"Marcus said he'd get in touch. Who knows, maybe he's planned a surprise vacation and he's working it out last minute?"

She winces at how far she had to stretch to make that sound even remotely plausible. It feels like this wasn't anything but an escape plan.

My head is spinning, my memory working overtime to try and come up with an explanation. I must have done *something* to upset him. I must have said something, looked at him a certain way, used a tone he didn't like. He's told me before that sometimes my tone is too harsh, or that I can snap at him, but it's just because I'm a bit stressed out. I'm at the tail end of my dissertation and four weeks out from my defense. Then there's the job market to worry about, publications, and what I'm going to do next.

Tears rush down my cheeks and I start to shake as Kat grabs one of my many fuzzy blankets, wrapping it around me. She doesn't say anything, she just lets me break down, sobbing into her chest. Even without confirmation, the data is enough for me to make this quick and succinct analysis: Brendan walked out on me and he's not coming back.

"It's okay," Kat coos. "You're okay, babe."

And maybe, just for kicks, he waited until the cruelest possible moment to do it.

"He couldn't even wait until my *fucking* dissertation was over!" I scream into her shirt.

"He's an asshole, Abi. He doesn't deserve you."

Toward the end, he became colder, and I'd be lying if I said I didn't notice. I tried desperately to build a bridge the only way I knew how: I bought him things, I went out of my way to make him happy, I kept the house cleaner, I wore more makeup, I changed the way I dressed...

And then he asked me to marry him, and I thought it all had worked. I had saved our relationship, and I didn't even care that everything else in my life suffered because of it.

Kat's phone starts ringing and she picks up.

"Yeah, yeah it's— I'm sorry, *what* did you just say?!"

She's on her feet in a split second, gently pushing me off of her.

"Tell him to call her or text her, or something! He can't just leave like that— I'm sorry, Marcus. I'm not mad at you, I'm— God, I think I'm going to skin him and wear him as a coat."

I stare at myself in the mirror, brushing away tears. My face is covered in bright red splotches, my eyes are puffy, and there's snot dripping from my nose. I wipe it all away on the sleeve of Brendan's hoodie.

He can have my boogers. He *deserves* them.

I feel helpless, and when I feel helpless, I lean into my background as a researcher, excavating memories and trying to figure out where I screwed up.

For the past six months, Brendan's been less affectionate. He's been hiding his phone, moving to the other room to text... the classic signs. I didn't want to believe it, so I tuned it all out. Things got lonely as he got more and more distant. There were nights where he could be lying next to me or not, and I wouldn't know the difference.

"Maybe he's sleeping with someone else."

"What?!" Kat hisses. "Abi, that's— nothing, Marcus. What were you saying?"

My gaze wanders over to her, running over the pair of distressed dark jeans, shiny black boots and Led Zeppelin t-shirt that's tied off at the waist, showing off the abs she's worked so hard for over the years. She's so strong, literally and metaphorically, yet somehow she always looks so polished, even when the world is falling apart around her.

Kat's my favorite superhero.

But as she stares at me, I know that pained look in her eyes isn't going to bring any good news along with it.

"I'll ask her, and I'll text you back, okay? Alright. Bye."

She hangs up, taking another one of her patented deep relaxing breaths.

"Marcus got through to him. He's in Oshawa, at his dad's place." She slides her phone into her back pocket, and flashes me a look that turns my stomach. "Brendan told Marcus he couldn't lie to himself anymore. Said he just had to leave."

I blink.

"What the fuck does that even mean?"

"I— I really don't know, babe." She runs a hand through her hair. "But Marcus had an idea, and I want to run it by you."

"What is it?" I mumble, face buried in my hands.

"What if we went out anyway? Dinner, dancing, and I'll rent you a hotel room for the night so you don't have to come back to... all of this. It took you forever to book those reservations, right?"

Leave the house when I'm a sobbing, snotty mess? I'd rather have both of my eyeballs plucked out.

"No. I'm just going to stay here and..." I trail off, not even sure what I would do with myself.

"Do you *really* want to be here right now, surrounded by sadness and his shitty cologne?"

"It wasn't that shitty," I hiccup, a giggle breaking through the tears.

"Abi, half the time he walked around smelling like a bear's rotting asshole. I hope he took that shit with him or I'm gonna toss it off the balcony."

I snicker. I told him I was allergic to get him to stop wearing that stuff, but he'd still wind up dabbing it behind his ears or spraying it on with the window open anyway.

"I don't know, Kat."

"Come on! I'll do your makeup, we can smoke a joint, and take a cab to dinner! Marcus is going to rally the troops. We can have a Brendan Sucks Party!"

I wish I could be angrier, but all I can think is that it's still somehow my fault that things ended up this way.

"I tried to be a good girlfriend, I really tried."

"You *were*," she assures me. "He was the one who couldn't handle it.

You were smarter than him, better than him, more successful than him, and he couldn't stand next to your fire. Baby, you're 23 years old and about to get a PhD. You're a wizard."

It really doesn't feel like it.

I stare at the engagement ring on my finger, suddenly feeling sick to my stomach at the sight and sliding it off. I get to my feet and take a few long strides toward the open window, and toss it straight out of my life.

"Holy shit, Abi!"

It's the first step toward letting go, I guess. Hopefully it gets easier from here.

"Okay, I'll go out, but only if you pay for my drinks. Because I'm going to drink a lot."

She flings her arms into the air, grinning.

"Yes! Of course I will!"

Kat was right, Brendan's the asshole here. This is entirely his fault, and to hell with him if he thinks I'm just gonna sit around and pick up the pieces.

I've been doing that for years, and I'm tired of it. Tired of being the good girl.

Tonight, I want to do something stupid.

the black dog

ABI

REYNOLDS VINEYARD
PRESENT DAY

Brendan hasn't said a word to me in two minutes.

When I walked up to him, he just *stood there.*

It was oddly anticlimactic.

I should have come out swinging, maybe chased him through the vineyard calling him a cheater, *anything* to get a rise out of him. Instead, we're both just sort of standing here as he slides his hands into his pockets, rocking back and forth on his heels.

His apathy only makes my rage swell.

"You actually made it... With your, uh, boyfriend?"

"Fiancé," I correct him, through a clenched jaw.

"Right."

He was so brave on Facebook, so callous, and now he can barely look at me.

"You're such a fucking coward," I growl.

"What?"

We stare at each other, and I take in those boyish features I used to fawn over as a teenager: his perfectly coiffed dark hair and those intense brown eyes that used to make him look like he was untouchable.

I remember watching him on the football field, shirtless, running plays over and over again with his teammates. He was perfect, and we were so in love; I really convinced myself that we'd be together forever.

What an idiot.

"You told me you loved me, you proposed to me, and then you walked away and never even looked back." I let out a pained laugh. "Brendan, you blocked me on everything and wouldn't even take my fucking calls. I had to go through three degrees of separation or talk to your *mom* to get even a half-straight answer about where you were or why you left, and even then it was just vague bullshit. Three goddamn years without an explanation, and then all of a sudden you invite me to this reunion? Why? So you can throw your brand new life in my face?"

"Jesus, Abi, you're fuckin' drunk. You don't want to make a scene."

No. He doesn't get to do this to me. I'm not crazy. I know what he did.

"What I *am,* is angry. You got away scott free, had a baby with Carly, and you left me to pick up after your fucking mess. Oh hey, speaking of that, how old is your son by the way? Looks like he'd be about—"

"Abi, I'm warning you," he snarls.

It's too late. I've got my mother's rage inside me, and right now, I'm fashioning it into a fucking shiv.

"Warning me? Brendan, all I've been asking for is an answer to the most simple fucking question on the planet, an answer that anyone but a limp-dick coward would have given me day-one."

Brendan's eyes are cold and steely, his fists clenched at his sides.

"That's it? You'll stop making a scene if I tell you why I left?"

"Yes!" I shout. "Finally, we're fucking getting somewhere!"

Brendan's scowl deepens, and he lowers his voice.

"Because every time I looked at you, every time we touched, I felt *nothing.*"

The words hit like a ton of bricks.

Everything I was afraid of back then.

It was me, I was the problem.

He didn't love me.

Could I have tried harder?

I feel my head spinning, and I swear my legs are about to give out.
He didn't love me, all the times he said he did.
He told me over and over that I was doing things wrong.
He never even tried.
And there it is, that moment of clarity.
It's like I'm floating above my body, watching myself as I smile,
Shake my head,
And toss my wine right into Brendan Howard's face.

call and answer

LOGAN

REYNOLDS VINEYARD
PRESENT DAY

Kat gasps as the wine splashes over Brendan, soaking his crisp blue dress shirt and leaving him sputtering as he stumbles backward, pinching the bridge of his nose.

"Holy fucking..."

Abi throws the glass on the ground, shattering it into pieces before she storms back toward the brick building. Shocked murmurs ripple through the crowd of people. It's not all scandalized faces though; some of them laugh, and one particularly drunk guest just starts applauding.

"OPA!"

I know there's something I should be doing right now, but I'm just... stunned.

"Uh, loverboy?" Kat asks, tapping me on the shoulder. "I don't know if you saw the look in her eyes, but I think you should probably go after her before she snaps Carly like a toothpick."

Oh, shit. That *was* the direction Carly took everyone for the wine tour.

I hand Kat my glass, sprinting toward the other building, trailing just far enough behind that I'm a little worried I might not catch her in time.

"Abi! Abi, wait!"

But she ignores me, furiously ripping the side door open and slamming it shut behind her. Someone mutters something about a psycho, but I don't stop. The only thing that matters to me is Abi.

I run at full speed, hot on her heels as I follow her into the winery. There's no sign of Carly, thank God, but that doesn't mean Abi won't find her.

"Abi!"

She says nothing, making a sharp right and heading down a long hallway. I hear sniffles and light, hiccuping gasps, like she's trying to hold back sobs.

"Go away, Logan!"

"Not a chance in hell, Shortcake!"

She reaches a large staircase at the end of the hall, vanishing into an unknown abyss. I have two objectives: Console Abi, and make sure we don't wind up in the newspaper tomorrow morning. Carly could be anywhere, after all.

The smell of must and alcohol hangs thick in the air as I scurry down the steps, finding a large wooden door. When I wrench it open, I spot Abi leaned up against a big barrel with tears streaming down her face. She's surrounded by beautiful brick work, dark wooden pillars, and racks on racks of wine that stretch all the way to the ceiling.

This must be the infamous cellar.

"I said go away," she murmurs, wiping her nose on her arm. "This is so embarrassing. Everyone was staring at me and I couldn't control–"

She buries her face in her hands, sobbing uncontrollably.

Yeah, I'm not going anywhere.

"So what happened?" I ask.

Abi begins to regain her composure, but I keep my distance as she takes a few breaths, staring up at the ceiling. I can *see* the pain ricocheting through her body like a bullet as she shudders and tenses.

"Do you know what he said to me?" She asks, her lip quivering as she tries her best to keep from breaking down. "He said that when he looked at me, he felt nothing. *Nothing,* that's what he said."

Her voice cracks, and my heart follows suit. I wish I could take this all away from her.

I wrap my arms around her, half expecting her to push me away, but all she does is hug me as tightly as she can.

"He really said that?"

I have half a mind to head back upstairs and finish what Abi started. I'll give him a swirly in a wine vat. Who the fuck says something like that?

"He wanted a housewife," she sobs. "And maybe that's not a bad thing, but that's not me! He couldn't stand the fact that I had a future, that I was going somewhere, when his football career died the moment we graduated!"

I want to tell her to forget about him, that none of what he said matters, but I can't. She's entitled to this pain; to have closure, in whatever form it ends up taking. It's not always the simple and clean outcome from the movies.

Sometimes it's dirty.

Sometimes it's painful.

"Back in high school I swore that I'd have it all together by the time I was 30, that I'd be someone. And then I get here, and I look around at everyone and they're so... They're just so..." She swirls her hand around as her face twists up into a knot of despair. "I look at them and all I see is how little I've accomplished. I'm fucking mediocre."

"There's not a single thing about you that's mediocre."

The tone of my voice surprises even me, far more firm and unwavering than I'm used to.

"You sound like my mom."

"Yeah, well, maybe she's right. The industry we're in? It's fucking hard. You're usually sitting in a room full of people who are just as brilliant as you are, and they're all competing for the same opportunities in a comically small pond."

Her shoulders slump as she grips the barrel next to her for support, her eyes unfocused and full of exhaustion. It feels like she thinks it's all over, that she's failed in some way, but I think it's just the beginning. If grief has taught me anything it's that sometimes big pieces of your life need to fall away to make room for something new.

Everything ends, but it's up to us to build new beginnings.

"There's nothing wrong with you, nothing broken about you." I slide my finger beneath her chin, tipping it upward so that she's forced to meet my gaze. "You are beautiful, and brilliant, and you've got a *huge* heart."

"You have to say those things," she snorts, that tiny bit of a cynical edge worming its way back into her voice. "You're my fake fiancé."

And it's in that moment that I know: It might be my last chance to set things right, to fix that mistake I made three years ago.

"No more faking, I don't want to do that anymore."

"What do you mean?" Her voice begins to tremble. "Logan, I can't lose–"

"You're not losing anything. I'm in love with you, Abi. I think I've *been* in love with you since the first night I saw you, I just didn't quite understand it at the time."

She stares past me, her eyes darting back and forth as her breathing begins to speed up... but I can't stop myself, I just keep fucking talking.

"I know that things have been complicated, and that not everything has ended up right; I even know you might not get another shot at that interview, no matter how much you deserve it. The only guarantee I can give you, the only solid promise I can make is this: whatever happens, I will be there."

I put a hand on her heart, feeling it hammering beneath my palm.

"Wherever you go, I'm right behind you. Is tú mo chroí."

She lets out a choked sob, and I can't quite tell if it's from sadness or joy.

"I don't know what that means."

"It means *you are my heart.* My dad used to say it to my mom every day. It was his way of telling her she was his reason for being."

The two of us just breathe together in silence for a moment, lingering in the wake of the long-delayed truth.

"I love you, Abi King. Always have, and that's all there is to it."

She shakes her head, squeezing her eyes shut to hold back her tears.

"It feels— it feels like I've always known you."

"Maybe you have," I murmur, rubbing my nose against hers. "Maybe in all those other universes we figured things out, and we're just lagging a little behind in this one."

In every future I imagine, each one worth living in, she's right beside me.

No matter how different, that part's the same in every single one.

So no matter how many times we've each decided to leave things be, to accept that we just weren't right for each other, that we would never get there...

This time, I'm absolutely certain.

"I love you too, Logan. Of course I do."

We make it.

I cup her cheek, nuzzling against her with the tip of my nose until I'm kissing her. And I don't want to stop. I can't stop. My confession opened a gate, and now there's no way in hell I'm going back to quiet pining.

Back to almost.

Everything has changed.

I pull away, grinning from ear to ear as Abi stares up at me with smeared lipstick, and mascara underneath her eyes. The truth seems to have relaxed her a little more.

"We said it," she laughs.

Above us, I can hear people milling about in conversation. The tour must finally be working its way through this chunk of the winery, which means it might not be long until they make it down here. But until then, I want Abi all to myself.

"Yeah." I breathe, the adrenaline still coursing through me. "Big step."

Abi looks as relieved as I feel.

"The biggest."

at last

LOGAN

REYNOLDS VINEYARD
PRESENT DAY

"Sunshine?" Abi murmurs. "You okay?"

I glance around the room... I'm sure Carly and Brendan wouldn't miss *one measly* little bottle of champagne. If I can't beat his ass, I'm stealing his booze. Lesser of two evils.

"I think we should celebrate."

"What did you have in mind?"

I snatch a bottle off of the rack, resisting the urge to try and flip it, even though that would look *so cool* right now.

"I can't think of a better way to christen the two of us, than drinking your ex-fiancé's wine off of your gorgeous tits."

"Logan!" She places a hand on her chest, lowering her voice dramatically. "That's stealing!"

"I won't tell if you won't," I purr.

Abi smirks, a little twinkle in her eye as she climbs onto the barrel and slowly begins to work the buttons on her blouse.

"Your secret crimes are safe with me."

She raises a brow, shrugging off her top before working the clasp on her bra and tossing it aside. The tour is still above us, and I can hear Carly's voice slicing through layer upon layer of brick and wood. We might not have as much time as I had hoped.

Maybe I can barricade the door...

Or maybe it's hotter if we get caught.

"What are you waiting for, Sunshine?" She teases her nipples. "Bust open that champagne."

"Oh, actually? It has to come from the champagne region of France for it to be considered champagne, otherwise it's Prosecco, Cava, Crémant— I should really shut the fuck up, shouldn't I?"

She lets out a giggle and I quickly get to work tearing the cork out. Foam spills over the lip of the bottle as Abi plucks it from my hand, a sly smirk tugging at the corners of her mouth.

"How about I pour, and you get down on your knees, Doctor?"

Drinking stolen wine in Abi's ex's wine cellar wasn't on my road trip bingo card, but when in Rome, right? I slowly work my way down her body, swirling my tongue over her pebbled nipples as she starts to pour. The sweat on her skin mixed with the sweetness of the wine is fucking delicious, and almost as intoxicating as her moans.

"Oh, *fuck*. Don't stop!"

I bite down on her nipple and hear her cry out, distracted just long enough to miss the bottle crashing down onto the floor.

We both freeze in a panic, staring up at the ceiling.

"Do you think they heard that?" I whisper, releasing her nipple with a soft pop.

Abi looks down at me, biting her lip.

"Might be even hotter if they did."

I'm grinning from ear to ear, my whole body feeling like it's on fire.

"You kinky little minx, Doctor King."

"I learned from the best."

She runs her hand through my hair, and my stomach swarms with butterflies. I want this forever. I want *her* forever.

"Tell me you love me again."

Abi's face lights up, eyes flickering with desire in the low light.

"I love you, Logan Flynn."

That's all I need to hear. We'll figure the rest out later when we get home, but in this moment, we're free to truly be us for the first time in years.

I return to the task at hand, licking the sticky remnants of wine off of her tits, and falling into a beautiful rhythm as my mouth slowly works its way down her body.

Moan, gasp, giggle.

Giggle, moan, gasp.

I spread her legs, kissing up each thigh before biting down. Abi's high-pitched keen fills the room, and she grips my hair tightly as I soothe the bite mark with my tongue.

"Too much?"

"I liked it."

"Good."

I start to tease her clit through her thin lacy panties, working her up until she's biting down on her knuckles. I love the idea of getting her so turned on that she might just blow our cover completely.

"I want these soaked by the time I fuck you."

I can see the anticipation building up inside her; it looks like it's killing her as much as it's killing me, but the voices above us are getting louder. Closer. I'm practically trembling with desire, but I refuse to stop. I can taste her through the lace, her arousal coating my tongue.

"More," she whimpers. "Logan, please."

Everything around me smells like wine and *her*.

Abi shivers, and the wetter she gets, the tighter the knot in my stomach becomes until I can't take it anymore. I *have* to get a good look at her glistening cunt. I push the fabric aside, my mouth watering at the sight of her, slick and pink and ready for anything.

"Whose pussy is this?" I growl.

She stammers and I spit on her cunt.

"Tell me, Shortcake."

"Yours!"

"Good girl."

I slide two fingers inside, breathing along with her as her back arches, and she starts to roll her hips to match my agile thrusts.

"I think they're getting closer."

Shit. She's right.

I got so lost focusing on her that I completely forgot to keep an ear out for Carly and her little tour. It sounds like pretty soon they'll be heading down the hall.

Right toward us.

But there's no way we're stopping now. I can still fuck Abi, clean up the mess we've made, *and* sneak out of here without getting caught.

Easy peasy.

Did I lock that door though?

I get back to work, my mouth and fingers working in tandem to push her right to the edge.

"Oh, *fuck*. Imagine if this is what Carly sees when she walks in." Abi's moan becomes a throaty laugh. "I'd kill to see the look on— oh my god!"

I push my fingers against her G-spot and she responds instantly, riding my face as she lets out desperate little snarls. My dick is so hard it's like I'm about to combust, but I keep stroking that spot, feeling her clench tighter around my fingers as she begs for more.

"Logan, I'm gonna—"

I want to taste her on my tongue every morning. I want those whimpers and moans etched into my memory, like a hook from a song you can't get out of your head no matter how long it's been since you've heard it.

My name is torn from her lips, her voice shredded and raspy as she tumbles over the edge. I keep working her through the last dregs of her climax and lapping it up like honey until her body goes limp.

Abi's slumped against the wall, her forehead glistening with sweat. I almost think she's too exhausted to keep going until she raises a brow.

"Are you just gonna stand there, or are you gonna fuck me, pretty boy?"

She doesn't have to ask me twice.

I press a feverish kiss to her lips, overwhelmed by my desire for her. My love for her. She's everything I've ever needed and more.

Abi wraps her legs around my waist, desperate to devour me, and I welcome it with open arms. I grasp her wrists, pinning her arms above her head with one hand as I guide my cock toward her slick entrance with the other.

"Beg for it," I growl.

"I don't think we have time for games, Sunshine," she purrs, tugging on my bolo tie and yanking me toward her.

I grin, kissing her softly.

"Indulge me."

"Please." The grit in her voice makes my heart thunder. "Make me yours."

"Oh, Shortcake." I sink into her, her warm, wet cunt with a single thrust. "You've been mine this whole time, you just didn't know it yet."

Her back arches, those pouty lips parted and begging to be kissed. She smells delicious, like warm sun on fresh fruit and I squeeze her wrists hard, every cell in my body finely attuned to her needs as I fuck her.

She's whimpering, shivering, and I'm so *fucking* close, I can taste it.

I want that ring on her finger to mean something real.

Because since the night I met her, there's never been anyone else.

But the sound of Carly's voice floating down the stairs slices right through this beautiful moment.

"Now, it's like I said outside, this is the crown jewel of the winery, the place where all the magic happens!"

The door handle rattles, and panic surges through me.

"Shit," Carly mutters from outside.

Huh. I guess I *did* lock it.

But... she's probably got a key.

"Don't you *dare* stop."

Sweat gathers on the back of my neck as the handle rattles again, louder this time.

I keep thrusting. Slowly. Methodically. And Abi just beams through it, rolling her hips to meet mine.

"You're a *bad* girl, Shortcake." I press my forehead against hers. "They're gonna come in here."

"Then we'd better give them a good show."

Suddenly, I don't care about the rattling door handle, or Carly muttering about her keys. It all fades into the background, and I pound into Abi until her eyes roll back.

When I look at her, all I see is the sun peeking through the clouds, showing me what the rest of my life could look like. That's never changed.

The difference is this time, I'm ready to take the leap.

"I'm coming!" Abi gasps, ripping her mouth away from mine and burying her face in my chest. "Oh, fuck!"

Someone kicks the door and I hear Carly's frustrated growl on the other side of it. But I can't stop. I'm dangling right on that beautiful fucking edge, totally willing to go to jail for this.

Can you go to jail for boning in someone's wine cellar?

I guess I'm about to find out.

"I think I left my key upstairs in the office. How about we take the tour up there for the time being? Oh! And I'll show you the..."

Her voice fades away, along with a smattering of footsteps, and the relief is enough to send me into a frenzy. I thrust harder, feeling Abi grip my arms tightly as we both reach our peaks.

"I'm right there!" She groans. "I'm right—"

She bites down into my shoulder as my own bliss comes crashing down on me. I squeeze my eyes shut, savoring as much of it as I can. Her sweat, her perfume, the wine... it all mingles together until I'm reduced to a shuddering mess.

Our bodies begin to slow down as we crawl back down to earth, and I find myself gazing into her big green eyes, and that smile that makes me feel like I'm home no matter where I am.

I knew we could never go back to the way things were.

I knew I couldn't leave here without making her mine.

"I love you Shortcake."

thank you aimee

ABI

REYNOLD'S VINEYARDS
PRESENT DAY

It's funny how three little words can change the course of your life.

But I don't regret them. I don't regret any of this.

The only thing I regret is that it took me this long to tell him how I feel. We missed out on three years of kisses, three years of dates, three years of lying in bed together and showing each other stupid shit on our phones.

I think about what he said to me in Irish.

Is tú mo chroí.

You are my heart.

He's mine, and the steadfast joy that comes from that simple fact keeps me calm.

Keeps me here.

Logan Flynn has tattooed himself onto my heart.

"Abi?" His voice slices through my train of thought as he hands me my blouse. "Don't wanna forget this."

"Are you sure? Maybe I could start a new fashion trend. I'll call it *Tits Out.*"

"I like it!" Logan chuckles as he buckles his belt. "But I think there are children outside. You don't want to be put on a list."

"True, true," I giggle, buttoning up my blouse. "Although, after what I did, I'm not really sure if I want to show my face anywhere around here."

"You wanna go home?" Logan asks.

"Actually, maybe we can see if Kat and Marcus want to head to the Black Bear? We can play one last game of pool tonight, since I don't think we'll get a chance before we leave on Monday."

"That sounds good!"

The residual pain from my conversation with Brendan still lingers, but I've come to the realization that maybe him being such a douchebag *was* the closure I needed.

He didn't love me, but Logan does.

And more importantly, I love myself enough to embrace the change that's occurring in my life. I don't know where I'm going to end up, but I know I won't be alone.

"I think I'm going to tell Frankie the truth," I murmur as I do up the last button.

"After you get the job?"

"No, after the interview." I run my hand through my hair. "If it doesn't work out—"

"It will."

Logan, always the optimist.

"If it *doesn't*... I've got money in my savings account. I can take a few months off of teaching, and maybe look into some more grants for my project."

"Hey, we could finally write that book we're always talking about," Logan replies. "That Andrew guy at Oxford University Press is still bugging me about it. I'm actually supposed to have a meeting with him when we get back."

Over the years, we've talked about writing a book on melding theory with research methodology, and all of the complexities and pitfalls that go into it. Logan's a methodology wizard and theory is my bread and butter. We'd be a killer combination, and I know we'd have a blast working together on a bigger project.

"That would be great."

He wraps his arms around me.

"When you tell Frankie, I'll be there for you, okay?"

"Do you think we'll get into as much shit as Roman and Imogen?"

Logan shakes his head.

"Nah. Especially not if you're already got the other job in the bag."

"Logan, I don't know if I'm—"

He presses a finger to my lips, his eyes lighting up as he smiles.

"*Show me how good it gets,* remember?"

"I remember."

He kisses me, and in that tiny little moment, I've never felt so at home.

"Come on, let's find Kat and Marcus and blow this popsicle stand."

He heads for the door, grabbing the handle and frowning when it doesn't turn.

"What the—"

I slip around him, rattling the handle myself before slamming my body against the door. It doesn't budge.

"You've got to be fucking kidding me."

"Here, let me try again. Maybe it needs my magic touch after all."

"Yeah, or a locksmith," I mutter, folding my arms over my chest.

He takes over again, jiggling and turning the knob from side to side for a few seconds before stepping back.

"Yeah, that's definitely locked."

"Magic touch, huh?" I tease.

Logan rolls his eyes.

"It's probably busted. That's why Carly couldn't get in."

"I'll text Kat. She can rescue us."

I tap the pocket of my skirt, my heart dropping when I don't feel my phone.

I could have sworn I brought it with me.

"What's wrong?" Logan asks. "You're turning green."

I scramble for my purse that's sitting abandoned next to the puddle of champagne on the floor and fumble through it with shaking hands.

Nothing.

"I think I left my phone back at the guest house, and I don't have her number memorized anymore."

"Okay, okay," Logan murmurs, nodding quickly to himself as he steps backward. "That's cool. I'll just body slam the door."

"You'll body slam the door?! Are you fucking—"

It's too late, Logan's already eyeball-deep in his stupid plan.

He takes a running leap, hurling himself against four inches of thick wood. His body hits it with a dull thunk and he collapses like a baby deer, sprawled out on the floor.

"Logan!"

I rush for him, turning him over onto his back, and he stares at me for a moment, blinking like he's in a daze.

"Are you okay?!"

His body shakes, laughter tumbling from his lips until he's red in the face. It's infectious, and soon, the two of us are slumped on the floor, holding each other while tears of joy stream down our cheeks. This night could not get any more chaotic, and for some reason, it's the funniest thing in the world.

"I can't fucking believe this!" Logan howls. "Jesus Christ, it's too perfect."

"Almost like it was fate."

Maybe we were supposed to go on this trip, supposed to have all of these stumbles and near misses. Maybe we were supposed to convince ourselves that we could never be together, only to get locked in my ex-fiancé's wine cellar. The world works in mysterious ways. It's like the universe got tired of the endless pining and longing stares and finally forced us to work our shit out.

Logan kisses me.

"I think we might have to start yelling for someone to rescue us."

"I think you're right," I chuckle.

We get to our feet, the two of us pounding on the door as we scream for help.

"There's a murderer in here!" Logan bellows.

"Logan!"

"What?! I'm creating a sense of urgency!" His eyes go wide and he starts slamming his fists against the door, causing it to tremble. "Fire! A bomb! The Sharknado!"

I can hear someone chattering above us, and Logan grabs a large broom in the corner and starts slamming it against the ceiling.

"Hey! Let us out of here!"

I sigh, glancing around the room for something to pick the lock. It's a large space, with part of the room disappearing around a corner. I wander off while Logan keeps shouting. No tools or tool boxes, just a hell of a lot of barrels, racks of wine...

And a window near the very corner of the room.

"Logan!" I shout. "I found us a way out!"

I hear the broom clatter against the floor and he jogs over, letting out a sigh of relief when he catches sight of the window.

"You think we can squeeze through that?"

"I mean, I was thinking we could yell for help," I reply. "But you do you."

He doesn't even wait, already forging ahead with another 'brilliant' plan, grabbing one of the barrels and dragging it all the way to the window.

"If I get stuck, you'll pull me out, right?"

I chuckle, shaking my head.

"I guess that's my first official duty as your girlfriend."

Logan lets out a dorky laugh, placing a kiss on my lips.

"I love the sound of that."

"Yes, it's all very romantic, but please don't get stuck. This night cannot get any more embarrassing for me."

"Hey, you fell in love with the guy who won *Emerald Bay's Most Embarrassing Bachelor*. I make no promises!" He calls, clamoring onto the barrel and rattling the window open.

"The title doesn't count if you gave it to yourself!"

I can feel the cool breeze rush in as Logan pulls himself up, trying to pull himself up through the window while his legs dangle behind him.

Actually, it looks more like he's wriggling like a trout.

"God, I wish I had my camera right now."

"Shut up! You try fitting this supple bottom through such a tiny space!"

We're the only ones in the room, but I still catch myself glancing around to make sure nobody else is seeing this.

"I think I'm getting it!" He squawks.

He keeps kicking, his body jerking and snapping as he finally manages to pull himself out.

"Come on!"

He shoves his face back through the gap, dirt smeared all over his chin.

"You know…" I climb up onto the barrel and hoist myself up with a grunt. "This is definitely *not* how I pictured my ten year reunion."

It's a bit of a struggle to get out, but with Logan's help, I manage to get to my feet.

"It's so much better," I laugh.

"Well, we made it out alive, Shortcake," he murmurs, pulling me close. "All thanks to you."

"I think you probably would have broken that door down eventually…" I stroke his cheek. "After a dislocated shoulder, some broken ribs, and—"

"Okay, okay," he chuckles. "I guess ruthlessly mocking me is already part of our relationship, so why would that change, right?"

"I think it's going to become an even more important cornerstone."

Whenever Logan kisses me, it feels like he's the puzzle piece I've always been missing, like I'm one step closer to being made whole.

"I love you," he murmurs. "I've waited so fucking long to say it, and I never want to stop."

"Me neither. Can we run down the street screaming it, or is that too dramatic?"

"A little, but I always appreciate some theatrics."

In a single heartbeat, I traded my best friend for the love of my life.

I have him.

Fully, completely.

And now, I want to embrace the rest of my life instead of trying to hold on to the parts of it that have already fallen away. I came back here wanting to seem successful, wanting to prove that I wasn't the social outcast I was in high school. I spent this entire trip worrying about Brendan and what the people here would think about me, when I should have seen what was sitting right in front of me all along.

And then I did.

"What the hell happened to you two?" Marcus laughs, the two of them rounding the corner.

I figure they probably heard all that noise we were making when we were trying to get out, but the second I lock eyes with Kat, her jaw drops.

"You guys were raw dogging it in the wine cellar!"

"I'm restricting your internet access," Marcus shakes his head. "That's disgusting."

Logan grins.

"Good guess! We also may have smashed a wine bottle—"

"Shh!" I cover his mouth. "You would be the worst criminal in the world!"

Marcus snorts, patting Logan on the shoulder.

"Don't worry, we won't sell you out. I'm sure Abi's told you, but Canada has a national no snitching policy."

"Nice job tossing that drink in Brendan's face, by the way" Kat says, looking me up and down. "You made him change his shirt, and the new one's *really* ugly."

"Well, he deserved it."

"What did he even say to you?" She asks.

I take a breath, letting the past slip away as I reach for Logan's hand.

"Nothing important."

As I glance around at my old classmates, I feel like I can finally start to close the door to this chapter of my life. I'm moving onto bigger and better things, no matter what happens. There's nobody to impress, nobody to brag to... I don't know if I was ever *really* interested in that anyway.

"You guys wanna get the fuck out of here and shoot some pool?" Marcus asks.

"Please," I sigh. "I think I've had just about enough of Reynolds Vineyard for a lifetime."

Logan wraps his arm around me and the four of us head for the exit. A few people gawk as we pass, and just next to the front gate, I spot Brendan and Carly in a heated discussion. It looks like she's really laying into him — until she spots us.

Brendan lingers behind her, hands shoved into his pockets. Even now, he's still too much of a coward to face me alone.

"I take it you're seeing yourself out after the little stunt you pulled back there?" She snarls.

For a moment, I think about asking her which stunt: tossing a drink in her pathetic husband's face or defiling her precious little wine cellar. But as quickly as the thought enters my brain, it vanishes. Whatever hatred or made up jealousy she has for me after all these years isn't going to dissipate any time soon, and I don't need to do anything to stoke that fire.

"Carly, you got everything you ever wanted."

My words are calm and soft, and clearly not at all what she expected.

"What?"

She clenches her fists, still ready for a fight.

"You're gorgeous, you got your dream guy, you have a beautiful baby, a beautiful property... and I hope it makes you happy."

I brush right past her, not even looking back.

"Damn, Shortcake," Logan murmurs.

"Pretty good, huh? And I didn't even cry!"

matilda

ABI

EMERALD BAY UNIVERSITY
PRESENT DAY

I stand in front of Dr. Paxton's office, the croissant I ate this morning bubbling away in my stomach. I think all this anxiety has given me a gluten intolerance.

On the drive back to Emerald Bay, Logan and I did mock interviews where we covered *everything*. By the end of it, I was completely exhausted, but it was extremely effective; I've never been more prepared for an interview in my life.

Just outside of the door, a moment before I get up the courage to knock, I'm startled by a buzzing in my pocket. I immediately whip out my phone to check the message, in a maneuver that's absolutely *not* just an excuse to avoid the meeting as long as possible.

SUNSHINE

Hey, I'm thinking we could do dinner Friday? The
Orchid?

I almost drop my phone. The Orchid is one of Emerald Bay's best and fanciest restaurants. Tucked on the edge of town, it's got massive windows that overlook the water, and the entire place is lit by nothing but candlelight.

ME

Logan, that place is really pricey.

SUNSHINE

Yeah, and it's my first official night out with my girlfriend that wasn't a double date from hell, so it'll be worth every penny.

ME

Maybe we can go to the Eclipse afterward and make out in the back row.

SUNSHINE

You're a genius, Shortcake! PS. I'll be on campus soon, just finishing up my meeting with that guy from Oxford University Press. Maybe we can do lunch?

Before I can reply the office door swings open, and I'm staring directly at Allister's willowy frame, barely filling the doorway. He's got thinning black hair, tortoiseshell glasses, and he's dressed more like a surfer than an anthropologist, with Hawaiian shorts and a bright yellow polo shirt.

"Oh!" He laughs. "Hello there! You must be Dr. King!"

"Yes." I blush. "Sorry, I didn't mean to lurk outside your office like a weirdo, I was about to knock, and—"

"Dr. King, we're all 'weirdos' in this line of work," he chuckles. "Now please, come in."

I quickly shoot Logan a text to confirm our lunch date before stepping inside, bracing myself for one of the most important meetings of my life. Once I'm in the room though, I'm quickly taken aback by my surroundings. Allister's office reminds me of the setting from a nondescript Sherlock Holmes story: dark wood with rich crimson furniture, tall shelves lined with books, and the faintest hint of tobacco lingering in the air.

If he told me he was an amateur detective, I wouldn't doubt him for a second.

"I can't tell you how sorry I am for the mixup with the interview," he says, taking a seat in his big leather chair. "I didn't even realize I'd scheduled it for New Zealand time, and, well… I'm not so good at the whole modern technology thing. A pen and paper is just as good as a computer in my books, and at the very least, it's much easier to catch your mistakes."

"Oh, it's really not a problem," I chuckle. "I just appreciate you making the time to reschedule."

"Happy to, happy to! Especially for someone with such an impressive CV."

He smiles, and I beam at the compliment.

He grabs a large legal pad and a pen from a side-table, and I can feel the butterflies start to return as he gets settled. This time, though, I'm not going to let it get to me. I run through every single thing Logan and I rehearsed: focus on my accomplishments and my goals. Make clear statements, and let him know my own expectations for the position. Most important of all, I've got to sell it, that version of myself I know exists deep down inside.

I'm getting this job.

I know I am.

For the first time in months, I feel like a weight has been lifted off of me. Even if the worst happens and I don't get this job? I'll be okay. I'll figure out a way to stay here.

"You got this," I whisper to myself, whipping out my phone.

ME

Interview went great. I find out if I got the job on Friday.

I head back up to my office so that I can grab my sneakers. These heels I borrowed from Imogen are murdering my feet, even if they're bright pink and absolutely adorable.

I tough it out as I walk down the hall, trying to put the interview behind me. Right now, I've got a whole new problem to tackle.

Telling the truth.

All of it.

Ever since Logan and I decided to make this leap, I've felt this nagging presence clawing at the back of my neck. I told him I was doing it today, and even though he offered to be there with me, I think it's best I have this conversation alone.

When I walk by Frankie's office I'm a little surprised to find his door is slightly ajar, but I stop in my tracks when I hear the unmistakable sound of Logan's laughter. This makes things a little awkward.

"Alright, I'll submit that paperwork today, Frankie!"

The door swings open, and he almost smashes into me as he flies out of the room. He's in a pale purple dress shirt, a blue tie, and the cutest little sweater vest with tiny ghosts embroidered on it. After a moment of catching himself before impact, he beams at me.

"Hey! I got your text. You wanna go out for lunch to celebrate your interview? I just cleared my credit card, so we can get as fancy as you want."

Frankie appears in the doorway, leaning up against it with a twinkle in his eye.

"That sounds— wait, hold up. You said you had that meeting with that Oxford Press guy."

"I did," he replies. "It went awesome! But hey, I'm just gonna grab my jacket. I'll meet you outside your office when everything's done?"

I see Frankie's smile grow behind him, and that familiar knot starts to form in the pit of my stomach.

They're up to something, I can feel it.

"Y— yeah." I nod. "Sure."

Logan tosses me a wink before sauntering down the hall, whistling as he goes, leaving me staring at Frankie who quickly motions for me to come inside with a nod.

"Got time for a quick chat?"

"Actually, I was just on my way to see you."

I decide to sit on the sofa rather than my usual spot in front of his deck. There's something about that chair that's always made me feel like I just got called into the principal's office, and I'm already working with a heavy disadvantage from all the anxiety.

"You want a drink?" He asks, heading for the mini bar he keeps tucked just behind a bookshelf.

"Frankie... It's 11:45."

"So?" He scoffs. "If people drink mimosas at brunch, I can drink whatever I want whenever the hell this is."

He seems oddly relaxed, especially for being at work. Frankie's absolutely a chill guy, but when he's here, he does his best to toe the line between 'Friend' and 'Hardass Department Head.' No matter how supportive he's been in the past, this isn't his normal work demeanor. Something definitely went down between him and Logan.

"So, how'd the interview go?" He asks, handing me a glass of whiskey before settling into his chair.

"It was good! He's going to be in touch next week, but I feel good about it. Even if I don't get the job, I think Dr. Paxton and I really connected."

"That's fucking awesome, Abi. I'm really proud of you."

He leans forward, holding his glass out for a toast, and I follow suit. Both of us drink in silence for a moment, but after that little break he pushes his drink to the side and puts on his serious face.

"Okay, I'm gonna come right out with it. I have a proposition for you, Abi. Logan's going on sabbatical starting Monday. I don't know how much he's told you, but he's going to be gone for about a year to write, get some research done, and hopefully scrounge up some more money for all of us back here in the department."

He didn't talk to me about this at all. I didn't even know he'd been considering it.

"That aside though, he... told me what happened on your trip."

"I see..."

I'm a little shocked, but this is his relationship too, which means it's his truth to tell as much as it is mine.

"Yes, but most importantly he told me... well, he told me he's in love with you."

"Oh, god," I whisper.

The whisky and the croissant from earlier aren't mixing particularly well with this chain of bombshells.

"It's—" Frankie laughs, moving to sit next to me on the couch. "Abi, chill out. You look like you're going to puke."

"I *feel* like I'm gonna puke," I murmur.

He doesn't look surprised, or concerned, or anything like that.

He looks like he's been expecting this.

"Abi, come on, you think I would've offered you a drink if I called you in here to give you shit?"

"I dunno, Frankie, I figure it might soften the whole *you're fired* thing. It's not the worst idea."

Frankie shakes his head, smiling at me.

"So, I've looked into it. Sure, your postdoc position means things are a little murkier than I'd like, *but* you're not a student and he's not your advisor." He swipes a hand through his hair. "To tell you the truth, I've never really dealt with anything like this before, but we'll treat it the same way we would if two professors in the same department started dating. One of you is going to have to leave."

"I know," I breathe. "I mean, that's what I expected. It's why I'm really hoping to get this new job."

"*And* it's why Logan's taking that sabbatical. We talked it through, and what I'd like to propose is that you teach his ethics and methodology courses, at least until January when you start your new position in the anthropology department."

"You mean *if* I start—"

"Abi, come on. Positive thinking, remember?"

"Right, no, thank you! But, I don't know... those are some big shoes to fill."

Logan built those courses from the ground up. They're incredible, ever-changing, and the assignments are tailor-made to give the students practical research experience. He's always said the best way to hone your skills is to get your hands dirty, instead of just reading about things in books.

"Hey, you're the one who said it. But you're not wrong, he's literally got clown feet."

I burst out laughing as Frankie takes a sip of his drink.

It's a good deal, and even if I don't get the other job, there'll be something else around the corner for me. In the meantime, this gets me more experience, and more importantly, a steady paycheck.

"I really thought you'd be mad."

"Abi, I'm gonna be honest… that guy has been in love with you for *years*. I think you'd have to be blind not to see it." I feel my cheeks start to heat up, but he only shrugs. "I'm actually surprised this didn't happen earlier."

"I mean… *technically* we hooked up before I even got the job."

This new freedom to actually be honest for once is pretty addictive, to the point where, apparently, I'm just telling him everything.

"Yeah, back in Toronto, right?"

I frown.

"Wait, how did you know?"

Frankie nods, his grin growing wider.

"I'd love to say I figured it out myself, but Logan told me that part too. I also want to say I can't believe I didn't recognize you, but I had my tongue down someone's throat for most of that night. Far as my memory goes I never saw a single other soul."

I can feel my body fully relax, all of that pent up anxiety and tension from the last few weeks melting away into nothing.

"You promise you're not mad?"

"This isn't like the situation with Roman and Imogen. Sure, you two could have disclosed a bit earlier, but honestly it sounds like there wasn't much of anything *to* disclose until your little vacation. In the end, there's no major ethics breach, just some workplace awkwardness."

He chuckles to himself, rattling his knuckles against his glass.

"You know, when he said you guys were going on a road trip, I have to admit I spent more than a little time looking for loopholes in some of the university's policies; I had a sneaking suspicion that something like this was going to happen."

"God, it's starting to sound like we were the only ones who didn't."

"Nah, it's not like that. It's more that it seems like you've known each other for decades. People don't have those kinds of connections often, so it's hard to ignore. Besides, if there's anything that dealing with Roman and Imogen taught me, it's that you can't really stop stuff like this."

"We tried to fight it," I mutter.

"Looks like it wasn't worth it, huh?"

Frankie wraps an arm around me, hugging me tight against his side, and I can't help but laugh as I think back to that moment of manifesting, way back at the falls.

Show me how good it gets.

"Not at all."

CHAPTER FIFTY-ONE
take a chance on me
LOGAN

EMERALD BAY UNIVERSITY
ONE WEEK LATER

I can't stop sweating.

I've fucked this woman on a pool table, called her a good little slut, and put a butt plug inside of her. So why the hell am I so nervous about a 'first' date? Still, even if it feels like we've done everything backwards, I wouldn't have it any other way.

"She loves you, man. You need to relax," I whisper to myself, smoothing my hair down in the bathroom mirror.

I look at my phone, checking Abi's last text from a few hours ago for what has to be the thirtieth time.

SHORTCAKE

Be there by 8:00!

Abi's still waiting to hear about her interview for the anthropology department, and just last week, she wound up getting a request for a zoom interview at a small college in Olympia. It would be a hell of a commute, but she'd only be teaching twice a week. We've got things covered with her handling my classes, but it would definitely take some weight off of her mind if she got it. Either way, we'll make it work.

I adjust my tie one final time before grabbing my keys, along with a bouquet of roses, and heading out the door. I have the perfect first date planned: dinner at a fancy restaurant, and then a walk up to Guardian Point to go stargazing.

Summer still clings to the air as I make my way to the Orchid, the weather practically perfect with no clouds in sight. Still, you can't be too careful about this stuff, and I double-checked the forecast to make sure there was no chance of rain.

There are kids zooming after each other on their bikes, soaking in the last bit of sunlight, and I smile as I watch a few couples walking hand in hand toward the bay.

All I can think about is Abi and our future together. Everything has finally fallen into place and while I could lament the moments we've missed out on over the last three years, I think it all worked out exactly like it was supposed to.

Taking a sabbatical was a no-brainer, and it definitely took some careful reading of university policy, but I managed to find a couple of small loopholes that are... Let's just call them open to interpretation.

And I fucking *love* it when things are open to interpretation.

By the time I arrive at The Orchid, I'm almost completely covered in sweat, and *deeply* regretting my choice to wear a suit. Luckily, the location itself is having none of my problems, the low-light, candle glow, and soft jazz music providing the perfect ambience I was hoping for.

"Good evening," The hostess smiles at me, doing an *almost* perfect job pretending I don't look like I just ran a marathon. "Do you have a reservation?"

"Yes, thank you. It's under Dr. Flynn for 8:00pm?"

Normally I'd just rattle off my name sans-honorifics, but you have to be as pretentious as possible when $150 plates are on the line.

"Right this way, sir."

This is pretty much the only place in Emerald Bay with a dress code, but even though I busted out my best suit, I still feel underdressed. Everyone looks so pristine, and as we walk I catch myself running my hand through my hair, in the vain, mostly subconscious hope that I'll end up looking a little less like a cartoon character who just got electrocuted.

We arrive at the table, nestled in an almost completely private corner of the room, and I slide into my seat as the hostess places the menus down. I'm not really sure what to do with the flowers I brought, so for now they'll just be living on my lap.

"First date?" She asks with a grin.

I nod, blushing furiously.

"Um... yeah sort of. First *official* date, at least. Is it that obvious?"

"A little." She pours some water, setting the overly-fancy pitcher down in front of me. "Your server will be here in a few minutes with the wine menu."

"Thanks."

Yesterday, I got a new key to my house cut for Abi. It might be fast, but I'm not really sure what speed we're supposed to be going at anymore. I want to rush us to where it feels like we should be, so we don't waste anymore time, which also feels like it could be a serious risk. But It's like I said, we kind of did everything backwards, and at this point I've pretty much thrown out the rulebook.

I check the time: 8:05.

The key feels like an anvil in my pocket, weighing me down more and more with each minute that passes by.

But it's cool. Maybe she forgot to charge her phone.

Maybe she left it at home.

And she's already on her way, I'm sure of it.

It's Abi we're talking about.

She wouldn't ghost me.

I sip my water, flipping through the menu to kill time and keep myself sane. Half of this stuff is in French, and I don't know enough about fine dining to really get what I'm looking at. That, and it's impossible to focus when I keep glancing at the front door every couple seconds.

I check my phone again.

8:10.

Fuck it. I can't help myself.

ME: Hey, straggler, I can get things started for you if you want. You want red wine or white?

I stare at the sent message, waiting for those three little dots to pop up. She's usually pretty quick to text me back.

But tonight?

Nothing.

I pull up the browser, swiping through local news to make sure nothing's gone wrong. No car accidents, no natural disasters... No explosions, no random acts of terror. None of the usual, or even the less-than-usual.

So where the hell is she?

"Waiting for someone?" The server asks, making her way to the table.

"Yeah." I chuckle, locking my phone. "Looks like she's stuck in traffic."

"Did you want a drink to tide you over?" She tilts her head with a sad little smile. "On the house."

Oh my god. This is the same as the last time, she thinks I'm a loser that got ditched. I even had flowers then too, there's no way this happens to me twice in the same—

"Oh my god, Sunshine, I am *so* fucking sorry!"

Abi's practically mowing people down to get to the table. I take the key out of my breast pocket, concealing it in my palm before she has a chance to notice.

"Lydia escaped and I had to hunt around for her while I was trying to get dressed, and I just lost track of time and I think I must have dropped my phone somewhere in my apartment— I'm *so* sorry!"

She's nearly out of breath but still stunning, in a floor-length crimson dress that fits her like a glove, showing off every curve of her body. Her hair is a bit mussed up, yet otherwise perfectly styled in wild dark waves. I reach up to brush a few strands away, carefully slipping the key behind a glittery rose barrette that's pinning some of her hair back. Everyone's expecting the classic dumb little trick where you pull the coin from behind the ear, so they're never ready for the swerve.

And my mom said spending hours learning magic tricks on YouTube wasn't productive.

"Is Lydia okay?" I ask.

"Oh, yeah! I found her sleeping in the bathtub." She shakes her head, laughing softly. "I was going to text you, and then I couldn't find my phone like I said, and—"

"Shortcake?" I laugh. "Breathe. It's okay. I was just worried, that's all."

"Yep, you're right. Breathing." She takes a few big ones, holding and releasing just like she learned from Iggy. "Oh, I also got great news."

"You got the job in Olympia?"

"No! I totally bailed on it and watched an episode of Real Housewives instead— Oh, are these for me?!" She picks up the bouquet of roses, giving them a quick sniff. "Logan, they're gorgeous."

I help her into her seat, kissing her on the cheek and making sure the key is still tucked behind her barrette. It's not like Abi to just ditch an interview, not unless she's extremely confident about something else, but I'm curious what it could possibly be.

"Actually, I sort of lied about why I was late," she says.

"You got me all worked up about a rat escape for nothing?"

"Not for nothing." She leans back in her chair. "Officially got my offer for the adjunct position *and* signed the paperwork today. I start in January."

I'm no Great Madame Mavis, but I *knew* Abi had that job in the bag the second her interview got rescheduled. I'm brimming with excitement, so much so that I don't really know what to do with my hands except reach out and squeeze hers.

Everything is falling into place.

"Why didn't you tell me?" I laugh.

"Because I wanted to see the look on your face! Also, I had to go and pick up my office key, *and* sign my contract, all in this dress!"

"You know, it's against the rules for you to be that hot on campus now."

She rolls her eyes, dipping her fingers into her water glass and flicking a few droplets at me.

"Oh, you wanna have a wet t-shirt contest in here, Shortcake? Because I've got a lot of experience, and almost zero shame."

She grins.

"Maybe I do. Show me those bosoms, Flynn."

"Alright, you asked for it," I sigh, loosening my tie and beginning to undo the buttons on my shirt. "But you're about to get us put on a list."

She snickers, but thankfully my commitment to the bit is interrupted by the server making her way back toward us. I quickly button my shirt back up and clear my throat as she approaches the table.

"You folks look like you could use some wine."

She sets the menu down in front of me, and this time *everything* is in French.

I default to Abi, sliding it toward her.

"You pick. It'll be super embarrassing if I try to pronounce *any* of this."

"Dangerous game, Flynn," she teases, scanning the menu with eager eyes. "How about the Salon Blanc de Blancs Le Mesnil-sur-Oger?"

"We have a 2002 or a 2004," the server says, grabbing her notepad and pen from her pocket.

"Which is better?" Abi asks.

"The 2002 is pricier, but it's worth it."

"We'll take it!" I chirp.

"Excellent choice. I'll be right back with a bottle."

She scoops up the menu and strides away, leaving the two of us grinning from ear to ear.

"So?" She prompts, nudging me under the table with her foot. "How about you? How's the first week of sabbatical?"

"Fantastic. I slept until 10:00, and then I got straight to work... watching Scooby Doo and the Ghoul School in my pajamas."

"A classic!" She gushes. "God, I can't believe I missed out on that! Why do I have to be the one with a real job?"

"Hey, you're welcome over anytime you want! But, actually..." I tilt my head, squinting at her. "Can you check your hair? I think there's something caught behind your barrette."

She tilts her head, a wry half-smile creeping over her face.

"What did you hide?"

I sip my water, wiggling my eyebrows as she starts to dig around for it.

"What is this?" She lets out a nervous giggle, holding the key out in front of her. "Oh, is it the key to your heart?"

"Oh, Shortcake. You got that a long time ago."

"Such a sap, Doctor Flynn."

She turns it over in her palm, chewing on her lip. I think she already knows what it's for, she's just a little too scared to ask.

"Well, being sappy is my bread and butter." I take a breath, trying desperately to calm my racing heart. "But, to answer your question, that's... Well, it's the key to my house. When you're ready, and I do mean when you're *really* ready... I'd like you to move in with me."

Okay. Got it out there.

It can't hurt me now.

Except if she says no.

Yeah, that would probably kill me, not gonna lie.

"I gotta say, Flynn, this is a hell of a commitment for a first date."

"Abi, I've licked your asshole, and that was *after* I proposed to you with a ring pop. I don't really think doing things by the book is on the table for us anymore."

I grasp her hand, leaning down to kiss her knuckles, something she's affectionately dubbed my 'prince charming move.' I've been busting it out at least twice as often since she named it, because how could I not?

This whole thing feels like a fairy tale.

"I want to be clear, I absolutely want to do things at *your* pace, okay? However fast or slow you wanna take this, I'm in. I just wanted to show you... I don't know, I wanted to show you where I'm at."

"My lease is up in like two months."

I don't think I've ever seen her smile so wide.

"Plenty of time to get Flynn Manor ready for you, milady."

The relief is so powerful I can feel a shiver run all the way across my body, but luckily for me she's far too enamored with the key to notice. We sit together in silence for a while, just grinning at each other like idiot-teens in love for the first time, until the server returns with our champagne.

"To your new job and to new beginnings."

"And to us," she grins.

"And to us."

"Did you know that there are only 9,096 stars in the sky that are actually visible to the naked eye?"

"Really?"

Guardian Point is the perfect place to go stargazing, the skies so clear that you can see everything. The trees that stretch toward the sky, the way the moonlight makes the water shimmer at practically any angle... no picture or painting will ever do this place justice. It was actually the place that first convinced me to move to Emerald Bay.

"Yep. You need a telescope for the rest of them."

"Makes these ones extra special then I guess, huh?"

She rests her head on my chest, staring up into the infinity above us.

"You know, I always wanted to be an astronomer," she sighs. "I liked the idea of trying to learn everything about the cosmos. I even took some classes in university, but I almost failed because I sucked at math."

I chuckle.

"I wanted to be a physicist when I was a kid. I liked to take stuff apart and figure out how it all worked, but I *also* sucked at math. Still do, actually."

"Algebra will get you every time."

"It's the stupid letters," I grumble. "What are they even for?"

"You got me. Maybe that's why we sucked at it. There was one specific thing we just couldn't quite wrap our heads around."

"Yeah, you're absolutely right." I nod my head sagely. "If I had to single out one specific thing, I think I'd have to say it was probably the math."

She snorts, slapping me on the thigh as I run my fingers gently through her hair. We're full of overpriced chicken, champagne, and shiraz, but it was all worth it. There's a softness to her features now, and a hell of a lot less anxiety weighing on her.

"I'll never get over how beautiful you are."

"Shut up," she laughs.

I've never had a love like Abi before, and I'm so lucky I'll never need to find another.

"I'm serious." I stroke her cheek. "Every time I catch you looking at me, it's like my brain stops working."

She fiddles with my tie, scrunching up her nose as she rolls it up and down my chest.

"What's going on up there, Shortcake?"

She lets out a contented sigh, a little smile spreading across her face. I could stare at her forever. That little button nose, and those eyes that tell you everything without her having to say a word.

"I just can't believe this is finally happening."

Her laughter rings out through the night.

It's not just joyous, but hopeful.

Magical.

I let my fingers dance through her hair, a lump forming in my throat as I remember some of my dad's final words to me.

Promise me you'll fall in love. Because at the end of the day…

"There's nothing else that matters…"

It hurts that he'll never meet the woman who changed my life, but I know that wherever he is in the universe, he's giving me that little wink of approval just like he used to.

"Hey, you okay?" She asks. "What was that you said?"

"Nothing," I grin, beaming down at her. "Nothing at all."

my love mine all mine

ABI

EMERALD BAY UNIVERSITY
FALL 2024

The last few months have been a whirlwind, but it was an easy decision to let my lease end, pack up my life, and move in with Logan. We even bought a few more rats for Lydia and Wednesday to hang out with.

I start my new position in January, and I'm excited to work in a new department with new people. I didn't realize how fast things would shift once I finally embraced the idea that my life could change for the better.

Show me how good it gets.

"Does anyone have any final questions, or do we want to get out of here for the weekend?" I ask, glancing around the lecture hall.

I stare out at a sea of blank and exhausted faces, more than a little relieved that nobody has anything to say. Teaching Logan's classes has been a challenge, but one I've been more than happy to rise to. I've done my best to follow in his footsteps while throwing in some of my own flare.

That said, regardless of how interesting the subject matter might be, I've felt my focus slipping for at least an hour now, checking the clock every 5 minutes or so since 9:00PM. Logan is supposed to be picking me up for our weekend trip to Portland; he rented an adorable little cottage near Cannon Beach for a short getaway, just us, the ocean, and a little bag of toys.

It's reassuring to know I'm not the only one who's excited though. He's been texting me *all* day, from mostly innocuous stuff, to the particularly spicy line: '*I can't wait to get my mouth on that sweet little pussy of yours.*'

Needless to say, it's been more than a little difficult to get anything done.

"Alright, well, have a great weekend everyone. Remember your papers —" I snort, watching a couple students already bolting for the door. "Are due *next* Friday! I'll have office hours that whole week to answer questions if you have them, but I will be unavailable this weekend, so don't even try it!"

I disconnect my laptop, toss out my abandoned coffee, and head for the door. Just before I make it out behind a couple of stragglers, my phone chimes in my purse, nearly making me jump out of my skin.

"Jesus!"

SUNSHINE

Come up to the sociology floor. I have a surprise
for you.

Logan and his surprises. He might act like a giant kid from time to time, but it definitely means that he's never boring.

I instinctively glance down at the ring he bought me in Banff, my little connection to both him *and* my Baba. I smile every time I see it.

Except I'm not smiling now, because *today* my ring finger is completely barren, save for the tiny white tan line.

"Shit."

I was in a rush this morning. Alarm didn't go off in time, and I was fighting with my hair and wardrobe... I guess I must have left it sitting on the nightstand. Maybe I can convince Logan to swing back to the house before we head out, because I don't want to go to Portland without it.

I head toward the Sociology building, slipping in the door, and around an exhausted student staggering outside like a zombie. There are still some people lingering in the lounge, typing away on laptops and sipping coffee. Strangely, I kind of miss those days of burning the candle at both ends just to get a paper submitted.

I step into the elevator, and the ride is quick for once. It usually stops at *almost* every floor and it can take me an extra five minutes to make it to meetings, but tonight it's blessedly empty.

When the doors open I'm struck by a peculiar sight: a trail of ring pops, still in their packaging, with tea lights guiding the way down the hall.

This has Logan Flynn written all over it.

I pick them up, one after the other, following the sugary path toward Logan's office.

And there he is, standing at the end of it, dressed in a black suit with a lavender dress shirt. He looks particularly fancy, his hair combed back into a deep side part, and he's even wearing my favorite pair of glasses.

"I suddenly feel underdressed," I laugh, gesturing at my black cotton dress and pair of converse. "All this to take me to Portland?"

He grins from ear to ear, making a 'come hither' motion with his fingers, and as I make my way toward him, I get the feeling this isn't one of his more impulsive surprises.

"I wanted to do this right."

He lowers himself slowly to one knee, reaching into his pocket, and pulling out a velvet box before popping it open. Inside is my ring, the same ring he bought for me in Banff, but it's a little different. He added two small diamonds on either side of the amethyst, and replaced the band, which had been starting to thin.

"I want to be the man you choose to spend forever with. I want to be there to cheer you on through every victory, and comfort you through every defeat. I want to get old with you, and sit on the porch while we watch our grandkids play in the backyard. You've always been the one, Shortcake. You're the stars in my sky, and I didn't know what my life was missing until you lit it up."

I got so caught up in the idea of spending a long weekend on the beach that I didn't even consider he might be planning something like this. Little tea lights flicker around us, filling the hallway with a beautiful golden glow, and I sink to my knees, grasping his face and pressing my forehead against his.

"I locked up my heart, but you stole it anyway," I whisper.

"Well, if you marry me, I'll keep it safe for you."

"Yes," I sob. "Of course, I'll marry you."

I'm shaking as he slides the ring onto my finger.

"A lot better than a ring pop, huh?"

All I can do is fling my arms around him, and the two of us topple to the ground. Our kisses go from playful to passionate in seconds. Maybe it's the filthy texts he's been sending all day, or maybe it's the proposal, but I'm practically clawing at his suit jacket.

"I want you out of these clothes, Doctor," I purr. "Fuck me."

"Here? Are you sure?"

I pull back, pressing my hands against his chest. His heart is pounding just as hard as mine.

"You've eaten me out on your desk at least twice over the past couple months, and now you're shy?"

Logan glances around, excitement brewing in his eyes.

"You know what? Fuck it. Dr. Barnes left half an hour ago, and the cleaners don't come up here until well past midnight."

We manage to untangle our limbs and he helps me to my feet, giving me just a second to breathe before he scoops me in his arms and carries me over to his desk.

He opens the blinds, revealing the rest of the campus stretched out before us. The sky is filled with twinkling stars, mingling with the few lights still on in some of the adjacent buildings.

"I'm thinking we could try exhibitionism."

He shrugs off his jacket, rolling up his shirt sleeves as he saunters toward me.

The edge to his voice has me instinctively spreading my legs, and he drops to his knees, slipping my shoes off before kissing all the way up my calf. His pace is torturous, but I know he's doing it on purpose; the deeper we've gotten into our relationship, the more I've discovered how much Logan loves to tease.

"I'm thinking we could try something new."

"Like?"

He pulls a small pink vibrator out of his pocket, setting it down next to me.

"Well, obviously we can still play with the toys, but I was thinking something more along the lines of..."

He slides his hand between my legs, teasing my asshole through my panties.

I stifle a giggle.

"So you want to..."

Logan grins, sliding my panties off and tucking them into his pocket.

"I really, really do, Shortcake."

We've had a lot of time lately for experimentation, with open communication and strong boundaries.

"I'm ready for anything."

He takes his time, working his way up from little kisses on my thigh to torturing my clit with his tongue, and I finally get to relish the pleasure that's building inside me all evening. He's deliciously slow, like he's savoring a meal, and all I can think is that I want more. More pressure, more pleasure, more everything. After the hours and hours of teasing, I'm ready to fucking explode.

"I kept reading all those texts you sent me," I moan. "Over and over. You're a dirty boy, Doctor Flynn."

He growls, only pausing for a moment to look up at me.

"You haven't seen dirty yet. Now come on my face."

I let out a gasp as he continues to devour me, his two long fingers sliding into my pussy and stirring me up inside. He's ravenous. I can feel his cheeks burning between my legs, but as much as I want to hold on to that sensation, and savor it like a bottle of expensive wine, I know I'm too worked up to make it last.

I feel like I'm flying, my nerves crackling and popping with each thrust or pivot of his fingers. I can barely think about anything except the pleasure that's flooding me, but the second he wraps his lips around my clit the feeling increases tenfold; I feel like I'm shattering, bucking my hips violently until I'm sure I'm going to collapse.

"I'm coming!" I grasp at him blindly, twisting his hair up in my clenched fist. "Oh, fuck, don't stop!"

And he *doesn't* stop until I'm completely spent, until I look up to see him greedily licking those fingers clean as he gets to his feet.

"Be a good girl and bend over the desk."

"Yes, Doctor Flynn."

I slip off of the polished wood surface, turning around and bending over just like he asked. I hear the familiar jingle of his belt, and quickly feel his cock rest between my asscheeks.

"I thought about this all day."

"Fucking me in the ass or proposing to me?"

"Both," he confesses with a laugh. "Now spread those gorgeous legs."

Something wet drips onto my ass and I gasp, my legs already beginning to tremble.

"Just breathe for me, okay? You say stop and we stop."

He begins to rub his thumb in circles around my asshole, all while he *slowly* slides his cock into my pussy. The sensation is almost overwhelming, and I find myself gasping as I claw at his desk.

A whole season of fucking this man and it's still always as exciting as the first time.

"*Fuck*, you're such a good girl," he moans, continuing to massage my asshole. "Just keep breathing. I want you to be nice and relaxed."

I follow his instruction to the letter, buzzing from head to toe as he slides a single finger inside. It's just like the pool table back in Blackburn.

"Grab the vibrator. I want you *soaked*."

Even on the lowest setting, it rattles my bones. The sensation is almost too much— his cock deep inside me, his finger thrusting in and out of my ass, and my clit pulsing along with the toy. I keep trying different angles, never keeping it in the same place for too long as Logan sets a slow and sensual rhythm for me to follow.

"You think you can take my cock?"

It's hard to focus as I get lost in the sweet rumble of his voice.

"Please," I whine. "I need more."

My heart slams against my ribs at the thought, and I keep myself right on the edge as Logan continues pounding my pussy. I've taken his fingers, and several plugs, but never his whole cock up my ass.

"You dirty little slut."

"Takes one to know one," I say, glancing over my shoulder to flash him a coy smile.

He pulls out of me in one quick motion, and I suddenly feel more lube on my ass. It's cold, but Logan is nothing but gentle.

"I'll take good care of you," he murmurs. "Any time you want to stop, you say... *berry*, understand?"

"I understand."

"Good girl. Now, remember to breathe."

Cool air fills my lungs as he lines himself up, pushing into me slowly at first. Even the tip causes tears to sting my eyes, and I turn the vibrator up to balance things out. The blend of pleasure and pain rocks my body, and the stinging sensation starts to feel... surprisingly good.

He pauses, letting me get used to his size and stroking my lower back as his dick pulses inside of me. I'm feeling a little bit dizzy, but in a good way. Almost like when that first drink goes straight to your head.

Deep breaths, I remind myself.

Deep breaths.

"Holy shit you're perfect." He smacks my ass. "My beautiful little fuckdoll."

Our bodies fall into a tender, almost soothing rhythm as decadent moans fill the room. Almost everything about this screams romance: the tea lights that fill his office, the splash of moonlight on the walls...

You can totally get fucked in the ass in a romantic way, right?

I turn up the vibrations again, trying to build to a beautiful climax as my fingernails dig into the fleshy part of my palms. I'm honestly shocked I haven't drawn blood.

"Tell me how good it feels," he grunts.

I can barely get a word out. It's all vowels, like my tongue is tangled up with my moans.

"Tell me you're gonna be my pretty little wife."

"Gonna be your pretty little—"

My climax rips through me, much sharper than I expected. I gasp and groan, struggling to focus through the haze, and when I start to come down I can hear Logan behind me, moaning my name.

"I'm gonna come. Oh, fuck, Abi! Tell me where you want it."

It's the *perfect* proposal.

"In my ass," I whimper. "Please, Sunshine!"

I turn the vibrator up one final notch, pressing it hard against my clit as Logan pounds into me. His hips are sharp, his breath shaky and jagged, and his body stills as he lets out a deep grunt.

"That's a good girl. Take every drop."

I feel myself come, for the second time in as many minutes, the toy slipping from my fingers and falling to the ground as the raging flames consume me from the inside out.

I keep myself breathing, my body still vibrating as I try to get my bearings, with the grain of the wood beneath my fingertips grounding me in the present.

"Thawasincreble."

I try to repeat the words, to separate them, but it's no use. Luckily, I don't need to be eloquent right now. Instead, I'm focused on the weight of his body, so comforting and warm; just like him, it's quickly become something I can't live without.

"I love you so much," he rasps. "I can't wait to start our lives together."

Sometimes I'm afraid this is all too perfect, that it's just a dream I haven't woken up from, but even if it is...

"I love you back."

I ran from one small town and found a home in another.

In the waves melting onto the shores of the bay.

In the mountains and the cedar trees.

In the halls of this very building.

And in Logan Flynn.

fully, completely

LOGAN

HALLOWEEN
ONE YEAR LATER

For a day that's supposed to be about me and Abi, we haven't really seen each other, and it feels more like preparing for a circus rather than a wedding ceremony. I'm running around, making sure everything's okay, answering questions I have zero authority over, all while thinking... I just want to see the woman I'm going to marry.

Between the bachelor and bachelorette parties and each of our mothers' insistence that it's bad luck to see the bride before the wedding, we've been away from each other for far too long.

Okay, three days. But I *miss her*. She's always there when I wake up in the morning and she's the last person I talk to before my head hits the pillow. You get used to that kind of consistency, and with her in the house, it hasn't felt so empty anymore.

I'm sitting on an old stone bench outside the church. The air is crisp, the sun shines down through the golden leaves making everything glow. Even the little birds who have stuck around are chirping non-stop.

I glance down, popping open the small red box in my hands.

Dad's cufflinks.

Well, they were his dad's, his grandfather's, and *his* grandfather's before–

You get the picture.

They're simple, gold with a diamond trim, and he used to wear them for every special occasion. I really wanted him to be a part of the ceremony, and these cufflinks are a good place to start.

I slip his watch off of my wrist, the part of him I've worn for so long, placing it safely away in my pocket. I think it's time to finally get it resized, maybe once we make it to Ireland.

I expected to cry more today, to feel that pang in my chest at the fact that he's not around to share this big moment, but... those feelings never came. Instead, it feels like he could be here, watching the chaos unfold and dolling out marriage advice.

You two should be a unit, but still be able to stand on your own... and for fuck's sake learn to do the dishes.

It turns out that whole dishes thing? Way more serious than I thought.

I fold my cuffs back, pinching the fabric together before securing the first cufflink, and admiring the way it glitters in the sunlight.

"I finally did it, old man." I glance up at the sky with a big smile. "Got a house, fell in love, I'm getting married ... the whole shebang."

Calm settles over me, and somewhere deep inside, I know that *he knows* I'm okay.

"Logan?" Roman calls, interrupting my brief moment alone.

He's dressed in a charcoal grey tuxedo, his salt and pepper hair pushed back. The guy looks like he's about to walk the red carpet.

"I'm fine, dude." I smile at him. "I just need a minute."

"Oh, I know." He grins. "I, uh... broke the rules for you."

I frown as Roman steps back, revealing Abi in her long violet wedding dress. It *was* white when she bought it, but she spent days dyeing it the perfect shade of purple to contrast her olive eyes. Her hair is styled in messy waves, with a few pieces held back by a hair clip that matches her dress.

Just looking at her makes me blush.

"Mom's gonna kill you, dude," I whisper.

Roman and Imogen aren't married yet, but he's basically my brother.

"You've got about ten minutes before Mrs. Flynn realizes you're both missing."

I grin.

"Thanks, man."

He waves me off, slinking back inside and leaving Abi and I alone. All I can do is stare at her because she's quite literally breathtaking. The way the sun makes her green eyes pop and illuminates her freckles? It still takes my brain some time to process that I get the privilege of marrying this woman.

"Can I sit?" She asks, gesturing to the empty space beside me.

"I don't know." I click my tongue. "I was kinda waiting for a big hottie to come along in a purple— oh my God, she's you!"

Abi rolls her eyes, easing herself down and grabbing my other cufflink.

"You know, that joke never gets old."

"I'll never stop telling it." I glance down as she fiddles with my shirt. "You needed a break, too?"

"I love your family, but there are just a *lot* of people around. Gets kind of..." She makes a vague and frantic gesture with one hand, chuckling to herself. "You know."

"The hovering?"

"Oh my *god* the hovering!" Abi groans. "*Abi, your dress* and *Abi, your hair*, blah blah blah! I mean, don't get me wrong, I'm grateful, it's just a lot."

She sighs, gazing up at me with big, fluttering lashes as she secures the cufflink.

"My mom told me that when she married my dad, she almost missed the whole wedding. She was so worried about other people, where everything was, and if everything was going to be perfect that it just... passed her by. When everyone was poking at me with brushes and eyeliner pens, that's all I could think about."

"That's funny, because I was thinking the same thing."

I kiss her temple, taking the opportunity to breathe in her perfume. Abi always smells so warm, like a crackling campfire. The scent has started to feel like home.

"So, what are you most excited for when we get married?" I ask.

I already know my answer. Dancing in the kitchen, dinner parties, cuddling in bed on rainy days, and movie marathons. What else do you do when you marry your best friend?

"Hmm..." She nuzzles against me. "Our honeymoon."

We're going to the UK for three months, and maybe even a bit of Europe. I want to take Abi to the church my parents got married in, and I've got family who can't wait to meet her. She'll fit right in with the Flynns. I've never had any doubt about that.

We're going to eat incredible food, go to museums, start writing that book together, and fuck each other's brains out. We leave tomorrow, but my bags have been packed for a week already.

"What else?" I ask. "Because me? I'm really excited to yell, *get away from my wife!*"

Abi cackles, her little button nose scrunching up and a twinkle in her eyes.

"When, pray tell, would you ever have the opportunity to yell that?"

"I don't know, maybe we're in Paris and some dude is hitting on you at the Louvre."

"Ah, yes, the infamous Parisian Wife Napper."

"Exactly! There are dozens of epic poems written about him!"

She giggles and nudges me with her elbow.

"Is that really what you're excited for?"

"To call you my wife? Hell yeah!"

I've already started practicing.

My wife is a professor.

My wife knits incredible scarves.

My wife secretly loves country music and if you breathe a word of that to anyone, I'll have to kill you.

It just feels good to say!

"What else?" She asks.

The sunlight hits her face in just such a way I can see all the glitter from her makeup sparkling, like little jewels on her skin. I want to make a Twilight joke, but I don't think she'd appreciate me ruining this moment.

"Getting super old and decrepit with you, and having insane conversations no one but us understands."

"We already do the second part," she giggles. "But yeah, I can't wait to be a crusty ancient goth with you, Doctor Flynn."

I brush a stray wave of hair away from her face.

"What about you? What else are you excited for?"

"Babies."

She breathes the word out, like revelation and relief mixed into one.

"Babies?" I ask. "Pl– plural?"

We've talked about it, but nothing too serious until now. We wanted her to get settled in the Anthropology department, publishing, lecturing, and building her passion project: a safe injection site right outside of Emerald Bay.

"Mmhmm." Abi pulls away, her eyes shimmering. "Two? Maybe three?"

She'd be such a great mom. When Kat and Marcus come to visit, the first person Dylan runs to is his aunt Abi.

I'm trying to figure out the best thing to say, but she skips right past that part, grabbing me by the tie before gently rolling it up and releasing it.

"I was thinking we could start tonight."

"I mean, we've got an extra five minutes right now."

I can make her come in two.

But Abi only snickers, reaching up and booping my nose.

"Are you ever going to stop being horny for me?"

"Are you kidding, not a chance!" I glide my lips along her jaw before nipping at her ear. "I'm gonna fuck you every single day. Maybe more than once!"

"So crass, Doctor."

"Hey, dorks!"

Frankie's voice rings out from behind us, a perfect blend of exhaustion and excitement. He's got a bottle of beer in his hand and a sly smirk on his face.

"Your moms are freaking the fuck out, *and* they're interrogating Roman."

"Well, I guess our time's up," I mutter. "He's gonna fold like a cheap lawn chair and confess everything. Probably even stuff he didn't do."

Abi snickers and I hop to my feet, stretching out my arm to her.

"Are you ready to get married to the biggest nerd of all time?"

She takes my arm, and I gently help her to her feet, making a big show of it all.

"I've been ready since the day we met, Flynn. How about you?"

I take a look around us, at the greenery and the sky, and the old brick-work of the church. If you'd asked me even two years ago if I thought we'd end up here, I'd have laughed it off, said you were crazy.

Abi and me? There's no way in hell.

We're just friends.

Best friends.

But despite all of that, despite *knowing* there was no chance in hell we'd end up together, if you'd have asked me, *really* asked me?

I'd have told you.

"I've never wanted anything more in my entire life."

academic glossary

The following is a guide to all of the academic terms located within this book.

Postdoc or postdoctoral researcher is a person who conducts research after the completion of their PhD. Most postdocs have temporary teaching appointments, often in preparation for a permanent faculty position.

All But Dissertation: Also known as *ABD* is a stage in the process of obtaining a doctorate. This is when your coursework has been successfully completed, you've passed your comprehensive examination as well as your research proposal and all that's left to do is write your dissertation. Fun fact: Writing your dissertation can take *years*. While the average PhD program expects you to finish in four years, the average PhD student takes around six to seven years to complete.

Judith Butler is an American feminist scholar whose work has influenced political policy, theory, ethics, and third wave feminism. Butler is most widely known for their groundbreaking work, *Gender Trouble: Feminism and the Subversion of Identity* as well as *Bodies that Matter: On the Discursive Limits of Sex* in which they challenge ideas of heteronormativity. Butler also developed the theory of *gender performativity*, in which they posit that "gender is not performed through a singular act, but through ritualized repetition." (Perlego). Butler uses they/them pronouns.

Postmodernism is a theoretical lens positing that reality is socially constructed. Postmodernists believe that there is no objective truth, but rather perspectives and experiences. It states that people construct knowledge through discourse with others and lived experiences. Michel Foucault is an example of a postmodernist philosopher.

Late Modernity is different than postmodernity. It's a concept posited by Anthony Giddens and Ulrich Beck that a very specific stage of societal development fueled by radical social, economic, and cultural change.

Pedagogy is considered to be the study of teaching methods. It's considered to be the theory of education, including the methods and systems that we use to disseminate and teach knowledge. Some of the essential components of pedagogy include: learning theories, teaching methods, and curriculum design.

Augustus Comte was a French mathematician and philosopher who is considered to be the the Father of Sociology and positivism, which is a research method that specifically uses statistics and hard scientific evidence.

Neoliberal/Neoliberalism is a policy-driven model that seeks to embrace private enterprises and transfer economic control to the private sector. Neoliberal policies are directly concerned with things like capitalism, the free market, limiting government spending, government ownership, and is often associated with the economic policies of Ronald Reagan. Many academics consider neoliberalism to be a threat to democracy itself as it tends to cause direct harm to things like workers' rights and marginalized communities.

Das Kapital written by Karl Marx, is a foundational three-volume text that analyzes and critiques capitalism. *Das Kapital* is the technical background to *The Communist Manifesto*. Volumes two and three of *Das Kapital* were completed and published by Friedrich Engels after Marx's death in 1883 with the help of Marx's notes.

acknowledgments

This book simply would not be possible without the following people:

My momma. You are the strongest person I've ever met in my life, and I don't know how much time we have left together but you have always been my hero. You raised me alone for seven years, we lived in basements, cars, and shitty apartments, and spent too much time in unemployment lines. But you always told me to have faith, to keep going despite the odds, and that the only thing constant in our lives is change. So much of Abi's relationship with her mom was inspired by my love for you. I don't know what else to say except that I love you, and I always will.

My dad. You stepped up to the plate and took in a kid who isn't biologically yours, but you raised me as your own regardless. It takes a real man to do that. Since I was 7, you've encouraged me to be myself, to be kind, to be confident, and to reach for the things I want. I love you so much.

My beta readers: Rebeca, MK, Lindsey, Aly, Tiffani, Aubrey, Cassandra, and Jordyn. Your comments and feedback helped shape this book into something truly special. I'm so grateful for you and your friendship.

My Street Team, aka "The Emerald Bay Faculty". Words cannot express how much I adore you all. You hype me up, you're the reason I'm in bookstores, you encourage each other, cheer on other authors, and your meme game is *unmatched*. You're the best found family a gal could ask for.

My husband. You're my Logan, and you always have been. I love you endlessly.

Dr. Spencer Reid. Thank you for being the fictional love of my life for 20 years and for inspiring Logan Flynn. Come home, the kids miss you.

about the author

Thea Lawrence is a PhD dropout turned romance author. After spending almost a decade in academia studying criminology (with a focus on carceral studies and prison theatre), she decided to shift gears for her mental health.

A lifelong storyteller, Thea has been an actor, burlesque dancer, screenwriter, and even dabbled in painting. Now, she focuses on romance stories with heart, grit, a dash of the forbidden, and a hell of a lot of spice.

She currently lives in Ontario with her partner.

IG & Threads: @thealawrenceauthor
TikTok: @thealawrenceauthor and @thealawrencebooks
Website: thealawrenceromanceauthor.com
Patreon: patreon.com/thealawrence
You can also sign up for Thea's monthly newsletter (signup is also available on her website!) featuring sneak peeks at future books, advanced links to pre-orders, deleted scenes from previously published works, life updates, author spotlights, and more.